KILLER TO
DIE FOR

Also Available From This Author

The MacMaster Chronicles
Honorable Assassin

This and other works by the author are available from:
RedPetalPress.com
Order from other fine bookstores

KILLER TO DIE FOR

BOOK TWO OF
THE MACMASTER CHRONICLES

a novel by

Jason Lord Case

NEW YORK

ISBN: 978-0-9825616-3-8

Published by Red Petal Press, New York
RedPetalPress.com

Book and Cover Design by Red Petal Press
Front Cover Photograph Elements courtesy of PhotoXpress

This book is a work of fiction. Names, characters, businesses, organizations, places, events, and incidents are the product of the author's imagination or are used fictitiously. Any resemblance to actual persons, living or dead, events, or locales is entirely coincidental.

Printed in the United States of America

This book is dedicated
to Antonia Orozco.

Chapter One
Hey, Stranger

The Central Tavern was nothing special, just an average downtown dive with an old hardwood bar running down one side of the long, narrow room. The washrooms were in the back and, while relatively clean, were serviced with very old porcelain and beaten up delivery fixtures. The satin and velvet wallpaper above the 5-foot wooden wainscoting spoke of a different time, a time when the central parts of the city had been more conspicuous, more fashionable.

Johnny was behind the bar, moving slowly. There was nothing to be in a hurry for. It was the middle of the day. The regulars for lunch were there. Madge was in the back making sandwiches and slapping pickles on plates so old they had varicose veins. Johnny already knew who would be there and what they would order. Johnny had been standing there for years seeing the same crowd drinking the same thing for lunch. Nobody under 40 years old ever entered this establishment before six at night.

Everybody in the place turned to look when the blond man entered. It was not that there were not plenty of blonds in Cleveland, but this man had the lightly tanned leather look that can only be achieved in warmer climates and was rarely seen in February. The phrase "You're not from around here, are you?" would have been as natural for them as a roast beef sandwich.

"What'll it be?" asked Johnny. He already had a draft glass in his hand, wiping it off with a clean white towel.

The stranger glanced at the handles poking up behind the bar and ordered a domestic beer. His accent marked him as a foreigner.

As Johnny drew the beer, he asked if there would be anything else.

The stranger was scanning the lunch menu when the sirens alerted everyone in the bar that there was something going on about a block away.

"I'll have one of these chicken sandwiches with french fries. Tell the cook to throw some Russian dressing on it as well." The foreigner was evincing no interest in the police cars or whatever had drawn them to the area. "I'll eat at that table." He took his beer to said table and draped his trench coat over the back of a chair. Under the trench coat he was wearing a padded vest, generally the style for people even younger than himself. He left the vest on and snapped at the bottom. He sat facing the door.

Outside, the police were looking for somebody. They were driving around the neighborhood with their lights on but their sirens off. They were obviously certain that the object of their attention was in the immediate area.

The tanned blond man with the foreign accent finished his beer and called for another about the time his chicken sandwich was delivered to him by the portly Madge with the stained apron that smelled of bleach and grease. He ate slowly, relishing his meal.

The stranger was only half done with his meal when the door admitted the next arrival, a beefy, red faced, uniformed patrolman. He walked up to the bar after a sweeping examination of the patrons and asked Johnny how business was.

"Same as always, Sam. Beer's cold and the food's hot. What'll it be?" Johnny had spoken with Sam many times, but the officer usually ate elsewhere.

"Looking for anyone new in the area. You ever see that guy before?"

"No. He got there about half hour ago. Had a couple of beers and a chicken sandwich."

"Did he look nervous when he got here?"

2

"No, just walked in… Just walked in."

"Thanks."

The stranger was looking at the officer with natural curiosity, the same as everyone else in the bar.

Once again the door opened. This time it was Ham, a regular customer of the Central Tavern. He was ten minutes later than usual and would probably miss his third draft as a result.

"Damn. Somebody just blew away three niggers down the street."

"What are you talking about?" Johnny asked.

"You know what I mean. Them greaseballs with their Cadillacs and their silk suits. Gimme a beer. Somebody went in that building they got down there and shot three of 'em. That's what I heard."

Everybody turned their gaze from Ham to Sam. Officer Sam Hardy knew what was going on and they all saw it as his job to enlighten them as to the veracity of Ham's story. He did not comment, however. Instead he moved from the bar where Ham was describing what he had seen in between slurps of draft beer.

The officer sat, uninvited, on the other side of the table from the newcomer. The stranger continued to eat, unperturbed but obviously curious.

After swallowing a mouthful of chicken with a sip of beer, he asked the officer how he could be of assistance. His accent marked him.

"What's your business in Cleveland?" was the direct, almost insultingly so, question.

"I'm in the import/export business. I'm in Ohio looking at glass manufacturing machinery. The M&R Verano Company. In two days I'll be west of Lansing, in Michigan, looking at a manufacturer's site. Spun glass."

"Spun glass?"

"Oh, uh, fiber glass you call it."

"I see. Do you mind if I ask your name?"

"Of course not. I'm Russell O'mara. Have you ever considered getting into the import business? There is a lot of money to be made in importing wool, mutton, beef and lamb. The difference in the currency, currently, makes beef particularly attractive. Now I'm not talking about your high-end steaks, since they need to be fresh, I'm talking about the strong-tasting free range herds that we use for broth. The possibility is there for the investment and we have the product down under, but I need a viable market for this one. I'm currently working with several concerns in Colorado on the import of sheep. There have been some concerns with the…", the stranger did not seem to need to breathe as he spoke. The spiel flowed forth unchecked.

Sam held up his hand, palm out and said, "Please, I'm only interested in why you are here, right now."

"Well, I'm telling you. I'm looking to bring back some viable glass forming products. I won't be buying them, of course; I'm merely here as a broker. I need to determine who has what we need and then establish an opinion of my own. There are businesses in Canberra that need the new equipment. Jars are a part of it. Kiwi jam is making a big splash in the States and we can grow some kiwi down under, let me tell you. We also got a need for spun glass insulation machines. If I can broker a proper deal this week, I can make me a good piece of change. Make it worthwhile to come up here in this miserable weather. How on Earth do you stand it up here in this climate anyway with all this snow and the salt on the roads and the…", once again there was an outpouring of information without the speaker seeming to even breathe. Sam held up his hand and apologized for interrupting the Australian's meal and made his getaway.

4

Once the officer was gone, the foreigner ordered another beer. The flow of words that had been gushing from his mouth stopped as if turned off at the tap. He finished his meal and slowly drank his beer. He paid for his meal and asked Johnny to call him a cab.

The Central Tavern went back to its regular routine. The television in the corner reported that the police were searching for someone who had entered a downtown building and wiped out the inhabitants. The police had found a huge cache of drugs and guns in the apartment and most of them wrote the incident off as gang related.

"No. I'm afraid the payment must be made in cash. It's not that I don't trust you, but things can be done with computers that I am not that familiar with."

"Was there a problem with the transferred down payment?"

"Not so far as I can tell, but I need the cash."

"Very well."

The living room was a simple affair. The furniture was clean but not new. The paintings on the wall were done in acrylics, so they lacked the quality and depth of work done in oils. The carpets were thick but not expensive and were a brown color that hid all but the worst stains.

The man making the payment was dressed unpretentiously. He had an insulated, checked shirt in red, a kind of lumberjack fashion and cotton work pants with a hammer loop on one side. He could have been a worker in any factory, a fork truck driver in a lumberyard or a long-haul trucker. There was no indication that he was wealthy.

The home was identical to half a dozen different houses in the subdivision. While it was a good neighborhood, it did nothing to single out the inhabitants. It was no mansion, no obvious seat of power for the rich and famous. It was just another home like all the others around it, in a neighborhood with manicured lawns and no sidewalks.

The guest topped six foot by a couple of inches. His sandy blond hair set off his well-tanned skin. His deep blue eyes missed nothing. He was wearing a padded vest and his trench coat and hat were thrown over the end of the sofa. One leg was cocked over the other, showing the flat sole of the cowboy boots. They were not the ideal footwear for February in Ohio.

"I'll need to confirm that the job was completed as contracted," the home owner said. His tone was as if he was discussing a roofing job.

"That won't be a problem. Turn on the telly. It's on all the news."

The man in the red shirt picked up the remote control and turned the television to a local channel where the newscaster was reporting the weather. Sports news and some commercials followed the weather report and then a recap of the day's news. The top story was of the killing of three drug dealers in a downtown apartment. This time the identity of the victims was given and photographs of them while they were still alive were aired. The police were asking for help in identifying a suspect in the shooting. The man seemed satisfied after the newscast was done. He excused himself and went upstairs. When he returned it was with a briefcase.

The guest had moved across the room when the resident came back down the stairs and he insisted the briefcase be opened so he saw the contents first. Despite the apparent ease of demeanor and casual attitude, the man was taking no unnecessary risks.

The briefcase was full of cash.

"Would you like to count it?" offered the resident.

"No, mate. If you try to cheat me, I'll just kill you too."

6

"I think I knew that."

"It's right then?"

"Yes. It's all there. The agreed upon amount." The homeowner was looking a bit stressed now.

"I'll be off then."

"Thank you again for your service."

"The money is thanks enough. A fair day's work for a fair day's wage."

"Yes. You know, you didn't need to kill the other two. I was afraid you were going to ask for something for them."

"We didn't contract them, so you don't need to pay. Just consider that community involvement; a public service. Blue light special is it?"

The homeowner laughed somewhat forcedly. He did not want this man staying any longer than he had to. Yes he had contracted the job, but now that it was over, the Australian assassin made him nervous.

He had contracted the job because the man he wanted dead had raped and disfigured his daughter. He had tried to get justice through the legal system and had run up against a brick wall. It was not long before his patience with the courts had ended. The lawyers stretched out the affair endlessly while the scumbag was still operating with business as usual. Justice was served now and the price had been paid. Now he started to think he had made a mistake. He thought he might now be subject to blackmail. What if this man told someone else what he had done and they wanted to squeeze him for more cash. His stomach began to hurt. He had done what he thought necessary. He had paid for that piece of walking filth to be cleaned from the street. He had balanced the books. Now he began to fear that it would not be over. That it would not be that easy.

In truth, he need not have worried. He was dealing with an honorable man.

Chapter Two
February in Michigan

Terry Kingston had no business trying to drive in Michigan in February. He considered himself a good driver and he was, in truth, competent on a good dry road but the roads are not dry in Michigan, in February. Nor are they good.

The State Administrators had neglected Michigan's infrastructure for so long that the roads were a disaster. The policy of trying to fix concrete roads with blacktop patches exacerbated the situation. Ice and snow combined with bad roads and a light, foreign vehicle could easily have been the formula for tragedy. Michigan's expressways have a seventy-mile-an-hour speed limit to top off the mix.

Four-wheel-drive pickups and Jeeps were flashing past and throwing slop on Terry's windshield as he drove the right hand lane about 55 miles an hour. The big diesel trucks were moving about the same speed he was and in the same lane.

The cell phone in his shirt pocket rang and he barely got it open in time to respond to the caller with "Gooday."

"No, it's not a particularly good day."

"Look, mate, I'm trying to be polite but I'm behind a huge bloody truck getting my kidneys pounded out by this shitty bloody road. I can't see a bloody thing through the snow and the salt and my windshield washers are frozen so I can't fix the problem. I may need to stop here and get a room for the night."

"I thought I had hired a real man."

"What you got, mate, is a man who knows better than to drive when he can't see what's in front of him."

"Well, what are you driving?"

"Japanese car."

"That's your first mistake. You're in Michigan, Mate." The man's voice took a hard, sarcastic edge. "A Japanese car stands out like a sore thumb. Get a Chevy pickup or an F-150 and you'll blend a whole lot better. Make sure you put some sub-zero windshield washer in the reservoir and it won't freeze to the windshield."

"Great. Look, as soon as the sun goes down and it's almost there, I'm done with this. I'll pull off and find a place to stay if I need to stay in the back seat for the night."

"Where are you now?"

"On US75 Northbound. I just passed Pontiac."

"Oh. Well, you got a rest stop coming up. Did you pass the weigh station yet?"

"The what? Oh, hell." The conversation ended for a moment as Terry regained control of the car. "All right, mate. That's it. I'm pulling off at the next exit wherever it goes and finding a place." Terry did not wait for a reply; he closed the phone, killing the connection and concentrated on driving. The snow was so thick he could not see the white truck ahead of him, just its taillights. The road salt on his windshield was dried by the defrosters, and the cheap windshield washer fluid was freezing to the glass.

The next exit turned out to be the rest stop his connection had mentioned, and he was grateful to pull off the road and into the area. One side of the little island was for cars and the other side was packed with trucks. The professional drivers were lined up with their engines thumping away, but there was no place for them to congregate inside the building. It was simply a toilet and vending machine affair.

A state worker was plowing the parking lot with a pickup truck. Terry let the truck plow around him and moved to a spot that had already been cleared. There were a couple of other cars in the lot, running. Terry could not have guessed they were gay men looking for temporary trysts with strangers. He naturally assumed they were seeking refuge from the weather.

After a few hours the snow cleared up a bit. Some of the professional drivers began pulling out. Terry was sleeping in the front seat of the car with the engine running and the heat blasting. He woke when a vehicle pulled up next to him. The sun was down but the snow had stopped. The heat of the engine in the parked car had warmed the windshield washer up to the point where it would not freeze to the windshield.

Terry took stock of his situation, unwilling to move immediately. He lit a cigarette and enjoyed the smooth American tobacco. He had been in America for a little over a month and was heading toward his second job. The job in Cleveland had gone well enough, aside from having to talk to the officer in the bar. He did not think there were any witnesses. He decided he liked taking out drug dealers because there was a lack of enthusiasm on the part of law enforcement in seeking the perpetrator. The drug dealers were always killing each other over territory, and it made for an easy explanation when one of them ended up dead. The last job had paid him better than many jobs would have because it was a personal job that an individual wanted done. Terry was already sure that the job in Michigan was not paying him enough to drive through this weather. He truly had no idea what the weather was like in the northern United States or that Michigan's weather was relatively mild due to its being surrounded by water. He would be surprised to find that the heaviest lake effect snows hit the eastern side of the lakes and pretty much bypassed all but the Upper Peninsula of Michigan.

Finishing his cigarette, Terry put the Toyota in gear and almost got stuck in the bank of snow that had been pushed up behind him while he was sleeping. He had no choice but to continue north from there, but the snow had stopped and the roads had been plowed. There was almost no traffic now, compared to earlier, so Terry let the cruise control take him down the road. Just before the city of Flint, he got a room at the Holiday Inn.

It was noon the following day when he met his contact at a restaurant in the commercial district. It was not difficult to pick him out, he was sitting in the only foreign car in the parking lot. His contact explained that Flint was a General Motors town and Michigan was the heart of the American auto industry. That was why it was unusual to see a foreign car there. He then went through some of the history of the town from the roots of the auto industry through its heyday to the present day. Terry listened, formed his own opinion and kept his mouth shut until the man was done talking.

"So, do you have the down payment, a photograph and address for the commission, a name and occupation?"

"Uh, no."

"What is it that you do have then?"

"The contractee wants to meet you personally."

"Is this necessary?"

"It appears so. I did not anticipate this, myself. I arrived at the airport from Chicago, yesterday. I usually handle all such transactions, but in this case I guess the man wants to pay attention himself."

"He'd better be careful or he may end up decommissioned himself."

"Uh, yes, well, that is not my problem. I would have done this in a civilized manner, but it seems our mutual friend does not understand protocol."

"So he wants to watch? That's going to be extra, a lot extra."

"I don't think that's it, but I don't know. He said he wanted to meet you and give you the down payment in cash. If it were me, I'd walk away. I don't do the heavy lifting though."

"I'll meet him but not on his terms, on mine."

"I'll let him know. So, the last one went quite well, yes? You met that one."

"I needed some cash."

"I don't know why; you've got all kinds of money."

"Because cash has a louder voice than anything else. I needed an auto anyway."

"Yeah."

"Don't start. I heard you the first time. I need a pickup truck."

"Or an American car. You're in Flint, Michigan. Get an old Buick if you want, a Chevy would be OK. They stopped making Oldsmobiles, don't know why. Make it American anyway; stay away from foreign cars.

"All right. I need to look around a little first. I need to pick out a spot."

"Well, there are malls on both sides of the city, all kinds of hardware stores and restaurants. There are closed factories but they are generally fenced in. Oh, this town has pawn shops, lots of them. Most of them sell diamonds pawned from failed marriages. Some of them have guns, they all have tools."

"Pawn shops. That's like a second hand store?"

"Uh, yeah, more or less. See, people take things in and get a little cash for them and then if they want them back they come back in with the money and if they don't, the pawn shop owner gets to sell it."

"Is there an internet café?"

"Uh, I don't think so. I tell you what, though, there are three colleges in this town…"

"Say no more. Call the man and tell him I'll send him an e-mail with the location as soon as I have his e-mail address."

"E-mail address? Are you serious?"

"Right as rain, mate. Take me to the biggest campus in town."

The cafeteria of the University of Michigan at Flint was packed with young people having lunch. They ran the full political gamut from liberal to conservative and every social strata was represented. The Hispanic members of society were notably absent in Mid-Michigan and the Orientals were almost nonexistent but the rich and the poor were there and everybody in between.

Terry had stopped in at security and gotten himself a day pass, which did not include a photograph. His name was Russell O'mara. He did not yet have the internet address to contact his newest contractor so he hung around campus admiring the fine young females.

In the cafeteria he saw one table filled with eight or so older students. They were in the definite minority but they were white. The black students seemed to have an attitude against anyone who did not look like them. That is, their group not their color. Some of the groups wore suits, unusual for a college campus but not unheard of. Some of the groups wore baggy, gang inspired clothing and moved in certain ways intended to intimidate others. Some wore jump suits, even though they were not there for athletics and could not have played sports with all the gold jewelry they were wearing. The whites were dressed more conservatively than the blacks, though some of the young women obviously spent a great deal of money on their clothes and makeup.

Terry got a cup of coffee from the lunch line and moved toward a table half filled with young white women.

He was careful not to choose the sorority girls. He was certain they came from rich backgrounds and were used to getting anything they wanted for the asking. The sorority girls were dressed better and looked better, but he knew their attitudes did not coincide with his purpose.

"Ladies, d'ye mind if I share your table?" was all that was needed. As soon as the young women heard his accent, he was in. One petite brunette was particularly taken with him and made no secret of it. She told him she stayed off campus and that she worked at a party store on Grand Traverse, just south of Hurley Hospital. She would be going to work at three o'clock and working until eight.

Terry could not help but think about how he loved young women as he leaned against the outside wall of the gas station and convenience store on Grand Traverse.

"You're not supposed to smoke at a gas station, you know."

"Vanessa, I hope you're hungry."

"Well, you caught me by surprise. Yes, I'm starving but I've also been in these clothes all day and I'm going to need to change and shower if I'm going out to dinner."

"I can wait."

The impish smile on Vanessa's face was adorable. It spoke of passion, restrained and refined. "I just live right over there. It's a small apartment but walking distance to school and work. Come on over and have a drink. I'll only take a minute."

It turned out that it took a bit longer than Terry could have predicted. Vanessa made him comfortable, poured him some rum, and then she took a shower. Instead of getting dressed, however, she walked back into the living room dripping wet and stark naked. She stood in front of him with the water dripping off her, grabbed the back of his head and

14

pushed his face into her womanhood. They never did get to the restaurant that night.

"Hello."

"I have the internet address."

"Right-o. Give me a moment." Terry held the microphone of the cell phone to his leg. "Vanessa, can I have a pen and paper?" Once she had handed them to him, he wrote down Hardjammin@jammin.com.

"What's that all about, lover?"

"Oh, just an opportunity to sell some things. I'll use one of the computers in the library to access the site."

"I've got a laptop and internet access right here. You can send your messages from right here.

"Thanks luv, but I think it might be better to use the one at the library."

Vanessa got a pouting look on her face, made a decision and hopped back off the bed. It was still relatively early in the morning and she didn't have a class until eight o'clock.

"Do you work today, dear?" Terry asked, realizing he had just opened a gap between them.

"Every day," she said curtly.

"Well, what do you think about taking today off and going to the theater. There must be some Hollywood thing you'd like to see."

"No. I need my job and I'm doing well in school and I'm not throwing that away because some Fancy Dan Australian Man comes along and makes me swoon." Vanessa was looking every bit the responsible business woman this morning. Her light brown hair was pulled back tightly and her conservative clothing made her look like a librarian.

"Well, what's that supposed to mean? I didn't ask you to go running away to the Congo with me."

"If you want to take me to the movies, you know where I work and you know when I get out. Now I need to get to school so you need to go."

"Right then. I would be charmed to accompany you if I may. I might be taking some classes soon."

"You can't get in until the fall semester. Oh, I suppose you could take some summer classes if you wanted. You can't get in now though. Come on, I'll just make it on time if I leave now."

The two of them walked briskly down the street and across the chipped surface of the Grand Traverse Bridge over the Flint River. Terry shuddered when he looked over the rail into the opaque water. There was a styrofoam fast-food box floating in the water.

The University of Michigan at Flint was generous with its computers and internet access, but Terry needed to leave his identification at the desk, something that made him a bit nervous. He stood out enough with his bushwalker accent and didn't want to be any more conspicuous than need be. E-mail was not his primary purpose. He did not want his new lady to guess what he was up to, and he did not want to implicate her or make her a witness that needed to be eliminated.

Terry brought up the satellite image of the town on the computer, located where he was and selected a spot for his upcoming meeting. It did not make him overly nervous to meet the client. Kingston could understand why giving money to someone you never met before, to give to someone else you would never meet, would feel like throwing money into the river. He thought again about the opaque water of the Flint River and accessed a web site to check on year round river levels. There was no data available on how often the bottom was dredged.

The words of Terry's Uncle Ginger came back to him as he sat there. Never trust or involve the constables. They can't and won't cover your back, but they can be relied on to act in certain ways and that can be employed if done so discreetly.

Terry sent an e-mail by accessing his private account. It would be no great trick for an accomplished hacker to determine where the computer was physically located and he did not want to be fingered, so he never accessed the account from a location he might be found drinking or sleeping. He had learned a great deal in his short life and one of such things was the necessity to move along after a short period of time.

Outside the cafeteria was an open patio that provided a sweeping view of the parking lot. In summer this would have been ideal, but to stand in the cutting February wind while waiting for an arrival was foolhardy.

Inside the cafeteria, some of the same girls from the day before were at the same table. Vanessa had back to back classes and would not be out for another half hour. Under the name Russell O'mara, Terry made light conversation. He was accustomed to a diversity of population from his time in Sydney, but he was still intrigued by the diversity of population everywhere he had been in America. He could not hide the fact that he was Australian, his accent gave it away, even though he had been studying German for some time now. Oddly enough his German was not tainted by the Australian accent as much as his English. Terry used his status to engage in conversations about ethnic background and found that people that would have been at each other's throats in their native countries were side by side in America. That is not to say that all was well in the great melting pot. The African-American members of that great society remained aloof and separate in social settings. In some places the racial tension was worse than others.

When Vanessa arrived, she joined their conversation. She was, it seemed, a mix of Italian and Irish with some Scandinavian thrown in somewhere along the line. Terry admitted he had no idea where his ancestry lay buried but assumed he was progeny of the criminal Irishmen that were sent to the Botany Bay Prison Colony. He described them as heinous and disreputable brigands, garnering huge peals of laughter from his audience.

Vanessa had one more class before she had to leave for work. While she was in class, Terry went back to the library and accessed his e-mail. The meeting was set for Saturday morning at Flint's Bishop International Airport.

The airport was perfect for such a meeting. The Office of Homeland Security, the Sky Marshals, the local and state police, FBI and CIA all had business at any airport, not to mention the hundreds of other governmental agencies that might be moving through at any time. With all the potential law enforcement, one might shy away from such a location if one had thoughts of nefarious activities, however, if that same person never tried to buy a ticket or board a plane, they were invisible, a non-entity. The one problem was the number of cameras that blanketed the area in a sea of watchful monitors. As much a benefit as a problem, the cameras had not been updated in a long time and the ancient video tapes they still used had been recorded over a thousand times. The resolution they would provide was severely limited and though the public did not know it, fully one third of the cameras did not even work. They were there for the illusion of security and as such, they were very effective.

Terry had about six hours to kill, and after a little more research he hopped a bus, transferred twice and found himself back at the restaurant outside the shopping mall. His automobile was still where he had left it, and checking the trunk showed his pistols were still in place. He had kept his eyes open while cruising around in the city bus and had seen lots of vehicles for sale. He preferred a private sale because there would be no paper trail.

The Buick was a few years old but it did not show much mileage on the odometer. Terry paid for it outright and took the title and registration with him. He would return in a couple of days and pick it up, he promised. The previous owner was very pleased, thinking to himself that the schmuck hadn't even tried to bargain with him and paid in cash.

Vanessa said nothing about the make of his vehicle when he picked her up at the end of her shift at the party store. The two of them went to dinner in a very comfortable Thai restaurant across the road from the theater. The restaurant was almost empty.

"Of all the places in the world, what made you come here?"

"You mean this restaurant?" Terry asked.

"No. This town."

"There's an incredible amount of opportunity in a place like this."

Vanessa took another sip of tea and looked at Terry quizzically. "Flint? What opportunity could you be talking about in this shit hole? Excuse me." She put her hand over her mouth as if trying to keep further words from flowing forth.

"There is a large, unemployed work force here. The past decade has seen the major employer shutting down its operations, so there are facilities and manpower available for an entrepreneur to take advantage of."

"Technically, yes. But, you're not from around here."

"That shouldn't matter."

The waitress brought their food and took the tea pot to refill it.

"It doesn't matter where you're from. But it does matter what you know. I'm going to educate you on some of the history and then you can decide if you've made a mistake or not. First, I'm going to eat."

Terry saw that his cover was working but that under further questioning, it had limited utility unless he could be more specific. That was the last thing he wanted to do. The more detail injected into a fantasy, the more chances of a contradiction arising. He counted himself lucky that she preferred talking to listening.

The food was hot and spicy, a real change from what Terry was used to, but Vanessa attacked it with gusto, obviously prepared for the heat. She was only able to finish half the meal regardless of the enjoyment she derived from it.

Afterward, Vanessa began her dissertation on the dangers of trying to form a business in a place like Flint. She went through some of what Terry's connection had already explained, that Flint was a General Motors town and that it had been the center of automobile production for decades. Then she explained what Terry had not known. The real troubles began in 1998 when the United Auto Workers had gone on strike at the parts plants and had shut down GM for a number of weeks, costing them millions of dollars. The following year, General Motors divorced itself from its parts manufacturing wing. They spun off the whole affair and renamed it Delphi. Then, they squeezed the parts manufacturer, who was not allowed, by contract, to supply anyone else. Delphi played some financial games for the first couple of years, claimed they were making a profit, then discovered their financial "irregularities" and went bankrupt.

"So," Terry asked, "what you are saying is that they shut down and left the work force out of work and available?"

"Not exactly. You see, both my parents worked at GM and later at Delphi. The company bought them off and they both retired. Don't get me wrong, I love my parents to death, but they were both overpaid for the kind of work they did, right to the end. All the UAW members were… are overpaid. Well, were overpaid. Now they hire people at half the wage, but they are not hiring here. Delphi is the largest employer in Mexico."

"So, what you are saying is that the people here are what?"

"They are used to being overpaid and underworked. The union protected them so well that they couldn't be fired no matter what they did. I'm not like that, but most of the people in this town expect to be paid more than they are worth, and expect to work less than they should. They expect overtime as a right and if they don't feel like coming to work, they don't."

Terry paid for the meal and the two left the restaurant. Even though the theater was right across the street they were forced to go around several blocks to get there, because of traffic. The roads were dirt and Terry couldn't help but ask why. Vanessa had answers for this as well that had long trains of corruption, fiscal mismanagement and payoffs among the African-American administration of the city.

The movie was quite good, a drama about lost love and the reacquisition of faith in the goodness of mankind. Terry did not express his feelings about the goodness of mankind.

After the movie, they stopped down the street in a tavern of questionable quality and had a few drinks. That is, Vanessa had a few drinks. After the first, Terry drank ginger ale. Once the alcohol took hold of his partner, Terry drove her home for some close, personal, non-verbal communication.

The next day was Friday and Terry spent it alone. He ate in diners and got a good lay of the land, still driving his Toyota. That night he took Vanessa to pick up the Buick. He told her it was his gift to her and it totally floored her. It may not have been new or flashy, but it was a good, dependable car with a 3800cc V6 engine in it. The company no longer built Buicks in Flint but that engine had been built there.

Terry gave the new owner the license and registration and one set of keys. He did not mention he had another set and did not need to. The Secretary of State administered driver's licenses and registrations, but was closed for the weekend. While Terry expressed concerns about driving the car without plates, Vanessa assured him that they would be just fine as long as one of them drove the car and the other followed. She explained the system to him. On the way back to her apartment, he noticed a couple of different cars with no plates and no tags, being driven.

Much to her surprise, Terry kissed her at the door, made excuses about needing to be up early and left her standing there.

Initially Vanessa was hurt, but that only lasted a minute. Her hormones and her emotions were both racing madly through her, spawning questions, anxiety and lust. She looked out the window at the Buick in the driveway and could not help but ask if this was a payoff, if she was being treated like a commodity. She asked herself if she would ever see him again when deep inside her she knew that any time he walked up to her door, he would have a place to stay. She got the bottle of rum out of the freezer and took a huge pull off it, grimacing as the freezing cold burning liquid hit her stomach. A few minutes later she called his cell phone number, but it went directly to voice mail. She was not going to be able to talk to him tonight. She shook her head and asked herself what the hell was wrong with her. She had only known the man two days and he was certainly not her first. He was the first that had affected her like this, however. She had to admit to herself that she was in love and it caused tears to roll down her face unchecked.

Chapter Three
The Precinct

Captain Cook was stumped. His men had been aware that there was a distribution hub somewhere in the city, but they had been unable to find out its location until today. They had been fighting the epidemic of drugs at the street level and trying to make connections higher up the underworld ladder, but it was slow going. The drugs that had been poisoning the city were in constant supply, and no matter how many street suppliers were apprehended, there was an unending flow. Then, this morning, someone had walked into a downtown apartment and shot three men, leaving a suitcase full of cocaine and a small arsenal of guns behind. There was no large stash of money on hand and Cook suspected that the cash had been taken by the killer.

The prevailing opinion would have it that the men had been shot by rival drug dealers but the logic was flawed in that rival dealers would have taken the drugs and guns with them.

There was something missing that was just out of the captain's reach; some little bit of evidence that linked the murders with something or someone. He was sure he could find it, but he did not know where to look. He parked his car behind The Woodsman Restaurant and got out. He did not bother locking the door. Everybody knew The Woodsman was a cop's bar. It was owned by a retired captain and full of cops every night. Nobody ever messed with the vehicles parked there. It would have been suicide.

Inside, the atmosphere was jovial and the music was more background noise than anything else. They were all there: Judge Appolitano, Jerry Francis the Assistant Prosecutor, Tony Terry the Court Clerk, Sergeant Brown, Lieutenant Kauffman, a dozen or so patrolmen, all the town hall secretaries they could talk into joining them, Sally the Stenographer and four guards from the jail. This was where they came to relax, knowing they might be recognized elsewhere. For anyone here to be recognized elsewhere could have been a very bad thing so, like cops everywhere, they congregated in their own company.

Jerry Francis joined him at a table with Frank Bertram, a guard from the jail. The three of them often drank together. All three drank Maker's Mark. There was some talk about the impending storm and how nobody could drive well in the snow. They talked about the pile up that had occurred in Kansas the day before, then Jerry broached the subject that was on both of their minds.

"Somebody is doing your job for you."

"What's that supposed to mean?" Kevin Cook asked.

"Come on, Captain, we both know that somebody just shut down the cocaine supply for the city, temporarily anyway." Jerry was smiling. He knew the police had been looking for that connection for months and had not found it.

"So, I'm supposed to cry about a couple of dead scumbags?"

"No, but I'd like to know who did it." Jerry's smile disappeared. "We can't afford vigilantes and I don't think it was gang-bangers. A junkie would have at least taken the coke with him. A rival gang would have wanted the guns. I don't know if there was a stash of cash, but it looks like somebody did make off with that, if there was."

"God damn dirtbags, anyway." Frank chimed in. "Who cares who shot 'em. Just means I don't have to deal with 'em."

Jerry was smiling again. Frank had been half in the bag when he had arrived and had not showed any sign of slowing down. "Regardless of the cost savings and your personal relief at not having to see them incarcerated in your jail, somebody killed them. It may have been a rival gang, but who? It may have been a vigilante. If it's isolated, we'll have a hard time pinning it on anyone. Does the MO match anything recent in the area?"

"No, but you know the niggers are always killing each other."

"Hey," said Frank. "Cool it with that nigger shit, you fuckin' cracker."

"You know I ain't talkin' about you. You Uncle Tom motherfucker." Kevin and Frank had been needling each other that way for years. Racial tensions run high in Cleveland and African-Americans are in the majority.

"I ain't in the mood to hear it today, bitch." Frank sounded almost sincere.

"I don't give a shit what you're in the mood for, an' I got your bitch right here." Kevin pointed at Lieutenant Kauffman who was shooting pool. Kauffman was smaller than either man and had a bit of a complex about his size. All three men at the table exploded in laughter and Jerry called for another round, telling the waitress that it was on Kevin's tab because he was a racist motherfucker.

All three of them were half in the bag when the subject of the killings came back up. Captain Cook told his friends what he knew. "The perps came in through a window. They used a fire escape but I think they came down from the roof instead of up from the alley. I can't prove it, but there was a plank on the roof that looks as though it came from the other side of the alley. Problem is, there is no roof access from that building. The perps needed to come from the next building down. Nobody saw anything from that building. There was one old woman that said she heard somebody on the roof in the middle of the night. If they were there in the middle of the night, they would have gone in then, while the dealers were sleeping."

"So you're sure it was more than one man?" Jerry asked.

"Uh, no. I mean, I don't have the report from forensics yet, and I don't have any real evidence yet. I'm just thinking that it takes a big set of brass balls to walk into a major warehouse and pop three heavily armed men, just like that. I don't see anybody in this town with a set that big. So, it's got to be at least two or some outside talent.

"You know the boys from Buffalo have been looking to consolidate their control of the region. I know the initial connections are in Buffalo. I just can't prove it. That's the pipeline though. I90, the cocaine highway.

"So, what? Did they bring in professionals? Did some of the local boys get squirrelly? Or is it something else? Nobody but the upstairs neighbor heard the shots, so it was probably muffled. There was no brass found, so they either picked it up or used revolvers. You know the gang bangers all use nines, autoloaders. This didn't look like it. I'll get the report tomorrow. Until then, Detectives Carmody, Quincy and Grady are on it." Captain Cook reached out and took one of Jerry's cigarettes. He only smoked when he drank.

Frank stood unexpectedly and announced his intention to go into the men's room and vomit. Kevin told him he never did learn how to drink and followed it up with several other derogatory comments. When the thoroughly intoxicated guard came back out, Kevin told one of the patrolmen to take him home. When the patrolman opened his mouth to protest, Kevin Cook told him to shut up and do what he was told. The patrolman, wisely, did just that.

"Why Buffalo?" Jerry asked suddenly. "Cincinnati I could understand. Columbus would make sense, but Buffalo? That doesn't make sense. The shit's produced in South America, so it must be coming into New York City."

"That makes sense." Kevin's face was getting that familiar blush that comes with drinking too fast.

Jerry Francis had been drinking slower and more carefully. As a member of the club, he was exempt from being pulled over randomly and arrested for being drunk, but he was not exempt from accidents. If he plowed into a little old lady on the way home, the cops on the scene would not be quite so forgiving.

"Waitress… Rosie, bring us a couple of hamburgers will ya? Captain Cook's sinking fast."

"Captain Cook is just fine, Assistant District Attorney Francis. You're buying the burgers."

"OK"

"If the shit was coming in at New York, and final destination was here, then it would be coming down Route 80, not Buffalo."

"Maybe it does. Maybe they ship it to Pittsburg and split the shipment there, sending some north to Buffalo and the rest to us, minus the stuff that stays in Pennsylvania."

"The street says it comes in from Buffalo."

"OH! The street says." Jerry's voice was loud and sarcastic.

"Those jackasses aren't smart enough to make up stories." Kevin Cook was slurring his words now.

"Sure they are. One man says Buffalo to three different people and the next thing you know the whole goddamn town thinks the shit comes from Buffalo. Street rumors aren't worth a fuck."

"True, but this source is inside. I'm pretty sure he's reliable but he won't testify."

"Can't you squeeze him?"

"If I want maggots. He's on a slab at the morgue. He was unlucky enough to be in the wrong place at the wrong time."

"You think he was fingered?"

"Naw. He got caught with the other two in the downtown affair. He was just getting into place. We couldn't get a cop in there, but I had something heavy on this piece of shit and I was getting somewhere, finally. Set him up as a buyer. He goes in there and gets lead poisoning and I'm up shit creek.

"Rosie, bring me a drink."

Jerry motioned for Rosie to forget the drink and bring the hamburgers instead. He had not known there was a man on the inside, and thanked the powers that be for making sure the cops all drank in the same bars. Kevin Cook might have ended up on a slab himself if he had been drinking elsewhere.

The hamburgers were pretty good and the french fries were bubbling hot from the oil. A glass of water came with the meal and Cook surprised his friend by actually drinking it. After eating, Kevin wanted to go home and sleep. Jerry had hoped for that. He drove Kevin home and watched him stagger into the building. It was not the first time and would probably not be the last.

Morning came for Kevin Cook accompanied by a pounding headache, a dehydrated tongue, a stomach ache and diarrhea. He considered calling in sick but rejected the thought immediately. There was too much to be done today. He looked in the freezer and found a half pint bottle of Old Crow. A few shots of that cleared his vision and got his saliva flowing again. He sat on the toilet for a while, and then realized he had left his car at The Woodsman. He swore once and called Dispatch to have a patrol car pick him up and take him there. He knew he was going to be late and hurried to scrape the dark stubble off his face.

When he reached the station, he went through the back way and slipped into his office, but not without being noticed.

Fortunately, he had written down his appointments for the day; he was scheduled to appear in court at 9:00.

Judge Appolitano looked none the worse for wear, though Kevin was sure he had seen His Honor drinking the night before. The truth was that the judge was as bad a drunk as Captain Cook. They hadn't spoken in the bar, but it was understood that the man coming up for trial was guilty. Cook had been in on the bust, and the District Attorney was not going to cut the defendant any slack. He had offered him a deal and the man had been rude.

Cook was sworn in and testified to what he had seen and done. The deck was stacked and the man was going away for five to ten.

When he returned to his office, the initial report from forensics was on his desk. The three men had been killed by the same caliber weapon, but not the same gun. Two separate .38s had been used. The ammunition had been hollow points in both weapons. At least one of the victims had been shot at close range, but there were no casings found.

"So we're looking for two men with .38 revolvers or one man with two .38 revolvers with silencers. That is, unless the killers stopped to police their brass, and I just don't see that. Nobody heard much of anything." Kevin's headache was returning and he rummaged around in his drawer until he came up with a small bottle of aspirin. He walked down the hall to the coffee machine and chased a couple of aspirin with black coffee. He knew it was going to give him a stomach ache, so he drank some water to try to buffer the pain.

The autopsies were not done, but there was no question about what had killed the three men. They had pulled two slugs out of each man. One from each gun.

"One from each gun. So we are looking for one man with two pistols." Kevin told Dispatch he was going to the crime scene, and pulled on his coat.

Halfway downtown, Kevin Cook stopped at a drug store for some Bismuth and another bottle of aspirin.

The crime scene was taped off, but there was a detective and two investigators there. Kevin was interested in the side alley and the building next door first. The board that Cook had seen the day before had been tagged and put into evidence. It had not been examined yet, but it was a 2-by-6 deck board, braced with 2-inch angle iron. The lag bolts connecting the two pieces were fresh, but the angle iron was rusty and the board itself was weathered. The killer had moved it to the roof from another building, and used it to traverse the width of the alley.

"When did he take it upstairs? Why didn't anyone see him do this? And… Wait a minute." Cook called to Phoebe, one of the Crime Scene Investigators and asked if she had a tape measure.

"Of course, Captain."

"Come with me; take notes."

Phoebe left her partner Brian behind and followed Cook. Everybody in the department knew he was a drunk and a womanizer, but they also respected his insight into criminal motivation and evidence correlation.

"How wide is this alley?"

"Twelve-foot four."

"Write it down."

"How long was the deck board on the roof?"

"Sixteen foot."

"Write it down."

"How long is that piece of conduit? No, not that one, the long one."

Phoebe almost asked Cook what that had to do with anything, but she had learned to keep her mouth shut. "It's fourteen-foot ten."

"That's close enough. Bring it." Kevin moved quickly toward the street and past the first building, it had no roof access. He didn't pause at the front door but walked up the steps of the next building. Phoebe was hurrying to catch up to him, but the almost 16-foot piece of conduit gave her a great deal of trouble on the stair well. The second floor was even worse. While there was a railing she could pick it over downstairs, she was unable to get it past the wall on the inside of the stairs above the ground floor.

"That conduit's a bit more flexible than a plank but you still can't get it up the stairs. That means the killers couldn't either. So he got it up there some other way or it was already there. Did we find any prints on it?"

"No, Sir. That is, we haven't tested that yet. There are no prints on the window or the fire escape; nothing on the door handle. Either they used gloves, or they wiped it down afterward."

Cook's head and stomach were beginning to hurt less as his mind got focused on the issue at hand. "Why would anyone go through all the trouble of hoisting that board to the roof and coming down the fire escape from the roof when he could walk in the front door? Why was anyone that interested in shooting these scumbags, and then leaving both the drugs and the guns? Why was there no money on the scene?"

Cook moved back to the scene of the crime. Detective Carmody was interviewing the postman. Detectives Quincy and Grady were nowhere to be seen. The blood spray and the outlines told the story well enough for an experienced investigator. The killer came in through the window, shot two men in this room, once while they were up, once while they were already down. Then he went into the bedroom and shot the man in there. The man in the bedroom had gotten off a couple of shots, but had not hit anyone before taking two himself.

If there was any money, it was stolen. The suitcase of cocaine was in the bedroom closet, so the man in the bed was the boss. The guns were in the living room and the bedroom, so the men in the living room were on guard. Cook's informer was one of them. Kevin began to suspect that the man was playing him as well. He had evidence against him, and could have sent him away when he was still among the living, but preferred to use him. He wondered now, who was using who.

"Why was the boss buck naked in the bedroom when his guards were in the living room? Was there somebody else in the bedroom?"

"What's that, Cap'n?"

Kevin Cook jumped half out of his skin. He hadn't heard the Detective come up behind him, and the sudden answer to his question startled him. "Shit, Carmody!" he said. "Let me know you're there next time."

"Sorry, Cap'n."

"That's OK, Carmody. I'm just trying to work all this out."

"Aw, who gives a shit? It gets a couple of bad guys off the street along with a suitcase full of crap and a dozen guns. I, personally, look at it as a favor. If the evidence points to anyone in particular, sure I'll take 'em down. I'm only gonna work that hard at it though."

"Where's Grady and Quincy?"

"Canvassing the area for witnesses."

"Right."

Captain Cook found both Quincy and Grady in the Central Tavern having lunch. More precisely, they were drinking lunch. Cook asked them what they thought they were doing, and found they were waiting for Officer Sam and someone named Ham. Kevin could not believe they were not pulling his leg, and kept waiting for some line about off color eggs that was not forthcoming.

Sam Hardy had been directed to stop at the Tavern. He should have been there by then, but such was the schedule of a patrolman.

Kevin ordered lunch for the three of them and told Grady he was paying for it. When Grady asked why, Kevin told him that it was penance for drinking on the job, and that he would be going to confession next if he didn't shut up. Quincy smiled but said nothing. He had paid last time and would probably pay next time. The alternative was much more unpleasant.

The coffee was hot and the reuben sandwiches were mediocre, but, coming from Ohio, none of them knew what a real reuben was supposed to taste like. The Detectives finished their drinks and ordered two more; Kevin drank coffee. It was not that he had anything against drinking on the job, but he chose the time and company to do so with great care.

Sam arrived, finally, in uniform and slightly dusty. He had been forced to stop on the way there and break up a fight on the basketball court of the local school. Some kid named Deron was jacking up another kid named Taylor.

"Deron Jackson?" asked Detective Quincy.

"Yeah. You know him?" replied Sam Hardy.

"I know his whole family. Did ya bust him?"

"Called another man to take him in and then moved on."

"OK. His papa gonna bust his ass tonight. Whad'ja charge him with, assault?"

"No, just disturbing. Judge'll let him out in the morning."

"His pop's still gonna beat his ass. Serves him right."

"So," interjected Kevin Cook, "you were part of the crew that canvassed the area after the killing down the street."

"Yes, Sir. Most of the men took their patrol cars around. I thought I could be more effective on foot. I see more that way, I talk to more people."

"And did you see anything out of the ordinary? Your report says there was a stranger here?"

"Yeah," Sam sat down and eyed the detectives' drinks. "That table. Guy had a foreign accent, Australian. A real salesman, kept trying to get me to get into the… What was it, beef industry? Something like that. Just kept talking about it. That and glass. He wanted to buy glass. Said he was going to Lansing, Michigan." He pulled a notebook out of his pocket. "Name was O'mara."

"But not a suspect?"

"No. This guy was just sitting here eating a hamburger and having a beer."

"Seen him since?"

"No. Johnny, that crocodile man been back in?"

Johnny said he hadn't seen him and the conversation changed to other theories.

Sam Hardy left, Detective Carmody arrived, apparently knowing where he could find his partners. Carmody ordered a hamburger, and they all discussed their feelings about the situation.

All three of the victims had extensive criminal records, and they had probably not been caught for more than 1% of their crimes. All three lived in the city, so they were obviously local distributors, merely running the local hub.

They were big for the area but not big enough. The police wanted a bigger fish and the FBI wanted all the big fish, but the question remained as to who wanted them dead.

The subject came up of Priscilla Porter. Priscilla had filed charges against Willy Brown, the man they found dead in the bedroom. She claimed he had raped her and then sliced open her face, but there had been multiple witnesses avowing that he had been drinking with them in a tavern on East Avenue all night, and he could not have been the perpetrator. The subject of her father also arose. Roger Porter was a manager at a local heating and air conditioning business. He was fairly well off and he had escorted his daughter to the hearings.

Grady said it might be worth a look. Quincy sucked his teeth, trying to get a piece of corned beef out from between them. Carmody said he'd look into it. Cook cut him off and told Grady he would be looking into it, and telling Carmody to follow him back down the street. He also told Quincy to stay right where he was until he had talked to Ham Hammonds. Ham would probably be here for lunch, he usually was, according to Johnny the bartender.

Carmody took the length of conduit that Phoebe had returned to the alley and followed Captain Cook to the second and then third building down the street from the crime scene. The conduit would go up the stairs of the third building but a 16-foot plank would not have.

Cook flipped open his cell phone and dialed a number. "Phoebe, do me a favor and go back up to the roof and have another look at that plank. Tell me if there is a way to tie a rope to that thing and drag it up the side of a building. Then check it for fibers. I want to know how that thing got up there. Call me back."

"Captain, dragging stuff up the side of one of these buildings is kind of a lot of work to go through to get across an alley…"

"I've got an idea, and if I'm right, we'll probably never catch this guy."

Detective Carmody kept his mouth shut at that point. He had seen Cook in this mode before and knew that while the pathways of the captain's brain were convoluted and arcane, they led more often than not to a theory that had more truth than not. Sometimes it was downright scary.

When she called back, Phoebe confirmed that there were fibers attached to the angle iron that was fastened to the plank. The fibers were nylon and she could see a length of nylon rope lying in the alley. It was her guess that it would be the same physical composition as the fibers.

"Carmody, remind me, who called the cops that day?"

"It's in the report. Upstairs neighbor. She heard a bang, she says it was gunfire in the alley. Officers came in, headed to the fourth floor, got stopped on the second when they saw two dead bodies through the open door.

"Nobody saw anybody leaving or entering the building. Smooth as a fucking snake, yet he left the door open for the officers to find the bodies. Why would he do that?" The gears were spinning in Cook's head now.

"He wanted somebody to find the bodies."

"Yes, yes, yes, but why? It's because he was being paid for the hit and wanted to get out of town quickly. He wasn't seen leaving the building because he used the board to get across the span, and then tossed the fucking thing back over the alley. How many shots did the caller report?"

Carmody did not need to look at the report for this. "She reported two and then a couple of minutes later a boom and three more."

"A boom and three more. By the time she heard three more, he was already over the alley. The boom was the deck board landing on the roof, then he let off three more to make sure somebody called the police. Leave the conduit; come with me to the roof."

On the roof, the two moved to the edge, dropped the four feet to the next roof that was the same level as the building the killings had occurred in.

The edge was raised and covered with half-round ceramic tiles. Toward the back of the building, there was a fresh abrasion on top of one of the tiles. There was a rusty substance mixed with the dusty clay underneath the hard exterior.

Phoebe was still on the roof across the alley, but she claimed there were no marks on that side.

"This son-of-a-bitch is slick. He came up here and set up his escape route before he did the killings. He dragged the board up here from the alley, not to get here but to get away. Then he tossed it back over here to throw us off. What we have here is a man who likes to play games and sit back and laugh. We got either a professional, in which case we may never see him again, or a fuckin' psychopath. I don't know which is worse. The motherfucker probably walked right back in front of the building and back down the street to the Central Tavern for a beer. Carmody, call the station. I want that Australian man brought in. What's his name? O'peckerwood or whatever it is. Have him picked up if he's still in the area. Check the hotels, motels and whorehouses. See if he has any credit cards we can track him with."

Detective Grady waited for Roger Porter outside the contractor's house. The neighborhood gave no natural cover for surveillance work. The trees were too young to climb, there were no sidewalks and nobody parked on the street.

The local police gave him a second look and he flashed them his badge. The school buses were dropping off the local children.

Priscilla Porter would have graduated the year before if it were not for the unfortunate incident that had occurred in her sophomore year. Grady saw her get off the school bus and head to the door of the house that was so much like all the other houses in the area. He could not see her face; it was masked by shoulder length blonde hair. He briefly thought of paying her a visit, but decided to wait for Roger. They had no evidence linking either of them to the killings, and couldn't even ask them to come downtown without something substantive.

Roger Porter arrived at home half an hour after his daughter was dropped off by the school bus. He parked in the driveway. Grady noticed that he used his key to get in the door.

The doorbell rang loudly and Roger Porter opened the door, stepping onto the concrete slab that served as a stoop for the house. There was no front porch.

"What can I do for you, officer?"

"Mr. Porter, I just have a couple of questions."

"About what?"

"Have you seen the news today, or last night?"

"No."

Grady knew Roger Porter was lying, at that point. He exhibited classic signs such as looking at his shoes. The detective thought quickly, asking himself why a man would lie to such a simple question. He counted himself lucky in that the man did not lie well.

"Mr. Porter, where were you yesterday at approximately 11:45?"

"I, uh, I would have been washing up for lunch. I went to lunch at about noon yesterday."

"Is there anyone who might corroborate your story?"

"Of course. I had Benny with me; he's an assistant. The customer was there. I talked to her after we installed the water heater, gave her my card, you know, told her to call if there were any problems. Made a pitch to get her to replace her furnace. She let us wash up in the bathroom and we went to lunch about noon."

"Did Benny eat lunch with you?"

"Yeah. Just another day. What's this all about?"

"There was an incident yesterday and we're just talking to everyone who might have interest in it."

"Oh, well, I was at work and don't know what you're talking about."

"OK. Well, I'll leave you then. Sorry to have bothered you."

Detective Grady went back to his car and pulled out a note pad. There was something wrong with Mr. Porter. He had asked what it was all about, but he did not ask what incident the detective was talking about. That was obviously because he already knew what he had denied hearing about. Perhaps Mr. Porter should be looked at a bit more closely.

Quincy and Grady tended to drink in the same tavern on a pretty much daily basis. Carmody didn't join them often since he was happily married for now and did not want his third wife to leave him. Police officers often have short and tumultuous relationships.

That night, all three of them were in the Brass Ring Tavern for a quick one after work, reviewing the case. Unlike members of many other communities, officers don't leave the job behind when they punch out. Part of the trouble is that they hang around with other cops when they're off duty.

The consensus of opinion was that the murders were a professional hit. Carmody told the others about Captain

Cook's theories, and Grady talked about what he considered the strange reaction Roger Porter had given him. Quincy had nothing to add that could be gleaned from the flushed and flabby Ham. As a black officer, he had not expected Ham to give him anything anyway. Ham was obviously of Polish or Czechoslovakian stock; many of that community had long-standing distrust of African-Americans and didn't like the police anyway.

Grady and Quincy had been working together for years and respected each other a great deal. Grady actually considered Quincy the better cop and it hurt him to see the racial tension that bubbled to the surface on some of the calls they made together.

Carmody went home after one beer, but Grady and Quincy stayed for a while, tossing theories around.

Chapter Four
Nothing Personal

Terry Kingston didn't like baseball caps and considered them of limited utility. He was willing to admit that they had a place, however. The baseball cap he wore to the airport had a lion on it, the logo of, oddly enough, a football team. Terry was also wearing a cheap pair of sunglasses. His trench coat covered his puffy vest and made him look much larger than he really was.

Rhinegold Sheer was dressed in a well-tailored suit as befitted a man of his stature. He did look a bit conspicuous standing in the lobby of the airport, but there were many people standing about, waiting for loved ones or business connections coming in from faraway places.

Terry sat on one of the wire benches that circled a concrete pillar, watching. He wanted to be sure his customer was alone and that there would be no surprises. He did not like meeting anyone who could implicate him. After watching for a while, the Australian rose slowly, kind of shuffled over to his contact and said, "Guten Tag, herr. Ich hoffe daß das Wetter zu Ihrem Mögen ist."

Sheer was clearly taken aback. He stammered slightly as he denied being able to speak German.

"Dieses ist merkwürdig. Mir wurde Sie erklärt, die Sprache des Vaterlandes daß sprechen Sie."

"I'm afraid I don't know what you are saying. If you do not speak English, we cannot do business."

Terry reverted to English, but put an affected German accent to it. "Herr Sheer, I was told you spoke German."

"No, I'm afraid not. I was born in Michigan and have no use for other languages. You are Sprange?"

"I am. No, I do not shake your hand. What do you have in the briefcase and why?"

"Well, money, of course, a couple of pictures and some directions."

"Why is this information being delivered by hand? These things I could have picked up without ever involving yourself. This would have been safer for me and much safer for you."

"Those in charge insisted on my taking care of this personally. See, there is a man…"

Terry Kingston put a finger to his pursed lips. "Come with me. We go to the bench and you tell me there. Not who or where, merely why."

Once they were seated on the wire bench, Rhinegold Sheer got a wry smile on his face. "They insist on having someone to blame if the news ever comes out. They need a scapegoat if things go badly. They keep themselves squeaky clean and make me the bad guy if things go south."

"These things do not go south as you say. They will be accomplished as you say. Your position is secure. Do not be concerned. I hope you will be adequately compensated when the job is completed."

"Yes, they have promised to take care of me."

"Ich bin froh. Dieses ist gut."

"Uh, yes. I guess. Look, I'm only supposed to bring you this stuff and make sure you understand what it is you need to do." Rhinegold was looking nervous now. "The target…"

Terry stood and walked away from the man immediately, leaving Sheer feeling perplexed and foolish. He picked up the brief case and followed Terry out the door. Terry was standing on the curb smoking a cigarette, he had donned a pair of driving gloves.

"What do you think you are doing? You set this venue. I'm not comfortable talking in there either."

"Cigarette?"

"No, I don't smoke."

"Too bad. Your American cigarettes are really quite good."

"Can we get down to business?"

"I am not sure. I seldom deal with the principals of a movement, and now I find I am dealing with an underling, an amateur. I begin to think that those who have no names will attempt to avoid following through on their commitment once the scene has been cleaned. I will need the entire payment up front. There will be no down payment, as you say, and there will be no further communication between us. We will never meet again once I have been paid. This is the way we will operate and that is the final word we will use. Have I communicated myself clearly to you?"

"You can't change the terms once we set them. Who do you think you are?"

"No, my American friend, who is it that you are thinking you are?" Terry moved in close so the smoke from his mouth was blowing directly in Sheer's face. "If your life were offered to me, I would take you without a moment's notice. I don't know what you are used to dealing with, but I was brought here because you want something done properly without the cowboy images and the gangster foolishness." Terry's voice took on a razor's edge within the German accented speech. Nothing more was needed to convince Rhinegold Sheer that this man was the genuine article. A shiver ran up and down the American's spine not caused by the weather.

"Now," Terry continued in a harsh whisper, "you will run back to your kennel and tell your masters that the job will be done when the payment is made. Full payment is to be forwarded to this account number. This will be done by midnight tonight or I will think there is no contract. This would be a bad thing for you, Herr Sheer."

Terry left the man with his tailored suit and his briefcase full of money standing on the curb, and stalked off toward the short-term parking lot, tossing his cigarette butt in the street.

It was not hard to spot Terry leaving in his Toyota. The car was small and its driver tall and wearing a baseball cap and sunglasses.

Terry sat in his hotel room, a mile from the airport after driving in circles for about ten miles. He was not being followed. He cracked a quart of beer he had bought at a party store and sipped at it. He had noticed how the laws involving alcohol changed as he moved from state to state. In Michigan a customer can purchase hard liquor on every street corner and in every grocery store along with beer, wine, soda pop and fruit juice. While this increased convenience, it destroyed the variety of choice. In short, Terry decided, while volume was high, quality was low.

Terry sat cross-legged in the middle of the floor with his single quart of beer in front of him, his book on speaking German on his lap, his cell phone on standby mode behind him and his revolvers on either side of him. It was the third time he was going through the book so he was reading rather quickly. He decided as he read that it would be the last time he went through it, but he would not stop without finishing it. He also decided that he would need to go back to some of the recorded lessons to make sure he did not inadvertently try to inject an inappropriate accent into his German. It had fooled Rhinegold Sheer well enough, but the man did not speak German.

The telephone rang with the introduction of a voice mail. Kingston rose silently, almost unconsciously practicing his balance and poise. This was the third message Vanessa had left. The night before she had left two messages, of differing levels of drunkenness and emotion. It was unsure whether she had slept late or was attempting to practice restraint today, but her message was brief and blunt. He could find her at the market and she would like to talk to him. He did not call her back.

Four hours later the phone rang again. Terry had finished the book on the German language, drank the one beer he would allow himself that day, eaten half a submarine sandwich and taken a nap. The caller was Terry's connection and obviously uncomfortable with messages. Terry took the time to brush his teeth before calling back.

"G'day mate."

"We need to talk," came the terse reply.

"We are talking."

"No, not over the airwaves we are not. The client is upset and thinks you are playing games with him. Just what did you do... No. Don't tell me. Meet me at the steak house where we first met."

"Check, mate. I'm on my way."

The steak house was full and the atmosphere was friendly. The floor was crunchy with peanut shells and the air was smoky and savory. Terry had a surf and turf special while his contact drank gin and tonic.

"Did you meet with this man?"

"Of course. I set up the meet, the man was there and I gave him my terms."

"Then why did I get a message about an arrogant German bastard treating him like shit and changing the arrangement?"

"The man was a dog and needed to be treated as such. Look, the original arrangement was that the payment is made by electronic transfer, I meet with no one and the job gets done, right?"

"Yes, but the client wanted…"

"Screw what the bloody client wanted. How can I say this? The man I met was not the client. He was a buffer. The men who pull the strings are the men with the money, and they will make the payment the way I want it done or they will not get the service and they can hire someone else."

"Did you at least take a look at the job?"

"No."

"It's a big job and must be handled delicately." The man signaled to a waitress and ordered another drink.

"How big?"

"National news big, and brain surgeon delicate. That's why they want a real professional. There's a thousand men in this city who will shoot somebody for a hit of crack, but a reliable professional is hard to find."

"Then they will acquiesce to my requirements." Terry smiled.

"Look, Mate," the American's voice took on the hard sarcastic edge. "These men are rich, powerful and desperate…" His speech paused as his drink arrived at the table. "Make no mistake that they will pay but at the same time they are not the kind of men one plays games with."

"Get to the bloody point," Terry tossed aside the shell of the lobster tail. He was getting tired of being told how rich and powerful the men were. If they had any testicles among them they wouldn't need him.

"Their time frame is limited. They want the job done soon and they need it done clean. It must look like an accident or it will only make things worse."

"Right-o."

"You will meet with them again to pick up the assignment?"

"No, you will take care of that and bring me the package. I've already exposed myself once. When you have the package, call me and tell me that the cruise has begun. I will tell you where to meet me. If things go bad for either of us, the code word is eagle shit. You got that?"

"Nothing will go wrong."

"Good. I would hate for anyone to die that didn't get paid for."

Both men got a chuckle and parted ways soon after that. Terry felt he was playing it safe and correctly. His contact was lamenting prima-donna foreigners and their cocky attitudes.

At midnight, American Eastern Standard Time, Terry Kingston phoned a number in Zurich, Switzerland from a pay phone. He pressed in a series of numbers representing account numbers and private identification numbers. These numbers accessed information that a transfer had occurred from a bank in Rio de Janeiro. There were other numbers he could have called to verify the money trail, but there was no need. The numbers he accessed also confirmed two other transfers out of the account. The smaller transfer was to a bank in Zurich; the larger, representing almost all that had been transferred in, was sent to an account in Berlin. The multiple transfers to accounts in multiple names occurred within seconds of each other. But for anyone seeking to track the transaction, there was a plethora of firewalls, security barriers, live and electronic monitors, and international laws to be negotiated. While it was an expensive system to use, it was totally secure. Security has always been a hallmark of the Swiss.

Terry smiled slightly. Payment had been made.

Sunday morning, the exchange of a manila envelope gave him the name and address of his target along with photographs and a history. The man who delivered the envelope told Terry that the target was out of town until Tuesday.

The entire day was devoted to the business at hand. A digital camera was purchased as soon as the big box stores opened, and photographs were taken of the man's home in Grand Blanc, a suburb about ten miles south of Flint. Then, pictures were taken of the plants that were still operating in the area that it would be likely that the man would be visiting. Third, pictures were taken of the local union halls and finally, the Region 1C union hall on Vandyke and Atherton Roads. This was where it would be most likely that he could find the President of the United Auto Workers, the target that had been paid for.

Carnival was over, the parades had passed and most of the tourists were departing. It was the day after Fat Tuesday in Louisiana, and tourists and revelers in both New Orleans and Rio de Janeiro were going back home. The Brazilian city seemed to take a collective sigh of relief after a raucous four-day party; Rio was on its way back to its normal daily level of celebration.

In a hotel room, one tall, slim, tanned woman was smoothing an antibiotic skin lotion over the shoulders of an equally well-built man. He had been wearing an ungainly shoulder harness in the parade the night before and it had chafed his skin. She needed no lotion. Her tan had no lines and her costume would have fit in a shirt pocket.

The couple could have graced a postcard advertising Rio. He was rippling with muscles, accentuated by the lotion that glistened on his tanned skin. His hair was swept back and though naturally dark, it had been bleached a bit by the tropical sun. His profile was much more European than much of the population. He had small traces of the native influence on his genealogy but not much. His teeth were small, even and straight and his eyes were green. She was not quite as tall as he, but taller than most women. She did not have the hard bulging muscle that punctuated his skin, but she was no frail flower either. Her muscles were long and sinewy, strong and flexible. She would have passed for at least five years younger than she actually was. Her breasts were full yet upright, almost artificial, though no surgeon had ever touched them. Her belly was flat right down to the bulge of her pubis and her legs were formed like a marble statue. She had the lips of a siren and the hypnotizing eyes of a goddess that would freeze a man in his tracks. Many young men dreamed of a woman like this, indeed, many dreamed of this woman, in the loneliness of their single beds.

Rio de Janeiro has been called the friendliest city in the world, but this couple was not here to make friends. Their aims were of a much darker sort. They were not natives of Brazil and though they could make themselves understood well enough, they did not speak the native Portuguese; they spoke a South American Spanish dialect more suited to the pampas of Argentina or the southern coastal city of Buenos Aires.

"What time did you agree to meet him?" the man asked.

"Six o'clock at the restaurant on Plaza Toromolinos.

"Is there a balcony? What restaurant is it?"

"El Toro Loco."

"The Mad Bull?" the man exploded with laughter.

"Yes, he is convinced that he is a sexual superstar and that he will rock my world." Her perfect lips split to reveal the large pearl white teeth inside.

"You'd better not fall in love with him."

"I'll try not to but it's going to be difficult. That bald spot on the top of his head drives me wild."

50

"You've always secretly lusted after short, fat men. I know."

"With lips like a grouper."

The two pealed with laughter and fell on the bed together in a creamy, sweaty tangle.

It was ten minutes after six when Perfecta Navaja met her new consort at the door of the Mad Bull Restaurant. She was confident he would not start without her in a mere ten minutes. Twenty minutes would have been too much.

Ten minutes earlier she had been a block away on a dark rooftop with Hernando del Fuego. He had been adjusting his scope for windage and she had been outlining what she hoped to do. The restaurant had a balcony and a deck and she wanted to sit at the rail of the balcony. Failing to get the man to sit outside would compromise their plan but not make it impossible.

When she arrived at the door of the restaurant, the general was waiting inside. His uniform was clean and fresh and his bodyguards were standing close. General Modiano had been making a lot of nationalistic noise lately. His speeches about the evils of the west and particularly the United States were following the lead of Hugo Chavez in Venezuela. It had caused a lot of very powerful men to conclude that he was a dangerous individual and that they wanted him to be quiet.

"The heat of the day has made it hard for me to breathe," she said. "May we sit on the balcony, in the open air?"

The general may have acquiesced to her demand at a different time, but his bodyguard reminded him that it was too dangerous to be exposed.

"Besides," General Modiano finished for them, "there is air conditioning inside. It is a symbol of the decadence of the Americans, but it has its place."

Not wanting to seem too insistent without real reason, Perfecta agreed.

The meal went well and the wine was exquisite. Perfecta insisted that coffee should be had on the balcony, knowing that it was going to complicate her escape. She was sure the pistol on the general's hip would be loaded, but she could not see the weapon since it was fully enclosed in a flapped leather holster.

The balcony was only lit by candle light and though the shot was not a long one, Hernando could not get a clear one past the four bodyguards that created a human shield in front of him.

Perfecta took it all in stride. She had been selected by the general to accompany him that evening, though that had been more skill on her part than luck. She had looked into his eyes and enchanted him. It had been a long shot at best but it had worked. Now she needed to steer him toward an open area where he could be quieted quietly.

She stood at the railing herself, her dress blowing slightly, showing her form underneath its sheer fabric. She expected him to join her but when he did it was to embrace her from behind. For Hernando to take the shot now would have silenced her more certainly than him. She turned and pressed her breasts into his chest while his hands explored her back. She stopped him when they reached her derriere and whispered "later" into his ear. "I want to go to a casino."

"Ah, I have chosen a gambler."

"And I have chosen a man who will be very lucky tonight."

"Come, we go to the Casino Carnival. Do you like roulette? Baccarat?"

"No. I prefer the feel of a pair of dice in my hand."

"I have champagne in the limousine."

"Hay, you are trying to make me a dirty girl."

"I cannot make you anything. I can ask you to show me something though. You remind me very much of my first wife."

"Oh, what happened to her?"

"She disappeared over 20 years ago. She was never found."

Inside the limo, the General was respectful under the watchful eyes of the bodyguards. Perfecta thanked heaven for that since she did not want her hand forced too soon. They drank a glass of champagne each and held hands like schoolchildren.

Inside the casino, the atmosphere was considerably subdued from what it would have been during Carnival. The costumes were gone and the tourists had slunk away with or without their money. Half the gaming tables were empty but there were still die hard, inveterate gamblers winning a stake or losing their mortgage.

They naturally gambled with the general's money and Perfecta was pleased to find that he was quite free with it. After losing a bit, they began to win when she got the dice. There was no chicanery involved, no loaded dice, it was pure luck of the toss, but it was an epic run as well. She rolled the dice dozens of times in a row, winning the general thousands of Real, the Brazilian currency. The table was in an uproar as she rolled matching numbers again and again. By the time Perfecta Navaja crapped out, she had cost the casino a small fortune.

The bodyguards did not lose sight of their objective and surrounded the general from the door of the casino to the door of the limo. Inside, Modiano tried to give her some of the winnings, but she would have none of it. The look of scorn and disappointment on her face was cutting. She made it clear to him that she was not a whore to be paid off at the end of the day, and if she spent the night with him it was because she wanted to, not because she was paid to do so. The general tried his best to mollify her but nothing he said came out right, and she almost got out at a traffic light but the door would not open for her. He finally got back in her good graces when he got on one knee and apologized for his actions. It was melodramatic and much more humbling than could have been expected of a man in his position. She was satisfied that she was gaining the upper hand, and he was satisfied that he was getting to bed this sleek and dangerous cheetah of a woman.

The general's compound was enormous, at least five acres of lawn alone. The house was huge and stately, constructed of cobblestone with a slate roof and 12-foot leaded-glass windows. The ornate iron work came from a different era and the massive slate steps to the castle doors would have fit a museum. The general had done very well for himself.

The master bedroom had a wide balcony with an imposing view, but it soon became clear that it was too far from any sort of cover and too dark to make for a definite shot.

Modiano slipped his arms around her supple form and grasped her generous breasts in both hands, grinding himself against her posterior. She stumbled forward slightly on her stiletto heels before turning around and kissing him deeply. She knew she had staged the play and the end of the fourth act was here. The finale was up to her now. The hero of the set was lost to posterity.

The two went into the bedroom and closed the balcony doors behind them. Perfecta took in every facet of the room, forming a plan as best she could. The general was ready for the climax of the evening and was not about to let anything stand in his way.

Perfecta started with his jacket and slowly undid the brass buttons. Then she removed his shirt and began to kiss his hairy chest. She fumbled with his belt for a moment and then dropped onto her knees before him. She looked into his eyes and slowly, languorously licked her lips. His shoes and pants were off in a quick staggering moment and he stood before her, urgent in his lust. She reached out with her left hand and grasped his turgid organ while her right fist flashed forward and smashed his balls.

General Ernesto Modiano collapsed with a groan. He was unable to take a breath or make a sound. The stiletto heel on Navaja's right foot demonstrated that it was worthy of its name as she buried it in the general's temple. Then she stumbled and fell as the shoe caught in the skull. A few seconds to remove the trapped footwear and she was ready to go. The general had been carrying a 1911 style .45 caliber pistol on his side. Perfecta liberated his side arm, the contents of the general's wallet, a .380 caliber Bersa Thunder he had on his bed stand and a Cuban cigar from his dresser.

There was, of course, no concealment in her flimsy dress for a pistol and no pocket to conceal it in. She put the smaller gun in her purse and strapped the .45 to her waist using the general's belt. Then she turned out the lights and began to scream obscenities in Spanish and English. "Oh, you animal! Oh! fuck me like a dog you fucking animal! Make me bleed! Oh! Oh! Oh! Yes, fuck me in the ass now!" Then with a shrill and incoherent scream she flung open the door and shot all four of the bodyguards who were clustered around the doorway. Two of them needed to be shot twice to keep them down. Then she shot each one in the head to make sure they never got up again.

Pulling the Bersa from her purse, she leaned over the railing and shot the doorman as he tried to run. The butler did not even attempt to escape. He simply stood in the parlor with a silver platter in front of him holding a tea pot and a couple of small, delicate cups. She drew down on the man and then, as he neither tried to run, nor raise an alarm, she let him live, shouldered her purse, liberated two AK47s from the mangled bodyguards and headed down the steps. The butler never moved. The doorman was trying to reach something near the front door but was convinced not to by a short burst to the head.

Whatever guards were on the grounds were no doubt heading for the house. There were too many on an estate this size to even consider trying to shoot it out with them. She threw down the Kalashnikovs, the gun belt and her purse. She slid the small autoloader under her dress and into her panties, then she screamed. She screamed again as she ran through the front door of the house and down the massive flagstone steps. She kept screaming until she saw the guards running toward her and then she yelled at them to get in the house and protect the general. Five or six men ran for the house and two grabbed her and hustled her down the steps. When they got to the limousine she ran around the far side of it and sat down on the ground. "I'm all right. I'm all right but the general is still inside with those men."

The two men who had escorted her got up and headed for the house, telling the driver to look after Perfecta. He got out of the limo and she rose from the ground, hitting him in the throat with a straight knuckle punch. He choked and tried to get a breath. She kicked him between the legs and the rest of his air evacuated his lungs. He fell in the driveway unable to breathe. Perfecta Navaja raced the huge engine of the bulletproof government limo as she charged the gates.

The wrought iron gates would have stopped any small car and most large, but an armored limo was more than a match for them. She left in a hail of bullets and twisted metal as she raced out of the compound and into the night.

The guards wasted no time in mounting a pursuit but they had not foreseen that Perfecta had an accomplice. As they rounded the first corner and headed down the hill, there was an old Chevrolet Suburban parked sideways in the road. The first car piled into it and the second pounded into the first. The taillights of the limousine vanished into the night as the distraught and damaged men evacuated their twisted vehicles.

The police and army went on alert but, unfortunately for them, there was no lack of tall beautiful women in Rio de Janeiro. The general had been with several lately. There was description of the escape vehicle once the limo was found abandoned, a couple of kilometers away. All they really had was her shoe size and the name Perfecta Navaja.

Gordon MacMaster had enjoyed Carnival a great deal. He was not on assignment in Brazil, he was on holiday. The vibrant and lively city served to perk up his usual cautious attitude. He had decided that if a man could not have fun at Carnival, then he didn't know how to have fun. The first day he had been restrained, a natural predator's response to a new environment. The second day he had cut loose and immersed himself in the crowd. Drinking and dancing and wenching for three days made him feel as if he were as close to Valhalla as he could be without the warrior's death. He had no doubt that he was going to die a warrior's death, he just didn't know when.

Portuguese is close enough to Spanish that people can communicate. Some segments of society look down on the other for their dialect, but not most. MacMaster spoke a good, Castilian Spanish so he had no trouble speaking with the people of Rio. He was mostly interested in the women whom he found exotic and full of Brazilian spice.

Maid service at the hotel began about noon, giving occupants enough time to get up and out, or to check out. When the maid knocked on the door of the MacMaster suite, she was surprised to find it opened by one of three half naked women, all of which looked like they had partied until six in the morning. The shower was running so there was another occupant of the suite. The maid apologized for disturbing them and started backing out when one of them said they would need more towels. She gave them an armful of towels and one of the party girls closed the door behind her. The maid shook her head and headed to the next suite.

In the hotel room, the one girl who had gone to sleep early, deciding she was not going to wait for MacMaster to get out of the shower, stripped off her skimpy clothing and joined him. The other two lay on the beds smoking and talking.

It was early afternoon before the big Scot was done with the women. He was fully satisfied and, to his credit, so were they. He scratched his hairy chest and yawned. The stubble on his chin itched so he went back into the bathroom for another shower and a shave. His hair had been cut a week before, parted to the side and still looked good.

One of the ladies had turned the television on and he had left it on when they departed. He stuck his head out of the bathroom, his face half covered with shaving cream when news of the assassination came across the cable. This was interesting to him. A person or persons had gotten into General Modiano's compound and shot five of his bodyguards and himself. Unlike so many of the sloppy suicide killings of late, these assassins had escaped in the government limousine. The news did not say that the assassin had been a woman. That would have been too embarrassing for the government, the general and his living relatives. They did say that a woman was being sought in connection with the incident. The name they gave as a person of interest was Perfecta Navaja.

"Perfecta Navaja," Gordon muttered to himself as he went back to the task of scraping the stubble off his chin. "Forget it. I'm on holiday."

Regardless of his assertion of disinterest, Gordon MacMaster could not help but look up the word Navaja in a Spanish-English dictionary. It was not there. Yet he knew he had heard the name correctly and that he had heard the word used in conversation.

It was almost dinner time and he had eaten nothing nutritious all day. He wanted a beer and a steak so he donned his loose fitting clothing and a grommetted leather hat against the sun. Underneath the blowsy shirt he wore a tight-fitting, elastic belly holster, like a cummerbund with a small .380 stuffed in it. The pistol would disappear in his massive hand if he were forced to use it, but with a seven-round clip it was marginally effective. He put a lock blade in his pocket and then took it out again, looked at it and smiled. "Navaja," he said.

The summer sun was punishing but the air conditioning was on in the restaurant. The beer was cold and the steak was bloody. After he had eaten, he sat at the bar and talked with the bartender.

Gordon was feeling more himself once the food and alcohol negated the effects of his earlier activities. He was about to switch from beer to scotch when his cell phone rang. He was somewhat surprised by it since he was off the clock, so to speak. The caller spoke in German and, while it took a gear change for Gordon to adjust his language, he did so smoothly.

"Colonel, so good to hear from you. I'm surprised to hear your voice. I would have thought you would ask someone else to make the call."

"Mack. You are one of the few I speak to myself. I have a situation you might be interested in pursuing, but I will not speak of it on this unsecured line. If you can get to a pay phone or a secure land line of some sort I will give you the details."

"Colonel, I'm vacationing in another part of the world. It would probably be too far away and too long a trip to make."

"Ah. I know where you are. Call me."

The pay phone on the street was damaged but the one in the bodega on the corner was not. Gordon was about to use it when he realized that he was just far enough from the tourist section that the gangs and cartels would be in power here. While that did not bother him, the phone might well be tapped. He bought a can of Agua de Coco, a coconut milk drink, and a pack of Fly Cigarettes. He knew Colonel Richter would wait for his call and understand if he did not call back.

The streets were coming back to life. It was too hot for reasonable men to work in the noonday sun, so they napped through the blazing heat of midday but were coming back out now. The detritus of Carnival had not been completely removed from the streets and lay about like a hangover on the sidewalks.

MacMaster chose a telephone in a tavern closer to the hotel. The police were more of a presence here and the gangs of youths were discouraged from hanging around in this neighborhood.

"Colonel. It must be very late at night in Berlin."

"Time is not the issue here, my friend. It is of the essence there, however. A General was killed in Rio last night and the woman who killed him had escaped the dragnet. It is believed that she is still in the city and a contract for her decommission has been created."

"Perfecta Navaja," replied Gordon, simply.

"Ah, I am glad to see that though you are on holiday, you have not allowed yourself to slack."

"A hazard of the industry."

"Yes, good. I have no other operatives in the area and I have no real information to go on, so I cannot truly expect you to accept or complete this assignment. I do feel that the compensation will be adequate for whoever completes this one, though. I knew you were going to Rio this week and I thought that you might be interested."

"If I had anything to work with, I might be, but I have no contacts and no idea where this perfect knife might be."

"Perfect knife. Is that what the name translates to?"

"Aye. Sounds like my kind of woman, no?"

Both men laughed and Colonel Richter agreed that it sounded like a match made in heaven. Little more needed to be said. Gordon agreed to keep his eyes open but did not think there was enough to even consider accepting the assignment. The Colonel quoted an amount for the job and the Scot agreed that it was a generous enough amount, but reiterated that he was on holiday and did not have enough to go on. This one would not be pursued.

Driving away from the limousine, Hernando del Fuego was grinning. "You killed him, didn't you?" he asked.

"Of course. You could not do your job so I was forced to do it for you."

"Ai, such a killing machine. You make me want to worship you."

"You should worship me. You should come to me on your knees with offerings."

"I'll offer you something later," he said, still grinning.

"Here, an offering, suck on this." She pulled the cigar out of her bra but it was broken in half. He threw half out the window and lit the other half with a butane lighter. "I have more as well." She pulled a large wad of bills from next to her other breast. His eyes lit up but she returned the wad to its home. With a small squeal she pulled up her dress and retrieved the pistol that had been stuck in her panties. He made some lewd comment that she did not quite catch and they took another turn to confuse anyone trying to catch them.

"They will lock down the roads out of the city. We need to get out of sight again. I don't think they saw this car but I'm going to dump it anyway. The Mercedes is older but better."

"No. Just go back to the house. I will dye my hair blonde and you can go to the Mercedes from there. It is the plan, right?"

"Of course, Perfecta."

"Ai, you know better than that! Andalucia. You will call me Maria Andalucia. Perfecta Navaja is dead, never speak the name again."

"I was making a joke."

"Never make the joke again. Now get us back to the house and I want you to serve me again before you leave. You know how horny it makes me."

Hernando puffed on his cigar but could not get the smile off his face.

Anastasia knew she did not look natural as a blonde but she needed to change her appearance dramatically. She had been seen by nine or ten men in the compound. Granted that most of them had seen her in the dark, and only three were close up, but there was the butler as well. He had gotten a good look at her in the light of the house. She knew she should have shot him, indeed, she had known it at the time, but there was something about the way he just stood there like a scolded puppy, frozen in his tracks, that had prevented her from eliminating him. If he had made a move she would have taken action, but he had not.

Hernando dropped Anastasia off in front of the house and drove off to swap the vehicle he was driving. Anastasia called him a faggot as he drove off and went inside to wait. She stripped and tossed her dress in the burn barrel inside the courtyard, lit it on fire and then walked back into the house. She made a mental note to buy herself another set of that brand of shoe. They had proved very effective at killing. They also lifted her buttocks in the air alluringly, as did all high heels, but that brand was better balanced than most.

The shower was turned on as hot as it would go and Anastasia was unable to resist her own fingers. It had been that way since she was a teenager. Nothing excited her so much as killing a man.

When her man returned with the Mercedes she was still in the mood and they spent the next hour satisfying each other.

The two did not arise until the heat of the day had made the room uncomfortable. Hernando was in fine spirits and cooked some breakfast for the two of them. Anastasia was in a kind of post coital depression. It was another long-term emotional problem for her. The first few times it almost led to her suicide, but over the years the effect had lessened. It would last a couple of days and then she would be back to her usual laconic self. She had not cried much since she was a very young child, but she did this time. It was not that she had any feeling for the men she had killed. It was her job to kill the general, and the others had simply been in the way. The emotion came from deep within her and she had never been able to explain it to herself or anyone else. The depression she was used to but the crying was new.

Her partner and lover tried to comfort her but she would have nothing of it. While she had been insatiable the night before, today she was untouchable.

The cigarettes that he had bought in the bodega were not for himself. Gordon MacMaster seldom smoked cigarettes. They were for the children. In most European countries and North America, giving cigarettes to children constitutes a crime; not so in the more liberal South America. Gangs of children roamed the streets demanding that tourists buy chewing gum, and begging cigarettes. Some of them had no parents and others had run away from home. Occasionally the state would round up the strays and return them to their homes, but many of them had no home and they were extremely difficult to catch, so it was more a token gesture.

The single pack of cigarettes was gone almost as soon as it was open, once the gang had homed in on MacMaster. They circled him like a school of hungry barracuda and forced him to keep his hand on his wallet. Once slipped from his pocket, it would vanish as surely as day turns to night. There was a reason for his generosity, however. The cigarettes brought them in and the chance of a real payoff got their attention. It was a real long shot but the man was asking if anyone had seen a woman with the general the night before. He wanted to know who she was, where she came from and what she did. The payoff was rich and one of them would be certain to come up with a story though the chance of it being authentic was unimaginably slim.

It confirmed the possibility of real information to him when the swarm had moved off and he had not told them where he was staying. Rio de Janeiro is a city of about twenty million people, and the urchins did not even need to ask him what hotel he was staying in. They were the real eyes of the city.

The hilly region of the city where the General's compound was located is northwest of the Lagoa neighborhood. It is primarily off-limits to the children, and manual laborers are only allowed in during the day. The buses do not run in the more affluent neighborhoods after dark. But it was not dark yet.

The hotels were more expensive, closer to the beaches, but that did not concern the Scotsman. He had taken accommodations between the pier and the airport, in the central section of the city. He found more life there than in the tourist oriented neighborhoods. The women were less inhibited and the food more genuine away from the beaches. The beaches were where the chatter was to be had, though.

A ten-minute cab ride to Copacabana and a two minute walk to the beach opened up a world of possibilities. Thousands of women in bikinis and hundreds of beach bars filled with half-sloshed tourists from all over the globe was the perfect place to make inquiries about the recent assassination. Unfortunately, nobody knew anything. He plied a few potential informants with drink but got nowhere. They knew nothing but the news and it was not even public knowledge that the general had been killed by a woman.

Going into the hills toward the compound would have attracted unwanted attention to himself, so MacMaster eschewed that in favor of taking a hotel room for the night. He watched the nightly news, which told him nothing he didn't already know, and then went to sleep. In the middle of the night he awoke with a thought, like a dream that he could not remember. It was there but he could not grasp it, like a ghost in a fog. He could almost see it, but the closer he got the less substantial it was. Finally it vanished and he was left grasping nothing.

Chapter Five
Competition

There exists no international community of killers for hire. There is no trade union for assassins nor is there any network that one can insinuate one's self into. The extremely specialized work of the international hit-man is retained more like a temp agency or a freelance truck driver. The word goes out that this work is available and if it has sufficient reward for the risk, it generates some interest.

Organized crime figures had their favorite hitters, men who were paid well enough to be middle class but not well enough to leave the organization. Attempting to leave put a target on a man's back more often than not. A hit on a hitter paid better than most local jobs so they almost always generated interest. Local jobs required less talent than the high-profile, international assassinations. The local men were simple thugs most of the time, the kind who walk up to a car and shoot the owner through the window as he is going to work. The upper stratum of specialist is inhabited by that rare sort of person who has both style and spine. The best killers are those who don't let anyone but the victim know they have been killed. Everybody knows they are dead but no one knows it was planned. This level of skill is beyond most men as it requires the artist to be within kissing distance of his victim.

When the word went out of the bounty on Perfecta Navaja's head, it did not generate an awful lot of interest. Yes, the payoff was sufficient, but the information was not. There was no background, no photograph, no address and an insufficient description. Everyone who was approached saw the same sort of scenario whereby the woman was apprehended and the blood money never paid because of a lack of identification. It was a hit on a hitter, but it was no local wise-guy trying to get away from the mob. This woman was new enough on the scene that she had just made her first enemies. She had done it properly however; she had made some powerful enemies.

The men who had seen the assassin were sequestered in a government building in front of a projection screen. While the local and regional police were kept in relative poverty as regards the newer technology, the federal government had a fairly modern setup. The guards, the driver and the butler were all shown an endless array of photographs of women who fit the profile of the killer. Long brown hair with brown eyes and tanned skin described almost every woman in the country and the technicians did not know how to narrow the field. If they had added the height dimension to the search they would have had many fewer choices they needed to review. It would have availed them naught since no photograph of Perfecta Navaja existed in their files under that or any other name.

Murders were not unusual in Rio de Janeiro though such a high profile victim was. The police had been accused of forming death squads and killing drug dealers and banditos out of hand for the past 20 years. Before that, military dictatorships had done the same. The victims were not always the criminal element of society; sometimes it was hard to determine why someone had been killed. In the favelas, the slums of the city there were often whole families killed by either the drug dealers or the police. In what has been described as the friendliest city on Earth, there is a subculture that the cameras do not see and the government does not allow to leak out; a subculture of fear and torture, violence and death that is as common as breakfast.

It is understood by both the police and the drug traffickers that there will be no migration of the territorial wars into the tourist sections of the sprawling metropolis.

Actions had been initiated some years ago by the heads of the organized crime cartels to expand their operations into the beaches and hotels, and while they had gotten a financial foothold, their soldiers were driven out in the most convincing manner possible. The casinos were run by the cartels, of course, but they were more efficient and demanding than the police when it came to the treatment of their guests. Employees of the casinos could not get away with stealing a half eaten hamburger from the trash and entrepreneurs were squashed in an extremely heavy-handed manner. So the tourists could be sure of a pleasant experience as long as they did not travel to the seedier side of town at night.

The Argentine assassins had been in town for a couple of months. Their cover was well established and they had created alibis for the night of the killing. The police never came to question them on the matter, but caution prevented them from attempting to leave town immediately. They continued with the routine that had been established over the past few weeks, cementing their identities. He was a writer and she was his wife. She did the shopping and cleaning and he did the drinking and writing.

This arrangement worked quite well for them, though everybody noticed that Anastasia had dyed her hair blonde and thought it was tacky. A week went by and they announced their intention to visit Paraguay and Bolivia. A writer needs to travel they said or he becomes mired in a tar pit. The next day they left with their passports, but they had miscalculated the extent and urgency of the government's desire for their capture. The head of the secret service had made a pledge to the president that their hides would adorn his wall before a month was gone.

It had not been expected that they would attempt to cross the Fraternity Bridge which connects Foz do Iguaçu with its neighbor, Puerto Iguacu in Argentina. That was a long and difficult trip from Rio. They had gone to Sao Paulo and then to Curitiba, Ponta Grossa and Cascavel in the Serra das Araras mountain range. They stayed a day in Cascavel recovering from the drive and then proceeded toward Foz do Iguaçu.

The couple was stopped at the border and asked to visit the emigration desk. They explained that they were not immigrating or emigrating, that they were traveling writers who needed to go to Argentina for research. It almost worked except for the pistol secreted in the trunk. The laws for transporting firearms across the border were prohibitive and they should have left theirs behind. The couple were arrested for smuggling and thrown into holding cells with nothing but a bench and a privy. The border patrol did not go through the local magistrates and courts; they relied on the federal courts to try anyone arrested at the border. The two could not announce themselves as Argentine citizens since their passports said they were the Chilean couple, Mr. and Mrs. Andalucia.

It was the first night when the guards made their move and their mistake. They had worked with impunity for many years, extorting money and favors from those they detained.

First was a middle-aged man with foul breath and rotten teeth. He had not shaved for three or four days and his uniform was stained with hot sauce and grease. He had cast his cloudy eyes on the statuesque form of Anastasia Viuda and desire flourished like an algae bloom. It was not yet midnight when he came around with his lustful demand thrust through the bars of her cage.

"You know what to do. If you do this we may let you go, if you do not, we will kill your husband and dump him in the river."

Anastasia knew that satisfying this creature would get her nothing, but there were ways this could be used to her benefit. She turned into an actress of lust and prepared herself for a star quality performance.

"Ai, you have such a nice little man there," she said and reached out with one slender fingered hand.

"Wait until you see how he tastes."

Almost choking on the stench of the unwashed manhood she obliged him, briefly. Then she stripped off her dress and got on her knees on the bench. The sight was more than the guard could resist and he slipped the key into the lock of the ancient cell door. He did not make it halfway across the cell, though. Anastasia Viuda launched herself from the bench, head first into his face. The sickening crunch of his nose being mashed filled the air and echoed. Regaining her footing, his intended victim kicked him in the stomach, doubling him over. Then she took her dress from the floor and wrapped it around his neck from behind, twisting the cloth until it cut off his wind completely, and then the blood to his brain. After he stopped twitching, she shook out the dress and put it back on.

The keys were removed from the guard's belt and used to free Hernando who quietly swapped his clothing for the guard's uniform. He checked the still body for a pulse, but there was none.

At the door to the block of holding cells, there was an anteroom off to the side where three guards were playing cards. Procedure prevented them from carrying guns into the holding cell area. They had played cards for the right to be the first to rape Anastasia. They had thought the winner had been the lucky one.

When he opened the door, Hernando del Fuego kept his back to the men in the room. One of them made a joke about how quick he had been. Then they fell silent again as

Anastasia walked through the door and into the room. She was smiling and cupping her breasts as if readying herself for all their attentions. Their good humor was short lived, however. As they watched Anastasia, Hernando grabbed a shotgun from the open cabinet by the wall and opened both barrels on them. The buckshot tore into them, blowing them into hamburger and temporarily deafening the escaping prisoners. There was no time to wait for their hearing to return, however, the two men in the guard shack were running toward the building with their pistols out. Anastasia relieved one of the dead men of his side arm and quickly and efficiently brought both men down. Seconds later, she stepped out of the building and shot each of them in the head.

The other side of the bridge was the Paraguayan border crossing and they were on alert, disturbed by the gunfire. It would have been suicide to try running the border so they reversed the Mercedes and headed back into Brazil.

Roberto Campena de Iguaca had been born in that region of Brazil bounding the national forest but had not stayed there. His family had chosen to move to Rio de Janeiro when he was still a baby and his father had clawed out a living in one of the favelas.

Roberto had been a lookout, then a guard, then a gang soldier. He had killed his first man when he was 12 and discovered that he liked it. Of the two kinds of residents, Roberto did not really fit into either category. There were people who wanted to escape the slums and make a life for themselves elsewhere, and there were those who wanted to rule the slums. Roberto Campena de Iguaca did not want to rule the slums but he did not really want to leave either. His ambition was to be the chief assassin of the men who did rule the favelas. He was a man in demand and his connections grew into a vast and branching network. In addition to the ghettos, he learned skills involved with tracking and killing in the mountains and jungles. He did not divide his attention between things the way most men do. He did not drink or smoke or gamble. The company of women was a necessity to him, one to be paid for, gotten done with and forgotten. He lived for his chosen profession and so became very good at it.

Roberto got the news of the assassination of General Modiano about the same time everyone else did. He got word of the reward before some. He was ready to take the job as soon as he heard about it. He had always resented women's hold over men. He hated the fact that he needed a woman every so often and while he did not often kill women for pleasure, he always accepted the contract. This contract was so ephemeral that it could not be called, however. No description and no way of identifying the killer led to a dead end. The reward was generous but the task was impossible. That is until the border incident was televised.

Special reports were common on Rede Globo, the most watched television broadcast in Brazil. This special report flashed across the screen before the nightly news, telling of the massacre of six border guards by a pair of psychopaths who attacked the border crossing, killed the guards and escaped.

Roberto saw the report and knew he was looking at a professional action. He did not accept that they had attacked the border crossing without provocation. That would have been ridiculous. Such persons as can carry out this sort of action never do so without a reason. They had not gone across the border. That eliminated most possible explanations.

Gordon MacMaster also saw the Rede Globo report and began to wonder why a couple would invade a border post and kill the men on guard there. A lot of scenarios played out in his mind that night, each equally implausible. It was more probable that the guards had stopped a carload of drug smugglers from Paraguay, on their way to the coast, though this seemed implausible as well. Paraguay has open ports in Argentina, Brazil and Uruguay, so it can operate an export trade even though it is a landlocked country. Most of the drugs would no doubt go down the rivers to lessen the risk of exposure. MacMaster learned later that the bridge was not at the Paraguayan border but at the Argentine border crossing.

American television would have no doubt splashed the mug shots of the wanted couple all over the evening news and front pages of the papers. They would have thusly captured the criminals in a couple of days, but they would also have made them celebrities and given them a venue for spouting whatever agenda they had adopted. The South American media did not do so. The pictures were never released to the public. They were released to the Secret Service however.

Roberto Campena de Iguaca had seen the report and had known that there would be video surveillance. He had not counted on mug shots. Additionally, he knew that the men who had survived the assassination of General Modiano were being held in the basement of a government building until such time as the truth was revealed. Midday, of the day after the attack on the border post, the men were released and Roberto was there to see it.

Most of the men were tall and upright. They had been in their uniforms for almost a week so they did not look fresh or bright, but they stood tall and walked with assurance. They had been members of the elite guard and would not have been easy targets even if they were available. A truck arrived immediately and drove off with them in the back. Presumably they were being redeployed elsewhere.

The butler and the limo driver were more accessible. Roberto preferred the butler because the man had been serving the deceased general for many years. He was either very fond of the general's memory, or would be a dead end, but it seemed a good place to start. Both the men had been living at the general's compound for quite some time and their outside contacts had been limited. When they were released, they were being cut loose of all ties, but they were not told this. Their clothes and personal items were still in the mountain hideaway and they needed to return there if they wanted them. Neither of them questioned the man who pulled up in the full-sized American car saying he had been commissioned to take them home.

"Who's the client then?" Gordon asked.

"Francisco Modiano. He is the dead general's brother."

"Look, I don't usually work this way. It could end up getting me snuffed out. I don't like it and I'm supposed to be on holiday."

The German accented voice on the phone did not miss a beat. "I told you before I don't care if you take the job or not. I thought you were turning it down before. I only called to let you know that the stakes had changed, that we have a picture of the targets and that they are to be brought in alive. The client will accept them dead, but he will pay twice the price for their live bodies."

"Three times the price, Colonel. I will not leave this city for less than three times the price."

"I did not say you would leave the city."

"These photographs were taken at the border in Foz do Iguaçu, right?"

"I must commend you, Scotsman. I cannot imagine how you knew that. You are correct, of course. They were responsible for seven deaths at the border station. The guards apprehended them without knowing who they were, and ended up learning a fatal lesson. It is thought that they went to ground somewhere in the Cascavel region."

"I need the photographs. I need them before the day gets much older and I need your commitment to the price. I'll need a vehicle and I need some history on the couple."

"By the time you get to the address I will give you, there will be an automobile and photographs there. You have my commitment on the price or I will call you on the cell phone and tell you otherwise. I cannot promise payment for the dead bodies of the targets."

"What has changed? The original contract was for their decommission."

"I did not ask what the change was for. I am only the middle man. You will either do the job or you will not do the job. I care not which."

"Give me the address. I'll consider it. Oh, and for your information, there were only six at the border according to the media. Is there something I do not know?"

"Six, I will make a note of that. My information is less immediate than yours. I have you booked on the flight to Cascavel under the name Boris Chercovski. Your plane leaves in and hour and a half."

"I say. That's right cheeky of you."

"I knew you would take the job in some form. I've readied a wire to pay you a retainer. My contact in Cascavel will phone me when you have acquired the vehicle, and I will send the retainer. Will this be acceptable?"

"Close enough. Ey, tell the man not to try giving me some beat up old piece of shit. I'll need a real car, a Mercedes and make sure the trunk works."

"I'll make sure he understands. If the vehicle does not meet your specifications, call me."

"I need to get to the airport."

The two said their goodbyes and MacMaster set off for the hotel to retrieve his identification as Boris Chercovski. He did not check out of the hotel, instead he paid for another two weeks stay. He made it to the airport in time to hop the flight to Cascavel. He had no luggage so he would need to shop when he arrived.

A man with a sign that said Chercovski met Gordon at the airport in Cascavel and transported him to a middle class dwelling in the city. The owner, a small and dapper man, was very gracious and accommodating, insisting that his guest have something to eat and offering him lodging for the night. He apologized excessively for the fact that the car was not a Mercedes but a Chrysler.

The photographs were obviously mug shots which explained why the couple had found it necessary to kill everyone in the border station. They could not afford to be detained. The history was more interesting in that there was none. They were detained at the border crossing for having a gun in the trunk of the car, taped to the underside of the spare tire. Their identification gave them Chilean citizenship, but there was no history available in the international databases other than birth records from Santiago. They had retrieved their passports from the border when they fled. That was the mark of a professional.

Gordon accepted lodging for the night once he had seen the accommodations. It was a separate apartment set off to the side, obviously created for a relative to stay, long term. A mother or grandmother would move here to live out their life in comfort under the care of the owner and his petite and beautiful wife and two daughters.

The two men sat drinking wine well into the night. The women of the house saw to their every need save one, and the Scot knew better than to even look at one of the females for too long. The two daughters looked long and hard at him, when their father could not see, but he did not return their attentions. He was here for business and saw no positive end for consorting with his host's women. The most he wanted to be was complimentary.

"Your wife is very beautiful."

Señor Diego sighed deeply. "Yes, she is a wonderful prize. She is loyal and beautiful but as with all things of great worth, there is a cost."

"I'm sorry, I don't understand."

"I was locked in a contest for Amelia's affections with another man in town. He lost that contest. She could see that he was shallow and of no substance. But, he has the charming tongue of a snake and managed to slither his way up the political ladder. He never forgot that I have the woman he wanted, my wonderful Amelia, and he married for political gain.

A short bellow of laughter came from Gordon's chest. "And he found that the home life is not so sweet as he might have had?"

Señor Diego got a crooked little grin on his face. "He married a cold, ambitious shrew and so, instead of going home to her loving embrace, he spends long hours elsewhere. But as I said, he never forgave me and has worked long and hard to prevent me from advancing in my position. I remain a clerk, while he is an alderman and poised for a run at the mayor's seat. If he is elected mayor, he will try to have me fired, or disgraced, or both. I may need you to come back into my life after the election."

"Is this why you have become involved with the Colonel?"

"No. I have worked with Colonel R. for about five years now. Mostly local stuff. There are connections around here and it becomes necessary to call in outside interests to, um, mediate a dispute."

"Yes. Mediation is a good thing. I want his name and address for future reference, in case I need to come back. Tell me now, Dom Diego, is there any way I can determine the real identity of these two killers? They are obviously well trained and very dangerous. You can make a substantial stack of reais if you can get me more information. Without knowing who I am really after, I may never get to them. If I make nothing off this you make only what you have already. If I make a jackpot I can spread the butter."

"I shall see what I can do."

Morning came and MacMaster was on his feet with the sun, prowling about like a big cat he reviewed what he knew and fell decidedly short of a plan. He stared at the pictures, memorizing every line and nuance of the faces. He wished he had better resolution photographs. He wanted to know the faces well enough to be able to locate them in the dark, by feel. The Scot was showered and dressed before anyone else was awake and was in the kitchen cooking scrambled eggs with cheese and peppers where Amelia Diego found him. She was mortified that a guest should find in necessary to cook breakfast and apologized repeatedly with real feeling and genuine remorse. He was embarrassed that he had caused her such shame and did not mention the incident to Dom Diego. Amelia served the breakfast along with coffee, fruit, and queijo de coalho a salty grilled cheese. Dom Diego commented on the scrambled eggs which were very seldom served but his guest remained quiet on the subject.

"I will stay home from work today. I will make some excuse."

"No, Dom Diego. I cannot expect any such thing. I will leave and reconnoiter the surrounding countryside. I will not return tonight, for there is much I must learn. Most of my experience was with a much dryer climate. This is so lush and beautiful but great beauty hides great danger as well, and I don't know how long the subject of my hunt will remain in the area, if they are indeed still here. I do not want you to call attention to the fact that you have company. It is best when no one sees me coming."

"The tree python strikes from above and the scorpion from behind its back."

"You understand perfectly, my friend. I wish there to be no connection to the things I do and yourself."

Dom Diego gave an extremely gracious goodbye and returned to the house while his guest popped the hood to inspect the power plant.

MacMaster was immensely pleased with the automobile that had been provided for him. A Chrysler 300 with a 6.1 liter V8 engine putting out over 400 horsepower. The engine bay was clean, the oil was clear and the antifreeze half filled its reservoir. It wanted for nothing and took its new master out on the road eagerly.

Cascavel was 132 kilometers northeast of Foz do Iguaçu where the fugitives had bungled their border crossing and massacred the guards. It took two hours at a reasonable pace because of the unexpected farm traffic on the road.

It took more time to get through the congested city of Foz do Iguaçu and once he got close to the border, parking was nonexistent. He finally got frustrated and paid a woman to park in her front yard. He paid her some up front with a promise of more when he returned. He also made sure she saw that he had a pistol under his jacket. Sometimes the promise of a reward was insufficient to ensure loyalty.

It was difficult for Gordon MacMaster to be inconspicuous. He stood about four inches over six foot and had flaming red hair. Rather than a tan, his skin was reddened by the sun. His legs were like tree trunks and his arms like the trusses of an unfinished sky scraper. The workers blues he usually wore were cut large to hide his powerful physique and his jacket was padded to make him look fat and hide whatever weapon he wore under it. His eyes were green with golden flecks and exhibited what came to be known as the thousand-yard gaze. He was always looking for whatever was happening anywhere around him. Many men had felt the impact of his huge, scarred fists, though few who did not deserve it.

In a country of medium-sized, brown-skinned people, the tall Scot stood out like a wolf among coyotes. He would be unable to escape detection if anyone were looking for him, so he made it a priority not to be a person of interest. Some street toughs noticed him walking in the city but decided that he was too large and confident looking to accost. If he had been a frightened looking tourist they may have given it a try, but he returned their angry glares with a calm assurance that spoke of a long association with violence. As hard as he tried to be innocuous, he could not allow himself to look vulnerable.

MacMaster bought a bottle of gin at the duty-free shop to excuse his presence in the area. He stood smoking a cigar and examining the area. The guard shack and accompanying block house were far enough from the nearest commercial building that they could not have been approached on foot without notice. There was an old shoe shine half a block away that afforded the Scot a good view of the situation. The old man was burned black by the long hours in the sun and spoke frankly when asked about the murders at the border.

"I have been here for most of my life, shining shoes and I never saw anything like that. The people that did this were not from this area and they were not from across the border. I hear things. The men in the upper floors of this building all get their shoes shined here. I hear things."

"I'll bet you hear a lot of things, old man. Tell me what you have heard lately."

"Oh, my memory is short and I can only think when I am not working." The man smacked his lips and Gordon handed him the gin bottle. After a couple of surreptitious swigs of gin the shine box opened and the bottle went inside along with some currency.

"The two who did this were together and were pulled inside. They drove a Mercedes. Nobody knows why they were pulled in or why they went mad, except the local police who investigated. I was gone long before this happened. It was late at night. I do know they started in the cell house and then killed the two in the guard shack. Those men have been abusing their power for years and it did not matter when they were replaced. They did not change. I have been here many years and the faces change but the nature of the men does not. They were probably just trying to get across the border and the guards wanted to shake down the wrong two men."

"Are you sure it was two men?"

"No. I say so because it makes more sense. Women are not the ones that kill, they are the ones that love, the ones that birth," he cackled. "We are the ones that thrust the spear in."

"Thank you, old man. You have helped much." The note was much larger than the bill but there was no change expected.

Though the evidence was slim, the Scotsman was relatively sure he was looking in the right place. It struck him that he really needed some friends in this city. He spat out the butt of his cold cigar and stepped into a barber shop for a trim. There was a line of people ahead of him but that was what he wanted. He talked the entire time, asking all sorts of questions. The most important of which, to him, was where the local police drank. As usual, there was one tavern, owned by an ex-officer where the precinct went after work for libations. After getting his hair trimmed, he called the Colonel and updated him on the search. MacMaster did not usually find it necessary to provide status reports but he was in a far from familiar environment.

The Chrysler was right where he had left it and a young man with a baseball bat was guarding it. The woman who owned the property was cooking furiously and insisted that Gordon have some food before he went any further. He tried to decline graciously, but she was adamant so he seated himself at the table for some rice and beans ands shredded beef barbecue. When the meal was done, she slid a cup of coffee in front of him and asked if there was anything else she could do for him. The offer was not banal or lewd, it merely represented a person doing what they needed to survive and provide for their family. Brazilian culture demands that when offered a cup of coffee, you do not refuse. The other offer was discretionary, however.

MacMaster declined any further services but tried to insist on paying for the meal. The Brazilian woman would not hear of it, so he paid twice as much as agreed for the parking space and that was acceptable to her. What he did decide was that he needed some company. As he drank his coffee he realized that to take a woman with him might cause some jealousy and the last think he wanted to do was anger the constabulary. What he did was take the young man, the woman's son, with him to the Brass Knob. It was not quite the end of the shift, so the place was almost empty. A couple of beers later the barroom filled up with off-duty officers, done with their routine and ready to have a drink. The young man left after the cops came in. He stayed long enough to establish that he had been drinking with the foreigner and then left. He had been compensated for his company as well. It only reinforced his idea that foreigners were crazy.

The normally taciturn Scot turned to his boisterous side in the bar. He had been moody for a couple of days and was done with it. He bought rounds for the crowd, he danced with one of the only women present, he translated old jokes to Spanish and pretended to be drunker than he was.

"Carmella. What a sweet name. Why would such a sweet and beautiful woman want to be a police officer?"

"That is my business." Carmella was not making it easy for him. As a female officer in a male dominated culture she was sure to have issues of her own.

"OK. I didn't mean to be rude. Can I buy you a drink?"

"You can buy drinks all night long but keep your distance."

"OK. Bartender, set her up. I go to the toilet."

Inside the bathroom, an officer gave him a bit of advice. "Leave her alone," he said. "She is the daughter of the Chief of Police and not for the likes of you."

MacMaster took the advice. He was not there looking for a woman; he was there looking for information. Half an hour later a beautiful, slim woman in blousy, revealing clothing walked through the door. Every man in the place would have been willing to accompany her, but she walked straight up to Carmella and kissed her on the lips, sensually. The bar held its collective breath during the length of the kiss, in appreciation.

The silence broke as the stranger in their midst howled like a wolf and exclaimed that the newcomer deserved a drink, in fact everybody deserved a drink. The tension broke in a wave of noise and alcohol and it was not long before the crowd had been primed.

The huge Scot had an immense capacity for alcohol though he was pretending to drink more than he actually was. He spent quite a wad of money in the bar that night but it was money well spent. Not every cop that patrolled the area was present in the Brass Knob but enough of them to make a difference. He made some friends and ensured that they recognized him. He established his whereabouts that night. He allowed the law enforcement community to know that he was Boris Chercovski, a former Sergeant from Austria and that he loved drinking with cops. Most important, he got them to loosen up and talk about the massacre that had occurred in the block house of the border crossing.

"Yes, my friend, it was a tragedy. They threw the two of them in the cell for trying to bring a pistol across the border. I can't tell you why they would be doing that. It was stupid. You can buy a pistol in Argentina as easy as in Brazil. It was stupid."

"So it was two men?" Gordon asked.

"Oh, no. One of them was a tall and tasty woman. I don't have a picture but I saw it. She looks good but she is like Carmella, I think."

"A lesbian?"

The man erupted in laughter. "No, no. I mean dangerous like the little snake of the forest that glitters like jewels, so pretty. If it bites you once, your family will never see you again."

The thumping rhythm of the juke box set a mood. A glance at the dance floor showed Carmella and her friend were doing a slow and sensual dance without touching each other. It was almost erotic in its fluid motions.

The door opened and a group of six young women entered. These women were obviously not officers but they were not professionals either. They were there for a good time. The crew wasted no time in getting them drinks. They had arrived in a group but it did not look likely they would leave as one.

By the time the sun went down, the remaining contingent was drinking shots and weaving like a schooner in a high wind. The Scotsman was buying rounds and felt extremely thankful for the meal that had been forced upon him. He had tried not to accept the woman's hospitality but appreciated it more than ever now.

"So, why have they not released the pictures of the couple to the press? That is what we would do in Austria. Get some help from the people. Somebody saw something."

"We would have. The federal government forces have jurisdiction in this case and they move slow."

"Slow, like that?" Gordon flicked his eyes toward the dance floor where Carmella was still dancing sensually, without touching her partner.

"I tell you, Boris. You do not want to even try this woman. They will find you in the river gorge."

"I'm not interested in that."

"No. Trust me."

"So, local police are hands off?"

"Carmella? Yes. We are hands off."

"No," he said with a grin. "I was not talking about Carmella. I was interested in the killings. It doesn't add up for me."

"No. It doesn't add up." The man staggered off toward the bathroom.

The ladies were working the crowd to their best advantage and Gordon got one of them out on the dance floor where he exhibited some unusual and very physical dance moves, picking the woman up and spinning her around. His strength and balance were appreciated wholeheartedly by the crowd, but he was feeling the effects of the liquor and needed to sit down before long. His dance partner, Marguarite, sat on his lap and made it plain that he would be enjoying her company for the rest of the evening. Before long, she took him by the hand and led him outside.

The butler for General Modiano was the man who gotten the best look at the assassin. Her face was burned into his mind, behind the black hole of a pistol barrel. He counted himself very lucky to be alive and did not know why he had been spared. During his incarceration and questioning he had worked with a sketch artist getting a picture of what he remembered. Now he was being interrogated by a man he had never met.

Roberto Campena de Iguaca had taken the butler and the driver to an open area off the road. The land had been cleared to construct a house that had never been finished. The foundations had been poured but the structure had not been completed. The two men did not know who Roberto was or why he was asking them the same questions the Secret Service agents had so many times already. It was easy to answer the questions and the .45 caliber pistol kept them from leaving.

The questions were the same and the answers were the same, but the man was not satisfied. He wanted to know the things they were unable to tell him. He wanted to know who the woman was. He did not accept that they had never seen her before and that she had been picked up from the Carnival procession and gone home with the general.

The limo driver had explained three times the way she had disabled him and stolen the limousine. He was being asked about it a fourth time and was getting angry. He had told the man all he knew and that was all he was going to say.

"No, there is something else. There is something you have not told me and you did not tell the police. There is something else that tells me who this woman is and where she came from and why you let her get away in the limo."

"I did not let her get away. She punched me in the throat with her knuckles, like this," he demonstrated. "Then she kicked me in the balls. I couldn't breathe. I thought I was going to die. If you don't believe me, kill me right now."

Roberto leveled the pistol and shot the driver through the eye. The gout of blood and brains that flew out the back of the man's head left no question of his being alive.

The butler dropped to the muddy ground and covered the back of his head with his hands, screaming.

"Shut up, you simpering fool. You have the option of telling me what I want to know or you will end up like this man."

"I don't know. I don't know. I don't know," he screamed. "I was bringing a tray of coffee to the guards. I was downstairs. I heard shots upstairs and froze. This woman leaned over the railing and shot the doorman. She pointed the gun at me but I did not move and she did not shoot me."

"Why?"

"I don't know. I was standing there with a tray of coffee and she was pointing the gun at me and she did not shoot me. I don't know why. Please don't shoot me. I didn't do anything. I didn't do anything. I don't know anything. I didn't do anything."

If the butler had known anything but what he had already said, it would have come out at this point. He was terrified out of his wits, beaten down from days of interrogation by the Secret Service and completely unable to withhold anything from this murderous stranger. The stranger reached this conclusion. A smile spread across his face as he reached down ad grabbed the sparse hair on the man's head. He pulled the butler's head back and looked deep into his eyes as he pushed the barrel of the pistol against his muddy forehead. The butler began to cry and blubber wordlessly. Roberto Campena de Iguaca silenced him with a bullet between the eyes and remained looking into the eyes, searching for something.

"Your deaths were too quick," he said, "and noisy. I should have cut your throats instead."

After leaving the border, Hernando and Anastasia did not stop moving until they were out of the city entirely. They knew they did not want to stay on the main roads in their Mercedes, it was too obvious. They took a road that was little more than a dirt two-track into the Iguaca State Park, northeast of the city. They backed the car into a little glade and shut off the lights. Hernando was nervous and wanted to stay awake, watching, but he was unable to stay awake after Anastasia Viuda was done with him. She rode him hard and put him up wet.

Morning came and Anastasia was once again despondent. Her cycle of excitement and depression was a familiar one with Hernando, so he was not surprised. He told her to lie back down and sleep while he drove. There was little doubt that they needed to get off the road, but there was so few places they could go without sticking out once they got out of the city.

The radio gave the news that there had been a massacre at the border bridge with Argentina. The details were sketchy but it was plain that the suspects had not come from Argentina, nor had they escaped to Argentina. Whoever they were, they were driving a Mercedes and were still in the area. Hernando saw children pointing at their car as they drove and their parents were paying too much attention. They needed a different vehicle and soon or they would be fingered for the killings.

The farm they chose to pull into was a family-sized affair. Fields of soy beans and wheat provided limited cover but there was a small rise before the house was reached so drivers could not see the lower story from the road. There was no real cover for the automobile except to pull it to the far side of the house, so Hernando did this.

"How should we handle this, Love?" Anastasia asked, deferring to his judgment out of courtesy more than out of a sense of inferiority. She knew it made men feel uncomfortable to follow a woman's lead.

"Give them the opportunity to swap whatever piece of junk they drive for this fine automobile. If they decline then we may need to kill them all."

"Let us not kill them unless it becomes necessary. There is enough blood on my hands already."

"It may become necessary. We are on half the radio channels and probably all the news channels. Shit! If that gun hadn't been in the trunk, we could be home in bed." There was a hint of blame in the man's voice. He had not taped that pistol into the trunk and he suspected that she had, though he did not know why she would have. He had only mentioned it once. Their relationship was torrid and tenuous and they could not afford to get in a disagreement at this point. Their arguments sometimes degenerated into violence and he could not put up with it right now.

Juan Carlos Ibrahim and his sons were in the fields while his wife and one daughter were in the house. The woman was gracious and though she could not get them to eat, she insisted they have a cup of coffee. Etiquette demanded that they accept the coffee.

It took the man of the house a while to get the news from one of his sons that there was a visitor at the house. They had been in the fields, tending the crops at sunup, after a hearty breakfast. Leaving the boys in the fields with the tractor, he walked back to the house. The strangers were finishing their coffee when he came through the door and he was immediately charmed by both of them. They looked like movie stars with their sun glasses and their tall muscular figures. They smiled and reiterated what they had told his wife, that the brakes were bad on the Mercedes and that they had to get to town to attend a meeting. It was imperative that they attend the meeting and they were willing to trade the Mercedes temporarily for whatever vehicle the farmer used, long enough to get to town and back. They would obviously pay the man for his hospitality.

Wiping his hands on the back of his pants, Juan Carlos drawled that he would be happy to take the couple to the nearest auto parts store where they could get repair parts and that he could repair the brakes on the car in no time. He told them, proudly, that his eldest son was going to be a diesel mechanic.

They eventually struck a deal whereby the couple would return with the farmer's truck and the spare parts needed for the brake job and pay him for both the truck rental and the mechanical repairs. They were so insistent that time was of the essence that the farmer gave them the keys to his old Toyota pickup, and they were off in a flurry of thanks.

The couple thought that it had gone quite well and were laughing about the situation, while behind them the owner of the farm was suspicious. He began to feel that he had been had. But, there was plenty of time to worry about that later. Back in the field he told his oldest boy to take the keys, pull the Mercedes onto the slab, jack it up and check the brakes. He would be back in a while.

The eldest son was happy to be doing the mechanical work rather than pulling weeds. He was a good mechanic for his age and studied hard when school was in session. He used the scissors jack that was in the trunk to bring the wheels off the ground, one at a time, and then placed house jacks under the frame as stands. The wheels were off the back in no time, but the brake shoes looked just fine under the drums. The drums themselves were not scored, but nice and smooth. The boy scratched his head and put the wheels back on the rear axle before proceeding with the front. The front wheels had disc brakes and, like the rear, they were in good shape.

Juan Carlos walked up as the inspection was finished and his son confirmed his suspicions. He stood looking at the Mercedes for a moment. It was easily worth four or five times what the beat up old Toyota could possibly bring. He muttered to himself for a second before his son broke in. He explained that the undercarriage of the vehicle was in fine shape and that the engine ran smoothly. He was of the opinion that if he never saw the Toyota again it would be a good swap.

"No. This is the devil trying to get me to take something that is not mine, for his own evil purposes. If I do not report this then I am as guilty as the people who stole this car. Yes, I will lose the truck but, God willing, the police will return it to me." He knew the police were corrupt but thought they would want the Mercedes and not the farm truck.

The telephone call took too long to connect. There was little to interest the police north of the border city, so there were few of them and most calls were about chicken thieves or church matters. The farmer's call about the Mercedes perked up the deputies' ears, however. The perpetrators of the border massacre had escaped in a Mercedes. It was a short time later the main roads were being watched closely and, like rural communities everywhere, they knew the local vehicles.

Deputy Carreras saw the Toyota and radioed his two counterparts. He knew they could get in front of the thieves as he pulled out behind them. The Toyota was moving the speed limit and all its lights worked. When the deputy turned on his lights, the driver put on the turn signals and pulled over. The deputy approached the truck close to its bed. He had his hand on his pistol but did not have it drawn. He never had a chance to get it drawn. When he looked in the window of the truck his career ended in the searing muzzle flash and accompanying hollow point.

"Oh, great. You had to shoot the son of a pig."

"Anastasia, you are still too soft. He was going to take us into custody no matter what we said or did. The farmer double-crossed us instead of just taking the Mercedes. Help me put this thing in the trunk."

Anastasia Viuda got the keys out of the ignition and popped the trunk of the police car. Inside, there was four shotguns and smoke grenades. She pulled the munitions out as Hernando del Fuego dragged the corpse toward the back of the car. Together they stuffed the body in the trunk.

"We need to get this out of sight as well. He called in our position so we cannot go forward, we must go to the side. I will drive the black and white, you drive the truck. We need to take the first road, right or left and dump the cop car. You see, don't you?"

"See what?"

"We should have killed the farmer and his wife."

"And all his children?"

"Yes."

Anastasia slammed the trunk and made her way back to the truck without a word.

The scanner was unintelligible half the time. It had good reception but the police radios had a limited range.

Parking a block from the police station allowed Roberto Campena de Iguaca to hear everything that was broadcast from the station. Sometimes the incoming calls were not clear enough to decipher. He had been sitting there for two days when the call came in, fuzzy and blurred, and was sent out to all officers. A small, white Toyota pickup truck with local plates, a tailgate made of boards and a large dent in the driver's side of the bed was sought in connection with the murder of a police officer north of the city. The suspects may well be the same pair that murdered the border guards. They had traded the Mercedes for the pickup truck and when the owner called the police they had tried to stop him and lost a brave officer in the altercation. The suspects had escaped in an easterly direction and every regional police department and state police office was contacted and put on alert. The suspects were armed and dangerous and should not be approached by unaccompanied officers.

Roberto had no intention of approaching them unaccompanied. He was simply going to kill them. He knew the price tripled for them if he could take them alive, but he still had no intention of attempting such a move. He would find them and shoot them. He licked his lips with the impending though of cutting their heads off as proof of a job well done.

The fugitives had moved east again, after heading out of the city. The police had a picture of them and he needed one, or at least a look at them. The clothing he had chosen for monitoring the police broadcasts was that of a middle-class office worker. It worked well for him when he wanted to look innocent and slightly naïve. He decided a change of appearance was needed for his next move.

The sergeant at the desk was well manicured and closely shaven. His uniform was starched and stiff. He obviously did not get dirty in his line of work. When he looked up at the shuffling figure with the wide hat and sunglasses, he immediately thought of a well-dressed beggar. The city had its share of homeless, and like any major population center, many were drug addicted or mentally ill. The man shuffling in looked as though he belonged in one of these categories. When the man spoke his voice seemed to confirm his status.

"I saw them!" the voice came from behind the man's hand. He did not raise his head to look at Sergeant Ortio nor did he take off his sunglasses.

"Who have you seen, sir?"

"I have seen Mary and Joseph in the Toyota pickup truck with the wooden tailgate. That will be the manger for the baby Jesus."

If Sergeant Ortio had not been looking at the dispatch in front of him, he would have tossed the man out on the street, but it was too much of a coincidence to ignore. He dealt with all stratum of society so he was able to handle almost any situation that arose. In this case, he knew that a little kindness would go a long way. "Would you like a cup of water or coffee or something?"

A consummate actor, Roberto knew better than to spend any more time in the police station than he needed to. He was not here to be seen he was here to see. "No, no, no, no, no," he said. "I just want to tell you that the baby Jesus is going to come into the world in the back of a white pickup truck with a wooden tailgate that has suffered the indignity of the wastes of the beasts of the fields."

"Where did you see this truck, and when?" Ortio asked.

"Ten minutes ago. Right out there." He waved his hand in a vague gesture that could have included half of Brazil.

Ortio knew that from the mouths of babes comes the truth and even madmen have their moments. He pulled out the pictures he had been sent and draped them over the edge of the desk and asked, "Are these the two?"

"Yes, yes, yes. Mary and Joseph in the pickup truck. I saw them. I saw them."

Sergeant Ortio knew there was little chance this vagrant with obvious mental problems could have heard about the manhunt before anyone in the police station, but he also began to be suspicious. Why was this man here, telling him this? This sort of coincidence did not happen to anyone, anywhere.

The shuffling visitor turned and began heading for the door. The room was deserted but for the two of them. Most of the city would rather rely on relatives to sort out problems than involve police. There was a saying in Foz do Iguaçu that translates to *If the police are called, both sides pay.*

Sergeant Ortio hit the button under the desk that locked the door to the outside, preventing the man from leaving. Then he came off the raised platform and around the end of the long tall desk. He grabbed the visitor by the arm, willing to use whatever means necessary to keep him there for a while. He had a nice, warm jail cell just waiting for this drunk to fill, and he could get whatever information he had in good time. What he had not anticipated was the strength and speed of a tiger under the disguise. The man punched Sergeant Ortio so hard in the stomach that he collapsed on the floor, unable to breathe. Had he been prepared he might have withstood the shot but he was not, and he was not well toned. Before he hit the stone floor, he had been relieved of his sidearm.

The hobo in the large hat and sunglasses stopped shuffling and moved with a sudden purpose. He strode to behind the desk and grabbed the copies of the mug shots and a black-jack. He hit the button to open the door and moved toward it. When the sergeant tried to reach out and grab his ankle, he hit him in the head with the lead-filled leather black-jack and sent him to dream land. He was not found until a half-hour later, by which time Roberto Campena de Iguaca was long gone, and the only description Sergeant Ortio had was of a shuffling bum with a big hat and sunglasses.

With pictures of both suspects in hand, Roberto was only one step behind the police and their lead was enhanced only by the fact that they had a larger force. It should never be said that the death of a fellow officer is not a motivating factor in a manhunt and Roberto knew this. Public safety officers see no lower form of life than a cop killer, and most of the world's armed public servants would rather shoot them than capture them. This knowledge was the only thing that allowed Sergeant Ortio to survive the night. If he had not been a cop, he would have been a dead man.

Anastasia Viuda and Hernando del Fuego had killed a cop and that made them public enemy number one. On the top of the most wanted list for the murder of a police officer was no place for a secret agent. There was no secrecy involved with that. Their careers were significantly compromised.

Chapter Six
Union Negotiations

Monday morning arrived with an influx of gloom that had nothing to do with the work week. The sky was overcast and the streets were dirty and filled with potholes and garbage. Terry Kingston had never experienced this sort of place. He knew almost nothing about snow, especially driving in it and he had never seen streets in such bad shape.

Nobody on campus had ever asked to see his temporary badge so Terry assumed he was free to roam about as he pleased. He got directions to the gym and had a good workout followed by an hour on the treadmill and stair climbing machines. He enjoyed the hot shower afterward and found himself craving something but could not put his finger on what.

He walked out the door onto the outlook over the parking lot and slid a foot or so before falling on his bottom. He rose, grinning ruefully and reminding himself that the surfaces were all very slippery. One of the young ladies who saw the pratfall was laughing at him, but he paid that no mind. He made his way to the cafeteria and had a turkey sandwich with mustard before returning to his car. The Buick that he had bought was not in Vanessa's driveway, nor was it down the street at the convenience store so it was undoubtedly on campus. But it blended in with all the others.

Grand Blanc was only ten minutes away. It was a much more upscale neighborhood. The union president's wife was at home if indications could be trusted, as the automobile had not left the driveway. It was covered with snow. Terry returned to the city and drove around until he found the unemployment office, right down the street from a flower shop. He selected a young black man from the stream of applicants flowing in and out of the office and approached him. A deal was brokered and the two of them walked down the street together.

The flower shop was expensive, they all were, but the purpose was worthy. Terry's associate bought a dozen red roses and included instructions and a dozen yellow roses with further instructions. The man did not understand why this tall German man wanted him to pay for the flowers rather than simply doing it himself, but a hundred bucks was enough to squelch any questions that might be asked. Terry paid the man and they never saw each other again.

The Aussie went to a pool hall for a couple of hours and played pool. He was not very good at it, having had no real experience, but he caught on quickly and was fascinated by the angles and spin. He grasped the concepts and physics involved and his mind swirled with possible applications in less genial situations.

Nobody had ever bought a dozen roses for Vanessa before and her reaction was even more enthusiastic that could have been predicted. By the time she got in the shower, she left her Australian lover lying on the floor gasping like a fish.

Tuesday evening was interesting at the Pikelfinger residence as well but nowhere near as satisfying. President Pikelfinger had been gone for a few days in negotiations with axle and suspension manufacturers that made component parts for two of the three remaining American auto makers. His wife welcomed him home in her usual loving but reserved manner and fed him dinner. Nothing seemed unusual until the dozen red roses arrived. The card read *"None of these can match your one rose."* It was unsigned.

Pikelfinger called the flower shop after getting no satisfaction from the delivery boy, demanding to know who had bought the roses. The clerk could not say, the delivery had been paid for in cash and the man had left no name. Besides, they were part of the Teleflora network and the purchase had been made at a different location. Nobody at that store had seen the purchaser. The flowers had been paid for in the City of Flint.

The message was obvious but Pikelfinger had been the subject of devious planning before. His wife said she had no idea what it was all about and he believed her. Mostly. He sent one of his cronies to the flower shop and that man bribed the woman behind the counter to come up with the details. Once again there was no name, but the purchaser was described as a young black man. That did little to narrow the field of candidates.

Wednesday came crashing in with a snowstorm. Terry insisted that Vanessa stay home, that nothing would be moving. Vanessa laughed at him and said she would be home later if he wanted to stay. The Toyota was parked behind the Buick so he threw her the keys and she took that. She didn't bother shoveling behind it, since the plows had not been through. She simply slid out into the street and spun off on her way to school.

Terry did not drive that day and suspected he would not leave the next, but by Thursday he would find that the snow had melted. He had no trouble walking down to the corner store to get some beer, and though he could not find any good beer there, he got a case anyway. At the last moment he decided a bottle of brandy would go well with it. He spent Wednesday watching American daytime television and getting piss drunk. He was worthless and sleeping by the time Vanessa returned. It had been a long time since Terry had gotten that incapacitated and was undoubtedly the result of feeling safe.

When Vanessa finally got home after school and work, she was prepared for what she found. The first shift clerk told her that her man had been in to get liquor and beer. She knew that there was no food in the house to speak of and the clerk had said that he had bought none. Vanessa was not prepared for the twin .38 Specials he had strapped to his sides. She had not seen them before, he had kept them in the trunk or carefully covered them with his clothes.

Passed out cold and snoring, he did not wake up when she came in the door, did not move when she shut off the television, and had not stirred when she got in the shower. When she reached under his vest, after she got out of the shower she got a bit of a surprise though.

She had seen the holster on the left side of his chest and was exercising her natural curiosity. She pulled the vest out a couple of inches and her new lover erupted. His left hand caught her right wrist and his right arm took her in the middle of the chest, lifting her off the ground and slamming her to the floor. Before the air had finished rushing out of her chest, she was looking down the barrel of one of the pistols. There was a very tense second when he recovered his memory of where he was and who he was looking at and she took two careful breaths. Terry very carefully de-cocked the pistol after pointing it out the window. Vanessa launched into a tirade of self-righteous vitriol. She was in her own house and he had almost shot her. What did he think he was doing and where had he gotten the guns? The basic questions were interspersed with statements and crudities that lasted about three minutes. When she paused for breath, he said, "Sorry, Love."

The invective renewed itself at the thought he could simply say sorry and it would be okay. Vanessa was on a roll and it was impossible to stop her. There would be no conversation, which requires a give and take, the words were on a one way course and flowed like a river, saying the same thing in a hundred different ways. When the woman needed more air he simply said "Give me my keys."

Thinking he was going to drive away and escape culpability for throwing her on the floor was another mistake and if he thought he was getting out of satisfying her that night it was the largest mistake he had made so far. She commanded him to get his drunken stinking ass in the shower and sober up a little. Meanwhile she broke into the brandy and got a little drunk. It was more of a surprise to her than to him that she had found herself aroused by the rough treatment and the closeness of death.

Afterward, with her head on his chest she asked if the pistol would have killed her. He told her that yes, it would have blown a large hole in the front and a huge hole in the back. She purred and he got very quiet. He was thinking about having to shoot his own dog in the head, years before. That had affected him worse than most men he had killed.

Then came the questions he had not wanted to hear. "Why do you have guns and are they legal?"

"I have guns because I need them and no, they are not strictly legal."

"Why do you need them?"

"Self protection."

"Who are you really?

"I'm Russell O'mara, the descendant of heinous pirates, thieves and murderers tossed into Botany Bay and left to die."

"Yeah, you said that, but I don't care about them. I want to know who you are."

"I told you."

"You can't even remember what you told me. You lied to me."

"I'm here on work visa to investigate the possibility of working with the governments of our two countries on bio-fuels."

"Save it for the bimbos. I don't believe that shit. Listen to yourself, you can't even say it convincingly." She scratched through his blond chest hair with her fingernails, then raised her head and started sucking on his nipple. When she had him fully interested she asked him again who he was and what he did.

"I'm an evil Australian man sent to corrupt the morals of America's youth," he said and rolled her over on her back. There was no more conversation for a while.

Terry passed out after their second torrid event and Vanessa lay there, physically satisfied but emotionally upset. She was in love with a man that she knew nothing about, that had almost shot her in the face and lied to her about who he was. She was setting herself up for failure and a broken heart and she knew it but could not help herself.

His toned body next to her, breathing slowly, did not help her think about what she wanted. She snuggled up to him and threw an arm across his waist. His shoulder blade tasted salty with sweat.

Thursday arrived with a small hangover and melted snow. The television announced a gun show at the convention center north of the city. It had been set up to run for three days: Friday, Saturday and Sunday. Terry asked Vanessa if she would like to go, but she was unsure until he promised to buy her a gun. She laughed and said she'd find out about that.

When she returned home, she had a permit from the Sheriff's Department to buy a pistol. She said the permit was good for ten days and he had better buy her a good gun or she'd make him pay in more ways than one. She did not specify what that was supposed to mean, but she did say she was hungry and they needed to go out to eat. He wanted to stop by a drug store to get a tooth brush. They ended up going to his hotel room for the night.

Flint had five registered stores that sold new pistols and several pawn shops. With a permit to buy in hand, it was not a difficult process. Once a firearm was in its new owner's possession said owner was expected to go back to the Sheriff's Department to register it. They did not do ballistic tests on the weapons, merely looked at them to determine that they were in good condition.

Vanessa liked the feel of a Ruger 9mm semi-automatic with a single stack clip. She did not really appreciate what she had until she and Terry went to the range outside of town and shot off a few rounds. It was far from ideal weather to be standing about outside, but her excitement made up for the conditions.

Terry bought her several hundred rounds of metal-jacketed practice ammunition and a full box of hollow points for when the need arose. He paid for her safety course so she could get a license to carry it with her. The safety course would not be given for another couple of weeks.

"Russ, have you ever shot anybody?" she asked him that night when they cuddled together on the couch.

"Well, now! What kind of a question is that? Do I look like some kind of a mad killer?"

"No. I just wanted to know. You could have been in Iraq or Afghanistan. Did Australia send troops there?"

"Only volunteers. I never volunteered."

"But you didn't really answer my question. Did you ever shoot anyone?"

"I shot a dog once." The expression on his face told the tale more than the words.

"Yours?"

"Aye. But that was a long time ago and there are such better things to be shooting now." He picked her up in his arms and carried her to the bedroom.

Union President Pikelfinger lived in one of those neighborhoods where it was difficult to set up surveillance unless one had an apartment available to them and there were no apartments. Typical, cookie-cutter suburbia in an upscale neighborhood where everybody knew when there was anyone new in the area. It helped people to feel safe that way.

Terry set up a candy-gram to be delivered Saturday morning. He could not be sure the man would be there. The note gave a time and place on Saturday afternoon for Mrs. Pikelfinger to meet an unspecified admirer.

Kingston wished there were some cliffs in the area. Driving off a cliff is a believable and understandable way to go that leaves very little in the way of evidence against it. It was not that he had anything against shooting the man, but the payoff was so much better if the entire affair is reported as a regrettable accident.

It could have been foreseen that a row would break out in the Pikelfinger home that Saturday. The note on the candies specified Wilhemina. There was no ambiguity and no chance of a mistake. The Dew Drop Inn was no fabrication either, it was a combination bar and motel right outside of town. Many illicit couples had hooked up in that bar and rented a room in the motel. Wilhemina Pikelfinger never had, but her husband, Richard, was now convinced otherwise. It was regrettable that she would need to suffer for her husband but any convenient avenue left open to the enemy is fair game.

The Dew Drop Inn was not such a difficult place to set up surveillance on as the Pikelfinger residence. There was nothing on the other side of the road except trees, but in the end of February there was no cover. There was no backlight from across the street, though, and the parking lot was double sided so a man could back up to the darkness and sit in his car undisturbed after dark. It was less clandestine during the day.

Richard Pikelfinger snapped. It was to be expected, with the stress he went through constantly, that something like this would send him over the edge. It did. He began ranting about her betraying him while he was working so hard to provide for them. It did not help that she reacted badly and started yelling at him about how he was never home. She did deny the allegations but the argument had been ignited and would not go out by itself.

After half an hour of heated argument, Richard left his home and his wife and went to a local bar where he proceeded to get potted on whiskey and soda. He was the only one in the bar drinking before lunch and it was not usual for him.

Wilhemina Pikelfinger managed to calm down a little bit. She had no idea who had sent her the flowers and chocolates, but was flattered. She was no longer the beauty she had been when Richard had courted her. A hot shower served to make her feel presentable and she spent quite a long time in front of the mirror. It had not been her intention to go anywhere that day. She was not having an affair, despite what her husband thought and the gifts suggested, but she was curious. Who had sent them? She began the incident with the best of intentions. She would find out whom it had been that had sent the flowers and tell her husband. That would end the story.

Sitting in the front seat of the Toyota did nothing to hide him during the day, so Terry Kingston was in the Dew Drop Inn when Wilhemina walked in. He had not expected her, he had expected a vengeful Richard and possibly some backup. The last thing he wanted to do was step into his own trap so he stayed away from her. He played pool and ate sandwiches, drinking lightly and watching the door.

Seldom occurring during the day, The Dew Drop Inn was frequented by older women looking for younger men. Nobody knew how the bar had gotten the reputation it had for this, nor why it persisted, but on any given night, a healthy young man stood a good chance of finding a willing escort if he could overlook the age difference. Thus it was little surprise when after a couple of drinks, Mrs. Pikelfinger had been approached. She had evaluated the young man and determined that he was not the one who had been sending gifts, and so, rebuffed him. He took it well and went away.

Half a dozen more drinks slid into Mrs. Pikelfinger and she loosened up considerably. The specified time had come and gone and her secret admirer had not appeared. She had been buying her own drinks, unusual in itself. She may not have been the knockout she was as a younger woman, but she was still appealing. She ordered one last drink but when she moved to pay for it a tall, slim man stepped up behind her and whispered in her ear. She turned with a smile.

"Brian! Are you my secret admirer?" The squint of her eyes and the crooked smile told the tale of too many martinis.

"No, Wil. I promised Dick I'd come over here and rescue you."

"Rescue me from what?"

"Come on. You have no business being in this dump."

"I was going to find out who it was who was sending me the flowers so I could tell Richard. I'm not having an affair, you know."

"I know. Dick didn't want to come himself for fear of what he might find. You know. What he might do."

"Well he had nothing to worry about. Bartender. Bring my friend a… what are you drinking?"

"I'm not. I'm driving. I'm here to drive you home."

"Well, I have a drink and I intend to finish it."

"Then I'll wait. I'll have a coke. You know, Dick sounded drunk on the phone. It might not be a good idea for the two of you to be together until you're sober."

"Oh, don't worry about that. I'll handle him. You can drive me home though. After I finish this." She hoisted her drink and waved it around as though it had some significance.

After waiting until she finished her drink, Brian poured Wilhemina Pikelfinger into the back seat of his car and drove off. Terry watched through the window, wondering what sort of relationship this man had with Richard Pikelfinger that allowed him enough trust to bring his drunken wife home. It seemed plain that she was drunk enough to sleep with whoever showed interest at that point.

Although there are a number of labor unions in Australia, Terry had no experience with them. He was without a substantive knowledge of union brotherhood. As he looked out the window he saw a man behind the wheel of a Cadillac in the motel parking lot. There was no snow on the Cadillac's windshield even though it was snowing outside. Then it dawned on Terry that he was not alone. Anyone trying to take Mrs. Pikelfinger to a motel room would have ended up with broken legs.

A serious argument might happen once she was home, but Mrs. Pikelfinger was not able to hold up her end of the disagreement. She ended up vomiting in the driveway and being carried into the house. The argument was carried on the following day with Richard unwilling to believe that Wilhemina was not having an affair. For her part, his wife was flattered and could not have been more pleased. Her husband was in a constant state of high-speed motion that allowed little time for her. The children were grown and gone away to college giving her a serious empty nest feeling. She wanted more appreciation out of life and her high-powered husband was not providing it. Her feelings had been building up for some time but needed a catalyst to energize the discussion.

The discussion was lively. It kept the president home for a couple of hours longer than usual. He was observed leaving the neighborhood about 8:30.

Terry knew he had found his way in, but the men who had waited for Wilhemina the day before also served as a warning.

The steak was pink in the middle when Vanessa cut into it; Terry's was blood red in the center. The steakhouse had a dimly lit warm lighting and the natural wooden furniture trapped a smoky atmosphere. Vanessa looked like a princess in her long dress and jewelry. Her hair was pulled up with a pair of long strands falling behind her ears, framing her face. Her rubies looked almost black in the low lighting but her bright red lipstick flashed and sparkled until she rubbed it off on a napkin. Her consort was no where near as elegant looking as she.

Terry had gone to the style that Americans thought was Australian. He had an outback style hat and tan khakis with lots of pockets. He kept the vest buttoned at the bottom to conceal the twin revolvers he had taken to wearing everywhere. Vanessa had stopped complaining and ended that particular conversation with a simple statement. "When the cops stop you," she said, "they are not going to be so easy. You can't just show them your dick and shut them up, like me."

The sun had gone down by the time they left the restaurant. They decided that since Vanessa had no classes the following day and did not report to work until afternoon, they would go to a casino in Detroit and do a little gambling. She had never been in a casino before and had no idea what to do. Terry had first gotten a taste for gambling on a

European cruise ship and while he was a bold hand, he did not always come out on top. In all, the couple had a good time but Vanessa had serious unanswered questions about Terry's financial base. The Aussie was betting thousands on a roll of the dice and did not seem concerned that he lost what she would clear that year in a matter of minutes.

After several hours of gambling, the couple went across the street and had an exceptionally good rack of lamb and a bottle of rosé. They got lost once on the way back out of Detroit, but eventually got on the expressway and headed back to Flint. By the time they had left, Terry had lost a substantial sum of money.

"Are you a smuggler?" she asked as they headed north.

"If that's what you would like to believe. There is a lot of intrigue and excitement in the world of smuggling I suppose."

"I just want to know, Russell. I want to know what I am getting myself into. Not that I'm complaining, mind you. It's every girl's dream to have a wealthy foreigner sweep them off their feet ant take them away to the South of France or whatever, but I need to know what you do for a living."

"I already told you."

"You haven't told me shit. A bunch of smoke and mirrors." She cupped her hands in front of her face to muffle her voice and said, "Pay no attention to that man behind the curtain." The allusion was lost on Terry.

"Look, my little wallaby," he replied, "If you knew everything about me that you wanted to, you might not like what you thought you knew."

"So, I'm supposed to keep my mouth shut and let you do whatever it is you do until you're done."

"That would make it easier for both of us."

"I don't want you coming in tonight. I need to think about our relationship."

"All right. I'll tell you what. I'll drop you and this Toyota off and I'll take the Buick out for an oil change and a tune up. I'll see you after work tomorrow."

"I.. uh, ok. I guess so. I'll see you after work then."

The Buick was less noticeable than the Japanese car. It was a nondescript color and model that blended into the landscape. Terry listened to the talk radio stations, National Public Radio and the news. It was becoming increasingly apparent that people died only two unnatural ways in Flint. People died in automobile accidents and they were shot. The percentage of murders in Flint was actually startling, given the size of the town. It managed to make the FBI's top five most dangerous places to live in America every year. This year it was number three; it had been number two the year before. Detroit was number one this year. The murder capital of America. Grand Blanc was nowhere near as dangerous, even though it was only 10 miles south of Flint; a quiet, affluent suburb populated by retired auto workers and some who still had jobs. The auto industry was deserting the area in a wholesale fashion and as the high paying menial jobs left, the crime increased. It was a savage cycle of violence and repression that showed no sign of ever reversing itself. Flint, Michigan had been the birthplace of the United Auto Workers and it would long stand as a grave site for it as well.

Richard Pikelfinger rose early every day that week and drove his Cadillac south on route 75, heading into Detroit to represent Local 882 in their negotiations with Detroit Axle Corporation. The UAW's Local 882 had been on strike for almost a week and it was beginning to shut down assembly plants at America's largest automobile manufacturer. It was on the verge of shutting down plants for the smallest of the three as well. Chrysler had recently been sold by a German company that had bought them out a decade earlier and were particularly sensitive to the costs of doing business. The automobile manufacturers had already negotiated deals whereby they could hire new employees at vastly reduced wages, but Detroit Axle wanted more. The axle manufacturer wanted to cut the salaries of the existing workforce in half. The union would not budge on this; they knew it was a slippery slope they could never crawl back up. If they allowed Detroit Axle to do this, then every auto manufacturer in America would insist on the same concessions. The union would be crippled.

It became clear why the men of power wanted Pikelfinger dead, but there was no end to it. The union would never elect or appoint a man or woman who would be able to accede to these demands. They would need to kill every man and woman that paid dues before they could get that kind of agreement. This promised to be a messy negotiation.

The Cadillac that Union President Pikelfinger drove was new, fast and solid. It's 4.4 liter supercharged engine put out 469 horsepower that accelerated smoothly thanks to the 6-speed transmission. While most of the automotive market was looking at making larger automobiles, Cadillac produced a muscle car. Terry knew there was no way the Buick could catch that machine. Thinking deeply about it made him realize that there was very little on the road that could. He had been thinking that a simple auto accident would be the way to go, but running him off the road was out of the question.

The convenience store on the corner made a good place to sit and observe. There were only two ways out of the subdivision and the most convenient one, the one that led to the expressway, led right past the 7-11. Smoothing his hair back, Kingston saw Richard pull into the parking lot and knew that his best shot was right there, but that he would need to kill anyone in the corner store as well. He was not willing to do that and it would not look like an accident that way. With a large cup of coffee in hand, Pikelfinger got back into the driver's seat and pulled out.

The president of the UAW drove well above the speed limit. On route 75 in Michigan, that meant he drove close to 90 miles an hour. Early in the morning the traffic was not dense so he could manage that speed safely, as long as there was no ice or snow to set him off course. His pursuer kept a comfortable distance behind him and tried to keep up but he was not used to the snow. Once Terry felt his tires slip sideways on the pavement, he gave up the chase. He had not formed a plan yet and was not expecting to punch the man's ticket today, so he backed off and let the quarry escape into the thicket of industrial Detroit.

The diner was half full of retired persons, there for the Senior Citizen's Special. The waitresses were almost the same age as the patrons though they moved a little faster. The eggs were fresh and the sausages had real casings on them. The rye bread was over-toasted and the potatoes were undercooked. It was a good, quiet environment for Terry to think. The coffee was hot and bitter and Terry was on his third cup after breakfast when he had a revelation of sorts. He regretted very little he had done in his life and that was part of his awareness. He had killed a lot of men, but there was not one of them that he felt had not deserved what he had gotten. Gangsters, pimps, drug dealers and thieves all knew what the potential outcomes of their scurrilous activities might be. They chose to break the civil and moral codes and laws of society and thus, faced the vengeance of the people. Much of Terry Kingston's life had been seeking vengeance for himself or for others. What came to mind in this seedy little diner in Detroit filled with geriatrics, some on oxygen and some smoking cigarettes, was that he did not really want to kill Richard Pikelfinger. He had been paid for the job and could not turn his back on the customer now. There are men that will not be trifled with and Terry knew he had been hired by just such men.

It passed through Terry's mind that he could disappear and never be found, but he would never work in this line of work again if he did. He would become the hunted and instead of watching for his target, he would be looking over his shoulder for the kill shot for the rest of his life. He shrugged his shoulders and threw some money on the table. People died by accident every day, he needed to arrange an accident, that was all.

The best kind of accidents involved natural forces: water, gravity, lightning, that sort of thing. The land around Detroit is relatively flat, without canyons or cliffs, but there are tall enough buildings and lots of water. Since Terry didn't know any Greek gods, he doubted lightning was an option, but electricity might be.

Auto accidents are a dicey proposition at best since the variables can hardly be controlled. As he pulled the Buick away from the diner, Terry realized he should have kept the receipt. He had wanted to rent a hotel room in the name of Richard Pikelfinger but since he did not have a credit card, nobody would rent him a room. It came as a real surprise and a shock as well. The world was being overrun by the plastic master. There was a way around it, though. He pulled into a motel that rented rooms by the hour. The hookers were not yet walking up and down the block. There was no reason to bring one in with him. It would have made him too memorable if it had been after dark, but right after breakfast, nobody was there to notice. All he wanted was the receipt anyway.

The 7-11 store on the corner turned out to afford the perfect opportunity in the morning. Richard Pikelfinger pulled his Cadillac into the parking lot and went inside to get a cup of coffee. This was the second day in a row and it looked as though it was his regular routine. He did not lock his car doors when he went inside.

"I got one for ya, Cap'n," whistled out of Carmody's mouth.

"What did you find?" Kevin Cook had just arrived at the station, unshaven.

"Vice picked up a hooker last night that claimed to have information about the Willie Brown case."

"Willie Brown? From the Saint Claire Slaughter?"

"That's right, Boss. I never forgot you asking why the man was stark naked with two other men in the other room. I figured he was sleeping off a long night but it looks like I was wrong. I got the tape of what the bitch did say; she wants a deal, of course. Vice thought they could run it by us since it's our case, but they want some of the credit."

"Who brought the woman in?"

"A guy named, are you ready for this? Jude Warrant." Carmody thought it was funny. Cook did not.

"Yeah, I know Warrant. I worked with him before. Heard every joke there is about his name already so don't even bother. Get him on the phone. Get me the tape. Where is the suspect being held? What's her name and why don't I already have this fucking information?"

Carmody backed out of the office door and moved to take care of the captain's demands. He had a secretary deliver a cup of coffee and a doughnut to the office while he did so.

Cook ate one bite of the doughnut and threw the rest away. He drank half the cup of black coffee and then pulled the electric razor out of his desk drawer and plugged it in. The dust of the stubble lay on his collar like fingerprint chalk.

Jude Warrant was on the other end of the line when the phone rang. He didn't have much to add to what Detective

Carmody had said. He provided the name, Tierecia Cargill, and her professional name Cherry Pie. She had been picked up not far from the crime scene on Saint Claire Avenue. She claimed to have been in the closet when Willie Brown was killed and that she got a good look at the man who had done the deed. Detective Warrant did not have a description yet. Tierecia was an experienced and canny woman and she wasn't going to give them anything until she had an immunity deal. They had offered an undisclosed plea bargain, but there was no way she would go for less than immunity from prosecution for past sins.

Detective Argent Grady cracked open the door as if he was worried about getting something thrown at him. When no projectiles were forthcoming, he opened it far enough to admit his body and closed it quietly behind him. He had the tape of the initial interview with Cherry Pie in his hand. The police had started taping all interviews years ago to head off a rash of accusations of police brutality. The brutality was real, but they needed to put on a good image, so they could clear themselves when it occurred.

Cook waved toward the VCR in the corner that was connected to the 13-inch black and white television in the wall niche. As Grady slipped the tape in, he made the comment that they wouldn't be able to use tapes much longer and the department would need to spring for DVD recorders. Kevin Cook cleared his throat and told him not to hold his breath.

The tape told him no more than he already knew, but it gave him a look at the woman's face.

When the tape of the interview was over, Captain Cook called the Assistant District Attorney for the county, Matthew Aspic.

"Matt, Cook. Tell me about this Tierecia Cargill that got picked up recently."

"Captain Cook, how goes the voyages of the Bounty?"

"Look, Assprick, I told you before that Cook was Captain of the Endeavour. Now, I don't have the time or patience to laugh at your jokes this morning. You have a suspect up on charges of prostitution that claims to have seen the man who killed those three dealers in the downtown apartment. She wants immunity from prosecution, right?"

"No need to get all huffy, Captain. I'm just trying to be friendly."

"Sorry, Matt, I've got a raging headache this morning, and I called to find out what you think about the woman's claim."

"Well, it's too early to say. Her lawyer is convinced that she has something, but he won't release anything until he has a firm commitment. I thought we could let her sit in County for a while and stew on it. She's got a couple of priors and is looking at 90 days in jail, minimum. That's not enough to make most whores turn over on their pimps, but maybe she figures it's worth it since the victims are all dead."

"So you got nothing on her, really?"

"Oh, the case is solid enough, but it's not like we can't get her again."

"I talked to Detective Warrant. Vice is willing to let it go if we can get something on this killer."

"OK. I'll let her mouthpiece know when he calls. I want the information first, though. We need to evaluate what she has before we make a deal."

"You know the procedure. I think we may have something here. I want to be there when she makes the statement. Don't leave me hanging."

"No problem, Kevin. I'll set it up and let you know when it comes out."

"Sometime before Easter, OK?"

"Sure."

"Thanks. Bye."

Cook hung up the phone and stared at it for a second. His head still hurt and the coffee was making his stomach too queasy for aspirin. He thought he should have had a shot of rum this morning. That would have straightened him up.

The morning sun and the steamy heat of Brazil felt like a soda bath on MacMaster's sun burned skin. The naked woman next to him was dragging herself to her feet and looking around like she had no idea where she was. The hotel room was clean and smelled of fresh paint. The window had been left open the night before and a gecko had slipped inside to capture the moths and mosquitoes coming through the window. The mosquito netting draped across the bed had kept the blood-thirsty insects off the room's inhabitants.

Gordon reached for the woman's breast but she slapped his hand. He was not sure she remembered him or the night before until she said, "You will not beat me with that meat stick again."

"That is not what you were saying last night," he replied with a grin.

"Last night I was drunk. Today I am sore and my head hurts."

"Sorry about that."

"Ah, do not apologize and do not think I want any more this morning."

The huge redheaded Scot slipped into the bathroom and turned on the shower. After bathing, brushing and flossing, he shaved and wondered for the hundredth time if he should grow a beard again. There was no bathrobe in the hotel room so he came back out wrapped in a towel, but his guest had left. On a piece of paper under a corner of the room phone was her name and address but no telephone number. He looked at it thoughtfully and then pulled an electronic device out of his travel bag. Opening the small unit revealed a tiny keypad. He needed a stylus to punch the keys since his hands were so much larger than the average man's. It would be unlikely he would need the address and to show up there in more than a couple of weeks could be a disaster. Marguarite might well have picked up a permanent man by then; after all she was a very appealing woman.

Thinking about appealing women caused Gordon to pull out the picture of the subject, Perfecta Navaja. The picture was of poor quality but it could not disguise the classic beauty of her face. There was something else in the look, though, something that appealed to MacMaster. It was a calculating, dangerous look in the eyes. He dismissed the thought almost immediately. He knew the woman was a stone cold killer and that was what made him see the look.

Breakfast was good and filling. There was more of it than Gordon was used to eating and he tried not to embarrass the women that were cooking at the street-side diner. They would have fed him lunch as well and not charged him for it. He tipped them generously.

The City of Cascavel was lively at night and bustling in the morning, but it is located right on the tropic line and midday at this time of year it was too hot to move about much. MacMaster was not used to siesta and wandered around until he found an open tavern. Inside it was dark and air conditioned, a condition that led to a crush of customers escaping the heat. With no need to make friends or probe for information, the Scot sat by himself and listened. There was nothing to be gained from this crowd. Nighttime would find him back in the Brass Knob, buying drinks and playing the life of the party.

The news came out that the body of a patrol man had been found stuffed in the trunk of his own cruiser. The location was remote, but the suspects were reported to have been driving a white Toyota pickup truck that they had traded a Mercedes for. That was enough to determine who had done the deed, but not enough to pinpoint their location. The trail was three days cold and the police were no closer than before. They could have been anywhere by now.

The pickup truck was useless now. They didn't even dare try to trade it in on another vehicle for fear they would be located through it. They had escaped the provincial forces yesterday, but they had no doubt made things worse. Killing the patrol man would energize the entire Brazilian police force against them. The border guards were not part of the same service and were often looked at as separate and corrupt, but when an officer of a police department was killed, it really hit a nerve.

"If we were not so far from something else, I would dump this truck in one of these ponds. As soon as we get a chance, we need to change to something else. We may need to split up as well."

"Hernando. You know as well as I that a man and woman in a car together causes no more reaction than feathers on a chicken. If you think we should split up, we can, but then I will not be there to watch your back and you will not be there for me."

"Let us find something that stands out less than this rolling neon sign. I don't want to leave you, I'm only thinking of you."

Anastasia Viuda turned her head to the side and rolled her eyes. Hernando del Fuego did not see the expression. An hour later the opportunity presented itself. A mid-sized Ford was right off the side of the road with the hood up. As they approached, they saw a man with a pair of jumper cables extended. It seemed like a gift from God.

The young woman in the car looked exhausted; her man was little better off. The scene spelled itself out: the fishing poles in the back seat told of a daytime expedition to a nearby stream or pond, the woman's sundress told of a city life that had little to do with agriculture, the man's expensive shoes told of an office life that did not involve physical labor.

It was a poor spot to have broken down. The man swore it was nothing but a dead battery and that he would pay for a jump. They had stopped to fish and the car would not start again. Hernando told him to keep his money, that they would be happy to help out the stranded couple.

The car did not start with a jump, however. The battery was flat dead and would probably never hold a charge again. Acting every bit the Good Samaritan, Hernando took the battery out of the truck, loosening the terminals with a pair of pliers from the toolbox in the trunk of the car. The Ford started immediately, bringing short lived cheers to the stranded couple. The cheers were truncated when they found themselves looking down the barrel of a shotgun. Anastasia held the shotgun on them while Hernando pulled his pistol from his waistband.

The man acted outraged and the young woman began to cry.

"Shut up, you stupid cow," Anastasia said. "I do not want to kill you, but if you do not shut up, I will shoot you in the face and then blow your man's balls off."

"Give us a chance. Let us get away into the woods and you will never see us again," the man said. There was nowhere for the young couple to have run to, even if they had gotten a head start.

"Shut up and take off those fancy shoes," Hernando told him. "Then get in the cab of the truck. No, I'm not going to hurt you. I feel sorry for you for being so stupid. That's right, now close the doors. Both of you."

The man was the first to die. Hernando shot him twice in the face, blowing the remains of his brain all over his companion. She started screaming and he shot her twice as well. Once the dead man had been relieved of his wallet, they were ready to go. The woman's purse was in the car.

The toolbox in the trunk yielded a screwdriver and it served to puncture the gas tank of the truck. Once the gas cap was loosened, the fuel began to run out in a small stream. The agents managed to escape in their new Ford before the fire spread far.

Chapter Seven
Cascavel

News that the pickup truck had been found was all the talk in the Brass Knob that night. The charred bodies of the perpetrators were said to be in it. It looked as though there was to a swift and decisive end to the mysterious episode. There was no mention of the fact that the bodies in the truck had bullet holes in them because that salient fact was being kept under wraps. The Federal Investigators were fairly certain that the bodies in the cab were not the couple they were looking for, but they were charred black and their clothes were all but gone. It was difficult to determine who they had been, but it was not difficult to tell that the woman was too short to be the fugitive known to them as Mrs. Andalucia. None of the local law enforcement figures had anything to do with the discovery, it was made on the other side of Prudentopolis, well over 200 miles away. It was clear to the officers of Cascavel that the fugitives were moving toward Curitiba, to lose themselves in the favelas. MacMaster did not subscribe to that theory.

Once he had learned all he could from the denizens of the Brass Knob, he excused himself, citing a headache. He checked out of the hotel, stopped at a market, dashing in just before they closed, and getting some meat, bread and mustard for sandwiches and a block of cheese along with a case of warm beer and a wool blanket. A couple hours later, he was halfway to the last known location of the assassins, but had to stop before he fell asleep on the road.

Roberto Campena de Iguaca had known of the discovery before Gordon MacMaster had learned of it. The police scanner had alerted Roberto hours before. He had been waiting for news on the scanner in the town of

Guaraniacu, about 50 miles east of Cascavel. He was 200 miles ahead of the competition by morning, in a motel on the outskirts of the town of Irati. By nightfall he was in Curitiba. Having no further information, he stopped there and made arrangements.

Dom Bravuria was one of the major players in Curitiba and Roberto had dealt with him on a couple of minor matters in the past. It would be a stretch to say they were friends, but they were associates so he was willing to speak with the man from Rio.

"Roberto Campena, what brings you to our humble town from the action of the big city?"

"Dom Bravura, your humility humbles me. Thank you for accepting audience with me."

The kingpin said nothing, merely rotated his hand to indicate he was busy and needed his associate to get the ball rolling.

"Yes, well, I'm sure you are aware of the attack on the border crossing a few days ago? I have reason to believe the couple that did that job also killed General Ernesto Modiano two days before."

"Roberto, you should know that I stay out of politics and I stay out of the affairs of the army. These are two very dangerous regions for a man in my position to be involved with and I have no reason to wish myself turned on a spit."

"Ah, I have misspoken myself and must clarify. The two killers have been contracted out and I was hoping, since it seems they have fled this way, that you might assist me in their final departure. I will of course perform the operation, I was hoping only for a finger in the right direction."

"Are these individuals from this town?"

"I do not think so, but they did flee in this direction."

"Well, if I do not know them, I can scarcely be able to assist you in locating them, can I?"

"Dom Bravura, you know everybody in this town. You have only to say you want something done and it becomes so. I implore you, make your network available to me and I will compensate you in time."

"What is it you are offering to me as compensation?"

"I can offer money, but I would not insult you in that way."

"No… I have no need of money. I do have a situation that a man such as yourself might be able to assist me with, however."

"As I said, Dom Bravura, say it and it shall be so."

"One of my lieutenants has a woman who has so tied him in her apron strings that he will follow her to the ends of his world, and I fear there may be other interested parties involved. She has been meeting with a man in hotel rooms. I have confirmed this, though he does not yet know."

"You would like me to eliminate this man?"

"No, both of them. I want it done so that there is no trace, no remains. I never want their bodies found while either of us are alive."

"I can do that. It would be my pleasure."

"And I would be happy to assist you with your endeavor. Marcello, find the people this man is looking for and give him the details of what we spoke of earlier. He is to be trusted, respected and assisted."

Marcello took copies of the pictures and provided Roberto with pictures and details of the other job. There had been a reservation made for two days off and nothing could be accomplished until then.

MacMaster stood on the edge of the freshwater lagoon known alternately as Lagoa Dos Patos and Lake Guaiba. It was the confluence of five rivers and one of the finest lagoons he had ever seen. He reflected that if he did nothing else in pursuit of the murderous couple, he had seen this. The sun was setting off to his right and some sort of sea birds were circling overhead. Some fishing ships were coming in for the night along with tourist vessels and yachts. Transport ships were docked off to his left; some were being unloaded, others were packing on freight. A butterfly stumbled its way in front of him and a cricket began to sound its creaky song. He found himself relaxing and wondering if he could retire to a place like this. He made a mental note to pick up some land on the margin of this lagoon as an investment if not a retirement spot. The town of Pintada was right behind him and the city of Porto Alegre was across the water.

It had only seemed natural to the tracking instincts of the Scotsman that he head for the coast. The pair he followed were going to leave the country when they got detained in Foz de Iguaça. He had no reason to feel that they were not engaged in the same activity now. They had killed General Ernesto Modiano, clearly why they were in the country in the first place, and now they wanted to vanish into the pampas of Argentina. Since the western borders were now closed to them, the sea ports would be the next easiest passage. To travel north into the rain forests would be the best way to lose pursuers, but the trip itself would most likely kill them instead. And so, Porto Alegre was the most logical and reasonable choice. The city was huge and one of the busiest ports in the hemisphere. It was possible to lose oneself on the docks of Alegre and slip away undetected and unknown.

Tomorrow he would engage a fishing expedition and go out for barracuda or shark or something. Tonight he needed a place to sleep.

The bellhop jacket and black trousers with the white stripe did not look as ridiculous as the hat the menial members of the staff were forced to wear. It looked like something from a 1950s movie but it reflected the style of the hotel.

All the clothing in the laundry looked relatively new, though the hotel itself was 70 years old. Roberto Campena de Iguaca had no problem finding his size though he noticed his shoes were wrong for the outfit and there were none to be had. The pillbox hat snugged down on his head was an insult to his dignity, but completed the disguise perfectly.

The laundry carts were normally only taken out in the early afternoon, to pick up the towels and sheets of the rooms that had been vacated. It was six hours later than would have been expected when the man dressed as a bellhop pushed the cart down the hallway to room 512. He did not leave the cart outside the door, but pushed it past and against the wall. Then he took the bottle out of the cart and knocked on the door.

It was more a feeling than anything else, that someone was watching him through the peephole in the door. When nothing was said, Roberto announced "Champagne."

"We didn't order any champagne! Go away!" was the annoyed voice from inside the room.

"Compliments of the hotel, Sir. You have stayed with us before and we wish to show our gratitude for your loyalty as a customer."

"Leave it outside."

"I'm afraid I'm not allowed to do that sir. You must sign for it or I will be accused of stealing it."

"Oh, very well." The door opened and a man, naked from the waist up, wearing no shoes, stood there.

Roberto's 9mm was silenced and nobody heard the three shots that penetrated the man's body, not even the woman who was in the shower, right next to the doorway.

126

The man's body was moved inside and then the laundry cart. Within seconds, the man's body was in the cart and Roberto was in the bathroom.

"Well, are you going to join me? Come on and wash the stink off your, Ooooh…" she started to scream when she saw Roberto but he stifled it with a towel in her face. Her resistance was worthless as he punched her into submission and bound her hands and mouth with duct tape and then hauled her to the bed.

"Oh, yes, chica. I can see why a man would be bound to you like he was chained. You are truly a prize. Such a pity nobody else will be able to enjoy your gifts. I imagine those beautiful lips are wonderfully talented." He threw her face first on the bed and invaded her from behind with the silencer of his pistol.

Having her slick, wet body on the bed before him was more than Roberto was able to resist and he dropped his pants, slicked himself up with hand cream from the bathroom and invaded her most private part.

The woman tried to scream as her assailant buggered her but the duct tape prevented any real sound from escaping. Her thrashing seemed to excite him more and he pounded into her savagely, then as he reached his climax, he shot her in the back of the head.

The mid-sized Ford had to be refueled a couple of times before its new pilots reached Porto Alegre. They had taken turns at the wheel and had driven straight through. When they got to the city, they parked the car in a hotel parking ramp. It would not be located for months if history was any indication.

Before finding lodging the two went to a local street market and purchased some clothing and food. They packed it all into an old-fashioned carpet bag.

Anastasia Viuda checked into a different hotel under the name Sandiana Torremolinos. It was the name on her credit card. Hernando took the back stairs to the third floor where she met him and together they went to the seventh floor where the room was. Neither of them had the energy for sex, even after they shared a half bottle of gin with tonic water. Anastasia took a shower and Hernando fell asleep while she bathed. She lay down next to him and curled herself into his arms.

The box truck had the name of a laundry painted on the side. It was a legitimate concern, open for business for at least 10 years and it evoked no comment when it backed up to the dock behind the hotel.

The two bodies in the laundry basket were covered with towels and blankets from the room. The "do not disturb" sign was hung on the door handle. The desk had been called and instructed not to disturb the couple in room 512 under any circumstances. The laundry cart was pushed into the back of the box truck and Roberto closed the doors from inside, still wearing the bellhop uniform.

The cell phone Roberto used was not his; it was not a registered account. The prepaid minutes were anyone's to use.

The construction site was not yet empty for the day, so Roberto was forced to drive around until the crew finished up. It was a couple of hours later when he pulled the box truck onto the premises, right behind a cement mixer. The cement mixers pulled in all day long, pouring foundations and pilings and the work would not end for another couple of weeks. The driver of the cement mixer circled around and backed up to a pit that was half full of fresh cement. Trucks had been pouring into it half the day and one more truck full would make no difference. The bodies hit the slab and sank into it slightly but the top had already begun to cure. The trough was run and the mixer dumped its semi-solid load over the still bodies in the bloody sheets. There was barely enough cement to cover the forms but cover them it did. By morning no one would know anything had happened here. Roberto climbed into the truck, made one more call on the cell phone and tossed it into the concrete as well. He followed the cement mixer through the gate and stopped to close the gate behind them.

After waiting for two days to complete this assignment, Roberto Campena de Iguaca was waiting again. This time he awaited news that the couple he really wanted to find had been located. He spent the time compensated by Dom Bravura with willing women and strong drink, but it did nothing for him inside. Inside he was driven by something he did not understand and could not put words to. He did not know the people he hunted, did not even know their real names, but once he had his sights set on them, nothing was going to stand in his way. Hunting killers was his very favorite sport. The couple in the hotel was a bonus, but they did little more than whet his appetite. They were not the kind of challenge he needed.

Tierecia Cargill had a good lawyer. He wasn't a world class, million-dollar lawyer but he knew better than to let his client give up her hand without getting the payoff first. It was a couple of days of negotiation while Tierecia sat in Cuyahoga County Jail. Cargill was no rookie though, she played it cool. Eventually, her patience was rewarded with immunity from prosecution for all misdemeanors currently and previously on record. This included any misdemeanors she might be suspected of subsequently, as long as they occurred before that day. It was a sweet deal considering what she had was not all that substantive.

"Let's begin with what you were doing there." Quincy asked. He and Grady were conducting the interview. Tierecia's lawyer was there as well.

"I was partying."

"What does that mean?"

"Come on. You're a brother. Tell me you don't do a little partying. I know you like to tap that ass," she leered at him.

"This has nothing to do with me or what I do or do not engage in outside the purview of my professional life. This has to do with what you were doing in the apartment of Willie Brown the day he was murdered."

"I was snorting his coke and sucking his dick. OK?"

"Yes. We like to be clear about that. Now how many men were there in the apartment."

"Three. But I wasn't into all three, now. I did Willie."

"If he had told you to, you would have done the other two as well, right?" Grady asked. He immediately sensed it had no bearing on the case.

The attorney whispered in Tierecia's ear and she responded to the question. "If it gets me somewhere, I do anyone. I do all three of them at the same time if they want it. I do you right now. Both of you."

"That's all right. Just answer the questions. Did you see someone else come in the apartment.

"Yes. He came in the window."

"What did he look like?"

"I didn't really see him very well. He was a white boy. He didn't have on a coat, it didn't have no sleeves."

"You mean he wore a vest?" Quincy asked.

"Yeah. A vest. He had on a black hat…"

"What kind of hat?" Grady asked.

"Just a hat."

130

"Did it have a brim, a cowboy hat, a pork pie hat, a yarmulke?"

"I don'ts know what a yammyca is and you'all gots to wear pork pies. This was a hat with no brim. A winter hat, fits tight, rolls up on the bottom. Y'know, condom cap. See what I'm sayin'?"

"A watch cap," Grady said.

"Whatever. I didn't see his hair. He was a white boy but he looked like he came from Florida. He had a nice tan. But he didn't sound like he came from here. Somewhere else. He sounded like England."

On the other side of the one way mirror, Captain Cook bit the index knuckle of his fist. The only way this woman could have known there was a foreigner in the neighborhood was if she had seen him or spoken to him, and by her own admission she was otherwise engaged.

"What did he do while he was there?" Quincy asked.

"OK. Get me. I was doin' Willie when we hears a window break. Willie tosses me on the floor an' goes for his gun. See what I'm sayin? Then pop, pop, pop, pop four times. Muffled like it was silencers. I hear that an' I'm in the closet. I don' need nobody poppin' a cap in my fine brown ass."

"So you're in the closet. How did you see this man if you were in the closet?"

"I'm lookin' through the crack, see? I see the door open and Willie shoots twice. Then I hear it again, pop, pop. Willie gets hit and he's down and I'm trying to make myself real small in the back of the closet. This guy steps into the room and says 'That's the way we do it, mate' like he's talking to somebody else, only I don't hear nothing else. Then he leaves.

"Why didn't he take the cocaine?" Grady wanted to know.

"Shit, I don't know."

"Why didn't you take the cocaine? You could have snorted that shit till the back of your head exploded."

"I ain't that stupid. I take that shit, they gonna find me and kill me."

"What about the money?" Grady was fishing now.

"What? Enough to keep me straight for a couple of weeks? Sure I grabbed what I saw, but I was in too much of a hurry to get out of there. I wasn't hangin' around to go looking into things. I didn't wanna end up dead too. I heard a bang on the roof, kinda like a big hammer pounding the wall. Then I heard three shots, not the pop, pop, pop. These was gunshots, outside, on the roof. That was when I ran."

"You didn't stop to call 911 or check to see if any of the men were alive?" Quincy asked seriously.

"Shit, Nigger. It's your job to check if any o' them was alive. It's my job to get my fine brown ass back on the street. Anyway, I got no car, so I'm running across the street to my sister's crib an' she ain't home. I'm inside the door, watching the street an' I see this guy…"

"The shooter?"

"Same guy. With the vest. He's walking down the street like he ain't got a care in the world. So, he don't see me an' shit I don' want him to, so I'm hiding back, see, by the old doorbells. They don' work no more but there's a little more room there. I look out a couple minutes later an' he gone. I don' know where he went but he heading for the river so I was heading the other way."

"So where is the rest of the money that was in the apartment?" Grady pressed.

Cook had heard enough. He grabbed the phone and called the Desk Sergeant instructing him to get Sam back to the station as soon as he could. Cook had already read Sam's report but there may have been something else he missed.

He called Carmody and told him to get back down to the Central Tavern and interview the staff there. The Aussie had just been fingered for the killings. The next call was to the IT department. He wanted to let them know who was next on the never-ending list of names to trace. Then he called Judge Appolitano.

The judge was less certain than Captain Cook that there was justification to search the financial records and airline tickets for a man based on a drug-addicted prostitute's testimony. He pointed out that the witness had said the shooter was English and the man they had interviewed in the Central Tavern was Australian. Cook was relentless. He was so certain that he had the right man he was willing to bet his career on it.

The warrant was finally signed and the IT crew got to work. If the name Russell O'mara had been entered into a network in Cuyahoga County, they would find it. That included airplanes, hotels, hospitals, credit cards, bank accounts, sewer and water, gas and electric and pharmacy records.

When Kevin Cook went home that day it was with a feeling of accomplishment. The name had not been found but he knew he was on the right track now. A couple of shots of rum and he went to bed almost sober.

Morning came without a hangover and no need for a hair-of-the-dog treatment. The captain called Information Technology before he even got dressed.

"IT, Billy."

"Billy, it's Cook. Tell me you got me something."

"Not much, but its something. A Russell O'mara bought a car from the Supreme Used Car lot a couple of days before the killing. He didn't pick it up until the day after. See it had an oil leak in the transmission pan, and he wouldn't take it until they had fixed it. So he picks it up, pays cash for it and they never see him again."

"Has anyone gone down there to talk to Supreme?"

"No. I got my information on the telephone.

"It's awful early for a used car lot to be open."

"They were open late last night. I think I should tell you, there may be other things to consider before you head down there. This is not the first time the Supreme car lot has come up in a search. I wouldn't go down there alone."

"Thanks, Billy. I'll be careful." Cook hung up the phone muttering about Billy not going into a pizza shop alone.

Kevin took his time for once and showered and shaved. He brushed his teeth and took out clean clothes. He took a garbage bag full of clothing to the car when he went downstairs and dropped it off at the laundry on his way to work.

By nine in the morning Grady, Carmody and Cook were all at the Supreme Used Car lot, talking to Benny, a used car salesman. Benny remembered the Toyota with the leaking transmission and the man who had bought it. His description of the Aussie was spot on, though he denied the man had an Australian accent. It was a foreign accent well enough but it didn't sound Australian.

The used car salesman, Benny, was smooth enough but the detectives noticed that the rest of the crew looked as though they had gotten caught with their hand in the cookie jar. They could almost hear the collective sigh of relief as they drove out of the lot.

Sam's report included the fact that Russell O'mara had indicated that he was going to Lansing, Michigan to look at a fiberglass factory. Judge Apolitano did not have jurisdiction outside Cuyahoga County, let alone outside Ohio, but there were others who could make things happen through different means.

The Woodsman was filled with the usual crowd that night. Cook was there with his friends, drinking lightly. He was waiting for another man, an associate more than a friend. Brock Dakota had promised that he would come around and listen to Kevin's spiel. Brock owed Kevin a favor, personally and Kevin was not shy about reminding him of it.

Brock was half Shawnee and half Germanic which made for an unstable drinking partner. The German half of him wanted to drink beer all the time and the Shawnee half wanted hard liquor. He was genetically predisposed to be a violent alcoholic and he sometimes lost the fight against himself. He would go for months without a drink and then months without a sober moment.

The Office of Homeland Security liked Brock Dakota because Brock did not have to be told anything twice. He had a bear trap memory when he was sober and no conscience when he was drunk. His superiors knew he would need to be sacrificed eventually, that he would become a liability, but they used him to their best advantage while he was still manageable. Captain Cook thought of him in much the same way.

When Dakota showed up at the Woodsman, he was already bleary. There was no telling how long he had been in the bag, but it worked well for the captain. If he had been sober, it would have been difficult to convince him of the necessity of finding the man they were chasing through whatever means needed to be employed. On a jag, however, the man was willing to bend the rules to benefit his side in the game. It would have been easy for him to blame the government and the white man for stealing his land from him but he did not seem to think this way. He had been born in Oklahoma, where his tribe had been relocated in the 1800s but he decided early that Reservation Life was nothing he was willing to put up with. As a half native, certain doors were opened to him in the federal government and certain allowances were made. When he was on the verge of ruining his career, he managed to heed the warnings that inevitably flowed his way and cleaned up his act for a while.

It did not take much convincing to talk the Homeland Security man into promising to do some research in Michigan. After all, the man in question was a foreign national, in the country, and suspected of killing Americans. It made no difference if the Americans were scumbag drug dealers, they were still citizens, and so afforded the protections any other citizen should reasonably expect. Homeland Security Agency needed no warrant to go snooping into the files of suspected terrorists, especially if they were foreigners. They had never convicted an Australian of being a terrorist before and Brock was eager to be the first to do so.

Dakota and Cook drank until closing time. Neither of them was in any shape to navigate the highways but somehow they both made it home in one piece. They were both late for work the following day.

It was afternoon before the information got to Kevin Cook's desk, almost quitting time. Russell O'mara had rented a hotel room in Flint and had been staying there for the past month. This information was gleaned from his credit card record. Very few hotels would rent a room, long- or short-term, without a credit card. There was no other record of his existence. The Toyota had never been re-registered in Michigan so it should be an easy pick-up. There was the business of inter-jurisdictional cooperation, however. The Flint City Police would not set up the surveillance outside the city limits. The Township police complained that there was no crime committed within their jurisdiction. The State

Police and the FBI were too busy with their own problems in Michigan to be excited about it. Finally, the Sheriffs took a cruise past the Holiday Inn looking for the Toyota with the Ohio plates. The car was not there and the desk clerks said they saw very little of the man who had rented a room under the name Russell O'mara. He made sure the room was paid for weekly but spent very little time actually in the room. The clerks promised to phone the Sheriffs Department when he showed up again.

Answering machines can be a wonderful and useful invention. They can also be used to set a person up if that person is gullible enough. Text messages are even better. Cheap disposable cell phones with purchased minutes on them can be used for many things and are relatively secure.

Richard Pikelfinger was asleep when the phone rang and his wife answered it. The woman on the other end of the line seemed embarrassed and claimed a wrong number. A minute later the vibrating cell phone alarm that indicated a text message went off. The message read *"Dick, I think I left my lipstick in your back seat."* As would any reasonably curious individual, Wilhemina Pikelfinger put on some clothes and took her husbands keys out of his jacket pocket. In the back seat of the Cadillac she found a lipstick and a used condom. She could not bring herself to touch either of the items. She closed the door and went back into the house.

The briefcase was not one of the stiff sided ones that were used for years, but one of the new expandable kind. There was a lot of paperwork in that briefcase, and it was heavy. Wilhemina set it on a kitchen chair and began to pull things out of it, putting them on the kitchen table. Before she actually riffled through any of them, she pulled a bottle of rum out of the freezer and took a long pull from it. Then she went to work. The papers were all union business or receipts

137

from gas stations or restaurants, except for one. That receipt was from a motel in Detroit; it specified what hour the room had been rented for and what day. There was no name on the receipt, but it was in her husband's briefcase. That was enough.

Wilhemina Pikelfinger took another long pull from the bottle of cold rum and shuddered as it warmed her stomach. As the wife of a powerful man, she knew there would be challenges to their marriage. There were always women working behind the scenes to improve their positions using their God-given assets.

The third drink of rum was enough to remove rational thought from the woman's mind. She was not the sort of woman who could be expected to do this. A messy divorce and a cutting settlement was the most anybody would have expected out of her. She did not have any training with guns and never accompanied her husband to the shooting range. He had gotten her a .32 caliber revolver some years before, but she had refused to be interested in it. Instead of following through and getting her carrier's permit, she stuck it in a drawer and left it there. That pistol came out.

"Richard, you no good bastard, who is she?"

"Wil, what the fuck are you talking about?" Richard's eyes were barely open.

"Who is she, Richard?" Wilhemina threw the cell phone with the incriminating text message on it.

"What is this? I don't know what this is all about. I... Shit, Wil, put that fucking gun down. There isn't anybody else." Richard's eyes were open now.

"You've been cheating on me, Richard. You've got some bitch calling you up in the middle of the night. Who is she?"

"Wil, there isn't… I haven't… Please, put the gun down before you hurt yourself. We can work this out. Somebody is setting us up. None of this is real."

"Oh, it's real all right. You had some bitch in the back seat of your car. I hope she was worth it." The pistol was wavering back and forth in her hand. The rum was making her weave as well.

Richard Pikelfinger leaped out of the bed in a desperate attempt to disarm his wife. It was the worst thing he could have done. She would have put the gun down eventually if he had just stayed where he was, but his sudden movement startled her and the gun went off.

It had seemed to make sense to Terry that swapping the Ohio plates with Michigan ones would help dim the spotlight on the Toyota. He had wanted to swap the plates from another Toyota of the same make and model but he had been unable to find one. He could have registered the vehicle in Michigan but felt this to be a bad move.

It was illegal to park overnight on the street in Richard Pikelfinger's neighborhood, and getting rousted by the Grand Blanc Police Department with an illegal license plate would have been a very bad move. The grocery store was open all night and had enough business to allow a man to sit in his car in obscurity. Security guards patrolled the parking lot but did not suspect people who were not outside their vehicles. After a couple of minutes of sending the text message, Terry went into the store and bought some beer. He didn't intend to drink it; he wanted the receipt to prove where he was that night. After stowing the beer in the trunk, he headed into the residential neighborhood only to find police cars and an ambulance at the Pikelfinger residence. Apparently his subterfuge had worked better than he could have expected.

Passing through the neighborhood evoked no notice and he slipped back out of the area without incident. He would need to wait until morning to find out the details.

Since he was only marginally familiar with the area, Terry immediately assumed that his target would be transported to Hurley Hospital, near Vanessa's place, or McClaren Hospital, just a couple of miles away. As a result, he waited in the Park-and-Ride lot right off the exit to Route 75 North, expecting to see the ambulance pass him on its way into the city. It did not. He was unfamiliar with the hospital south of the city, closer to Grand Blanc, where they took all the patients from that area.

Around four in the morning, commuters began pulling in and consolidating into one vehicle. The price of gasoline was forcing a lot more people to share the ride to work. The ambulance never passed this entrance to the expressway. Another hour passed and Terry remembered the beer in the trunk. Two beers and half a pack of cigarettes later, he fell asleep in the front seat of the car.

The inside of the car was quite warm when he awoke. While not officially spring for another week, the weather was much more pleasant than when he had first arrived. The problem was not the weather but the beer he had consumed. It was time to return some of it to nature and there was no spot to do so at the Park-and-Ride. Since he was only a couple of miles from the hotel, he got back on the expressway and headed north. After pulling off the exit and crossing the overpass, Terry saw something he had not expected. There was a Sheriff's car parked in the empty lot of the unused Eastern Michigan University building. It stuck out like a cactus in the desert.

Terry did not make the turn onto the southbound road to the hotel, he just kept heading west. There was no reason for him to believe the police were looking for him, he had been very careful, but there was no sense in taking chances. He drove the perimeter of the airport and headed north again. He still needed to relieve himself but that could wait a little while. He had thought to dump the car in the airport lot, but if they were looking for the car, he might never make it out of there. He pulled into a restaurant lot and backed into a spot. Since there is no provision in Michigan for a front license plate, the numbers are easier to hide.

Steak and eggs made a good breakfast. Kingston deliberately limited the coffee this time. He did not need to be any more jittery than he already was. He went over his recent actions, everything he had done in the past couple of weeks, but he could not think of anything that might have given him away. He privately cursed the need for credit cards in America and chewed over the few times he had used his. Russell O'mara had registered the Toyota, even though he had changed the plate, and Russell O'mara was the name on the card. If they were looking for him, it was for something that had to do with the car that he had purchased in Ohio. He tried to work through it logically, but could not. He did not know what his mistake was, or if he had even made a mistake. Maybe the cops were only taking a break to have a cup of coffee and a doughnut.

Picking up a different car would not be a problem. He could drive Vanessa's Buick if need be; getting rid of the Toyota was more of an issue. The 24-hour grocery store parking lot would be the best place to leave it but there were no sidewalks in the area. The place was not designed to be walked to or from and he did not want to call a cab. The anonymity of these huge parking lots was just what the doctor ordered, however.

Terry left the restaurant and drove to the mega-store. To call it a grocery store was to sell it short since a customer could get almost anything there in one form or another.

Within the doors was everything from asparagus to work boots. Terry took an inconspicuous parking spot and went inside. He bought a new set of clothes and changed into them in the bathroom by the exit. His vest was discarded with the old clothing and some regret. He had grown quite fond of the vest since it had hidden his pistols so effectively. He kept his trench coat but tossed his hat out in favor of another baseball cap. Before he left the store he bought a gallon of bleach some paper towels and some liquid drain cleaner.

The headline of the local newspaper read *"Union President Pikelfinger Accidentally Shot."* It gave an account of an accident whereby Wilhemina Pikelfinger had shot her husband once through the chest by accident. Richard was expected to recover since none of the major organs had been hit. He was reported to be in serious condition, however.

The bus was going in the wrong direction, initially, but that did not deter the Australian from hopping on. He changed buses twice without incident and found himself back in the downtown area. He kept thinking that it was nothing and that he had overreacted, but there was a nagging doubt in his mind. He could not figure out where he had slipped, but something was wrong. He thought of the statement Rhinegold Sheer had made in the airport about the customer needing a scapegoat. That did not read correctly with the desire for a clean hit, one that looked like an accident.

Pulling the cable rang the bell and the bus stopped. The sidewalks were broken in this neighborhood but they existed as a holdover from the past. The minivan was as innocuous as could be expected. There was nothing distinctive or memorable about it; not the color, make or model. Kingston negotiated with the owner for a minute and bought it. There was plenty of space in the back and a higher seat for a better view. Like any minivan, it looked like it belonged to a family man and this one was made in America. He took the license plate out of his coat pocket and jammed it into the seam of the lift gate panel. It could be clearly seen there, but it could barely be read.

That night when he cruised back toward the Holiday Inn, the Sheriff's car had been replaced by a State Police car. There was nobody in the car which said the officers were inside the University building. It was not being used and had large, mirrored windows so it made a perfect stakeout spot. The empty, marked car in the parking lot gave up the trick, though.

With his twin 38s in the pockets of his trench coat, Terry backed the minivan into a spot in the parking lot. He was wearing his baseball cap and carrying a cane. He walked with an exaggerated stoop and a pronounced limp. He moved slowly, making every effort look painful. He was not disturbed as he went to his room but he knew he needed to move quickly. While inside he wasted no time. Anything with his fingerprints on it was wiped down or thrown in a duffel bag. Anything with a possible DNA trace such as the sink and tub were doused with bleach and drain cleaner.

Downstairs the clerk was not the most alert creature on the planet but, to his credit, he did eventually notice that the room that had been flagged had also been accessed. He wasted no time calling the Sheriffs Department, but it took that much longer for the Sheriffs to call the State Police and for the field office to call the team on stakeout. By the time the message had returned, full circle, the site was clean.

The two officers moved quickly once they got the message that their suspect had possibly slipped past them. They went through the lobby, picking up the clerk with the pass key on the way. The elevator was going up while their suspect was going down the stairs.

Knocking on the door generated no reply so the officers went in using the pass key and with their weapons drawn, but there was no one inside. The room was orderly and smelled very strongly of bleach. The three shrugged their collective shoulders and went back downstairs. The two officers returned to their lonely post across the narrow parking lot and the clerk returned to his desk. Once again, it took him a minute to notice the key card left by the courtesy phone. It was for the room he and the officers had just invaded.

Back in the minivan, heading south to the hospital, Terry kept his eye in the rear view mirror. Nobody followed him but there was no doubt in his mind that the jig was up. He needed to finish the job and get out of town. There was no more time to spare.

The hospital parking lot was huge and well lit but the minivan was parked on the side where the lights were fewer and further between. The sun had been down for an hour or so and visiting hours were almost over. There was no charge for parking at this one; the ones in the city had parking ramps with guards.

Terry stepped into a stairwell and was struck almost physically with a memory from childhood that stopped him dead in his tracks. He remembered cowering under the stairs in a similar stairwell in a similar hospital on the other side of the world. It played with the force of a hallucination, the scene he had in his dreams, where his mother's brains were blown all over the wall of her hospital room. His gorge rose and he almost vomited on the floor. He began shaking and stepped out of the stairwell emotionally impacted beyond his capacity. It had come unbidden and it struck him too powerfully to ignore. He stepped back outside the building and lit a cigarette, trying to gather his emotions, trying to squash the feelings. Nothing had affected him so powerfully

144

in years and he began to doubt his ability to reenter the facility. A couple of drags from his cigarette and his stomach began to rise again. The minivan was still warm and he sat inside it for half an hour steeling himself for what he needed to do.

The stairwell was out of the question. He could not bring himself to reenter it. Instead he went to the front entrance of the structure and limped up to the receptionist with the cane. Putting on his best German accent he asked for the room number of Richard Pikelfinger. It was on the fourth floor and yes, he could have visitors for another half hour.

A more exclusive facility, this hospital was less densely occupied, better staffed and more expensive than either of the other two regional facilities. Prim nurses walked the halls in their starched whites and various levels of interns and assistants hurried around in their blue uniforms. The fourth floor was quite busy. Richard Pikelfinger had lots of company. It would be some time before they cleared out. Terry noted with satisfaction that the man's room did not share a hallway with the nurse's station.

The tenth floor was given over to the terminally ill and geriatric near the point of expiration. It was easy for Terry to find a room that had no occupant there. He needed to wait out the visitors' hours and he wanted to make sure the nurses had made their rounds before he made his move. The bathroom had an exhaust fan so he sat on the edge of the tub and smoked for a while. He was still extremely uncomfortable being in the hospital. It amazed him how deeply the old emotional scars went and how badly shaken he was by the environment, in a place that had little similarity but purpose, on the other side of the world.

If he had made a detailed plan about how to complete the job, Kingston reflected, he would certainly not have counted on having Wilhemina shoot the man. That was a bonus but also a negative. It changed the playing field from private to public. It struck him suddenly that incapacitation might be as good or better than actually killing the man, and wondered if he should run that past his contact before taking further action. He rejected that thought with regret. Given his perceived status he could no longer stay in the Flint area and if he did, he would be ineffective.

He turned his thoughts back to the stairwell. It had been the bottom, where the steps met the floor. It had been the little boy, terrified beyond reason, hiding under that first flight of stairs. The memory had the horrifying fascination of a bad accident on the road. His life had been changed that day. If that day had not occurred, he would not be here, now. He would never have come to America. He would not be hunting a man, now. He would not have chosen to kill people for a living.

The hallways of the geriatric ward were empty and silent. The patients were too old or heavily drugged to notice anyone or anything. The stairwell was silent as well. Terry's boots made no echoing clang on the stairs, the way the ringing noises of Bradley's boots on the stairs of the Goulburn Medical Center populated Terry's nightmares. He took a deep breath and then worked his jaw as if he were chewing on something. Whatever phantom he was chewing on got swallowed and after another deep breath, Terry Kingston was himself again. That unexpected apparition from his past was conquered.

A calm and deliberate purpose filled the Australian's mind as he moved toward his target. His last thought before opening the door to the fourth floor hallway was, "Expect no mercy, take no prisoners."

The hallway was empty of nurses and visitors as he moved slowly and quietly down to Richard Pikelfinger's room. The door was open but he closed it behind him as he entered. Pikelfinger was unconscious. He had tubes running into needles in his arms, wires running to sensors on his chest and head and tubes running into his nose and mouth. The beep-beep of the heart monitor and the low susurrations of a vacuum pump were the only sounds in the room.

There was only a moment's pause. "Look at this poor bastard. I don't think I really need to do this," ran through Terry's mind before another voice asserted itself. "Once you've been paid for a job, you see it through or that's the end of it for you." It was difficult to remember if Gordon MacMaster had said that or if it had been Uncle Ginger.

Stepping forward, Terry clamped his victim's nose shut and pulling out the drainage tube, slapped his hand over the man's mouth. Nothing happened for a few seconds and then the man's eyes opened. Terry had hoped the man was sedated enough to pass on without a fuss but such was not to be. He began thrashing about, trying to dislodge his assailant but in his weakened condition, he was unable to do so. The beep-beep of the heart monitor went into a flat monotone drone.

Keeping his head down, Terry stepped through the door and was almost bowled over by a nurse and the intern who were responding to the alarm that went off when the heart monitor went dead. Echoes in the hallway indicated more staff moving toward them. It was a moment's decision on Terry's part. "The monitor's gone flat. I think something's wrong," came out with his full Australian accent. He knew it was a blunder before he was done saying it.

The intern looked at Terry for a second and then dashed inside the room with the nurse. By the time they were inside, two more people in blue scrubs were heading down the hallway. Instead of turning and running, Terry pointed into the room and said, "I think he's dying."

"Sir, visiting hours are over. You'll have to leave now."
It was a line rehearsed so often that it sounded like a line in a
play.

Terry did not say another word until he got outside the
confines of the hospital building. Once he did his words
were not pleasant or pleased. He had not expected the level
of response that his actions had initiated. He had not
expected witnesses. He could not afford witnesses. He
actually considered going back into the building and
eliminating the nurses and the intern, but quickly rejected the
idea. He could not afford it. It was a bad move. He swore a
couple more times, pulled one pistol out from under his
trench coat and laid it on the seat next to him, covering it
with a newspaper.

"What happened to take no prisoners?" was all he
could think as he put the van in gear. "Well, I tried to be as
bloody foxy as I could. Worked out pretty good 'til right at
the end. Time'll let loose on this one. Or not."

Brock Dakota was happy to be in Michigan. It gave
him a reason to sober up. He had been on a slippery slope
for several months and had needed something he could get
his teeth into. This seemed just the thing. A foreign national
that was going around killing drug dealers was the sort of
thing that could turn him into a crowd favorite if the news
stories were spun that way. "Christ," he thought to himself
as he pulled out of the Detroit area, "they'll turn him into a
fuckin' Robin Hood if I let 'em. Glad I thought to pull the
prints of the crime scene. Dead bodies make compelling
evidence."

Chapter Eight
Porto Alegre

Gordon MacMaster had not thought he was going to have any luck in finding the couple of fugitives he had accepted the job for. Brazil was huge and there were villages not on any map. It was a good place to disappear to, if one needed to become a wraith. What he did not count on was his own insight being so keen. He knew what they were going to do before they did it, or at least as they were doing it. He always asked himself why people did things and, though he often came up with an empty bag, he had a good track record for putting himself into the minds of others. They were in Porto Alegre. He was in Porto Alegre. They were staying in a nice hotel and he was in the lobby bribing the desk clerk to tell him what room the woman in the picture had rented.

Two hundred dollars was easily enough to convince the receptionist that he should point out the room. The Scot considered eliminating the man as well but then decided that there was no need for it. The man was old and obviously knew what would happen to him if he admitted to having anything to do with whatever was going to happen to the woman in the room. The Brazilian insisted that Sandiana Torremolinos had rented the room alone but MacMaster doubted that she was alone. He was congratulating himself as he gained the seventh floor and slid the key into the door of the room directly across the hall from the one occupied by his prey. This had been only the fifth hotel he had investigated, looking for the couple. He also felt good about the fact that he did not need to leave a paper trail here. A few bills slapped on the counter, a fake signature, and the room was his.

Downstairs, the old man was congratulating himself on his windfall. He did not know that the men who had approached him earlier were not associated with the man who had just rented the seventh floor room.

Hernando del Fuego slid out of bed slowly and quietly so as not to wake his partner but she awoke, regardless. Sleep left her in an instant, the way small birds awake, and she was alert. Hernando smiled at her and padded into the shower stall.

The hotel they had chosen was far enough from the docks to have some class but close enough that they did not need transportation. They had planned on going to the waterfront that morning and securing passage to Argentina on a cargo vessel. The dock house coordinator would tell them which ships were leaving for where, and when.

When Hernando came out of the shower he found his partner sitting cross-legged on the bed with their pistols disassembled before her. She was working with a tissue, cleaning the mechanisms. Hernando smiled, involuntarily this time, and told himself again how lucky he was. His smile vanished when he thought of how much he would miss her after it was over.

With the pistols cleaned, loaded and concealed on their persons, Hernando and Anastasia were ready to head for the docks. They were both hungry but they knew food could be had in the dockside taverns. Hernando was dressed more or less as a dock worker and the disguise worked well for him. The rough cloth would blend in on the wharf while the cap would help with the disguise. His vest was cut a little longer than was usual to cover the holster in the small of his back. Anastasia Viuda was not so easy to conceal. She was too tall a woman to ignore and automatically attracted attention wherever she went. They had discussed leaving her in the hotel room while he secured them passage but she was not about to sit around waiting for him. Her clothing was dramatic in comparison to his. She wore a full-length dress cut in a gypsy style, with the three tier crinkle pattern from the waist down. The long leather coat covered her shoulder holster and concealed her pistol. It was early enough in the morning she could keep the coat on without raising questions but that would not last long. Wearing a black leather coat in the midday sun would be suspicious and uncomfortable. Inside the carpet bag was another set of dockworker's clothes for Hernando and a set for Anastasia as well.

The door locked automatically behind them as they stepped out and headed down the hall. They heard the door open behind them but they could not imagine that they had been discovered so quickly and easily. They were not alerted to the danger until they heard an unfamiliar voice speaking Spanish, behind them.

"Stop and turn around slowly. I have a .40 caliber pistol pointed at your heads. Drop the bag and don't make any sudden moves"

"I'm sorry sir," Hernando began in Portuguese, "do we know you?"

"No. Do not move. Keep your hands away from your sides. Drop the bag."

Anastasia Viuda turned to Hernando del Fuego and began screaming at him in the border dialect that mixes Spanish and Portuguese. "I told you that bag was bad luck. Look what you have done now. He's going to rob us because you were too stupid to throw that nasty old bag away."

Hernando played the game back at her and began hollering, "This is what you think of me? You stupid cow. Where did this thing come from that you are so smart that you can tell me where we are going to go and what we are going to do and as for your stupid premonitions and seeing ghosts you should be taking pills for that."

"You fool," she replied, even louder now. "You know I'm right. I saw the aura around that bag and told you it was going to be bad luck but you just had to have it because it was like one your mother had. Give him that thing and remember forever that it was your stupid decision, not mine."

As loud as Gordon MacMaster's booming voice was, he could not shout down the couple who were bickering as if it was an every day occurrence. He told them to shut up, then he demanded that they shut up, but they ignored him as if he were a wall fixture in the hallway.

"Stupid decisions, you want to talk about stupid decisions? What about checking into this hotel that is obviously full of criminals. Perhaps this is where you belong, with the thieves and the whores." Hernando was now yelling at the top of his voice.

"Whores? Why you stupid, little, blind cockroach. Your mother's a whore. Give me that bag before we end up dead." Anastasia reached out and grabbed the handle of the carpet bag and wrested it from his grasp. He was protesting meaninglessly, while she threw the bag at Gordon MacMaster's head.

The fraction of a second it took to bat the flying bag away from himself was enough for Hernando del Fuego to draw his pistol and fire. The round went through Gordon's wide, billowing shirt, but did not touch his skin. The second round went wide to the other side as his target spun back into his hotel room. By the time he was inside, he was facing two pistols in the hallway as Anastasia Viuda fired a third round.

The hotel door slammed behind him and the Scotsman dove over the bed to take a position behind it. The Argentine couple did not follow him into the room.

Roberto Campena de Iguaca was still an hour away when the confrontation exploded in the hallway of the hotel. Dom Bravura had no organizational strength in Porto Alegre, nobody in that city worked for him, but the octopus of organized crime did not work in such absolute ways. Favors were exchanged and payments made in sometimes unusual ways. The men in Porto Alegre had located the couple Roberto was after and Dom Bravura had provided the conduit for the information.

The fly in the ointment was that some members of the local underground had wondered what the interest was and had discovered the reward themselves. Rather than risk his own life, one of the gangsters had sold the information to the local police who were as corrupt, or more so, than the local mob.

So, when Anastasia Viuda and Hernando del Fuego exited the lobby of the hotel, they were in for much more than they had bargained for. He had re-holstered his pistol, but hers was in her hand, in the pocket of her coat.

The couple was attempting to look as though they were not running away from something when they ran into what awaited them outside. The gangsters were sitting at a wrought iron table pierced by the support shaft of an umbrella. The presence of the police had kept them from entering the lobby of the hotel. The police were lounging against their car across the street from the hotel. Four of the officers swung into action when the couple emerged through the large glass doors. Automatic weapons were leveled. The pair did not have a chance. They were disarmed and handcuffed, then stuffed into the back seat of a cruiser and driven off, not, however, in the direction of the local jail. Following at a safe distance was a local tough guy on a motorcycle.

The police cruiser was driven into the residential suburbs where the couple was escorted into a middle class home. Anybody seeing it done knew better than to say anything about it, but the man on the motorcycle was in a different category than the frightened members of the local population. He took note of the street and the number and rode off with the valuable information.

Gordon MacMaster was feeling incredibly chagrinned. He had underestimated his opponents in a drastic fashion and it had almost cost him his life. He grudgingly admitted to himself that they had played him as smoothly and effectively as he had ever seen a spontaneous swindle affected. It had been improvisation at its finest.

From behind the bed, he could hear the footsteps retreating down the hall and knew his quarry was escaping. He also knew they would shoot him without a second thought and that they were both armed. He launched himself out the door, his pistol in hand and followed the pair down the stairs. They were moving quickly and he was a half dozen flights behind them when they emerged from the building into the waiting arms of the police. By the time he emerged from the building, his pistol was in his pants pocket. His tourist shirt marked him as being from out of town, but the police had not marked him as a target, nor did they know that he was hunting the same reward they had just acquired. He turned and walked away, embarrassed and ashamed of himself. He also congratulated himself at surviving the encounter. He made note of the men at the bistro who were not watching him, but the police in action. He made note of the fact that the police did not enter the hotel to determine where the shooting had come from or who had done it. They simply took the Argentine couple into custody and drove off. He took note of the motorcycle that followed the cruiser, an

1100cc crotch rocket. The cops could no more outrun that bike than they could outrun radio waves.

"You might as well forget whatever plans you had. The police have them now and they will keep them. If it were local dealers or gangsters, you might have a chance of negotiating with them, but not with the police. They will take you and sell you to your competition as well. You might as well ride off into the sunset."

"Forgive me, Arturo, for not understanding the subtleties of your local culture, but what are you trying to tell me, that they have been arrested?"

Arturo glanced wistfully at his empty beer glass and Roberto raised his hand to signal another round for his associate.

"They have been taken to a house, by the police, where they will be sold for the reward or ransom to whoever it is that…" Arturo left the statement unfinished as the bartender delivered the foaming glass of beer.

"Where is this house?"

"Ah, I am not able to tell you. I am able to tell you who knows, however. He followed them and is waiting on someone to bid on the information. He knows the address is worth something to someone, but he does not know who, and so the information is worthless without a connection to tell him who wants it. I am that connection and that is why we are speaking, now."

Roberto said nothing, took a sip from his glass of brandy and pondered momentarily on how much fun it would be to shoot this fool between the eyes at that moment.

"For 2000 reais, I can bring him here. He has the information you desire, but he also knows that he cannot do any more than sell it to the highest bidder and that would be you. The decision must be made quickly though. They might be moved soon." Arturo decided he had warned this man of the impending danger of any sort of continued action in regard to the fugitive couple. If the man were fool enough to initiate something, he would be the cause and the recipient.

"I will give you 200 reais to bring the man here and then you will be happy."

"200? No, Sir. 500."

"All right. 500."

"I require payment up front." Arturo took a deep drink to cover his nervousness.

"No. If you get money up front you will get drunk and fall down in an alley and I will need to find you and shoot you between the eyes. Bring the man to me and I will reward you."

Arturo knew when he had been bested and got up to go. He was not sure how long it would take to find his knowledgeable associate but since he was to be sober, he would not stop looking until his search was done. Deep inside he also knew how necessary it was for his continued health that he carry this mission out with alacrity. Roberto had known Arturo for a long time; long before he had been afflicted with alcoholism. Roberto was not the sort of man you took advantage of cleanly.

Gordon MacMaster took a different approach to the situation. He found the local watering hole for the constabulary, The Raging Lion, and began buying drinks for the crowd. He dropped names from the Brass Knob in Cascavel and established himself as Boris Chercovski. He did his best to stay as sober as he could, while appearing to drink vast quantities of beer and liquor. He told stories of apprehending evil doers in Austria where he had been a sergeant in the police force. In all, he used every bit of personality and charm he possessed to insinuate himself into the closed culture of the tavern.

The officers were a bit leery at first but as is common with all men, the flow of free alcohol loosened their tongues and their minds. The lines of cocaine started appearing on the bar at about midnight. Not everybody was willing to partake in the stolen goods but Gordon took a snort just so as not to alienate anyone. It turned out to be top quality product. The cops only stole the best.

The Raging Lion closed at four o'clock in the morning. At about 3:15, MacMaster asked about the couple he had seen taken away from the front of the hotel that morning. He did not get the precise response he was hoping for.

A tall thin lieutenant pulled his service revolver from his holster and stuck the barrel under Gordon's chin. "You are not to ask these questions and if you do, I will personally see you floating in saltwater. Do you understand, puto?"

"Yes, I understand. I meant nothing by it, I was only making conversation."

"Good. This is the last time I will hear you ask this?"

"Yes."

A scan of the crowd confirmed that most of them did not know what the problem was. A couple of them were starting to move in on the lieutenant to diffuse the situation and others were standing there with their mouths open, clearly shocked. On the streets this was standard operating procedure, but not in the confines of their chosen restaurant. A lot of noise ensued and a lot of voices tried to shout each other down. The Brazilian re-holstered his weapon and everybody breathed a little easier. They were all a little upset by the episode.

"Hey, Boris, do not mind Ramirez, he's a hot head. He doesn't know when to keep it in his pants. He wasn't going to shoot you." The speaker was a Sergeant.

"Right. But... I tell you I'm not used to that. The last time someone did that was when I was coming across the

Austrian border from Poland. I was very young, maybe eight years old and the border guard stuck a gun under my chin like that. He took money from my father to let us go. It makes me think very bad thoughts from the past."

"Forget it. It's late. What do you say I give you a ride back to your hotel?"

"Yes. I'm staying at the Continental."

The sergeant was as drunk as his new friend and barely able to control the vehicle. After a harrowing ride to the Continental, Gordon got out, thanked the man and headed inside. He saw the officer had not moved by the time he got to the elevators, so he took one of the elevators up and then another one down. By the time he got back down, the sergeant was gone. Gordon MacMaster walked out the back door of the hotel and across the street to the Hotel Flamenco where he had actually rented a room.

Regardless of the Scotsman's capacity for drink, he was unable to stay awake once he got to the hotel room. About five hours later he roused himself and got into the shower.

Roberto was having a bit more luck with locating the couple he was after. Arturo had produced the wannabe gangster that had followed the police into the suburbs. For a fee he had divulged his knowledge of the address and a few of the details of the neighborhood. He could not provide an exact location within the house, of course, or the number of guards to be found.

It had been late enough in the day when the information had finally reached him, and he was slightly intoxicated by that time, so he had not even considered taking the task in hand that night. He had driven past the location to ascertain what sort of assault he might need, what sort of weapons and tactics would be appropriate.

Of course, Roberto considered the possibility that Arturo's friend had given him bad information for good money. That was one of the risks one took when buying information on the street. The only thing keeping this from happening was reputation. Roberto did not have much reputation in this town but Arturo knew him and would not try to bilk him. The same could not be said of this other man.

The next morning, dawn lent a different light to the area. There was an obvious undercover car parked in the driveway and the garage door was down. There were no windows in the garage door but there was one in the side. It could not be accessed from the street and the hunter did not chance sneaking around the side to look in. If he was going to do it, he would need to do it tonight. The window of opportunity was about to close. He could feel it. Whoever was putting up the money must know about the capture by now. Tonight might be too late, but there was too much traffic this morning. There was no available spot for surveillance on this building. Roberto took a couple of cell phone pictures and left.

Lieutenant Silvio Ramirez had made a mistake when he overreacted the night before. Had he sat and said nothing, there would have been no indication of culpability but shoving the snout of a pistol under Gordon MacMaster's jaw was enough to indict him immediately. His actions indicated more than just knowledge of the incident, it was implicit guilt.

It was a simple matter to call the station and ask for Lieutenant Ramirez, but Gordon knew the man could not have reported for work that early, given his level of intoxication the night before. He was correct. The man was scheduled to appear for the afternoon shift, starting about two in the afternoon. He told the desk sergeant he did not want to leave a message and hung up.

Cops everywhere tend to keep their residences private. Unless the town is very small it is unusual to know where all the cops live. Porto Alegre was not a small town.

The Hotel Flamenco had large windows on the front of the building. They were mirrored to reflect the light and much of the heat from the sun, but were merely tinted from the inside. Gordon stood at the end of the hallway and observed the street very carefully. He did not see any surveillance vehicles. There were no men sitting in parked cars or full sized vans at curbside. The sun was not punishing yet so, dressed in sandals, a flowered tourist shirt and shorts with extra pockets on the legs, the Scot headed toward the lot where he had left his car the night before. He had struggled with the fact that he was unarmed. He had left his pistol in the trunk of his car when he had gone into the bar. It does not surprise the police that they are armed, but it tends to surprise them when other people are.

Halfway to the parking lot, in a dirtier section of the city, MacMaster saw five young men lounging outside a corner market. They looked like men, though they had very little facial hair, and they carried themselves like men. Their brazen stares and outthrust chests marked them as still unsure of themselves but unwilling to let strangers, especially tourists, know that. Three of them had tattoos on their arms and hands.

"Hola, companieros," did nothing for their attitudes.

One of the boys spit on the sidewalk, another adjusted the toothpick he had between his lips to the other side of his mouth. The one who stepped forward was obviously the leader of this little group of toughs. "What makes you think we are your companieros?"

"Well, if I was your age and hanging around on the street, anyone who offered me 100 reais would be my friend and companion." Gordon MacMaster had a huge smile on his face that did not extend to his green eyes.

"What is it you want us to do for your 100 reais, eh. Maybe you're some kind of a pervert, eh?" The leader was direct and the gang laughed. "Maybe you like a little boy, yes?"

"I need some information. I need to know where a certain man lives and I will pay for this information. I will also expect some discretion along with it."

"I still think you are some kind of faggot, but I will take your money."

"Good. What I need is the address of Lieutenant Silvio Ramirez. He is a policeman from this area of the city. Somewhere around here."

While they spoke, the other members of the little group were moving into position around them. Gordon could not believe they were intending to rob him right out in the open like this but steeled himself nonetheless. He saw the shop owner come to the doorway, look out and shake his head, then close the door. It was obvious he had seen this scenario before.

The attack came from the left side and the youth was fast, but he did not find the unsuspecting tourist he thought he had. The swing flashed past the stranger's chin as he pulled his head back. The boy's wrist was grabbed and that was all he was good for that day. Gordon wrenched the hand and broke the wrist while deftly sliding the brass knuckles off the opened fingers. He twisted the body to keep it between him and the two in front of him, while he lashed out to his right with a foot. The sandals he was wearing were not designed for fighting but they were leather, not foam rubber. The young man shrieked as he collapsed with two cracked ribs.

MacMaster heard the knife snick open behind him and sidestepped the lunge. The young man recovered quickly and slashed at him but to no avail. The tall, red-headed stranger was much faster than he looked, and as the arc of the knife flashed past him, he stepped in with a straight punch. The knife fighter fell to the sidewalk, with one tooth missing and two more loose, totally unconscious. When he came to, he would adopt a different weapon of preference.

The leader of the group and the other remaining undamaged youth headed for other parts immediately, leaving their companions behind. They wanted nothing more to do with this tourist.

The thought of forcing one of the young men to talk crossed his mind, but then Gordon thought they probably didn't know what he wanted to find out anyway. He left them where they were and walked on. No police arrived all the while he was there, but he was glad he did not have a gun in his belt all the same.

There was a better way to find out the information, but the assassin did not know what it was. He could get chummy with Silvio Ramirez in the bar but that might not work. He could follow him home but cops were naturally paranoid, especially dirty cops. He was getting more worried about the time as well. The person who put up the reward would not want to waste any time either. That gave a moment's pause as he wondered why it was not the government paying the reward. Perhaps it was, in which case the couple was already in custody and had already been transported. It might be that someone else is offering the bigger reward.

The voice from behind him was that breaking tone of a boy coming of age. "I can help you. Keep moving and do not look at me. If they see us talking they will kill me."

Nothing more was said until a couple of blocks later. Gordon's shadow directed him into a little shop full of clothing and then into the back room where there was a table and chairs with a refrigerator and stove.

"Foolish boy," came from behind him as he entered the room. "If they saw him come in here they might burn the store down. Why don't you use what little wit God gave you and stay out of the affairs of others?" A wizened little man in loose fitting clothing was wringing his hands before him.

"Tio Paco, this man has money and he can take care of himself. Nobody saw him come in here that matters. He took out three of the Thirteens like this." The boy was flailing around awkwardly but the shopkeeper got the point.

"So he has made enemies and now you want them to be your enemies. This man will leave and the enemies he has made will still be here. Why have you done this thing? Why have you brought him here?"

"Look," Gordon said from the back room, "I have no wish to complicate your lives. I was only looking for an address. I will go now although I would like to try on one of those hats."

"Hai, Señor." It was as though he had not thought his guest could hear him or understand him, though that was obviously a game. "I do not wish to put you in danger. The boys today do not know what they are doing. It's not like when I was a child. They have no respect for the old ways. They have no respect for their parents. Please accept my apologies but this is very dangerous. The Thirteens are taking over with their drugs and their guns. They come from California and Mexico City and corrupt our youth with their broken dreams. You are very lucky to be alive and if you do not leave immediately, you will not live the night through."

The white hat did nothing to disguise the Scotsman but the shirt did change his look a bit. He kept the shorts with the extra pockets; one of those pockets held the brass knuckles he had liberated from his assailant. He was surprised that they fit on his hand but then they had slipped right off the young man's fingers, obviously too big for him. He thanked Tio Paco for the moments respite from the heat, and indicated what he had been looking for when he approached the gang members. Paco said he could not help and he wanted nothing to do with trouble. It was obvious to him that the tall red-headed stranger was trouble.

Nino on the other hand knew an opportunity when he saw it. He whispered to meet him at the Rio Rojo.

The white-hatted tourist had no idea where the Rio Rojo was, but assumed that it was in the direction he was already moving so he simply kept walking toward his vehicle. On the way, he stopped at a pay phone and made a short international call before continuing on. At the top of a slight hill, a faded sign over a closed door indicated the Rio Rojo. It was a bar, just opening for the day. Inside there was air conditioning, actually colder than was comfortable at that time of day but it would be very welcome later on.

Gordon ordered a ginger ale and sat with his back to the wall at the end of the bar. Nino came in the back door. "Tio Jose," he said, "I must take this man into the back. He is in danger and it could be bad for the bar."

The bartender nodded and looked toward the outside door. There was a small diamond shaped window in the door set too high to be seen through from the outside. The windows were set with six glass bricks apiece so they let in little light and more importantly, little heat. The place was designed to stay cool.

Inside the back room, the walls were stacked with cases of beer and liquor. There was a walk-in cooler with what must have been a month's supply of cold beer and a freezer with meat and vegetables. There was more supply than there could have possibly been demand from the bar. There was also a door to an office.

The boy knocked on the window and said, "Tio Carlos, I need to talk to you."

"Menino Perdido. Are you in trouble again?"

"No, Tio Carlos. I bring a man who needs some help and is willing to pay for it."

"You are in trouble again. Come in and bring the man with you."

The man and his small escort squeezed into the office that stank of cigars and while the boy showed no concern, the Scotsman did not like looking down the barrel of a double-barreled, sawed-off shotgun. In the confines of the small office there was nowhere to go. If 'Tio Carlos' pulled the trigger there was no hope.

"Pull up your shirt," the man said. "I want to see if you have guns."

For the second time that day, Gordon was actually glad he was not carrying a pistol. "I have no gun today. I do, however, have this." He pulled the brass knuckles out of his cargo pocket and laid them on the desk. "I was forced to take them from one of your local tour guides."

Tio Carlos smiled and pointed his weapon to the ceiling. "What is it you are in need of then, my friend?"

"Tio, this man was looking for an address…"

"Shut your mouth, little lost boy. I will deal with the fact that you bring a stranger to my office later. I have told you some of the rules we operate under and you know better than to do this."

"But, Tio Carlos, he fought five Thirteens and won. He is a hero."

"I have said for you to shut your mouth and now you are ignoring that. Go. Out into the bar. Get an orange soda and sit there in silence. Now."

Menino Perdido slunk back out the door dejectedly.

"Who are you and why are you here?" asked the man, in English, still holding the shotgun but not pointing it at his guest.

"I was merely looking for the address of a friend and I was assaulted by some young men who thought I could be taken advantage of. Your young friend, who seems to have a lot of uncles in this city, brought me here thinking you could help me."

"And who are you?"

"I am Boris Chercovski. I am a retired Sergeant from Austria seeking a contact in this city."

"And who is the friend you seek?"

"A Lieutenant Ramirez."

The business end of the shotgun went from vertical to horizontal again. Tio Carlos had not liked the answer.

"Whoa there, cowboy, I think we may have gotten off to a difficult start here."

"Why do you need to find this Ramirez? Speak quickly or you will die now."

In his mind's eye, Gordon MacMaster saw a pair of dice rolling across a green felt table. He knew this was one of those moments in his life that he needed the correct path if he wanted to keep traveling, since the other path led only to the cemetery.

Tio Carlos was a difficult man to read and that exacerbated the tension in the small office. He was not a large man but had excess skin that indicated that he had either been fatter or stronger when he was younger. He wore a silk shirt with short sleeves and dark glasses that gave no indication of his mood.

"He has something I want and I intend to get it from him." The dice were rolling.

"And this thing what is it?"

"It is not so much a what, as a who. He has kidnapped a pair of fugitives."

"That is ridiculous. He is a policeman. Why did he not arrest them?"

"There is money to be made."

The shotgun went back to the ceiling and fate's dice rolled to a stop.

"Please. Take a seat and start from where this makes me any money. A man such as yourself, a stranger in this town, needs friends if you are to succeed. Lieutenant Ramirez is not really a friend of yours, is he?"

"No. In fact he is a stupid pig who almost shot me last night in the Raging Lion."

Mention of the Raging Lion was enough to open Carlos' eyes a little. He began to take the stranger a bit more seriously.

"I would very much like a cigar, if you have one. I am out and, well, I am feeling a little nervous."

Carlos produced a pair of cigars from one of his desk drawers and a moment of silence ensued where they both ignited them and savored the thick heady smoke. Then Gordon began his tale. "The couple I seek are killers from Argentina. They are the ones who killed your General Ernesto Modiano. This has placed a huge bounty on their heads, one I am perfectly willing to share with any man who assists me in their capture. It is a requirement that they are brought in alive, however, and though I am not sure why this is, I do not question it. Dead they are worth little, but alive they are worth a lot. They were taken away by the police yesterday morning, but they were not taken to the police station and they were not arrested. At least the newspapers and television know nothing of it. I am merely attempting to make some money and, as I said, I am willing to share the score."

"So, Boris, Boris Chercovski, you speak very good English for an Austrian. Much better than your Portuguese"

"Yes, thank you. You speak a very good English as well."

"Give me a good reason I should believe you, or help you."

"Aside from the money, I have no reason. As I said, I was on my way elsewhere when I was assaulted and then your little lost nephew approached me."

"As you say, he has many uncles. This is because he has no father or mother. We have adopted him and he has been good to his family, but I think he may have made a mistake this time."

"I do not think we are dissimilar men. We are both trying to make a living and doing so by whatever we are good at. I am good at finding people and you are good at, uh, distribution." Gordon made a sweeping gesture with his cigar.

Carlos narrowed his eyes, though they were still hidden by the dark glasses and said nothing. This large stranger was extremely perceptive and could be a liability if he were allowed to live. On the other hand, there was an opportunity here if one were cautious.

"If we have similar goals, there is no reason we could not work together," Gordon continued, though he began feeling as if he were losing the argument.

"Do you know anything about the man you are looking for?" Carlos asked suddenly.

"Lieutenant Ramirez?"

"Yes."

"No. I know that he became very upset when I mentioned the kidnapping and he almost shot me in the face and told me to stop asking questions."

"Ah, that would not be unusual for him. Ramirez has family in the upper levels of the government. He is a

Lieutenant because he cannot control himself. If he were a more reasonable man he would be the Minister of the Interior or some such, but he is not."

Gordon relaxed a little. He saw the dice on the table and knew he had a winning roll. There was still great danger but there was also great opportunity.

Chapter Nine
Ohio

"Yes, the job is concluded."

"Brilliant. Actually, I have the news on my desk. It worked out even better than could have been expected. The UAW was thrown into total disarray. I don't know how you managed to leave him alive with brain damage, but it was a stroke of genius."

"It needed to look accidental."

"Oh, but it was so much more rewarding than could have been expected. The next time they want someone decommissioned, you are the man they will be looking for."

"I'll probably be unavailable, but do not tell them that."

"Check.

"Do you have anything else for me?"

"Nothing local. There's always something in Central America, Columbia, Mexico…"

"No, I don't think so. I do need to get out of here, though. I think I'll try the American Southwest. Texas. Probably remind me of home."

"Look, joker, don't get too cocky. There are a lot of border guards and Immigration Services checkpoints down there. If they haul you in, they might make a connection."

"I'll need American papers then. Look, I've got to get out of Michigan. I'll call you from somewhere else and you can tell me where to go to get papers."

"All right. I'll work on that."

"Good day then." Terry hung up the phone and took another look at the headline on the front page of the local newspaper. *Pikelfinger Suffers Suspected Stroke*. The article outlined how he had gone flat-line in the hospital room and been revived by the alert staff. It reiterated the previous day's story of his being shot by his wife.

According to Terry's paper, it was impossible to immediately determine the extent of the brain damage the Union President had suffered and so the upper echelon of the union was in abject confusion as to how they should proceed. The Vice-President was of the opinion that he should take over immediately and prevailing wisdom said that eventually he would, but a lot of people feared that he was too cozy with the heads of the company that they were in strike negotiations with. It led to a tense situation for the union and anything that threw the union off was good for the company. To the newspaper's credit, the back story was left to the public's imagination. They reported the facts as they knew them.

The longer the strike lasted, the weaker the union's position would get. This was in contrast to previous years when the company would suffer vast losses from plant shut downs. This year sales were down and a strike was the perfect solution for the company who would have been required to pay for any other form of workforce stoppage. While they were on strike the UAW was paying the workers and the automaker was getting a free ride. When the strike ended, the union would be more desperate than the automakers and the wage concessions the company wanted would be granted. Richard Pikelfinger would have never granted the wage concessions, but his successor was in favor of them all along. His view was that saving the industry was more important than the short-term integrity of the union's income.

None of this had any impact on Terry Kingston. As he stood in the entranceway of the Toledo, Ohio train station, he reflected on deed done. It had been close to perfect. He had left almost no witnesses. The shooting had been done second hand and nobody got fingerprints or DNA. Nobody knew his name. So why did it feel so wrong?

The drug dealers in Cleveland had caused him no internal conflict. They were predatory animals preying like cannibals on the body of society. They should be dead. He thought briefly of a joke about Tennessee that claimed "He needed killin'" was a reasonable defense in court.

"Ashes to ashes, dust to dust
Even steel suffers from rust
Slow or fast, heart or head
The best of us will wind up dead"

The short poem of his own devising summed up his overall view on life and the corporeal nature of his profession. He spat on the floor causing an oriental family to look at him in surprise, then he stuffed another couple of quarters into the phone.

"Hello, Dumpling."

"Russ! Where are you?"

"I'm sorry about this, Dumpling, but I'm afraid I'm in a place called Grand Rapids and I won't be coming home."

"What do you mean? You have all sorts of stuff here. Clothes, razors, your toothbrush…"

"Look, Dumpling, I found another woman and she's better than you. She has money, she's better looking and she's a better roll. So, I won't be coming home. Put all that stuff in a box and leave it on the stoop, I'll pick it up when I come through town tomorrow. No hard feelings, eh, love?"

Vanessa began screaming into the phone and Terry hung up. He chewed his lower lip thoughtfully, looking at the pay phone on the wall in the train station. That was what he had intended, a sharp and somewhat rude cutoff. His imagination brought images, not far from actuality, of Vanessa slashing at his remaining clothing with a butcher knife and throwing it onto the lawn. He had not envisioned her setting the whole lot on fire in the yard, but he could not have planned her actions better if he had done so himself.

172

Toledo, Ohio was a depressing sort of place and the train station was in a neighborhood of warehouses and factories. Terry would not have expected to find women hawking their wares on the street in a place so devoid of personality, but they were there. They looked miserable in the cold wind that blew between the block buildings. There were no trees to mute winter's sting; there was no bus stop respite.

The minivan would not last long in the parking lot, unlocked, with the keys in it. A quick wipe-down was all that was needed. The vehicle, while not prime fodder for a chop shop, would be taken by some worn out old hooker or some angry child and driven to death or wrecked from the sheer malice and thoughtlessness of youth.

Standing out in a crowd is not a desirable trait for a man on the run. Having a memorable countenance or excessive height is detrimental. Terry took stock of himself and saw that he would indeed stick out in the group waiting for the train. Most of them were black. There was the one oriental family, who kept very close to each other as if to drift a few feet away would be to tempt the tides of fate to catch them in a whirlpool and suck one of them away.

There were no stores in the area that would be open to sell him some new clothing, if they even sold clothing. The train was set to arrive in half an hour and he would be heading elsewhere on a self-contained thousand ton bullet. A change of clothing would come elsewhere.

He stepped outside the door and lit a cigarette. "He needed killin'," kept repeating in his head.

Brock Dakota was not having much luck to this point. The Sheriffs and State police had bungled their jobs, in his opinion. He was short and pointed with those in charge and did not accept excuses. Nor did he make any friends.

Things began to come together simultaneously, though if Dakota had not been there to connect them, they would never have been associated. The Michigan State Police and the Genesee County Sheriffs could not really care less about some drug dealers that got shot on the other side of Ohio. They did not believe there was an international terrorist with a European accent executing America's law abiding drug dealers. They saw Brock Dakota as an arrogant elitist with some agenda of his own that had nothing to do with the area or the needs of an area in recession and dying from the loss of jobs. It was bad enough that the people of Flint were determined to kill each other. The mayor kept slashing the police department's budget, so there were no local officers to count on for assistance. The skyrocketing price of gas was restricting their ability to patrol and their overtime had been cut by budget constraints. The State Police did not need to import threats from Ohio, and the County Sheriffs saw it as doing somebody else's job as well as their own.

Within a couple of days, the disparate elements he searched for were paraded before Brock's hawk-sharp eyes.

First to attract the hunter's attention was the Toyota. It was brought into impound without a license plate and no identification tag. This vehicle, however, had an alternate location for its identification number, as well as the plate. That number could only be removed with a grinder since it was stamped into the steel of the body. Dakota's mouth watered when he heard that they had located the car. His nostrils flared as if he was sniffing out his quarry.

The next bit of information was brought to him by an alert member of the sheriff's department though there was a day's delay. The staff at the hospital had reported seeing a man who had spoken with an Australian accent leaving the room of Richard Pikelfinger when the monitors went dead. They had not gotten a good look at him, but the initial report of a stroke had been inaccurate and now it looked as though someone had tried to kill him. One of the sheriffs mentioned it, sort of in passing. After all, Richard Pikelfinger was no drug dealer.

Last, but not least, a woman had been arrested who claimed to have knowledge of a Russell O'Mara. He had bought her the gun she had been pointing at the unruly customer at her job in the party store on Grand Traverse.

The young lady was in custody for carrying the weapon without a carrier's permit. There was no trouble getting an interview with her downtown.

"Your name is Vanessa Migliori?"

"Yes."

"My name is Brock Dakota, I am with Homeland Security. This is Captain Devon Whitefield with Immigration and Naturalization. Your attorney, Mr. Packer will be here shortly."

"Why are you talking to me without my lawyer?"

"You, missy, are in a lot more trouble than you seem to think. We can level charges of aiding and supporting a terrorist and make them stick. If you decide to be unpatriotic, you will be shipped to Guantanamo Bay until you decide to be more cooperative."

"Oh, bullshit. I'm no more a terrorist than anyone else in this town and Guantanamo Bay got shut down last year so save the speech."

"Your employer is Rashid Farahani, yes?"

"What?"

"Rashid Farahani, expatriate Iranian?"

"Uh, yes."

"Your boyfriend is Russell O'mara, yes?"

"No. I mean, yes, he was. He called me a couple of days ago and told me he was in Grand Rapids with another woman who was better than me and to leave his clothes on the porch so he could pick them up. That no good bastard used me for a place to stay and a quick piece and then dumped me like yesterday's newspaper."

Brock's eyebrows went up and he almost smiled.

"He lives with you?"

"For about three weeks."

"Is he there now?"

"No. I told you. He called and said he was with another woman in Grand Rapids and didn't want to see me any more. He said she was better." For a moment, Vanessa's eyes quivered and she looked as though she was going to cry.

"Is that where you got the 9mm pistol you were brandishing at the Good Times Party Store on Grand Traverse?"

"Check with the Sheriff. I bought that gun legally. It's mine. That is, he bought it for me. He paid for it. He bought me that Buick in the driveway too. He didn't mind spending money."

"But you do not have a permit to carry it concealed in public, do you?"

"No, not yet, but I'm going through the process. I went to the safety course a couple of days ago and I sent the application in. They told me if I'm not a felon or wanted on some charge, that Michigan could not turn me down for a license. So that's why I wear it at work. Plus, look at the condition this town's in. Would you work there without a gun?"

"But you do not yet have the permit?"

"No. Neither did Russ but he carries two guns."

"Do you mean Russell O'mara?"

"Of course."

"What sort of guns does he carry?"

"Two .38 revolvers. He has a holster for them under his coat, uh vest, I guess it's a vest. The first time I saw them they scared the shit out of me. I didn't believe in guns before, but I do now."

"Why?"

"You're shittin' me, right?"

Brock changed direction to get back on track. He knew he had a nervous and inexperienced detainee before him, but she was not stupid, just naïve. "So what did Russell O'mara tell you he needed the guns for?"

"He didn't say."

"What did he say he was doing in the country?"

"Coordinating governmental approaches to biofuels or some such bullshit."

"Was it bullshit?"

"How the fuck am I supposed to know. I'm busy. I never checked up on what he was doing, I have too much to do of my own. He called me and said it was over and to leave his clothes on the porch."

"Did he come by to pick up his clothes?"

"I burned them."

"Burned them?"

"Yes. I doused them with lighter fluid and burned them. The no good son-of-a-bitch can have what's left of them now. I used his lighter fluid, too." No longer looking as though she were about to cry, a small half smile crooked her lips.

"But did he come by to get them?"

"I don't know. I have a very busy schedule. I work and go to school. If he stopped by, he didn't pick up his stuff."

"We will need access to your apartment. I'll have the clerk bring a release form in."

"What if I refuse?"

"Sign the form and we'll use the key to get in. Refuse and we'll use a sledge hammer and you'll end up paying for the damage. I don't particularly care how we get in, but we are going in."

"Don't you need a search warrant?"

"We'll have one within the hour."

"What the heck is going on anyway? What did he do?"

"This will all be made clear to you, later. Now tell us, where did you meet Russell O'mara?"

Folding her arms to indicate that the interview was essentially over, Vanessa told them that all that would be made clear to them when she thought they needed to know and that she wanted her lawyer. She was feeling very much the innocent victim and had no problem giving then the information they wanted, but she would be damned if they would treat her like a schoolgirl, even though she was. As far as she was concerned, they were abusing their privileges. She signed the permission form, but without some form of reciprocity, she would not say another word.

When the lawyer that Mr. Migliori, Vanessa's father, had retained showed up on the scene, he was furious. They had grilled his client without legal counsel. She had not shot anyone with the pistol that was legally hers. She had not been wearing the pistol but had concealed it under the counter. He demanded that she be released immediately and began to threaten lawsuits and investigations.

Brock was satisfied that he knew what Vanessa Migliori knew. He left Captain Whitefield from Immigration to answer the expected questions and headed for the young woman's apartment, with the key. He knew he should be waiting for the CSI people to dust for prints and look for DNA, but he also knew that most people were sloppy and left clues as they exited.

The apartment was a mess. There was food on the living room table and a half bottle of rum. An open bottle of cola lay on its side; some of the fluid had leaked onto the table top and ran down the leg to the floor. The bed was not made and there was a towel on the floor in the bathroom. It looked as though Vanessa had gotten drunk the night before and hurried out the door in the morning. There was no immediate evidence of men's clothing, there were no boots in the hall or ties in the closet, which was open.

Dakota was careful not to touch any surfaces that might have fingerprints on them. He could not have forgiven himself if he destroyed evidence. He carefully pulled back the curtains over the kitchen window and saw the flying saucer style grill in the front yard. It was definitely not picnic season.

Feeling there was nothing he could learn from the apartment, he stepped to the door and heard the bottle of rum calling him from the table. He saw his hand shaking as he reached for the door handle and shook it a couple of times to gain control. He knew he would not drink until this case was over and done with, but he wanted a shot right then and there. He could almost taste it. He shook his head and exited the apartment, locking the door behind him. One shot had never been enough in the past and he knew that to start drinking now would incapacitate him for the rest of the day.

Downstairs he saw the burned remains of a pair of jeans, a couple of shirts and some underwear. A can of lighter fluid for old-fashioned cigarette lighters lay on top of the charcoaled cotton cloth. The paint was burned off the can and the plastic cap had melted. It confirmed that Vanessa Migliori was not lying and it told him that Russell O'mara used a liquid fuel cigarette lighter. Then Brock began to question where the rest of the wardrobe was. He saw no socks, no ties, and only one pair of jeans. So they could not have been living together. There was not enough there. "Where are the razors?" he asked himself softly. "The toothbrush is missing. A comb, a belt, flints for the lighter,

179

cell phone charger, books, laptop… There's nothing here, and it wasn't at the hotel either. So all I've got so far is burned cloth and a red shot spot in the driveway."

The hotel had reported that Russell O'mara had checked out. A check of the credit card number gave them an address in Australia. A check with the authorities in New South Wales led to the conclusion that there was no such address and, indeed, that there was no such man. Russell did not exist in Australia and for all the evidence he left behind he barely existed here either. But there had to be a paper trail. Credit cards were handed out like religious flyers around the turn of the century. All you needed was an address. But if they did not get paid, they did not last long. This card was getting paid so someone knows O'mara and takes care of this little bit of financing for him.

The officers who had been on surveillance when their subject walked in, cleaned up and walked right back out again, were embarrassed by the incident. Their subject had thumbed his nose at them and they had let him. Brock understood how that could have happened. He had come in disguised and driving an unknown vehicle. It was at this point when Dakota realized there was more. If the man was merely being careful he would not have gone to those lengths. He knew the police were watching the hotel. He had cleaned that room like it was a lab, even burning out the drains. There would be no fingerprints in the Toyota and unless he missed his guess, none in Vanessa's apartment.

'Cops should never take it personally' was a mantra from the days before the World Trade Center Bombings. The Office of Homeland Security did not even use this phrase, never had. As far as the OHS trainers were concerned, it was personal and very deeply so. Brock Dakota took his job personally and he was going to make it his personal mission to show this arrogant Australian that America would not put up with this sort of behavior.

The nurses and intern at the hospital had very little time to devote to Mr. Dakota's investigation. He met them separately, in the cafeteria. One of the three nurses had gotten a good enough look at the man with the accent in the hallway. The intern had seen him face to face. Tall and blond is a pretty standard description for Australian men, but so few of them made their way to Flint that the man's accent sent off alarm bells. The staff who had heard the man's voice concurred, the accent was Australian, not English, not Canadian. The intern was more positive in his answers. The nurses could not be relied on as witnesses, they could easily have been swayed in court since they had not gotten a good look at the subject. The intern refused to work with a sketch artist.

The man from Homeland Security stood over the prone body of the President of the United Auto Workers and chewed on his lower lip. He reviewed everything he knew internally, seeking that one tidbit that would drop his target in his lap. The diagnosis released to the press was comatose due to respiratory failure and there was no direct evidence linking the Australian to the President. But he had been here!

The Toyota was abandoned. It would have sat where it was for a lot longer if the license plate had been left on it. There were no prints in the car. The hotel room had been dusted for prints but was clean to the point of sterility. Vanessa Migliori's apartment might give them something. Brock doubted they would find anything and wished they could use all the tricks the TV shows used. DNA evidence would be something to have, though as a foreign national, he would not be on an offenders' database.

Back in the local station, they had an answer on the credit card. It was paid online. A trace of the e-mail address led the investigators to an accountant in Georgetown, Grand Cayman. The source of the funds and anything about the owner of the card was refused. The best they could do was watch the account number and see if it popped up again. The OHS alerted the card administrator who red flagged the account.

Kevin Cook was busy with other matters by the time the call came in from Visa. Initially, Cook had no idea why the call had been routed to him. He was not looking for identity thieves or stolen credit cards, he was homicide, dammit. He actually hung up the phone and returned to his roast beef sandwich.

When the phone rang again, it was his friend and drinking associate Brock Dakota who had a few choice words for Cook's failure to act. Kevin was confused and could not make the connection between the two phone calls until Dakota explained that he had asked Visa to call. The credit card was used in Cleveland. Russell O'mara was back in Ohio and he, Dakota, was still four hours away.

Hanging up the phone for a second, Cook looked wistfully at the remains of his quickly cooling roast beef sandwich and picked the receiver back up. Visa reported the card had been used in the Van Beuren Plaza, at the Parkway Liquor store. Kevin had been in The Parkway himself, he knew it was a large and bustling business that would soon forget who had used what card when. He scratched his neck and took one more bite of lunch then pulled on his jacket. Detective Grady joined him on the trip.

The proprietor of the liquor store did not recognize the name O'mara but he was helpful. He pulled the tape out of the VCR and handed it over without question. There was a time stamp on the tape so it would be a simple matter to match the image to the card user.

Back at the station, Cook found the quality of the tape to be questionable. It had been re-recorded many times and was at the end of its usable magnetic life. The image was grainy and shaky but it was the only image they had. They matched the time Visa had given them for O'mara being there but the quality of the picture was so poor that they did not have an image they could use.

The hits began to come in with regularity: liquor stores, restaurants, a shoe store, and finally a hotel. The process had taken days and there was still nothing to work with but the hotel was a sure thing. Grady, Carmody, Quincy and Cook were on the scene with half a dozen uniformed officers. They had the outside doors to the hotel blocked off so nobody was going to leave short of jumping out a window. The manager's key card opened the door to room 436 and there was their perpetrator, in bed with a young blonde woman.

The man Cleveland's finest apprehended that day was 5'9", with dark brown hair and eyes. He had a spindly mustache under the kind of cob nose one gets from drinking too much for too long. He did not speak with an Australian accent and had, in fact, lived in Cleveland his entire life. Under interrogation he admitted that he had found the credit card on a Trailways Bus in Toledo, Ohio. He had gone to Detroit to gamble in the Casinos and had hit the jackpot on the way home. At least he thought he had. Then half the police force came charging through the door with guns drawn.

Chapter Ten
Porto Alegre

The neighborhood was impossible to survey from a regular automobile during daylight hours. Children chased each other around the trees and women watched from the windows. There were no lawns inside the city, the houses faced right on the sidewalk.

Lieutenant Silvio Ramirez lived in one of the newer houses in the area, one that had a garage and a driveway, though it still had no lawn. The garage was situated 30 feet back from the street, leaving enough driveway for one car. It was an extravagance that most builders would not have included in this city.

When Silvio went to work in the early afternoon, his car was replaced in the driveway by another, obvious undercover police car. The garage door never opened, nor did it have a window in it. The garage itself had a window in the side but it was not a functional porthole since it looked out on the wall of the neighbor's house. There was a lot of vegetation growing between the two buildings, almost deliberately, making passage between the buildings difficult. The far side of the house butted directly against its neighbor. There was no access that way and there was no access to the back of the building without going through or over another dwelling and then over a wall.

Roberto mused that the rear of the building would be the least expected direction of attack but the one that would leave him most exposed. He wanted to get in and out with as little fuss as possible but he saw his time frame shrinking as well. If he were unable to access the interior of the house by tonight, he might never again have the opportunity.

Ramirez would likely return before midnight, have a beer or two and go to bed. That would likely be the last chance to do the deed cleanly. Roberto Campena de Iguaca went to a local hotel to get some sleep.

Carlos had made a telephone call and within minutes, the information that his visitor had required was in hand. Menino Perdido knew where the street was and was more than willing to show the man they knew as Boris Chercovski where it was.

Gordon was generous with the boy and his pseudo uncle and promised to deliver more if the information was accurate and the prize obtainable. He further explained that he was on his way to pick up his car when he was assaulted by the street toughs. He had a couple of kilometers left to travel and refused the offer of a ride. He liked to walk and was undeterred by Carlos' reports of the dangers of the city streets. Armed with the address of Lieutenant Silvio Ramirez, he bid adieu to his new associates and walked on down the road.

The Chrysler was unmolested in the parking lot of the Raging Lion. Only the youngest and stupidest of criminals would have targeted cars in that parking lot. As the engine warmed up, MacMaster did some deep breathing exercises and did his best to clear his mind. He could not be sure he had the right address but he knew once he was into this mess there was no turning back. Abducting the couple from a hotel room was one thing, abducting them from a group of armed officers was a completely different proposition.

The house was of whitewashed stucco with the ubiquitous red roof tiles. A relatively steep roof angle prevented people from venturing onto this unstable surface. The houses in the neighborhood had similar constructions, though some had flat roof sections as well. Many had interior courtyards in the tradition of Spanish and Portuguese houses, often with flowering trees to provide shade for guests and a respite from the choking heat that could come in summer. Silvio's house had no outside access to the garage for persons, only an overhead door for cars. The one car that fit in the driveway had a spotlight on the driver's side making it conspicuous. Parking in the street was forbidden.

The front windows were small and guarded by wrought iron bars. The overhead door to the garage would make noise being opened even if it were not locked. The back door was unavailable to the general public since it was walled off from the other buildings around it and had no back alley.

"The only way I'm going to get in that house properly is to be invited in," mused the Scotsman sitting briefly across the street with his car's engine running. "That would be far better than sneaking in or breaking in. I stand less chance of getting shot."

The parking lot of a restaurant two blocks away was a good fit for the Chrysler. The food was good and the one beer he drank was cold and refreshing. Something about the establishment reminded the Scot of the Balkans but he could not put his finger on the similarity. The take-out food came in a white paper sack with the name of the restaurant printed on it.

The white hat and the bicycle complimented the reflective vest. Lieutenant Ramirez could not see the face of the delivery man who pounded on his door though the logo of the restaurant was familiar. He had forgotten to get food for his captives and did not particularly care if they went hungry for a couple of days. In a life of soiled righteousness, they represented his exit strategy but he had not planned to keep them for long. As Ramirez opened the door, he prepared to unleash some verbal venom on the incompetent delivery man.

The first bullet took the delivery man in the small of the back and passed through the soft flesh and organs without resistance. The second one hit a rib and deflected upward into the chest. The gory hole that opened in his chest sprayed blood in Silvio Ramirez's left eye.

Ramirez stood with his mouth open a fraction of a second too long. The third bullet took him in the chest, and as he stood staring stupidly at the hole that punched its way into his body, a final shot entered his right eye and blew out the back of his head. Silvio's dreams of retirement had just come to fruition.

Seconds passed between the door opening and Roberto Campena de Iguaca grabbing the fresh corpses and pulling them into the house. It was quite late and though the city was still very much alive, this section of street was deserted, or almost so.

The silencer on his pistol had prevented anyone being awakened by the gunfire. No one else was guarding the house and its captives. Roberto was feeling very strong. The couple was found in the garage, bound to metal chairs that were in turn fastened to rings set into metal stanchions. The construction was not new. These were not the first people to have graced these chairs. A stainless steel kidney tray of scalpels, clamps, spikes and other devices sat shining on a table beside the chairs.

The captives did not appear to have been damaged. Their mouths were gagged and in addition to the handcuffs, they were tied to the chairs by lengths of rope. Roberto stood looking at them as they blinked in the artificial light that flooded the garage. He found himself attracted to the woman and decided that he would definitely rape her before the escapade was over. He savored the thought of doing it in front of her companion. A small smile cracked his face as he pushed his gun into his waistband, pulled his leather gloves tighter on his hands and went to the kitchen. It would be a few hours before anyone came to relieve Ramirez. There was a can of beer in the refrigerator but nothing looked palatable, then he thought of the delivery man and went into the hallway to pry the sack out of his hand. A minute in the microwave oven and there was dinner. Prior to the operation, Roberto could not have eaten but now he was hungry.

The purr of the engine was the only noise Gordon MacMaster heard as he turned the corner. He was driving slowly, not wanting to be noticed. This was the second time he circumnavigated this block. The first time he had seen the car parked at the curb in front of the Ramirez residence and had thought there was a changing of the guard going on. He knew there were "No Parking" signs on that block and was surprised that the cops would be so brazen considering that they were holding captives. Perhaps he was too late and they were already dead or being transported to the general's brother who would make it so.

The second time around, a man was stuffing two others into the back seat of the parked car. They were both handcuffed with their hands behind their backs. It was too dark to see the gags that filled their mouths.

Turning the headlights out, MacMaster steered the vehicle into a driveway, just far enough that he could observe the operation. It was clear he needed to act now. The transfer was taking place and he was being cut out of the loop.

Anastasia Viuda woke when the light went on in the garage. She had been sleeping for lack of anything else to do. Chained in the dark did not leave much for options. The light hurt her eyes and she blinked repeatedly to clear her vision. She did not know the man who was looking at them like a predator surveying a flock. He was not one of the four men who had taken them from the street outside the hotel. He was obviously not here to rescue them. Their captors had not told them why they were being held in this garage and they had not been allowed to speak in their own defense.

The mystery deepened when the stranger cut the ropes that fastened them to the chairs. He used a scalpel from the tray and watched them carefully. He obviously had respect for their abilities, though they had never seen each other. He moved them at gunpoint through the house and out the front door past the cooling bodies of the hapless delivery man and the corrupt police officer. The bodies rated a passing glance.

Questions raced unasked through Anastasia's mind. She chewed on her gag to no avail.

The automobile that had pulled off but had not discharged a passenger had not escaped the notice of Roberto Campena de Iguaca. He had heard the engine shut off but he had not seen the interior light and nobody had opened the door. He was much too old a hand and way too paranoid to allow someone to watch him that obviously. He was no expert in the devices available to the public for recording, it was not his business to record images, but he suspected he was being filmed. If it was another man or team of men here for the same purpose, they would simply have tried to shoot him. Ergo, the observer must be an undercover police officer. His reasoning led him to believe he was being observed by one of the men who had secured the prize he had stolen. The possibility of this worried him since those men had the resources of the police department behind them.

Roberto took some shells from the glove box and refilled his clip, checked his spares and started the engine.

"I do not know who it is that is in that car. I tell you that I will kill you both before I will let some one else take you from me. I would rather see you dead anyway, the only reason you are alive is that you are worth more to me that way.

"No, do not try to speak, there is nothing you can say that will save you and I do not believe you have information for me. Anything you say will be a trick to get me to release you. That will not happen until I have the money that has been promised. Until then you are to keep your mouths shut and you will do whatever I say. The reward was simply for a living captive, there are many stages to life and many have begged for death before the end of their lives."

Roberto had told them more in the first minutes than the others had in the past day. Both captives felt both a tiny relief and a heightened sense of urgency. They were to be left alive but only until they were delivered. Their final moments could not be imagined after that event.

The man took a left hand turn and then another. The vehicle in his rear view mirror did the same. There was no doubt he was being followed, and there was so little traffic on the roads at that time of night, the follower must know he had been spotted.

Then the car was gone. He had not lost him, though he had been formulating a plan to do so. The car had pulled off somewhere else, broken off the chase. Its absence affected Roberto worse than when the car had been there. While he thought he was being followed, he had something to focus on, now he was looking for whoever it was that took over the chase. He circled blocks and pulled over without warning trying to spot his pursuers but could get no sight of them. Finally he gave up on it and headed north out of the city and onto BR116 heading to Rio. If there was anyone following him he would know about it in short order and he would deal with them.

It took longer than half an hour to leave the populated section of the metropolis behind. It sprawled out over the countryside in the geometric perfection of planned communities everywhere. The couple in the back seat had stopped squirming around and so had stopped demanding so much attention of the driver. More and more his eyes were on the road ahead and not in the rear view mirror. Once he had escaped the lowlands and was headed into the mountains, the drop-offs and hairpin turns took most of his attention.

A forward tail almost never worked. One of the fundamentals of following a vehicle is that the subject cannot know you are there. Whoever had stuffed the couple into the back seat of that Lincoln Town Car knew he was being followed, so there was little that could be done. Gordon MacMaster knew the Lincoln could not outrun his much newer car, but he also knew that the rules of the game were in question. Something had happened, something out of the ordinary.

Driving well over the speed limit is a dangerous practice for someone who does not want to attract attention, but in this situation it was warranted. Luck was with him as MacMaster headed north on BR116. There are other ways to get to Rio from Porto Alegre but none is so efficient. He rolled his mental dice and chose to follow the most logical path.

An hour outside of Porto Alegre he pulled the Chrysler off the road. If his plan worked, the Lincoln would be behind him and was an unusual enough vehicle that he would spot it immediately. If his plan did not work he would switch to plan B. Unfortunately, he thought, he did not have a plan B. He cracked a beer and took a sip, grudgingly admitting to himself that he did not really have much of a plan A.

There was enough room in the dark back seat of the Lincoln that when Anastasia moved over against the door,

Hernando could lie down on the seat. He slid off the slick vinyl and onto the floor, with his lower back against the transmission tunnel. In this position it was not difficult to pull his hands under his backside and out in front of himself. The driver could not see what he was doing, though he did realize the man had fallen onto the floor.

It was easier for Anastasia to perform the same maneuver Hernando had. She did not even need to lie down until the chain of the handcuffs reached the inside of her knees. Then she lay down on the seat. This was the point where an exclamation from the front seat indicated that the driver was aware that they were up to something.

Slowing the car down to pull over, Roberto took one hand off the wheel and put it on the pistol lying on the seat next to him. He cursed his own greed silently, knowing it would have been so much easier to have shot them both while they were in the garage and left with nothing but their heads in a bag. That had been his plan in the first place and that, he decided, is what they were getting now. He had told them to accept their fates and they decided to play games. The time for games was over.

Roberto was not the only one deciding that the time for games was over. Hernando del Fuego threw his arms over Roberto's head and hauled back. A vomitous choking sound came from his throat as Roberto's wind pipe was closed off.

Anastasia grabbed the pistol just as the business end of it pointed at her face. She pushed it away and it went off into the passenger side rear window. The report was deafening in the confines of the car; the glass showered the roadside. She maneuvered the driver's elbow across the side of the passenger's head rest and tried to break it backward but failed. The driver's forearm was trapped against the back of the seat, and she was trying to take possession of the gun.

192

Instead of pulling off the road as he had been in the process of doing, Roberto floored the accelerator. The car surged forward, increasing the tension on the Brazilian's throat but when he hit the brake it threw everyone forward, loosening it a little. He got the fingers of his left hand under the handcuff chain. It did nothing to relieve the pressure and with no hands on the wheel, the vehicle was out of control.

There was nothing in Roberto's emotional make-up that led to panic, but he was panicking now. In a matter of seconds he would be a dead man unless he did something, so he did. He floored the gas pedal again. There was no hesitation as he closed his eyes and anticipated the collision.

The big Lincoln hit a sign on the far side of the road that did little but bounce it back into the road again into the path of a southbound farm truck.

The farm truck slammed into the trunk area of the car, spun around and clipped the rear bumper of the northbound Chrysler charging up on it from behind. The truck came to a stop on the other shoulder, facing the wrong way. The Chrysler ground to a stop in the gravel, the Lincoln rammed into a tree. Roberto was the first one out, but he exited without his gun and bolted into the woods.

The stench of gasoline from the car's ruptured tank filled the air for a second, but the engine continued to run since the electric pump was still moving the fuel. The lights from another vehicle outlined the car and sped past.

A spark from the engine and the gasoline ignited like the surprised exhale of a titan. The visceral world opened to the bowels of Hell and man's greatest ally turned to feast on human flesh.

The driver's door was open and Hernando del Fuego slithered out head first. His pants caught fire and he rolled in the dirt and grasses to extinguish them. Inside the Lincoln Anastasia Viuda pulled off her gag and screamed in anger.

The flames were running up the passenger side of the vehicle, where the broken windows let in the smoke and the heat. Somehow her handcuffs had twisted into the passenger side seat belt. She was trapped.

Hernando pulled the gag from his mouth, looked back once, said "Sorry, chica" and ran across the road toward the Chrysler but veered off when he saw the driver. He ran to the farm truck instead, pulled the stunned driver out and jumped into the cab.

Anastasia screamed again, this time in rage. She pulled against her restraints, but could get no further than the driver's side of the car and could not release herself. As she screamed a third time, the window behind her exploded and a hand reached in with a knife to cut the seat belt from her and drag her through the broken glass. She took a few minor scratches but had no time to be concerned about it. Her savior was bitter fruit. She recognized the huge redheaded man that had confronted them in the hallway of the hotel. She moved to reach back into the car for the pistol she had dropped but he pulled her away, physically lifting her from her feet and carrying her across the road.

The gas tank finished evacuating its contents leaving a passage for the fire to enter the tank full of fumes. The Lincoln exploded, flipping over on its roof and spreading shrapnel. The driver of the farm truck was gaining his feet after being flung to the dirt and was caught in the chest by a piece of the flying debris. He went down and did not rise again.

Anastasia's rescuer thumbed the button on the electronic key, and as the trunk lid rose, he stuffed her inside. This was no mean feat as she struggled the entire time, but handcuffed she was no match for the brawny man. She was inside the trunk and the lid went down. Lashing out only hurt her feet and hands. She had lost her shoes back in Porto

Alegre. A string of insults questioned her captor's manhood, ancestry, morals and sexual preference. He did not reply and she did not stop. She had been gagged for too long and now she would release the pent up volumes of frustration. After a while, she paused to catch her breath and realized that the man who held her probably spoke English, so when she began again it was in his native language. This turned out to be frustrating since her command of English was not as good as might have been wished and Gordon MacMaster roared in laughter when she told him she would fuck him like a sheep.

The farm truck was badly damaged from its collision with the Lincoln. It had a ruptured radiator and could not be expected to move more than about four kilometers before it overheated. When the steam started leaking from under the hunch-backed hood, Hernando had no choice but to turn it sideways and block the road. The next vehicle on BR116 was a tour bus. It was running at sun-up this morning, with a load of very sleepy passengers. The driver saw the farm truck and locked up the brakes, skidding to a stop inches from the disabled vehicle. He instructed his passengers to stay where they were and got out to investigate the scene.

Running from the cover of the trees, Hernando del Fuego smashed the bus driver across the back of the head with a jack handle that had been in the bed of the truck. He jumped into the driver's seat of the bus and loudly announced that he would be their replacement driver and that every body should relax and enjoy the ride.

The invective from the trunk had not yet ceased when Gordon saw Hernando driving the tour bus away from the smashed farm truck and directly at him. It was not moving fast yet but it was picking up speed. Gordon switched to the left side of the road but the bus did the same. It was obvious that Hernando had recognized either the vehicle or the driver and was trying to take him out of the equation.

Playing chicken with a tour bus was not on MacMaster's agenda this morning. He weaved back and forth then pulled completely off the road and ran half on the shoulder, half on the dirt. If he ceased his forward momentum he would have stayed in the soft dirt at the side of the road but he was enough of a driver to know that. He spun the vehicle around and followed the bus south. The stream of insults was moderating slightly and now a steady river of lies was coming from the trunk. Anastasia Viuda was trying to convince him of several implausible scenarios to get him to allow her to exit the trunk. He had not yet spoken to her but he continued to listen. Her rhetoric brought a wry smile to his lips despite the tense situation.

Roberto slunk back out of the foliage looking like he had been in an auto wreck. He had heard the screams and curses of the woman and though he had not seen what had happened to her, he knew she was not in the Lincoln. He saw the body of the farmer lying in the road. The sun was just rising but more light was created by the burning Lincoln. The Brazilian jungle is so dark on a moonless night that bats are the only thing that can hunt.

The lights of the tour bus sped past to the south and then the Chrysler 300. Someone had called the police from a cell phone but it would be a while before they arrived. Roberto could not remember passing any farms or houses before the incident and he did not want to wait around for a government inquisition. The next citizen who drove up donated his vehicle to Roberto's cause. It was an elderly man driving north in a Honda. Roberto limped up to the car and asked for help in a shaky voice. The old man got out, to lend some assistance, and Roberto chopped him in the throat with an overhand slice. His breath cut short, the man staggered backward. Then the man he had stopped to help threw an arm across his face and hauled back snapping the samaritan's neck.

Following a bus is easy but getting it to stop is no mean feat. With no way of knowing how much fuel the tanks held, it was impossible for Gordon to know if he could outlast it. He did not know if Hernando was armed, though he had seen the handcuffs. Any attempt to pull along side the bus would be suicide. He could leave the chase and still gain the reward for Perfecta Navaja but it seemed ridiculous to stop with his target in view. Shooting the tires of the bus was not even an option.

Some police cars and fire engines passed them going north, to the crash scene. With the sun up, more traffic would be heading each way. Then they hit the road block. Someone had called the police from their cell phone on the bus. Two police cruisers were nosed together at the center line. Four cars were stopped in the lane ahead of the bus and more were taking up the other lane. Hernando saw the only opportunity he had and accelerated in the left lane, passing the stopped cars and slamming the bus into the cruisers. The officers dove for cover in a hail storm of broken glass.

The bus was fully capable of continuing. With the engine in the back it had sustained no real damage to the drive train, but it stopped anyway. The officer was just rising to his feet when Hernando del Fuego hit him in the side of the head with his handcuffs and dropped him. The keys were right where they should be, in the little pocket on the handcuff pouch. It was a matter of moments and he had one hand free of the restraints and in less time it was filled with the officer's service weapon. The .45 caliber Taurus felt good in his hand. It felt like he was about to break free.

The risk was too great for Gordon to justify when he saw the bus slamming into the cruisers. If it was a decommission job he would have followed through, but not for a secure and return job. He pulled the car up short and got out. He could hear Anastasia Viuda kicking the inside of the trunk lid and demanding to be released. Nobody else could hear her at that point but there was no way for her to know that.

The first of the shots split the dawn. One of the officers got a shot off himself before he too breathed his last. Hernando was going from one officer to another and putting a slug into each man's brain. It was a study in efficiency. After securing the pistol, he shot the one officer who was already on his feet, then shot one that was just rising. A third man dodged behind one of the cars filled with screaming women that had been stopped at the road block. That officer discharged his weapon but was brought down by a round to the ankle and another to the head. Then Hernando finished off the first officer who was recovering from the handcuff blow.

Hernando spit on the face of the final victim as he removed his other hand from the restraint. The man driving the Chrysler was almost an afterthought. He looked back and saw him standing by the side of the vehicle, too far for a sure shot. The red hair and the massive chest stood out and Hernando surmised that it was the same man who had confronted him in the hotel. A thousand questions flooded in and then drained back as irrelevant. This man was a professional and Hernando was his only remaining target. The Argentinean was convinced that his erstwhile lover had burned to death in the back seat of the exploding Lincoln.

The Honda flew past at highway speed. MacMaster only got a glimpse of the man driving it. He saw Hernando trying to get out of the way, then shooting twice at the windshield before being hurled onto the hood and rolling over the roof of the car.

"That's one way to slow him down," Gordon said out loud.

Leaping out of the Honda, Roberto Campena de Iguaca quickly availed himself of one of the dead officers' guns. Once armed, he gladly turned his attention back to his prize.

There was no room in the trunk of the Honda for a full grown man, that was obvious and Roberto was not about to try stuffing Hernando in there. He wanted him in the back seat but there was a bit of a snag. Hernando was unconscious and the process of getting him in the back seat was way too awkward and difficult as he was unconscious.

There was no way to be sure that the Chrysler he was looking at down the road was the same one that had followed him in the city but the scarcity of such vehicles in Brazil made it unlikely it was any other. The driver was still standing by his vehicle, immobile, waiting. If Roberto were to focus his attention on securing his prize, this man would undoubtedly become active, but if he did not move soon, there would be more cops and a lot of questions for which he had no real answers. Then he realized he had help, even if they were unwilling. The tourists were deserting the bus now and either running down the road or into the woods.

"You! And You! Do not move. I need you to help me put this man into that pickup truck." The man's voice came out as a catching growl due to the livid bruise on his throat. The gun in his hand spoke louder than he could have.

Moving to the truck, the Brazilian pulled the door open and found the driver hiding on the floorboards.

"You too. Grab this man and put him in the bed of this truck."

One of the men he had made the demand of turned and tried to run. He got a slug in the back for his cowardice and flopped in the road trying to reach behind him as he screamed. A second slug silenced the screams. The two remaining men saw no option. They picked up the now barely conscious and feebly protesting body of Hernando del Fuego and hoisted him into the bed of the pickup truck. The owner of the truck still had nothing to say as he watched its tailgate heading south. He was almost run down by the Chrysler as MacMaster negotiated the wreckage and followed the pickup.

Both drivers knew they needed to get off the main road. They were also sure they each needed to kill the other. Until now, MacMaster had managed to fly under the judicial radar, he was not a wanted man anywhere and he wanted to keep it that way.

Anastasia Viuda had stopped thrashing around in the trunk. This may or may not have been a good thing, Gordon reflected. He wondered if Hernando would survive without hospitalization. Knowing that the man was destined to be killed by the general's brother anyway, he was somehow still concerned. Not for the first time, he wondered how the situation had gotten so out of hand.

The trail of dust indicated where the pickup had pulled off the main road. Nothing but a dirt path, the trail might have been un-navigable in the rainy season but was dry enough now. Roberto's vehicle was more suited to the path since it had more ground clearance and four wheel drive. Anastasia was protesting loudly as the car pounded up and down on the road, kicking up clouds of dust.

Around a wooded corner, suddenly, there was the truck, blocking the road. There was Roberto Campena de Iguaca, standing in the bed of the truck, training a .45 on the approaching car. There was no time for contemplating the situation; it was act or die.

Gordon MacMaster slammed his foot to the floor and gripped the steering wheel like he was going to rip it from the column.

Roberto opened fire on his unknown enemy, shooting him through the windshield. Then the car struck the back bumper of the truck and pitched Roberto head first into the windshield he had just shot.

Nobody was moving at capacity speed after this. They were all battered and bleeding, but they all moved, part of that predatory breed that would never lie down and die until they could no longer stand for themselves. Anastasia had been waiting for the car to stop; she had found the emergency cable and only just realized what it was. Hernando was playing possum in the back of the truck, waiting until Roberto eliminated the threats against him or was eliminated himself. While he had been knocked around badly by the collisions, he had no broken bones.

Gordon MacMaster reached across his chest and opened the car door with his right hand. His left arm would not respond to his demands and blood was running from his fingers. If he had moved a little faster he could have succeeded in terminating Roberto, but to manipulate the door handle and retain his grip on his pistol was awkward. By the time he got out of the car, the Brazilian had rolled off the passenger side of the car and moved toward the back where he was surprised and pleased to find the trunk opening and Anastasia Viuda rolling out. Nobody saw Hernando slip over the side of the truck bed and cat-foot down the side after Roberto.

Roberto's pleasure at finding Anastasia was short lived. He almost had time to cover her with the pistol when the articulated jack handle flashed out. The business end gained speed as it flipped around on its rivet and cracked into Roberto's hand with enough force to break bones. He did not have time to finish the scream that began to issue from his mouth before the handle arced back and smashed him in the side of the head. He fell to the ground and had no time to rise. Hernando half fell onto his back and Anastasia administered the coup de grace, splitting the back of Roberto's head.

Hernando pried the pistol from Roberto's hand and crouched behind the car. He had seen MacMaster and knew the game would not be over until one of them was dead. Then he had an idea.

"Gringo," he said, in Spanish. "There is a way we can both survive this."

Gordon did not answer, he was trying to stem the flow of blood from the bullet wound just above the elbow. The slug had passed outside of the bone but his arm was bleeding a colorful stream.

"Gringo, I have a proposal. You can take this bitch with you and you will get the money for her. I will go my way and we will both survive." This time Hernando spoke in English.

The look on Anastasia's face would have done credit to a hunting lioness. Hernando had left her in the back of the flaming Lincoln and so, as far as she was concerned, his life was already forfeit. To offer to trade her life for himself was merely a garland on his coffin. She turned her head to him and looked directly down the barrel of the stolen weapon.

"You forget," MacMaster was speaking Spanish, "I have already experienced your little game. It made me a fool in the hotel. It will not work again."

"You make yourself a fool now. If we make no deal, we both will die and her as well. I will shoot her first and you will have nothing to work with."

"Do it then. Shoot her or send her out."

"Go, woman. I am done with you." Hernando del Fuego was looking her right in one eye. Her other eye was still looking down the barrel of the weapon.

"Bastard," was all she said. Then she stood to her full height and stepped out from behind the car, knowing if she was greeting her own death she would greet it standing tall.

"Get down on the ground and put your hands behind your head." Gordon shouted in English. Anastasia said nothing and neither did she comply. She simply kept walking toward the back of the truck.

The incident in the hotel had shown how tricky and spontaneous the couple could be and MacMaster did not believe for a second that the woman he knew as Perfecta Navaja was actually surrendering. It was some kind of trick.

"Stop where you are." The accented Spanish might have been difficult for a second-year student to understand, but the pistol needed no interpreter. Anastasia stopped in her tracks and looked almost scornfully down the barrel of his gun.

"I know you want me alive. That stupid policeman told us about the reward. I... oh, you have been shot." It was impossible for her to hide her pleasure at the fact but her smile faded quickly. "You will need me to wash that. The infections the jungle holds will be much worse than the wound."

"I will deal with the wound. Drop to the ground. I will shoot you. You are too much trouble to be worth my time. I should have shot you already."

"But I will be no good to you dead."

"You will be no good to me alive if you do not listen."

"Oh, you need me now. I'm the only one who can get you out of this mess and back to where you can see a doctor."

"I need no doctor and I've had about enough of you as well." Gordon MacMaster was in a bit of a conundrum. He did not hunt women any more than he shot children. There was no romantic assassin's code of conduct that forbade him from shooting women; he simply didn't like to. He was on the verge of breaking his own rules for this woman, however, when the game changed.

The sound of a new player in the drama was beginning to invade. A farmer or hunter may have been running down the two-track but so little motor traffic used these trails that Gordon assumed it to be police. It made sense that someone had called from the site of the bus crash and the police who were heading for the burning Lincoln had turned around and pursued them. It seemed far-fetched that they could have known to turn down the dirt road, but there was someone coming regardless.

The same way Gordon had been blinded to the truck parked in the road, the approaching vehicle could not see the crash sight. Coming around the corner, the driver took the scene in as a flash picture: the woman in the road, the body lying behind the car, the other man diving into the bushes to the right. He saw the car and the pickup truck but he was already turning the corner to the right and could not recover quickly enough. The passenger side of his military transport vehicle smashed into the back of the car hurling it forward into the back of the truck. Without a seat belt, the driver smashed the windshield with his forehead. The four soldiers in the back of the truck were tossed around but not incapacitated. They were ready for a fight.

Cursing softly to himself, Hernando checked his ammunition. He did not know there was a military base nearby. He gazed through the tall grasses and bushes at their automatic weapons and began to drool. With one of these in his hands he could clean the entire situation. The only problem was convincing one of the young soldiers it was time to make a donation.

Gordon MacMaster had dropped to the ground when the truck came around the corner. He had merely desired to hide from the inevitable confrontation but it had saved his life. Between the size of the truck and the speed it was moving, it jammed the Chrysler hard into the back bumper of the pickup. It would have crushed him if he had been standing. As it was, he ended up jammed under the none-too-spacious front end of the car.

Anastasia knew an opportunity when it presented itself. Her mind calculated the angles in a millisecond. There was no way the military could have been mobilized in the amount of time expended, therefore, the truck full of men was on a different mission. She ran to the transport screaming, "Help me, they have kidnapped and raped me."

Some of the young men piling out of the back of the truck thought they might have forgiven themselves for doing the same thing. Though she was dirty and scratched, with torn clothing, she still presented an attractive prospect. The trouble was that they were without leadership. There was no one in charge because this was not an official mission and without supervision, the young men did not know how to respond.

The driver got out of the cab and stumbled toward the back, blood streaming down his face from a cut on his scalp. The four young soldiers were in the prime of life, healthy and strong, but without the assurance of experience.

"Aje! Look at this," one of them began. We won't need to pay for it after all. Somebody has even handcuffed her for us."

"Idiot," another responded, "don't let your gun think for you."

A third chimed in with, "There is some thing going on here. Where are the men who cuffed her? Are they police?"

"No. Probably Columbians," decided the first. "They shoot each other all the time. I'm going to take advantage of their generosity."

Anastasia could not hear what they were saying, but she could see what they were talking about by knowing what they were looking at. The thought flashed through her mind that five such men would rape her to death if she did not gain the upper hand and soon. She was all alone and compromised.

The driver finally spoke up. "We are in a deep hole here. You, get me some water to wash off this blood. I need to think. One of you, secure that woman. Two of you take a look around. See if you can find the men who were driving these." He indicated the two vehicles with an upward nod of the head.

The two men indicated accepted the driver's leadership. He was older and had been driving young recruits to the whorehouse in the jungle for a number of years. They were no trackers though and while one walked past Hernando del Fuego, the other followed a deer path. Both missed the fact that there was one man trapped underneath the car that they had rammed.

The first aid kit in the transport cleaned and disinfected the driver's scalp, then they turned their attentions to their new captive, asking her who she was and what she was doing there in handcuffs.

Anastasia's fertile mind had already evaluated the situation and so she made a play she thought might work for her. "I am the lover of Colonel Esteban. I was kidnapped from our compound in Rio. He will have men searching for me. These fools have been using me as a slave."

Her story did not work the way she had wanted it to. Being the concubine of an officer did not afford her the respect a wife might be afforded. Their thoughts tended toward a more likely explanation, anyway.

The driver sat on the ground next to the wrecked transport. "We cannot go back to the base and tell them that we wrecked a truck on the way to the cantina to buy some pussy. We're supposed to be on patrol. What the hell are we supposed to do now?" As he sat there his gaze drifted to the pickup truck and he noticed a pair of shoes behind the rear wheels. "Aje. There is a man under the truck and another one behind it. Get them. Why are you standing there looking stupid?"

"What are you talking about? There is no one behind this truck." The one soldier was looking at the blood soaking the ground behind the truck, but the body was missing.

"He went into the woods. Follow him and bring him back. Must I do all the thinking here?"

"Yes, Sir."

"Come out from under there, you are under arrest. Move, now. I will shoot you if you do not."

"Idiot!" came out from under the accident. "If I were able to get out of here, don't you think I would have? I can't move. I'm pinned to the ground."

The soldier was unconvinced and continued to yell and threaten but Gordon MacMaster was thoroughly stuck. Anastasia Viuda was telling the strangers that he had kidnapped and raped her and that he was a dangerous murderer and should be shot. Fortunately for Gordon, they did not exactly believe her either and told her they knew who she was. She changed tack and began wheedling to get her hands out of the handcuffs but was unsuccessful at this as well. Had she been able to generate tears at this point, it would have been a useful tool and may have given her the edge but she was unable to sprout them now.

Hernando was perfectly willing to shoot Roberto when he saw the Argentine slinking into the woods after the young soldier, but he was unwilling to give away his position so he watched them pass. He wished the young private well but did not think for a second that he would survive the encounter. Hernando was not old in years but he had learned that age and treachery often trumps youth and vigor.

Since the pickup truck was still capable of running, one of the soldiers started it and drove it a few feet forward but this did little to free MacMaster. It was the Chrysler that pinned him to the ground. Given enough time he could have worked his way out from under it.

The driver had what seemed a perfectly reasonable idea when he took a piece of solid wire and bent up a facsimile handcuff key. He waited until his associates had hoisted the front of the car up with the scissor jack, then freed Anastasia's hands and secured Gordon's. The driver had no idea who he had encountered, but he knew with certainty that the woman was the less dangerous of the two. Because of the Scotsman's wound, he cuffed him in front rather than behind his back. One of the young men took some alcohol and gauze and cleaned around the bullet hole.

Chapter Eleven
Justification

Little Rock, Arkansas was big enough to lose yourself in but not the sort of megalopolis that Los Angeles promised to be. Terry didn't really like the huge, sprawling cities with no sidewalks. They were actually better for his purposes, but they had never felt right. Living on a farm meant that you knew who your neighbors were for miles around, but living in cities with no sidewalks meant you might not know who lived next door and they might not welcome you if you brought over some lemonade on a hot day.

A couple hundred thousand people is by no means a huge city and Little Rock still manages to maintain some of that famous southern hospitality that seems absent from the more modern cities. Terry thought he was replicating the southern drawl reasonably well but the truth was that no southerner would be fooled by it. His neighborhood consisted of lower-middle-class houses and apartments, the structures of which had passed their prime. The population was working class men and women struggling to raise families under the declining economies of the age. Terry's lifestyle was by no means ostentatious; he lived in a one-bedroom apartment on the second floor of an old Victorian mansion. The subdivision of the structure had happened in the fifties or sixties so it had a good solid hardwood door. The windows looked out onto the intersection of two streets, both of which had sidewalks.

It had taken Terry two weeks to stop imagining that he was being watched, though it was not all his imagination. Most of his neighbors worked too hard to care about new additions to the population, but curiosity is a natural reaction to any kind of change and Terry did evoke some curiosity. He wore a vest or a jacket constantly though it was much warmer in Arkansas than it had been in Michigan. Spring was just over the horizon and most residents of the city were discarding outerwear if they had worn it at all. Most of the interest and questions were generated by the single mothers in the area. Terry was not initially seen with a woman and he walked everywhere he went. He never used a credit card at the corner store.

One of the things that surprised Terry about America was that more people didn't drink beer. The level was much higher in Australia and was seen as part of the natural order of things. He knew nothing of the decades of anti-alcohol legislation, and the age of prohibition was a hazy myth in the back of his mind. He, however, had no qualms in tipping a few. After the initial couple of weeks, the taverns called and it became widely accepted that the newcomer had no driver's license because he was a drunk. The truth was, his driver's license was being forged in a print shop in Kansas, he was meeting with new contacts, he was learning Spanish from members of the bilingual community and he had learned how to cut off his drinking whenever he decided to. It was one of the things Uncle Ginger had taught him.

One of the things he learned about the Spanish speaking communities was their jealousies. The Hispanic men were very protective of their women and suspicious of anyone coming into their communities. Their nationalistic attitudes may have been justified or it may have been nothing more than the feudal politics fed by thousands of years of colonialism, but it made it a difficult culture for acceptance. Terry did not care. Terry was not trying to become a part of the hard working, poorly paid immigrant community. He was hiding among people that did not talk to the police and who drank almost as much as he did. While he did stick out like a sore thumb among the short, dark-haired men, his story was accepted and repeated without question.

Terry had always had a facility for language, he simply had not known it. Looking at the enormity of the South American continent and understanding a little about the brutal brand of politics that holds sway in the emerging nations, he acknowledged that he should have learned Spanish already. German had been of little utility for him.

"My parents came from Spain," the old woman explained. "So I am exempt from their bickering. I have always found it fascinating that within one set of people there can be so much prejudice. The Puerto Ricans hate the Mexicans and everybody else who is not Puerto Rican. The Mexicans hate the Dominicans and the Colombians hate the Mexicans and on and on…"

Terry found this statement fascinating and was very careful to determine what faction of the Hispanic community he was with before opening his mouth. He also discovered that while the old woman was teaching him Castilian Spanish, none of the sub-sets actually spoke this most proper Spanish and within their communities they had completely different dialects. It was not that they could not understand each other, it was simply that they had their own ways of speaking as different from each other as Terry's was from an Arkansas accent. The enormity of the task gave him pause and then he carried on with his lessons. Later, he thought about the divisions between cultures and visited the local library. Books on Latin America were not that plentiful but there was a number of American History books and a nice historical novel about Mexico. While he did not become a scholar on the subject, the books helped Terry to relate to the community and get a feel for what lay south of the Rio Grande.

The Spanish radio station was indecipherable at first, but as he learned more he listened better. It seemed that the announcers spoke so fast that by the time he recognized a word, the sentence was finished and they were on to the next, but with perseverance and dedication it all came with time.

Rosalita was from Colombia. She was not brazen in her attention but it became obvious she wanted the Australian. She had no way of knowing what he did for a living or that he would, one day, disappear without warning, leaving her waiting like a sailor's wife.

Terry spent about a year learning, exercising, walking, drinking and reading. Then he left.

"What do you have for me?"

"Well! Stranger. It has been a while since you've done anything I've known about. Are you sure you haven't lost your edge? Is this line secure?"

"I'm calling from a public line at a highway rest stop. I've got an American passport, Arkansas driver's license and a couple of credit cards that have never been used. I'm legal and bored out of my mind. I'm ready for something south of the border now."

"What?"

"Yes."

"Okay. I... wait a minute. Look. Your old friend has come up missing in a location I will disclose later. We have some information coming in and should be able to send you close. This job started as a simple snatch and grab. I don't know how it turned into the bucket of rats that it did. What is your general location, I need to transmit some information."

"Route 40."

"Go to Sherwood Avenue and Eighth Street in Russellville. The Fontengras Building, third floor. Belly Button Printers. There will be a package there for, um, Jack Straw. It will have what we know."

"Is he alive?" There was no doubt in Terry's mind whom his contact was referring to.

"We think so, but he has been off the grid for a couple of months and out of touch for a week. He has not been paid and nobody else has either as far as we can tell. My information has a few days lag time but it gets here eventually."

"All right then. The Fontengras. Belly Button. Jack Straw. In Russellville."

"Eighth and Sherwood."

"Bottoms up." The line went dead.

Terry went into the rest stop and ordered a cup of coffee and breakfast. The food was surprisingly good. The newspaper had nothing that was real news in it but he took a look to give him something to look at. He was not thinking about anything around him for once; he was thinking about Richard Pikelfinger. He had not thought much about the man since he left Michigan, but going active again brought the feelings he had experienced after the killing. He had decommissioned a number of men for a number of different reasons and he had never had much of a problem with it. Most of the men he had targeted had been very bad men who had done something bad enough that others were willing to pay for their deaths. Some of the men Terry had killed had made him feel good, like a boon to society. Richard Pikelfinger had not even died fully and yet there was a nagging feeling that it was the wrong thing to do, that it had been a mistake to take the job. Then he thought about Vanessa and the statements she had made about the union and the UAW workers. There was a storm in his head as the winds of conscience blew against the bulwarks of his chosen profession.

"More coffee?"

"Thank you, dear. One more cup is all I need."

"All right. I'll leave this here and you can pay it on the way out."

The waitress left and Terry found himself wondering how much she was paid for her services. It was certainly not union wages. He shook his head and drank the hot coffee like it was a shot of whiskey. He knew he performed an essential service. His last thought as he threw the newspaper away was that the good he created more than offset the evil he might have done.

Terry's natural caution was misplaced in Russellville. There was nobody watching the Belly Button Press on the third floor of the Fontengras Building. The package was there and required no ID. Terry thought Jack Straw a strange name for parents to have named their son but it served as well as any other.

The package contained a pair of mug shot style photographs showing a beautiful couple. Mr. and Mrs. Andalucia had been detained at the border between Brazil and Argentina, according to the scrawled handwriting on the photograph. The letter gave them different names. Sandiana Torremolinos was listed as another alias for the woman as was Perfecta Navaja. Perfecta Navaja was the woman wanted for murdering General Modiano in Rio.

Andalucia was the only name associated with the man but there was another photograph of him as well. It was a grainy black and white photo, almost a surveillance camera still. If the letter had not indicated they were one and the same, Terry would not have been sure. The letter purported it to be of the man entering a safe house of the Argentine Secret Service in Bolivia. It gave no detail as to why he was there or what side of the road he walked, simply that he was there.

The reward was offered by the general's brother, Francisco Modiano. His telephone number and address were included, along with a photograph of him with his wife. Clipped to the photo was a short biography of the man. It seems he and his brother had been in collusion with each other, working both sides of the fence. The General controlled a lot of the police and politicians in Rio and this allowed his brother to know who was being raided when and where. It had worked out well for them and they had amassed huge sums of money, but unavoidably they had made some enemies as well. When the General died, it changed the dynamic and put a lot of pressure on Francisco. The police and the other drug-invested families began to attack his supply lines and interfere with his cash flow. They never attempted to assault him personally and that may have been because he lived in the northern suburb of Itaborai where he had police protection in addition to his personal security force.

The last communication from the agent who was not named in the letter was from Porto Alegre. That was where he had provided the name Sandiana Torremolinos. There was nothing further but a recent newspaper article that spoke of automobiles set on fire and policemen shot in the street. The connection was uncertain and provided nothing but a possible location to begin looking. There were more questions created than answered and Terry felt he may be wasting his time. After all, there did not seem to be any compensation offered. There was no doubt that he would take the assignment, however. He owed Gordon MacMaster too much to ever desert him in a possible time of need.

Terry's flight out of Dallas was directly to Rio. A twin engine prop-plane took him to Curitiba. Once in Curitiba, he began to feel the enormity of the task he had set for himself. The weather was good, the people were friendly and giving and the accommodations were cheap. He felt like he was on holiday, but he knew his business could not wait or he was already too late. He purchased a throw-away cell phone and contacted Colonel Richter's office to give them the number. An emergency device, the phone would not last longer than the job.

The thought that Gordon MacMaster may have been killed was dismissed without serious thought. The Aussie knew the Scot was alive and that he just needed to find him.

The first place to look might be a tavern or two.

"I need a friend," seemed like an absurd statement at first. A man did not walk into a taxi dispatch office and declare that he needed a friend.

"I will be your friend, señor," came from more than one of the drivers. It was a joke with most of them. They did not know what was going on.

"Señor, we are not in the business of buying and selling friends. We provide a transportation service." This was the dispatcher speaking from behind his glass wall.

Terry slid an American hundred dollar bill under the glass and the dispatcher became very quiet. "You, reading the newspaper, what is your name?"

"Juan."

"Juan, you are going to be my friend today."

"What does that mean?"

"You are going to drive me around to different places and help me find another friend of mine. We will investigate a local story for my service."

"And what makes me so lucky that I am to be your friend today?"

"Because you did not make fun of the concept. You are a serious man and I need serious men on my side."

"What do I get other than your friendship?"

"Friendship should be enough but I think four hundred dollars will more than compensate you for the day."

"Yes. A little sugar to make the bitter go away."

"Speaking of bitter, take me to a coffee shop so I can have a cup of coffee. After that we will be driving south."

The driver looked up at the dispatch window. The dispatcher told him he would be paying for his own gas if he went freelance for the day. The driver grinned and hitched up his pants. "Blondie," he said, "you will be filling my tank. Yes?"

"Yes."

"We go now."

The coffee house was homey and the cab ran on ethanol. The road south was clear enough though it rained much of the way down. The driver said little but answered Terry's questions with an uncanny knowledge of recent events in the area. He tried to get Terry to talk, indicating that if he wanted help then he had come to the right place, but Terry did not want to enlighten this walking encyclopedia of current events.

"This is where the big American auto burned. You see where the trees are burned." The heat and humidity did not seem to bother the cab driver.

"Were there any bodies?"

"Yes. Dead bodies. There was farmer killed in the explosion. His truck was found back there, where the tour bus was hijacked."

"A tour bus?"

"Yes, sir, let me try to tell what I know of this. First the American car burned, exploded. The farmer was killed and his truck was found down there. The engine was seized up. Then the tour bus was hijacked. The driver of the bus is my wife's cousin. He's okay but then there was another. An old man I do not know was killed right here, his neck was broken. It might have been from the crash."

Terry lit a cigarette and tried to imagine the circumstances. He did not know if he was in the right place or if the people he was seeking had ever been here. "So the tour bus was hijacked here, when they stopped to help?"

"Ah, no. The farmer's truck was stolen…"

"Yes, yes. Now I remember. Go on."

"The bus hit a road block down that way and the crazy man killed four cops and stole another truck. He put somebody in the back of the truck and left."

"So they did not find them?"

"No, they went into the jungle. The jungle keeps its secrets."

"Show me where the police were killed." Terry was beginning to think he was following a dead end. If the cops couldn't find them, the trail was cold. "Are there any witnesses I can talk to? It would be worth money to them and to you."

"Yes, I can arrange that."

It actually took three days to get in touch with all the witnesses that were in the area. The bus driver was first and he had very little to say, he had seen little, but he did provide a passenger list the following day. It was a dead end since none of the passengers were local. The witnesses to the shootings were, however, and they were happy to invite Terry in for coffee and conversation, once he flashed a cheap tag that said he worked for the BBC.

The man whose truck had been stolen gave the best description of both the man who had stolen it and the victim who had been in the bed of the truck. Neither of them was of the slightest interest to the fake reporter. The women in the lead car were most helpful though. It was an off-handed comment about almost being run down by an American car that caught Terry's interest. The woman described getting out of her car after the murderer drove off in the pickup and having a big white car with a big redheaded man try to run her down. Yes, he was going the same way as the pickup, south. There was no mention of a woman, however and no indication there had been one involved.

The following day, before Terry had finished his breakfast, Juan found him. "Blondie, we have good news. The truck was found, along with a car that smashed into it on a side road. The tow truck brought them in yesterday. Perhaps this helps, yes?"

"Yes. Take me to them."

The most telling piece of evidence involved the trunk of the Chrysler. The trunk lid was undamaged even though the back of the car had been smashed in by a collision with some grey-green vehicle and the inside of the trunk was spattered with dry blood. Someone had been in the trunk or just outside it.

"That paint, that comes from the army." Juan said.

"This paint?"

"Yes, sir. That is the color the Army uses on Jeeps and trucks."

"So this one was hit by an army truck?"

"It popped the trunk but it did not hurt the trunk, so it hit low on the car."

Terry looked at the clasp and hasp and decided that, no, the trunk was not popped open by the accident. It had already been open. Inside the trunk was a scrap of cloth that could have come from a woman's dress; in fact it could have come from almost nothing but a woman's dress.

The bed of the truck had some blood in it, as could have been expected.

The tow truck driver was only too happy to take a couple hundred dollars to show Terry where he had pulled the vehicles from and he didn't even need to drive there. Juan took the two of them in the taxi.

Much in the way a river wears its outside bank, the dirt road had been expanded to the left of the accident by the vehicles that had skirted the scene. Under and around the accident there was what looked like dried blood and many boot tracks. Juan could not be sure they were military boots but they were cut similar and of different sizes. There were also tracks leading into the forest, one of which was barefoot. None of the tracks were pristine as the rain had washed them out. A quick walk into the soggy underbrush revealed nobody.

"Juan, do you have any friends at the army post?"

"With some money, anyone can buy friends there."

"Yes, but I do not need them to tell you what they think you want to hear. I need to know what happened here. I need to know where these men went. This happened a couple of weeks ago, yes?"

The tow truck driver smelled money and said. "I know all the repair shops and body men. If any of them have repaired an army truck I can find out about it. They usually do their own work but I know that man too."

"I need you to be quiet about this. Tell them nothing but find out what happened. I will pay well for this information, but only after I confirm it to be real."

"Yes, Blondie, we can do this for you."

"Good, Juan. Tell me, where does this road lead?"

"It is a little town of whores."

"What?"

"This road leads to a town where the whores live. Nobody likes to talk about it. It has no real name. Some call it Woodytown. It is not on the map and no one ever admits to going there, but there it is. Many of the soldiers go there to sample what they cannot get at the base. Even the officers. After all, young soldiers in the prime of their lives need to be regulated, but they also need release. The women provide this."

"How far?"

"Perhaps five kilometers from here."

"Go to the base, find your friends in the business. Find out what has happened here, if anyone has taken prisoners, if any soldiers have been killed. I am walking to the town. Pick me up in two days."

"I can do this, sir, but it can be very dangerous to walk alone into such a place." Juan was clearly afraid of seeing his cash cow amble off.

"I am capable of taking care of myself. Remember, tell nobody anything. They do not need to know, and I will pay well for the truth. Lies on the other hand will be rewarded in other ways. In three days."

"I tell you this is a bad idea. Bandits and drug dealers live in these forests."

"I'll be good. Pick me up in the Plaza de Putas in three days."

"I'll be back, I hope you will be there." Juan said as he turned.

"We'll be back." The tow truck driver said. "You are not going to cheat me out of my share."

The rutted, seldom used road did little to increase visitors' anticipation of the nameless little compound. The town itself was much cheerier and more modern than could possibly have been expected. There was a dry goods store selling chocolate, coffee, rice and beans. The aged owner had set himself up as the importer of fancy and revealing clothing and had a guaranteed market for his produce without government oversight. There was a wide array of condoms and lubricants, feminine hygiene products and cigarettes.

This was the only store here and it did not sell liquor. If a visitor wanted to drink, he needed to cross the street.

Aside from the dozen little cottages that had sprung up, obviously from the hand of the same man, there was little to call this a town. The centerpiece of the community was the pleasure palace. The sign above the door proclaimed in sun bleached lettering that it was Jardim de Prazeres, Garden of Delights.

Terry stood in front of the sundries store with a candy bar and a warm bottle of soda pop. It was the lay of the land that interested him. He had no idea what sort of reception he might receive so he thought it best to plan a way out before he went in.

The Garden of Delights was set up more like a movie version of an old west saloon than any building the Australian had ever seen. It was almost a parody of the style, it was so perfect. It had the plank walkway in front and the swinging double doors. The upstairs was undoubtedly where the ladies attended to their customers. It was not hard to imagine the sound of a honky-tonk piano emanating from the barroom or of drunken cowboys staggering out the door to duel in the street. A movement of the curtains told him he was being watched as well as watching.

Behind the Garden of Delights was a massive water tower with heavy angle-iron legs and a cylindrical chamber. This tower was the same grey/green as the paint that had transferred at the accident. The color the military used for its trucks and hardware. The paint looked relatively fresh. As Terry crossed the street, he became aware of a mechanical throbbing. Some kind of engine was running. He walked to the end of the plank walkway that served as a porch for the establishment and the noise increased. He had already determined that there was a diesel generator behind the building. It had become clear at that point that the military was taking good care of their recreational location.

Before entering the building, Terry turned to get a view from there. He had already gotten a view from around the perimeter of the enclave. He pinpointed the cabin his pistol was hidden behind. This was the pistol Juan had secured for him. He pinpointed the more heavily travelled road out of the village to the West. He noticed for the first time that there was a huge tank marked diesel fuel but not a single fuel pump for vehicles.

The inside of the saloon mirrored the outside, like a Hollywood version of the old west. There was indeed a honky-tonk piano on one wall. There was green, felt covered poker tables and paisley covered chairs. The bar stools were tall and spare but the bar was polished to a rich luster. The place was well maintained and very clean.

There was no bartender and no women in the saloon which surprised its newest visitor. A town that existed for one purpose should be ready to provide that service at the drop of a hat. Then he realized how early it still was and that the place was likely open late. He debated leaving and returning at a more appropriate hour but he knew he had already been marked and there was no where else to go. The bartender's area was accessed from a door behind the bar so if he wanted a drink he would need to get back there, raise a fuss, or climb over the bar. He was about to pound on the bar when a woman in a long velvet dress began wafting down the stairs.

"Good morning, stranger. Most men don't show up here before four." Her voice was warmer than her velvet dress.

"Good morning, beautiful. I don't seem to be able to get a drink here. Is there anything to drink in your room?"

"It is a bit early for drinking, no?"

"No."

"Then follow me." Her dress swayed back up the stairs with the same smoke-like grace she had descended and he followed her into a room with a bed, a dresser, one chair and a spittoon.

"What do you prefer? I have aguadiente and rum."

"No beer?"

"I can get you a beer if you want."

"Yes. Get several; whatever you would like to drink as well." The currency he shoved into her hand was more than enough.

When she had returned with the beer he asked what her name was.

"Lu-la," she said with a charming lilt to her voice.

Terry and his new friend, Lula drank a couple of beers and some of the strongly flavored aguadiente, then she got some fruit juice and they started on the rum. The difference in the language that Lula spoke and the Spanish that Terry had learned was vast but rather than allowing that to be a liability, the couple laughed explosively over the mistakes.

Without changing the subject too abruptly or introducing a businesslike air to the room, Terry asked about strangers wandering into town without vehicles. She noted that he had come into town on foot.

"Am I the only one lately that has walked into town?"

Lula turned her head to hide her reaction but it was simultaneously obvious that he was on the right track and that she would not talk about it. He knew he could find somebody in this town that could point him in the right direction.

"I think I would like to stay in town for a while. Who do I talk to about renting one of those cabins?"

"Oh, I don't think you want to do that. Just get some of this and sleep for a while and then move on. When the

224

officers come into town, they get a little upset when there are strangers. The officers use the cabins."

"Does that happen often?"

"Officers have a day every week…"

"I meant strangers."

"No. We don't get a lot of strangers here, especially gringos."

"But there is one here now, yes."

"No." Once again she looked away.

"I meant me."

Lula smiled broadly, her beautiful teeth like marshmallows in a sea of jelly.

"There is a doctor here, yes?"

"He comes in town once or twice a week. He treats the girls who pay him in trade. There is a dentist as well. He will work all day and party all night about once a month and then crawl back to his ugly wife."

"How do you know she is ugly?"

"He tells us. He says she is so ugly she scares the cats." Lula giggled, obviously half drunk.

The bell rang for lunch and Lula rose, still graceful and steady if yet a bit bleary. "I go to get you some food from the kitchen. We should eat when we drink. Then you can tell me how you like it… or maybe you have some kind of skill you can trade."

"What is the town in need of?"

"You will need to talk to AnaMaria about that. She handles all such trade um… negotiations. You know you will need to pay, just for being here, in my room. Nobody gets away without paying, even if they are unable to um…"

"No, I'm not unable. I will pay you as well, but I don't need that sort of service."

"All men need that sort of service. Unless you're a faggot."

"No, I'm not a faggot, I just need friends more than I need pussy."

Lula raised an eyebrow and floated out the door, still in the velvet dress.

When she returned, Lula found Terry looking out the window at a tanker truck. It was painted the faded green of a military vehicle and was pumping into the large diesel tank.

"I should have asked if you wanted to dine at the table, I'm sorry. I just assumed that you would be eating here since we did not complete our business yet." She had a tray with plates for both of them. The fare was simple but nutritious.

They sat on the bed with the tray between them and ate dried beef and rice with onions and garlic, collard greens and farofa, toasted manioc meal with nuts and prunes. Lula apologized for the lack of fresh fruit or vegetables, the supply truck was late and food spoiled quickly in the jungle.

The effect of the large meal, the early alcohol and the tropical heat was predictable, siesta. Terry lay down on the bed and fell asleep. Lula cleaned up the dishes and took them back downstairs, and then she returned, stripped to her underwear and lay down next to him. She had not met a man in a long time that did not want what all men want. He seemed fully normal and claimed he was not gay. She was reflecting on all this when she dozed off.

The two of them awoke at the same time in response to a banging on the door. A man's voice was hollering "Get up. you lazy whores, the soldiers are here. Wash your asses and get downstairs, it's time to make some money.

"Arturo, you pig, I am making money."

"Then finish up and get downstairs or charge him double."

Terry put his finger to his lips and quieted Lula's response. The wad of bills from his vest pocket was more than sufficient to convince her he could afford to rent her attentions all week. He peeled off some bills and handed them to her. Then he told her he needed to piss.

The room had no private toilet, such things were done at a communal room. At present there was a line in front of the room as the women waited to take care of nature and improve what nature had given them with makeup and scented oils. It might not be free for a while so Terry opted to urinate in the spittoon instead. She looked down at his unit and decided that he would be capable of satisfying all but the most jaded of women.

"So, you do not want to use that thing, yet you are willing to pay to be here. What is it you are really after. It's not the rum, you can get that anywhere. You walked into town but do not look like you walked the whole way. Do you have an auto?"

"No, I have a man coming to get me in a couple of days."

"So you expect to say here for a couple of days?"

"That was the plan."

"What is it then?"

"Get a couple more beers and we'll discuss it."

Lula slipped her dress over her shoulders and floated out the door in search of more beer. She was stopped multiple times on the way: Arturo wanted cash and the soldiers were all waiting for the women who were in turn waiting for the bathroom. Lula had to thread her way through a gauntlet of young soldiers in the prime of their lives to make it back to her new friend.

"So, Terry, what is it you are after if my womanhood is not good enough for you?"

"Lula, I never said you were not good enough. You are an incredibly beautiful woman. It's just that I am looking for a man."

"So!" she said, turning cold. "You are a pato."

"No, no, no. I am looking for a friend of mine that I think was lost in this area."

Lula looked away. This was the third time she had done this when he had mentioned strangers. There was no doubt in Terry's mind that he was making progress.

"You know what I am talking about now. I will pay you for solid information."

"That is no help to me. Arturo will find the money and take it."

"What is it then that I can do that will help you, help me?"

"You can get me out of this place."

"Why don't you just leave?"

"Ai, you are so naïve. Some women have escaped but they always had help. And I don't know if they actually escaped to something better, to the same thing, or if they were killed and left in the forest."

"And you think I would do something different?"

"I think you are a man who knows what he wants. You get what you want but you do not need to steal it."

Terry took a sip of his beer and thought for a second. If he gave his word to this working girl, he would feel honor bound to follow through. Much of his life he had held his word to be his bond and it was one of the things that cemented his reputation with those who directed him. "If Kingston said he was going to do it, it will get done," had been heard more than once.

"How do you know I will not kill you and leave you dead in the forest?"

"How do you know I will not do that to you?" she replied.

"You need help to get out and I need help finding my friend."

"What does he look like?"

"His hair is red and he is taller than me. He stands out in a crowd."

"Ai. I have a story to tell but you must pay me first. That is the one rule that is beaten into us in this life. You must pay me first."

Terry was of two minds. He knew he had other avenues he could explore and he knew that if he secreted this woman away from the compound, he could never return. Yet he liked Lula and would like to help her. He felt that if she knew where MacMaster was, then there were others in town who knew. It might be as easy as going down to the bar and asking the bartender. He lit a cigarette and offered her one which she refused.

"No."

"What?"

"I said no. I cannot pay you first. I have already paid you for your services and you have given me nothing so I am not obliged to do more."

"You paid for the pleasure of my company, a good meal and my time. Whether you use me or not, my time costs."

"Yes, but I have paid for it. This other thing you ask for is not the same, true? I will do what you want but if you ask too much I will need to go elsewhere. And I cannot pay you first. Tell me what I want to know or I will go downstairs and drink and you will not get what you want."

Lula knew that Terry could get the information he wanted for nothing or next to nothing so she had no choice but to acquiesce. If Terry walked out the door her charade was over and she would be left with nothing. Her desires depended on getting him to stay there. She put a hand on his chest and pushed him slowly back onto the bed. He did not resist as she undid his pants and went to work.

Lula was still sleeping when Terry slipped out of bed. A few die-hard drinkers were downstairs pickling their livers in rum so he slipped out the window onto the roof of the awning and down. While there were still some holes in the picture, it was more complete now than it had been.

The cabins were reserved for the upper echelon of the army base but they were almost never all in use simultaneously. They were used for other things as well. They had no electricity run to them, but they did have toilets. It would have been a simple matter to run lines from the generator to the cabins but it had never been done. None of the cabins had lights in them, not even candles were lit. The officers were not on hand today and it was impossible to tell if anyone was inside.

It took a little while longer than he would have expected to secure his pistol from behind the cabin. It was not the cabin he was directed toward, either. He slunk down to the farthest cabin from the saloon and twisted the knob slowly. It resisted. The door was locked and he could not tell who was inside.

Lula had told him about the four men who ran the town and the saloon and that they slept in whatever bed they wanted to, with whatever woman they felt like sleeping with. She told him that on days when the soldiers visited, the town's rulers slept in empty beds or in the unused cabins.

Terry could not know who or how many were in this locked cabin. He peered in the window but it was too dark to see. There was a door in the front and one in the back, which seemed like an excess given the size of the thing, but neither door gave a shudder. There seemed no way in. Terry slipped back into the woods to consider his options. He wished he could smoke a cigarette but it would have been a bad idea.

After about 45 minutes, the Australian had come up with nothing that would be quiet enough to suit him and was about to slip back to Lula's warm embrace when he heard footsteps scuffing through the dirt in his direction. The man was not staggering as could have been expected of any of the remaining soldiers, he walked upright and with purpose. Using a flashlight to guide him, he walked directly to the cabin Terry was watching and unlocked the door.

The flare of a match or lighter and then the soft glow of a candle lit the interior.

Nobody was patrolling the grounds, although it seemed as if they should. Nobody saw Terry slip up to the window.

Inside the cabin, the man stood in front of a woman in pitiful condition. Chained and shackled, she sat on the floor, naked and dirty. She looked as if she had been starved and the bruises attested to the beatings. Her dyed blonde hair was growing out black. The man spoke softly to his captive and she spit at him and threatened to kill him. He slowly shook his head and then slapped her repeatedly. He spoke again, holding his hand on the side of her face and instead of replying, she tried to bite him. He slapped her again and then positioned himself behind her.

Terry Kingston had seen enough. He knew what was going to happen next and while he admired the woman for her spunk and tenacity, he knew it would be a mistake to interrupt now. The screams and curses were punctuated with the occasional sound of a blow and the grunts of pain and pleasure.

Terry sat back on a log, disgusted with himself for not taking action but counseling himself on patience. Lula had told him that many of the women had been through this sort of abuse at one point or another, usually just after they had arrived in "Woodytown." Most often, the women were already prostitutes, working in one of the major cities, when they were captured and brought to the jungle. It did not take long to determine that there was little chance to escape without help and the punishment for trying was public and brutal. It was not long before a woman lost hope in a place like this. The woman who had been brought here last was apparently an exception. She had actually been captured on the road in. The soldiers that had captured her assumed she was a whore being rescued by family or lover and had returned her to the compound. It was expected that she would be punished so they were not surprised when she was taken to one of the cabins and chained to the floor. As a reward the soldiers were allowed to gang rape her. Lula had not known of any men being brought in but it had happened fairly early and she had not witnessed their arrival. She had perked up her audience's ears when she mentioned that their truck was banged up.

The design of the saloon was such that it would be difficult to get back on the overhang so the foreign visitor was forced to wait until the festivities died down and everyone was either upstairs or elsewhere. It did not take long. He saw the rapist leave the cabin and head to a different one. The interior flared briefly and then went dark again.

The throbbing of the generator stopped and that was the signal for the night's activities to come to an end. Candlelight illuminated the stairs and shone out the window of the rest room briefly, then the whole place went dark. Without the moon, there would be no navigating this area at night, but there was just enough to show the way in. Terry slipped off his boots before he entered and made his way up the stairs to Lula's room as quietly as he could. It was not easy, as the interior of the saloon was dead black, but he managed to get there without stumbling over anything. Lula stirred as he slipped back into bed with her.

It took a while before the Australian fell asleep. He reflected on the nature of men and women and concluded that pimps were as necessary as whores or at least as unavoidable. He thought fondly about the first woman he had been with. She had been a whore too, paid for by Uncle Ginger in the red light district of Sydney. She may have been the first but she was far from the last.

Breakfast was no different from the day before as the supply truck had not arrived. Lula was in fine spirits, happier than anyone had seen her in a long time, though her visitor could not have known that. She had hope for a change and though it was tenuous and would likely vanish like a puff of smoke, it lit up her being and radiated from her smile.

Soldiers are not paid much in any country and the young, fresh ones are paid almost nothing, but they have few expenses and many are willing to hand over their meager pay for a night of drinking and wenching. The money Terry gave Lula should have covered him for a couple of days but in usual form, Arturo demanded more and without a standard of any kind, Terry handed over some more. Arturo was curious now as well. He wanted to know what sort of man he had staying upstairs who could afford this kind of rent. Lula had given him the money with the specific instructions that they were not to be disturbed. That was all right with him but he had noted the change in Lula as well, the man had changed something in her, made her skin glow and her eyes sparkle. He spoke with his compatriots about it and they agreed it was best to watch that sort of situation. There was no telling when a young man might fall in love with a whore and do something stupid.

Chapter Twelve
Bondage

The cell stank with mold, vomit and the putrid stink of a thousand prisoners. The jailers were less than enthusiastic about their charge and blamed him for existing and disrupting their world. They blamed him for not meekly accepting his fate. And they blamed him for the death of Sympatico.

The prisoner could not help the fact of his existence and the innate struggle for self preservation. Meekly accepting his fate, however, was not something this man was prepared to do. Sympatico was a swaggering, sadistic animal who opted for guard duty so he could exercise his will over other men with impunity.

A concrete block of a building, only one in a row of ten, it became unbearably hot in late afternoon and slowly leached its heat at night. Its purpose was to detain errant soldiers until they sobered up or went to trial. It was not for long-term storage of prisoners. Conditions in these cells were too brutal for extended stays.

The prisoner had arrived three weeks before, brought in injured, by a patrol. He was a huge bull of a man, muscular and ferocious looking. His hair and beard grew quick and wild, soon giving him the appearance of a pirate or a wild mountain man. Lieutenant Sympatico had thought he was an open target and had entered the cell to administer some of the justice he was so fond of. He had found to his eternal dismay that the man was not as debilitated as he had assumed. Instead of curling up in the corner and accepting the beating, the prisoner had taken the baton and crushed the soldier's wind pipe with it. Sympatico died gasping for air as the prisoner dashed for the fence line. The prisoner did not escape and the soldier did not survive. Now, charged with murder in a military brig, Gordon MacMaster awaited his fate.

Some prisoners prowled their cage like lions, some screamed and cried and others beat their fists against the walls. Gordon MacMaster knew the futility of all this bluster. It wasted energy and gave the guards pleasure. MacMaster sat cross-legged in the shade and conserved his strength, ignoring the horrendous itching from his clean but uncovered wound as it healed. He ignored the insects for the most part, unless they were large enough to eat, then he did so. His water came when it rained and then he stuck his cupped hand out to get what he could. Fortunately, it rained a great deal here. Unfortunately, the roof leaked so the inside of the cell was wet on the days it did not rain. MacMaster had not bathed since he first arrived so the smell of his body was beginning to overwhelm the stench of the cage.

As the sun came up this morning and burned the chill off the concrete, MacMaster reviewed his situation carefully, trying to find benefits and cracks. He decided his Portuguese was getting better and almost smiled at the thought. He decided he was losing weight but he had never been fat. His body had no excess reserves and was consuming muscle now. He decided that there was no possibility that the military tribunal that was scheduled to try him would vindicate his killing of one of their own. Nobody from the outside world knew he was there, so there would be no miraculous wave of media resentment or heavy handed action from the British consulate. If he did not escape soon, he would die in a Brazilian prison.

The door was unlocked for the first time in days and a guard entered leveling a pistol at his unmoving form. He was told not to move or he would be shot and a second guard entered behind the first with a bowl of biological material that was supposed to pass for food. None but a starving man could have choked it down, but Gordon MacMaster was indeed starving. He had been fed almost nothing for weeks.

If they decided to feed him, then the trial must be beginning soon.

With something in his stomach, it was easier to concentrate. Gordon thought of the woman he had been chasing, the one the soldiers had left at the Plaza de Putas. She had been an amazing specimen. He thought of the man who had deserted her to the fiery embrace of the burning car and the other who had taken them both from the police residence. Hope may spring eternal but he saw no hope coming from that quarter.

He reflected that it was a good thing he had kept in contact with Colonel Richter but that it was unlikely there would be any help coming from Germany and if there was, there was no way of letting anyone know where he was. Brazil is vast and one man is very small.

It was not until the next day that MacMaster was given access to a lawyer; a dapper military lawyer who kept urging him to plead guilty to a manslaughter charge and avoid the murder charge that was sure to follow if he did not. He assured his foreign client that there would be no longer a sentence than five years, but that the sentence for murder would be execution. Some men may have been swayed by this argument.

Days later, the lawyer returned. His client had been starved since he had been there last and the prospect of starving to death loomed over him. It was a more effective persuasion than the plea deal, but still the stubborn Scot would not crumble. The trial was set for a week away and once the date was set, they started feeding him once a day.

The guards had lost the cavalier attitude that had been their initial hallmark. Gordon was never allowed out of his cell without chains. The arraignment was nothing more than his plea of not guilty and he was returned to his cage. The trial was set for another week away.

It was plain to MacMaster that his lawyer was less than enthusiastic and would be ineffective. The self-defense plea would have held water in some places, but not here. The prospect of a firing squad became very real and immediate. There was no 10 years of appeals and judicial wrangling the way there might be in a more "civilized" country. This was a military trial and the defendant faced military justice. In some ways, it may have been a blessing that he had been detained by the military. The civilian prisons were the worst kind of corrupt, overcrowded stink holes imaginable. Here he had a cell, foul as it was, to himself.

Breakfast on the third day was better. A chicken farmer had donated some eggs in a reciprocal agreement and the supply truck came in as well. No soldiers showed up in the morning. When Terry asked about it, Lula told him that it was officers day. The enlisted men would not be coming around today. She also told him, with genuine sadness, that she might be needed later. There was a certain Colonel that found her favors irresistible and insisted she join him when he visited. She hit upon the idea that she could pretend to be ill and avoid having to serve him, but she explained that Arturo knew all the women's cycles and he would undoubtedly beat her after Terry left if she faked it.

More than whom they were, Terry was more interested in finding out how they arrived. The jeep-like vehicles employed by the army were much more appropriate for navigating the jungle trails that passed for roads in so much of this country. Juan had come close to bogging his taxi down repeatedly.

Juan and his friend arrived this morning in the tow truck. It was good cover since a breakdown could occur anywhere. They were told that there was nothing broken down here, but if they wanted to tow the junk car from behind one of the cabins, they could buy it for a little bit.

"Juan. I have been waiting for you. Manuel, you brought the tow truck?"

"Señor, I hope you do not mind, it was a long and dusty trip so we thought it might be acceptable to have a beer."

"Of course, it's on me." Terry winced inside at the "dusty" comment since it was raining outside but went with the flow.

"Your vehicle is ready at the garage. We replaced the radiator and the bearing assembly on the passenger side. She will ride as good as new."

"Thank you, Juan. Finish your beer and we will go."

Arturo took his opportunity to get a good look at the man who had been sequestered with Lula. He was not sure he bought the broken down vehicle story, but it did explain some of the episode. While the two newcomers were having a beer, Arturo tried to engage his mysterious guest in conversation, but the man's answers were short and to the point. He was sure to invite them to return soon, as the trio left the building.

As soon as the stranger had left, Arturo paid a visit to Lula. She was very lucky that it was officers day and equally lucky that the Colonel was coming in that day. As a prostitute, it was necessary for Lula to be an actress as well, but Arturo had seen better actresses and believed nothing his women said anyway.

Outside of town, the driver stopped the truck in the middle of the track and announced that the information they had was worth a lot of money. A bit of wrangling over the price ensued. The information was indeed worthy of the price. The location of the emergency repair on the wrecked transport had been found. What's more, the location of the prisoner they had returned to camp with. There was no mention of the woman but the pieces of the puzzle were coming together.

MacMaster was not surprised when the shackles were removed, just outside the room that was to be his courthouse. It was nothing more than an office in a long row of offices set up like a motel, but without the swimming pool and ice machine.

The showers were cold and the soap was harsh but he was given clean clothing and his boots were returned to him, if only temporarily. The military had found it to be quite a deterrent to would-be escapees to be without shoes.

If there was ever an opportunity it was now, but he was feeling so debilitated from exposure and hunger that he doubted he could manage to hit hard enough. Three officers sat across the table from him and two guards were directly behind him. All five wore side arms. He saw it would be impossible to make a stand without making a lot of noise.

The trial was quick and decisive. The prosecutor and the natty defense attorney presented their cases and court was adjourned for the judges to consider their decision. It was obviously not so much a question of the verdict, as a deliberation over the sentence.

The restraints were clamped on the defendant's wrists and ankles and he was led back to his cell.

Roberto Campena de Iguaca sat at a table in the seedy little cantina and drank stiff liquor. He was unaccustomed to the alcohol and did not use it for recreation but for its numbing effect. The hospital staff had been required to shave part of his head so they could stitch the wound in his scalp. Roberto had shaved the rest of the hair off himself. The cast on his hand made his skin crawl but the pain killers and alcohol kept the ache to a minimum. Dom Bravuria had furnished him with a place to sleep while he was in town.

The ladies of the night tended to frequent the more upscale hotels. The streetwalkers had their own district where they plied their trade and few of them ventured this way. That was one of the reasons Roberto was here. He liked women but had never respected them. He saw them all as whores, a feeling that had followed him since early childhood in the favelas of Rio.

At this point in his life, women were not on Roberto's menu. He was more interested in killing Perfecta Navaja, no matter what she was calling herself today, than he was in bedding anyone. She had humiliated him, had bested him in combat, broke his bones and split his skull and she would die for it. He only needed a little more recuperation time and he would go after her.

Roberto was getting drunk and nursing his bruised ego, not paying much attention to what was going on around him. He had seen the two men at the bar but had not noticed the looks they had given him. He did not realize what a target he made of himself; with his head stitched together and the cast on his hand, he looked like a mugger's dream, easy pickings.

The sun went down and the crippled criminal rose to leave. He was unsteady on his feet and shuffled as he walked. The two men who followed him out of the bar had no idea who they were after. In their eyes he was merely an easy target. They walked up behind him and he turned slightly, just enough to see who it was on his tail. The lead man reached for his intended victim's right shoulder but came away with a handful of loose fabric as the man turned to the left. A cast can be an effective weapon when there are no broken bones beneath it, but Roberto's hand was still in bad shape. What the man behind him could not have known was that Roberto had fastened a brace around his wrist and was carrying a bayonet strapped to his forearm. It was the old-style spike with a barrel ring on it. When he left the cantina, the spike had been slid forward and the ring was locked down.

The lead man of the pair coughed slightly as the spike slid into his left lung. Then he made wheezing, gurgling sounds as he tried to take a breath. The spike was dragged down as the man dropped to his knees. Behind him, his partner did not know what had just happened. He saw the other man drop, saw the barrel of the pistol in Roberto's left hand and opened his mouth to say something, he wasn't sure what. Whatever it was he was about to say never came out, as the first round crashed through his teeth and spine.

Roberto shook his head, wiped his blade on the mugger's clothing and then shot each in the head, once. Muttering about sloppy and incompetent criminals, he walked quickly down the street. It may be just as well that this had happened; now he would need to leave town, now he would need to go back to the forest and find that woman and kill her.

There were no automobiles in this section of town, the streets were too narrow and convoluted. The police would show up at the scene of the attack but not until morning.

A few blocks away a man was unlocking his motorcycle from where he had chained it to a pole. Roberto slipped up behind him and drove his spike into the base of the man's skull. He caught the helmet and put it on as the man fell to the cobblestones.

It was very difficult to control the motorcycle with the cast on one hand and the uneven surface of the road, but before long he was out on the flat blacktop. He had not wanted to leave quite so abruptly but his hand had been forced. He did not stop until his physical condition forced him to pull over to the side of the road. With the motorcycle hidden in a thicket, Roberto Campena de Iguaca lay on the ground next to it and passed out. He was full of pain killers and alcohol so he slept like a dead man.

There was a hundred yards of gravel and rubble between the tree line and the wire fence that surrounded the army depot. Bushes and grasses grew from between the boulders and were constantly battled against by the younger troops. The concrete base of the wire fence was patrolled all day and all night by young soldiers, both vigorous and bored. Most of them could not lend credence to the fact that a military encampment on friendly soil needs to be patrolled. Their reasoning was standard in 'nobody who does not belong there has any reason to try to get in.' Their typical attitude proved how quickly people forget the past and how it repeats itself to those who do forget. In March of 2006, the Army was forced to invade the favelas of Rio to recover 10 assault rifles stolen from an army base by drug dealers. The rifles were never found, and some say they did not exist but were used as a ploy to invade civilian areas. Nevertheless, guards were punished in the incident, and civilians died.

Terry Kingston knew nothing about the history of the Brazilian Army and did not think he needed to. He was light-loaded that day and needed no extra baggage. He carried weapons, some granola and jerky, a good pair of wire cutters, a wad of money, a cell phone and a pack of cigarettes. A pack of matches completed his inventory and caused him to curse the fact that he wanted a cigarette. If he had no means of making fire he could forgive himself for wanting one and not being able to have one.

Terry sat quietly, almost sedately, in the underbrush outside the rubble field. His collar was cinched tightly around his throat to keep the biting insects from drawing his blood. His wide floppy hat was adorned with local weeds and grass. When he was not watching the guards he could almost have been asleep but he was practicing keeping his other senses alive. Too often men become so visiocentric that their other senses dull and atrophy. Terry was listening to the trees growing, the insects buzzing, the wind travelling and the monkeys howling in their arboreal homes. He watched toads making their laborious way across the forest floor in search of grubs and beetles, and snakes slithering after them. He smelled the smoke and the diesel fumes of the base intermingled with the eternal rot of the humus.

The day was overcast and smelled of impending rain. A crew of soldiers was clearing the tenacious trees and bushes that sprang from the rubble field on the other side of the base. He had seen them earlier, though they had not seen him. Non-commissioned officers were evident from time to time, checking on the activities of their subordinates. A huge kettle of water was boiling to wash clothing in and the latrine detail was beginning to burn the cut-down barrels full of human effluent. Such unsavory practices were undertaken on Officers' Day, when the upper echelon was enjoying its respite.

The guards were seamless in their back and forth plodding. While the sun was up and the rain withheld its sodden glory, they performed like a machine. It remained to be seen how well they performed after dark, when scourged by the weather that gives the rain forest its name.

Roberto had waited an hour for someone to come along that was delivering to the base. He stepped into the road that served as an extended driveway and told the driver that he would help unload the truck if he could get a ride. Naturally the driver was suspicious and wanted to know why the man wanted a ride into an army base if he was not a soldier. Roberto showed him a plastic bag of candies and spices. He explained that the cook wanted to use spices that the army would not provide and that he had a sweet tooth but the canteen had no sweets. Then the driver noticed the cast on Roberto's hand. "How can you help me unload these chicken crates and reload the truck with the empties from last week with only one hand?"

"Oh, I have a tool I use. See?" Roberto pulled out his pistol and pointed it between the driver's eyes.

"I see. Yes, you will be of great help, Señor."

In the passenger side of the truck Roberto entered the compound, and with spices and sweets he weaseled his way into the confidence of the cook, though never letting the chicken rancher out of his sight.

"Stranger, I do not think so. The army, well, our former Major, had some buildings built on the other side of the main road. It is a source of relaxation for the men and if you are seeking a woman, then that is where you should be going. They call it Woodytown."

"I seek a particular woman. She is tall and thin with a good chest. Brown hair, long. Her face is beautiful, even without makeup and she was with a big man with red hair."

"Ai. The man, he is here. He has been convicted of murdering a man, Sympatico, and they will probably give him his last meal in a couple of days. That is what I hear. But there is no woman here, and there was no woman with him when he was brought in. If he had kept his temper, he would have been released with a little, um, donation, but he insisted on killing Sympatico."

The truck was unloaded and empty cages were going back in place. The Brazilian gangster eyed the cement block cells, wishing he could have a few minutes alone with his foreign adversary. He would be glad to save the army the price of a few bullets and do the job himself. The simple act of killing no longer gave him the pleasure it once had, he needed to make each murder unique for it to even become memorable, but this one he would have savored. The big red head had been stuck out where it did not belong.

Roberto Campena de Iguaca smelled blood and he had a taste for it but would need to leave the table without sampling this vintage.

Sitting in the underbrush and watching the unending waltz of the guard patrol was no stimulating experience. The guard was changed every four hours and that provided the only lapse in their antlike movement. Even after the sun went down, the rain blustered in and the lights came on, the guards marched back and forth unhampered in their clockworks. They met every five minutes in the center of the fence and five minutes later at the corner of the fence. That left a couple of minutes as they walked away from each other, that a quiet man could get through the fence and possibly six more before any hole in the wire was detected. The razor wire on top of the fence was a deterrent to attempting to scale it.

Terry Kingston was an artist in farm and field, but even he could not move about at night in those forests. The rain kept the insects down, a small blessing, and it was not a cold rain.

Morning came without sleep and the watcher moved about the perimeter of the base, upset that he left footprints in the mud but acknowledging that there was no other way. He pinpointed the row of cells with a grimace. They looked like torture devices in themselves. Through the lens of the scope, Terry saw that there was only one cell whose door was closed. The rest stood open. A less-than-enthusiastic-looking man walked back and forth in the mud, guarding the one man in the one cell. Terry watched that one spot for hours, unmoving. Nothing happened. There was a prisoner but it was impossible to tell who.

The diesel generator was easier to get a fix on. It sat in one corner of the base, waiting for the frequent power failures to come. It had an electric start, with a bank of six batteries hooked to a main lead. The lead could not be cut by anything short of a full-sized bolt cutter, but the individual leads were not so sturdy. Terry took his cell phone out of its plastic bag and looked longingly at the cigarettes and matches that shared the bag with it.

"Well, MacMaster, ye've made a shite of it this time. A bloody firing squad in Brazil of all places. Well, it had to end sometime.

"Oy, that's a different guard today. Let's try it again."

The Scot's Portuguese was good enough by now that he could communicate properly. It was by no means flawless but it was understandable.

"Soldier," he said, "your partners were too stupid to take advantage of a situation that presents itself. I can make you very rich if you can help me get out of this cell. Money greases the wheels everywhere and Brazil is no exception."

The young man who had pulled the guard duty this morning did not turn around but he did reply. "How are you going to do this for me?"

MacMaster's spirits rose a little. The guards who had been assigned to this detail had been, not incorruptible, but too aware of the spotlights shine to succumb to Gordon's wiles. This young man seemed to be less concerned with the consequences or less aware of the focus.

"My friend, I can get you out of this country with half a million dollars in your pocket if we can put a little distance between this base and ourselves."

"I think you lie. I think you are trying to make a fool of me and will kill me as soon as you get the chance."

"No, no. I have the money in a Swiss bank account. All I need you to do is bring a cell phone. You will put in the number for the bank and I will put in the reference number. This will put us in contact with a bank officer and you can check the balance on the account. I can make you a very rich man. I know they do not pay you enough here. I know that an obviously intelligent man, such as yourself, should be making a life for himself in a place like Texas where money flows like water."

"This is impossible. I cannot bring you a cell phone in full view of every one. I will not do it."

"No, not during the day. There is five hours time difference between there and here. If you call at five in the morning it is ten in the morning there. The banks open at eight. If I have a cell phone at three, or four is even better, I can contact the bank when it is open and you can get the balance checked. This will show you that I have the money. Get me out of here and the money is yours. It does a dead man no good, so I am willing to part with it. You can spend your life in this miserable mud pit or you can live like a king in America."

"How will you get me to America? I do not believe you."

The bait had been taken and it was time to set the hook.

"I know a man in immigration. For $10,000, he will get you a green card and you can stay in America for as long as you want. Half a million will set you up in business and you will be able to live the life of a king. Or, you can stand there in the mud like a duck and, for the rest of your life, curse yourself for being a fool."

"Why have you offered this to me and not the men who usually stand guard?"

"I did. I told them what I have told you. I offered to make them rich men but they were too stupid to take the opportunity before them. You are not that stupid." He phrased it as a statement, not a question. He wanted it to sound as if the deal was a plan in operation. He was not pleading with this man, he was dealing with him.

"I will speak to the Duty Sergeant. I can probably get night detail but not today. They are going to shoot you in a week."

"My sentence hasn't been handed down."

"Boris Chercovski, they will shoot you in a week."

"Oh. We must move quickly then. I will prove to you that I have the money and as soon as I am away from this dump I will transfer it to your account or whatever account you choose."

"I will think about this. I will probably not accept your offer, it sounds too good to be true, so it is. There may be something we can do, however, to keep you alive and make me rich."

The hook had been set, now the Scottish mercenary needed to play his fish. The line was light, but despite the man's words, he was hooked deeply.

That day lasted longer than most but Gordon spent the day productively whispering in his guard's ear. He provided information both real and fabricated to convince the Brazilian of that his intentions were honorable and that his wealth was real. He also found out that the guard's name was Andreas Castro. He had spent the past few days going over the plan in his head and repeating the details to himself. He thought of every possible argument that could be presented and fabricated counter-arguments. He knew the new guard was interested because he continued to listen. The guards on the job previously had told him to shut up as soon as he had begun speaking, but this one was different. Once he learned the man's name, there was more of a bond immediately.

It rained all that night and all the next day. The rain was the prisoner's ally that day in that his guard was forced to stand in it wearing a plastic poncho over his uniform. He had not brought the cell phone that day but he had brought an attitude with him that was workable like putty. By the end of his duty that day, there would be no turning back.

It was the following day the guard brought the cell phone. He walked into the cell before the sun rose, relieving the night guard half an hour early. The tired young man had been standing there all night and was glad to take the opportunity.

Inside the cell, the numbers were entered and once the guard had determined that he was indeed speaking with a Swiss banker, there was a bit of a delay. The banker needed to find someone who spoke Portuguese. Gordon offered to speak to him in German but Andreas would have none of it. It did not take long before a competent interpreter was arranged and the Brazilian was convinced that there was a substantial sum of money in the account. The euro was worth about a dollar and a half at that point, so the 350,000 euros would actually work out to more than the 500,000 dollars the Scot had promised.

The next move was predictable. Andreas backed out of the cell and redialed the number, including the code and attempted to transfer the money into his account. At most banks this would have been sufficient information to conduct the transfer, but not at this one and certainly not for this account. It had been specifically arranged as such. There were security questions that needed to be answered.

"That is why I had it arranged that way, my friend. If I die in captivity, that account goes to charity. I won't need it. I'll be dead."

"So, how are we supposed to make this transaction? How are you going to convince me that you are not trying to play me?"

"I am trying to play you, Andreas. I need you to get me out of here. Then, I am your prisoner and I will have no choice but to make you a rich man. I have no doubt that you will accompany me to the United States where we can both live in luxury. All the fine cars and hot women you can handle."

At eight o'clock that morning, Gordon was taken to the shower and cleaned up. This was only done on days he was to appear in court, so he assumed his sentence had been handed down, and he was not disappointed. He was to face the firing squad in a week.

"There you are, you big, cheeky bastard. I hope you're ready to run, mate. This is not going to be easy." Terry was gratified that sitting through the days of surveillance had finally paid off. He assessed MacMaster's physical condition as adequate, but it was obvious he had lost some weight.

"Looks like the showers. Good thing, I don't need you stinking the joint up."

MacMaster was shackled as he moved about, but Terry had seen them carry the shackles into the cell, so he was not bound while inside. Outside of the showers, the guards moved their prisoner into a different building that had no visible designation. Terry had no way of knowing his friend and mentor, under the name Boris Chercovski, had just been sentenced to death.

Out at the road, Terry called Juan and told him there was work to be done and to pick him up. There was no discussion about it. The way Terry paid his compatriots ensured their immediate compliance.

On the way back to town, Terry smoked until he got dizzy.

Chapter Thirteen
The Cup is Half Empty

The hotel welcomed its newest guest and honored the 'do not disturb' sign on the door. He had come in looking like he had not slept in a week. It had been no week but long enough to feel like it. He showered, slept 12 hours and then showered again. A plate of restaurant food and two beers and he was ready to get to work. The sun was rising when he called his taxi. Juan was officially off duty, but for Terry his cab was never off limits.

"Juan, why is security so tight at this camp?"

"What do you mean, sir?"

"There are guards walking up and down outside the fence. That happens when a country is at war but not otherwise. What are they hiding in there?"

"Young men need to keep busy or they get in trouble."

"This is more than that."

"I don't know, sir."

"OK. We have another hour. Manuel will perform his part?"

"You don't need to worry about Manuel. He is excited about it all."

"OK. Get me as close to the gate as you can, but they cannot see me."

Terry was having some serious second thoughts about this whole affair. Killing people was one thing, trying to rescue them from a guarded military installation was another entirely.

The circumlocution of the compound took half the day, slipping quietly through the undergrowth and pausing frequently. Terry was in no hurry. He had all day.

Once he was in position, he sat perfectly still and meditated. He thought about all the people he had known in his life, all the places he had been. He thought through the plan he had in place. His final conclusion was that it was much too dangerous to do as a freebie and nobody else would ever get this much of a favor. In fact, if Gordon MacMaster needed this kind of help again, assuming they made it out of this one alive, he would need to look elsewhere. It was way too dangerous.

The blackout came at 10 o'clock in the evening. Right on time. Before the lights went on again, the sound of gunfire blossomed near the main gate. The alarm went off and most men either hid or moved toward the sound of the guns. The guards on the fence were no exception.

Kingston had no way of knowing what the protocol was for the guards in case of an attack, but they moved predictably, regardless of what they were supposed to be doing. They moved away from the back corner, where the generator was. It only took Terry a couple of minutes to get through the fence. The man in charge of the generator had not yet reached his huge diesel charge. Terry yanked out a nine-inch tanto blade and pierced the oil filter for the generator then ripped it in half with a twist. He was dressed in black and the blackness around him was complete until the headlights of some jeeps began to impale the darkness. He had swapped out his usual boots for leather moccasins so he could move quietly.

By the time the soldier got the generator going, Terry was in the man's workshop.

The lights went out again as soon as the generator man saw the oil drenching the surrounding area. He cursed loudly and headed toward his workshop. In the workshop, instead of an oil filter and a gallon of oil he found an Australian and a stun gun. There was no struggle, the surprise was too complete. The man went down in a crumpled heap and was stripped, bound and gagged in no time flat.

Wearing his latest victim's clothes and working in semi-darkness, Terry sidled up the front of the cell block. He had counted on the guard remaining at his post for the plan to work. He wanted to access the cell quietly and lock the man in it afterward, but the guard was not there.

"MacMaster," he hissed once, then louder. There was no response. Scenarios flashed through his mind like a high-speed train. Had MacMaster been executed? Was he asleep? Had he been moved to a different cell? Had he been transferred to a different base? Had he been handed over to the civilian authorities? Had he escaped?

"Mack, it's time to go." Still nothing. Ignoring his inhibitions, Terry thrust the stun gun through the bars of the door and pushed the trigger. In the crackling light of the electric charge, Terry saw that the cell was empty. There was nothing more he could do. He stood perplexed for a moment, then accepted the fact that he had failed, and moved on.

The front gate was open and teams of men in jeeps were heading out, down the driveway and around the perimeter fence.

"Oye, Sandiana, you are ready to begin your new life, yes?"

"Yes, Arturo, I will do anything you say." Anastasia mumbled through swollen lips. She had spent what seemed like an eternity chained to the floor of the little bungalow, abused and raped every day. She knew she was not the first woman to have been chained to this floor, but it did not lessen the humiliation. At first she had thought she could trick one of the men into freeing her hands, but they were too well versed in feminine wiles to be tricked. They were brutal, but they were careful as well. They were not particularly sadistic, but they also had no empathy for the women.

Three days ago, Anastasia had stopped resisting. She had tried to trick the men, overwhelm them, fight them and beg them. Nothing had gotten her anywhere. Now, when the men visited her she lay on the floor and whimpered. When they told her to get on her knees, she did so. When they told her to open her mouth, she did so. When they told her to spread her legs, she did so. She was starving and beaten and had no more will to resist.

Arturo had seen broken women before. He had broken them like animals, removing their will to resist. This one, this Sandiana Torremolinos, had resisted longer than most, but the end result was the same, it was inevitable. He knew that once she healed a little and got a little food in her that she would probably need to be returned to the shack for a while to remind her that she was not special and that he controlled every aspect of her life. He considered freeing her that day but decided against it. He raped her and slapped her repeatedly but she offered no resistance, now. He forced her to say, repeatedly that she was nothing but a whore and all she was good for was fucking and sucking; that all she had of any value was her cunt, her ass and her mouth. In a couple of days he would let her shower, eat, and sleep in a real bed. For tonight she would stay where she was. He pissed on her before snuffing the candle and locking the door.

Darkness enveloped her and for the first time since she could remember, Anastasia Viuda curled into a ball and cried like a baby. She had taken all she could take. The debilitation and humiliation had taken their toll and she finally crumbled. This proud, efficient killer had been reduced to a wet quivering jelly who cried herself to sleep. Then the dreams came.

All people dream but Anastasia could never remember her dreams. She would remember these dreams. She would remember them for the rest of her life.

The matron was speaking, not the Argentine dialect, but something more northern, like Columbian. She was slapping Anastasia but there was nothing the victim could do; she was only about three years old.

"Pay attention, you stupid little shit." The matron was yelling. "This is the most important part of your entire useless life. No, you will not cry. You will never cry. You must never cry. You are to be hard like the stones of the mountain."

The scene moved back, away from her and Anastasia could see herself sitting in a chair that was too big for her... no, she was tied to the chair. The matron was smoothing her apron and wiping sweat from her brow on a hand towel. Anastasia saw herself sitting bolt upright and she was not crying. The welts on her cheeks from the matron's hands were bright and angry, almost as angry as the child's eyes.

A man entered the room in a surgeon's gown. His face was bare and his head shaved, even his eyebrows had been removed. The matron turned to him and said, "This will be the one."

The man looked over the bound child and licked his lips. "Prepare her," he said.

The scene changed and she was still bound, but this time to a table, an operating table. Her head was as bald as the man's; shaved. Another man entered. He was wearing a surgical gown as well but his face was covered with a white cotton mask and his eyes glittered from below a surgical cap. He took an anesthetic face mask from a hook and connected it to a tube. He turned the valve on a tank and then placed the mask over the frightened little girl's face. "Don't worry," he said, "this won't hurt."

Anastasia awoke gasping for breath. This had seemed so real. She could feel herself there, with those men, with her head shaved and her arms and legs tied to that table. Where was that? Why was she there? What had happened and why did she not remember any of that, until now?

She sat and caught her breath, shaking. This was not a dream; this was a memory. Something had happened those many years ago and she did not know what. The scenes in her mind brought on panic, but she was chained and shackled and her thrashing only served to tear the flesh on her already raw wrists and ankles.

It was hours in the darkness before the prisoner fell back into sleep. While awake, she remembered the two dream sequences vividly as if they had just happened, but had never seen them before in her memories or her dreams. They were real and frightening. Anastasia Viuda screamed inside and struggled outside, but got nowhere. Eventually she collapsed in a heap and began to cry again. As she cried, a piece of her mind, a dispassionate, analytic crevasse in her mind's polar region whispered to her, "You must never cry." She burst forth in an inhuman wail and her eyes poured out her grief on the floor.

Chapter Fourteen
Marco Polo

"Brock, it's Cook, I got something for you you're not gonna believe."

"Kevin Cook! How the hell are you?"

"I'm doing fine, Brock, how are you?"

"Fantastic. What can I do for you?"

"I got evidence on that triple homicide last year. You remember? You chased the perp to Michigan and lost him in the Flint area."

"I remember. What did you get?"

"Well, you remember the plumber?"

"No."

"Oh, well there was a man with a motive, uh, Roger Porter. He owns a heating and cooling business in Cleveland. His daughter was raped by the vic. They pressed charges but nothing came of it. We thought he had good reason to want one of the victims dead, but he had an alibi."

"Yeah, I remember now."

"Well, this mook fucked up on his taxes. He claimed a large deduction for business expenses that he delivered no receipts for. I think it was money paid for the hit on Willy Brown. Obviously, the IRS wanted to jump into him. I have the luck of thinking about the move first and asking for a red flag to be sent to me before anything was done."

"Interesting. I didn't think you could do that at the city level."

"I can't. I told them you wanted it done."

A palpable silence gripped the connection as Brock digested this misuse of his name.

"Do you wanna piece of this one, Special Agent Dakota? After all, he dragged you into Flint, Michigan in the winter. The least you could do would be to thank him with a long stretch in Lucasville."

"I can be in Cleveland in 15 hours, give or take a couple hours. Arrange a hotel for me and get the package together. If it's worth anything, I'll get on it. Until then, perhaps we should bring this Roger guy in and squeeze him."

"You know it won't stand up in court. The tax charge isn't shit. If I bring him in he'll lawyer up and I won't get shit. Better we do it subtly. I've got a plan."

"If I'm coming to Cleveland, you'd better have something for me."

"I'll have it. It's already in the works. I'll call you back when it's solid."

It had not been easy for Catherine to get close to Priscilla Porter. The rape and the scars on her face had made the girl reclusive and self-conscious. She had been the butt of jokes in high school and had not even attended her own graduation. Catherine worked hard to get close to her, however and it had worked.

Catherine wanted to do what her mother, Phoebe, did. She wanted to be a crime scene investigator. Phoebe had pushed her to get close to Priscilla, without telling her why, but Catherine was canny enough to know what it was her mother wanted.

Desperate to give his daughter an ordinary life, Roger Porter was saving money for cosmetic surgery. He had spent all his savings on the darker edge of retribution and had nothing to spare. In the long run he would recoup his losses, but for now he was deeply in debt and struggling. This had caused him to make a mistake.

Priscilla had a hard time trusting people. It was not that she had ever trusted Willie Brown, she didn't even know him. She had been with a friend of hers and had stayed when she should have gone. The event had scarred her much more than physically; it had destroyed her belief in the goodness of mankind. Her inherent distrust included women as well as men, and her initial reaction to Catherine's overtures of friendship had been to reject them. She still had the feeling that she would betray her.

Priscilla had graduated high school and had needed a job, since her high school experience had been so bad that she refused to register for college. Phoebe knew a lot of people in Cleveland and worked her network to get Catherine and Priscilla jobs in the Police Department Dispatch Office. They worked nights as Cathy was attending classes at the local Community College. They both lived with their single parents, though they made no attempt to get the two together. Phoebe had divorced her husband and Roger's wife had died.

Priscilla had played around with drugs when she was younger, but that had gone by the way after her ordeal. She did not trust herself to lose control, especially around men. It was different with Catherine, however. The two of them began to spend time together, alone. Both their parents worked days, primarily and they took to going to one house or the other after work and drinking. One day, right after Phoebe had left for work, her daughter showed her friend the ecstasy. Phoebe had supposedly brought it home and stashed it in her bedroom closet. A tab of this and a few shots of liquor brought the two so close that they were in bed together before either of them knew it.

It was wonderful for them both. It was not like either of them were virgins, but neither had been with a woman before. They had not expected this to happen, they had not wanted this to happen but once it had, there was no turning back. It changed the dynamic for Priscilla; her feelings were much stronger and her opinion of their relationship was

260

skewed. After that, she did not want to let Catherine out of her sight. She did not want to let her go to classes and did not want her to go to the store alone. Miss Porter began showing up in the school cafeteria and the library, monopolizing her new lover's time or spying on her. It was not long before the suggestion was made that they move into an apartment together.

"Cat?"

"Yes, Pussycat?"

"I love you."

"Oh, Priscilla, what we have is very special but I don't know if I'm ready to commit myself completely."

"What are you talking about? Why?"

"I just get the feeling you're keeping secrets from me. There are things you won't share and it makes me feel left out."

"Cat, I love you. I'll tell you anything you want to know."

That was the beginning of it. Priscilla Porter was so desperate to hang on to her love she might have invented things to tell her. As it was, the only thing Catherine was interested in was the details of the murder of Willie Brown. If the truth be told, the death of Willie and his two thugs was very low on the list of judicial priorities. If they had not suspected the same man in the assault on the UAW president in Michigan, there would have been little follow through and without a little leverage, there couldn't be. Catherine provided the leverage.

"Mr. Porter, we've asked you here to clarify some things we are a little fuzzy on. My name is Kevin Cook, Captain Kevin Cook, and this is Special Agent Brock Dakota of the Homeland Security Agency."

Roger Porter looked more than a little concerned when he asked, "Am I being arrested? Should I have a lawyer? Don't I have the right to a lawyer?"

Kevin forced a smile and said, "You always have the right to a lawyer if you get arrested, but we have not arrested you yet and we might not if you cooperate with us." It was a lie but he thought it was an artful one.

"What is it you need from me?"

Brock stepped in, looking every bit the federal agent. "Take a look at this copy of a document you filed with the Internal Revenue Service and then compare it to this one, from said agency affirming that there were no receipts filed with the return for this money."

"So what, I forgot to file the receipts for expenses. What's the big deal?" The relief was evident on the contractor's face.

"It may not be an issue, that is, it may not have been an issue until we got this. Tell me if you recognize the voice on this tape."

The camera was rolling and every word being said was recorded, Roger should have known that. When Kevin pushed the button on the tape recorder and Priscilla's voice came from the speaker, the true nature of the interview was revealed.

"I saw him come to the door like some kind of Jimmy Cagney figure, y'know with a black hat and a trench coat. We get people coming to the house but this guy was different. He pulled down the street a little and smoked a cigarette while he watched the whole neighborhood first, like he was lookin' for something or someone. He got out of the car and he had a vest underneath the trench coat. Very geeky, y'know, insulated, like they wore years ago. Anyway, he caught my eye 'cause he was blond and handsome with a real good tan in the winter. Not, like, one of those fake tans but a real one, kind of like a permanent one. If I was still into men, I would've done 'im."

A patch of static covered the next couple of seconds of tape where someone else's voice had been covered up.

Roger's face turned purple with emotions yet un-cataloged and he reached for the tape recorder to turn it off. Dakota did not allow it, gripping the man's wrist with a fierceness. The tape rolled on.

"A foreign car, kind of an off white. Anyway he came to the door an' Dad let 'im in, so I went to the vent to listen."

Again the patch of static broke the monologue.

"Yes," Priscilla's voice continued, "you know, that heat vent in the bedroom I keep covered when I want to sleep an' the television's on."

At this point, the full implication of what he was hearing poured on Roger's head like boiling oil over a castle wall. His legs began to twitch under the table

"The guy had a funny accent, like English but not. Maybe New Zealand or Australia. Anyway, he says 'turn on the telly.' So Dad does and they listen to the news for a minute. Then Dad comes upstairs and gets something from his bedroom. When he goes downstairs, it wasn't so easy to hear but I know I heard, 'If you try to cheat me, I'll kill you too.'"

Dakota turned off the tape recorder and eyed Roger Porter who was looking like he had just been sentenced to death.

"So, Mr. Porter, is there anything you'd like to tell us?"

"I… uh… I'd like to, uh…"

"Would you like a cup of coffee?" Kevin asked.

"Yes, very much."

"I'll get a cup of coffee. You give your statement to Agent Dakota." Kevin left the interrogation room but went no further than the one-way glass outside.

"Shouldn't I have a lawyer?" Roger asked.

"We haven't arrested you, yet."

"I just don't know…"

"Oh, you know! We have you, if we want you. Conspiracy to commit murder. You'll get 20 years to life for this. If we want to charge you, you'll go away for a long time. However, if you cooperate, we might be able to offer you a deal. If you call a lawyer, we'll be forced to charge you and I won't guarantee you anything at that point."

"But, they'll kill me. If I talk, I'm a dead man."

"We can offer you some protection. The truth is we don't want you. We know you're guilty and we can run you through the system and get you sent away, but it's a waste of our time and a waste of your life. We know why you did what you did and while we will never be able to justify it, we can give you a chance to make it right. If you force our hand, I will personally make sure you spend at least the next couple of years in jail, before you even get to trial. Do you know how much power we have?"

"You mean Homeland Security?"

"Yes."

"But, I'm not a terrorist. I'm a tax paying citizen. I'm not…"

Brock cut him off with a hand gesture, a kind of non-contacting backhand. "I already know what you are. You are a man who takes the law into his own hands. You cheat on your taxes and you have people killed."

"I… but I…"

"Don't talk, listen. Give me his name and the names of the contacts you used to find this man. Give us names and dates and we can work on getting you out of this. Think about what's going to happen to your daughter while you are in prison. Think about what Willie Brown's friends are going to do to you while you are in prison, and what his friends on the outside will do to her."

That was the last straw. Roger Porter began spilling like a broken fountain, telling everything he knew, everyone he had spoken to regarding this matter. He was no lawyer and did not know that his coerced testimony would be inadmissible in court. He promised to appear and testify against any and all men involved this affair.

Outside the mirrored glass, Kevin Cook grinned like a jackal. The rest of the department, including his superiors, had written the killing off as good riddance to bad garbage, but Kevin saw the larger implications. He saw the promise of a much better job with Homeland Security, and he had promised Phoebe that she and her daughter would be coming with him. Of course there was no guarantee that any of this would happen, but it looked more and more likely as time went by.

The Woodsman was almost empty this evening. The weather was bad and many of the regulars had stayed home. Brock and Kevin were there, Quincy and Grady were shooting pool and Judge Apolitano drank at the bar.

"So, did we get enough?"

"We got something, but it didn't do that much for us. I already knew most of it, though I had no confirmation. Did the tapes of the first part of our little interview get destroyed?"

"Yes, I took them myself."

"Good. I want a copy of his confession and I need to be kept in the loop on this. I have a couple of other irons in the fire."

"I'll get us some more drinks."

Kevin did his best to get Brock drunk before he broached the subject again. It was not that he was not drunk himself by that time, but he had a feeling that the HS man was holding something back. When the subject was addressed again, Captain Cook did so by lauding his own efforts in getting the confession from Roger Porter. He bragged about how he manipulated Phoebe to get her daughter in tight with Priscilla. He mentioned the fact that there needed to be some form of reciprocity. He did not remind Brock of his earlier promise, or say that he expected the three conspirators to have jobs with Homeland Security, but subtle hints were dropped in that direction. He may have been drunk but Cook functioned well enough in a state of inebriation that he would remember every word spoken.

"Hah, you think you're so good, why didn't you tell me the perp's car had a leaking transmission?"

Cook did not know how to respond.

"You see, if you want to be good, you need to pay attention to every aspect of the crime."

"I did know that, actually. The used car salesman told us it had been leaking but this guy, this O'mara, wouldn't buy it until the transmission was fixed."

Brock looked at his compatriot out of one eye, his head making little circles over his neck. "Everything is important, didn't they teach you that?"

"Sure, but what difference does it make that his transmission leaked. How did that help us?"

"Pay attention. I got to thinking about it and went back to the impound lot, pulled the dipstick. The transmission was full, but it was leaking. This was a long shot. They way I figured it, the scumbag at the Super Duper Used Car Lot put some Stopleak in the tranny to get it to stop leaking 'til after they sold it. It worked for a couple of days, then started leaking again. But the tranny was full."

"So he needed to buy some tranny fluid."

"Right. It was a long shot but some of the parts stores have cameras for shoplifters. It was like pulling teeth to get the cops to even think about looking at them so I got a probie down from the Soo to go over them."

"What's a Soo?"

"Sault Saint Marie, in the Upper Peninsula… of Michigan.

"Oh… right, but why didn't you tell me this? I could have had Kauffman go over the tapes. I mean, what-the-fuck, you couldn't let me know? I been sitting down here for the past year thinking I'm part of the team and then I find out the game went on without me?"

"Look, Cook, I got this all in hand. I told you, I got this."

"You got what?"

"I got the bastard's picture."

"Good copy?"

"I got enough to use the facial recognition software at the airports."

"I thought that was something from casino TV shows. When did we get that installed at the airports?"

"It's just at the major airports. The government doesn't want the public to know all its tricks. The goddamn civil liberties people get all over us about this shit. Problem is, by the time something comes through, 'cause we got so many we're lookin' for, we don't usually catch 'em 'till they're gone. Mostly it's used for terrorists, and we can't scan every face that goes through. We got selective software. If they got a turban or a head rag, the system targets them first. Tall blond men are kind of at the back of the bus, y'know?"

"So do we have anything?"

"Not yet. Maybe never. He's probably gone for good."

"Are you sure you got the right picture?"

"Pretty sure. Tall blond with a vest on. Bulges on the sides like he's packin' both sides."

"So we got a real picture of him. I need to see it."

"I'll get you a copy."

"Why didn't you send me one before? I could have had Sam confirm it. I thought we were friends, partners."

"Shit, Captain, don't ever think you're in my league. We may be on the same side but you'll never match me. Shit. You can't even drink like me."

"We'll see about that, you ugly bastard. My sister could drink you under the table."

The rest of the night degenerated into insulting each other's sisters and imaginary girlfriends. Brock left the next day knowing what he had suspected was true. Kevin stayed in Cleveland knowing he was never going to get what he had been promised.

Lula was chained to the floor of a cabin where she had been found deserving of Arturo's attentions. Bonito, the bartender, was allowed to work on Sandiana. Arturo was very pleased with Lula, who had learned that there was no point in resisting or restraining. Lula gave it her all and was becoming a splendid actress. Afterward, the two men shared Aguadiente in the tavern.

"Oje, Arturo, what did you do to the wild boar in cabin one?"

"I broke her like a wild horse. It was almost a pity, I love the birthmark on her rump, it looks like lips. That one has so much fire."

"Had. She is lying there like a dead woman. I had to spit on it to fuck it. She just lies there, eyes open but like she was dead."

A few choice jokes and insults flashed through Arturo's mind but none of them surfaced. If his latest acquisition was comatose, she was all but useless. She was probably acting, like a possum, playing dead. He let her have the night to herself, naked and stinking, chained to the floor.

With morning, Arturo visited Lula first. By all indications, Lula was ecstatic to see him and offered herself up in the most explicit ways. She played it so well that Arturo took the chains off her wrists. He left her shackled to the floor by one ankle but with the chains gone from her arms, she could at least stand up. Arturo did not use Lula this morning.

Sandiana was another matter. Where Lula had greeted him like a dog greets its master, the new girl, who had been so full of fire, looked like she was dead. She might have been sleeping but her eyes were wide open. Her tears had washed tracks through the dirt on her face and the mosquito bites rose all over her body. It seemed clear that she had taken more than was necessary to gain her compliance. She did not respond when he lifted her head by her hair and slapped her. Her jailer cursed. He could see now that she would never have made a proper whore; rather than accept her lot in life, her brain had shut down. His only option now was to sell her for whatever he could get. He reached for his keys and unlocked her chains. He would need to get her to a room and let her recover. She would either try to escape, remain unresponsive or, less likely, become what he considered all women to be in the first place.

Bonito was wiping down the bottles behind the bar when his first customer entered. He had heard the motorcycle and knew it was no soldier, the military motorcycles had a deeper sound. The customer was definitely not what he had expected, not that he had expected anyone this early. The man had the same amount of stubble on his head as on his chin. A long line of stitches was visible across the scalp. The man's right hand was in a cast and he wore a long-sleeved jacket, too heavy for the weather but good for riding, blue jeans and boots. There was something sinister about the way he swung his head back and forth when he entered, the way he took in everything in the room.

"Good morning, sir, what can I get you this morning?"

"Tonic water."

"Yes, sir. Perhaps it is too early for anything more potent."

"I need a woman."

"We have just that, sir. Our women are the most beautiful in the country and they are ready to serve you for whatever it is you desire."

"Not just any woman, I need a particular woman."

"Tell me what it is you like and I'm sure we can find one to your liking."

"If she is here, she arrived recently. She is tall, with long brown hair, thin, with big tits. She goes by the name Perfecta Navaja."

"A dangerous sounding woman. Perhaps you like to be tied up? We have women that will do this for you."

The look that his first customer gave him sent a shiver down Bonito's spine. There was something about this man that was frightening. He was definitely not the kind of man who wanted to be tied up. Years of tending bar in this and other places had made Bonito a good judge of character so he could tell that this one was trouble. "Or, perhaps not," he finished weakly.

"Has such a woman come to this place recently?"

"No, sir. Women do not often come to this place."

"She would not have come here on her own, she is not your usual woman. She would have been brought by soldiers, young soldiers."

"I don't know what you are talking about, sir. We are a reputable night club. Perhaps you should look somewhere else for what you want."

"Perhaps you should tell me the truth before I decide you don't like me."

"And, sir, if I decide I don't like you?" Bonito's charming and solicitous attitude disappeared in a vagrant breeze.

"I am a man who does not need bartenders and whore masters to like him. Tell me where she is and maybe I will kill you quickly."

Bonito reached for the pump shotgun under the bar. He knew it was loaded, he loaded it every morning. The sense that there was something wrong with this man had progressed through several layers to this point. It was never a good idea to kill your customers, but this one was not a customer and not a soldier. He was here looking for a sister or a lover and he would be nothing but trouble until he was dealt with terminally. He would not be the first to come into Woodytown on his feet and leave on his back. If Bonito had been quick enough he would have written the stranger's epitaph, but he was not. As he raised his weapon, the stranger shot him three times in the chest. The buckshot from the shotgun tore through the ceiling of the tavern and into an upstairs bedroom.

One woman screamed upstairs, a man cursed. One door flew open and a man in his boxers came out and leaned over the rail with a revolver, searching for a target. There was no one to be seen, but the tavern doors were not swinging. If any one had just left, they would be moving a little. That meant whoever was shooting up the place was behind the bar, in the kitchen or under the stairs. Another man joined him on the mezzanine, this one sported a shotgun. The first man turned his head for a millisecond to gesture toward the kitchen door, it was a millisecond too long. Roberto Campena de Iguaca stepped from under the stairs and shot both men through the railing. He noted their locations and shot them again through the floor.

Arturo was looking in his latest captive's eyes. The pupils were so large it looked as though she was on heroin. They all but covered the corneas. She was freed, but lay on the floor with the sagging weight of the dead. Arturo was looking in her eyes when the gunshots sounded and her pupils went from black moons to pinholes. It was as if the sound of gunfire had sparked her back to life.

The second round of gunfire cracked from the tavern and Arturo turned to the door, forgetting about the woman he knew as Sandiana Torremolinos. Sandiana did not, however, share his concern. She came out of her trance in the same way she woke from a sleep, fully aware and ready to act. When Arturo dropped her head to the floor, she bounced back off the boards.

As he pulled his pistol from the back of his pants, she kicked him in the back of his left knee. It did not damage him, but surprised him and he did not stand a chance after that. He collapsed on one knee and started to roll, but she had already grabbed the wrist and elbow of his gun hand and pulled the wrist while she jammed the elbow. The pistol fell from his grasp and he reversed his spin, punching out at his unexpected adversary. She ducked, deflecting the arm and jabbing him in the side with her long and broken nails. His left hand fastened on a hank of hair and he pulled her up while his right punched her in the face. It was the last time. Anastasia Viuda shot him once in the chest and once in the face. Blood flew all over the walls and the floor. Arturo's perforated corpse lay prostrate and Anastasia spit on it.

There were three other men who needed to die here, and then she was going to take a shower.

As naked as the day she was born and carrying a 9mm pistol, she slunk from the shade of one cabin to another on her way to the tavern. In the fourth cabin she heard a noise, but the door was locked. Instead of cursing herself for leaving the key chain behind, she peeked in the window and saw Lula, as naked as herself except for the chains on Lula's ankles.

Anastasia listened closely but could detect no further sign of life from where she was. They were not coming to investigate the shooting in the cabin because there was trouble in the tavern. She made the decision and slunk back to the scene of her humiliation and vindication and slipped the key chain off Arturo's belt loop.

When she returned to the cabin where Lula was chained, she was astonished at the woman's composure. It was as if being chained naked to the floor was business as usual. Lula explained that it was not the first time it had been done but, obviously, something was different this time.

"I killed Arturo."

The smile that split Lula's face was like the coming of the dawn.

"I need you to do something for me, now."

"I want to see him." Lula said.

"Later. First we need to kill the other men."

"What? The two of us, naked, with one gun are going to kill all three of them?"

"Yes, if you pay attention. I need you to get inside and tell them that Arturo has been killed in the far cabin. I need all three of them together, in the open and I will kill all three of them before they can take their hands off their dicks."

"Yes. I can do that."

"Do this and we will be free, make a mistake and we die. Is there a question?"

"No, Mistress, no question."

"Then go."

Questions did begin to invade Lula's mind as she walked down the dirt road to the tavern, but none would have been sufficient to give her direction once inside. She found herself looking down the barrel of Roberto's gun. He almost shot her but stopped at the last moment.

"Whore, get over here."

Lula, who so often used words to her advantage, had nothing to say. Her mind was assimilating the situation. She could see the bodies at the top of the stairs and the man who had so obviously shot them. She walked across the floor trying to calculate how she could get out of this mess alive.

"How many men are in this house? Lie and I kill you."

"This morning there were four. One of the men at the top of the stairs is still moving. I don't see Bonito the bartender and Arturo is… in one of the cabins."

"What cabin?"

"The last one, on the far end."

He looked her up and down, appreciating her figure. "Why is your ass hanging out?"

"I was engaged," she said with a nervous smile.

"Where is Perfecta Navaja?"

"I don't know Perfecta Navaja."

"Liar. Go behind the bar and get the shotgun. Bring it to me."

"No, he will shoot me."

"He's dead, and if you do not do everything I ask, you will be dead too."

There was not much of a choice at that point. Lula saw the spike of the bayonet protruding from the cast, and the pistol. Somehow she knew he would kill her without a second thought. "I need to go over the bar or through that door and through the kitchen."

"Go over the bar. Do it now or you will not take another breath."

Lula's composure was gone and she was shaking like a leaf. She hesitated for a split second and saw Roberto's arm draw back in preparation for a killing stab. There was no more time to spare. She ran across the floor and slapped her hands on the bar, vaulting over it and landing in a pool of Bonito's blood. She slipped and fell on her back with a cry. She grabbed the shotgun and tried to stand but slipped again on the blood.

"Get back here, whore."

Lula's head was spinning with one fear battling another. Many have chosen the wrong path under this kind of pressure. Lying there, naked and covered with a dead man's blood, Lula tried to rack a shell into the chamber. With no experience, she could not have known there was a button on the side of the receiver that needed to be held in. She struggled with it for a second and Roberto decided she had made the wrong choice. He fired three rounds through the face of the bar. Lula screamed and he fired another round. Lula fell silent.

He could wait no longer. Spinning from under the stairwell, Roberto covered the mezzanine with his pistol but he had no shot. The women were not coming out of their rooms and the only men up there were lying on their faces. He dashed up the stairs and saw that, as Lula had said, one of the men was still alive. He picked up their weapons and put a bullet in the live one's brain.

The doors did not lock from the inside but some of the women had placed chairs against the handles to prevent them from opening. Roberto opened the ones that did so easily and shot the women inside, if they were easy to find. They did not have many places to hide; he shot them in the closets, under the beds and one, climbing out the window. To get to the woman who had injured him, he had no compunction against killing every man, woman and child in this town. He was beginning to think he had made a mistake, however, as he had still not found her.

At the end of the row was the bathroom, and this door was locked from the inside. In his most reasonable tone, Roberto asked if the person inside would open the door. Understandably there was not answer, so he blew the lock and handle off the door with the shotgun and kicked the door open.

"Where is Perfecta Nevaja?"

Of course, the woman cowering in the bathtub had no idea who Perfecta Navaja was. All she could do was cover her face and beg for mercy. Roberto Campena de Iguaca had no mercy. He grabbed her by her hair and half lifted her from the tub.

"Where is she?"

"Aiee. I do not know."

"She is here, yes?"

"In the cabin with Arturo." she squealed in a last ditch effort to save herself.

Roberto felt his manhood rise but had no time for recreation. He dropped the woman back into the bathtub and stabbed her through the heart. He could not chance getting shot from one of the upstairs rooms when he went outside, so he systematically forced his way into the remaining rooms and massacred the women inside.

Satisfied there was nobody dangerous left on the second floor, Roberto crept back down the stairs. Instead of rolling over the bar, he took the side door into the back area. There was no one in the kitchen or the pantry, and only one body behind the bar. He had not seen her body, but he had felt certain that he had shot the whore who had come through the swinging doors, naked. Then he saw her wet, bloody footprints heading out the back door. He muttered a curse. She had gotten away from him and with a shotgun as well.

Behind the second cabin, Anastasia Viuda racked that shotgun twice, showing Lula how to hold the button in on the side. She reloaded the live shell after satisfying herself that it was buck shot. There was no sense in angering a man with bird shot.

Lula's description of the man in the bar was understandably vague. She was agitated to the point of incoherence and as they stood, waiting, the gunshots continued from within.

The sound of the gunshots was having an unusual effect on the Argentine assassin. With each report, she could feel something inside her head buzzing for a moment. It was not a sound that she could hear, not a tickle on her skin, it was something inside, like a spark. While every blast made Lula tremble, it calmed Anastasia down and made her feel stronger, more confident, better. Despite the fact she was starved, filthy and bruised, she stood tall and actually smiled.

The gunshots ceased and Lula made a small mewling sound in the back of her throat. She cast about like a frightened animal preparing to bolt. Anastasia grabbed her by her rich black hair and growled in her ear. "If you run, I will shoot you. You have one chance to live. Point the barrel at whoever comes out that door and pull the trigger. This is a 12-gauge shotgun and will kill anything in front of it. I will watch this corner, you watch that one."

Lula nodded numbly. She was still trembling timidly but felt more focused.

A flash of movement, a bit of color that was not from the forest and Lula did just what was expected, she pointed the gun and fired at it. Whatever she hit screamed.

Both women ran toward the sound and found what they had not expected. The old man who had been running the sundries store was lying in the bushes, bleeding. The pain in Lula's face mirrored the pain in the old man's. He had not been one of the abusers, he had been a kindly old man who had no interest in the intimate company of women.

The buzzing inside Anastasia's head hit her stronger, like some kind of an alarm bell and she spun back behind the building just in time to see Roberto fire his pistol. He fired again and Lula screamed. The bullet had caught her as she cowered behind the dying old man in the bushes.

Anastasia ran to the corner and pulled around it, pistol first, but Roberto was not there. She checked the far side of the building and he was not there either. Slats prevented her from looking underneath the cabin.

"Where did you go, you bloodthirsty bastard?" she half-muttered half-thought. "Show me a little skin and I'll give you your last reward."

She slunk down the side of the cabin, following the same direction, hoping to catch her prey from behind, when the alarm bell in her head rang again. She turned around but there was no one there. Above her, Roberto launched himself through the open window from inside, and knocked her to the ground. The pistol went flying. The bayonet locked to his cast missed her chest by less than an inch. He had no weapon in his left hand but he punched her hard in the face as he pulled the bayonet out of the packed dirt. She tried to roll away from him as he rose but he kicked her in the stomach.

As he retrieved her pistol he spoke. "I wanted to take you back for the reward but killing you will be reward enough in itself. A woman like you would have made me a good partner, but it is much too late for that."

The alarm in Anastasia's skull, which had begun as a little tremor, was now vibrating physically. She felt stronger than she had any right to be and she gathered her legs under her for what she knew would be her last move on earth.

The shotgun blast came from the side of the building and though the aim was wide, it still pulped the hand holding the pistol, spinning the man around.

"Stay down. This bastard is mine." Lula walked from the bushes, racking the shotgun. Roberto screamed incoherently and ran toward her with the bayonet extended before him like a lance. The second blast did not go wide; it caught the Brazilian assassin in the face, tearing flesh from the bone. The third shot removed his head entirely.

The vibrating in Anastasia's head stopped and she almost collapsed again. It was as if it had been feeding her adrenaline and it stopped once the danger ended.

The two women supported each other as they staggered back to the tavern. Lula was streaming fresh blood from a scalp wound caused by Roberto's last round. It ran down her already blood soaked body.

Inside there was nothing but the stench of blood from the bodies of the dead. Lula cried as she saw her sisters mutilated bodies and Anastasia closed the doors to block the view. Between the two of them they were able to drag the body of AnaMaria out of the tub so they could wash themselves off. After that, food was the only thing Anastasia could think about. Lula refused to eat anything; the morning's experience was more than her stomach could handle. Anastasia ate until she vomited, ate some more and chased it down with half a pint of rum and a beer.

It seemed there was little in the way of practical clothing for riding until Lula brought out the dominatrix outfit. Tall boots, long gloves and a leather bodice coupled with riding breeches provided some protection with an oilskin duster covering it all. Lula was dressed in men's clothing, cinched tight with a belt. Anastasia wore the motorcycle helmet and Lula wore a leather executioner's mask over her bandages.

Anastasia Viuda took two liters of rum, smashed a few bottles and set the Jardim de Prazeres on fire. The dry, unpainted wood of the tavern crackled like a symphony behind the women as they rode down the less traveled of the two trails.

Chapter Fifteen
And He's Treading on My Tail

"I got you now, you son-of-a-bitch. What have you been doing in Dallas? And, more importantly, what makes you think you're getting off that plane in Rio?" Brock Dakota was as happy as a clam in a sandbar. It had been over a year since he had started looking for this Australian assassin and he finally got a lead. The CIA would pick him up in Rio de Janeiro and a clandestine operation would bring him back to the States, or he would end up having a terrible accident. Assuming the CIA didn't screw up, and they seldom did.

"Next we contact the FBI in Texas." Brock was talking to himself now. "Find out if there are any unsolved murders there. This slick bastard was down there for a reason and I want to know what it was. You think you're so fucking professional, I'll show you professional. Now, what is going on in Rio that would cause you to hop a plane there? I know you didn't go there for a vacation."

The phone rang five times in Cleveland before Captain Cook picked it up. "Cook, you degenerate drunk, I'm going to want Roger Porter and your man Sam Hardy down in Dallas in a couple of days to do a line-up ID."

"You found him?"

"He took a flight out of Dallas. Went down to Rio. He's been living in Little Rock, Arkansas under the name Walter Suffolk. I got the men down in Rio waiting for him."

"I'll get somebody to cover Sam and we'll meet you down there."

"I don't need you here."

"Hey, I got a better charge. Three counts of murder one beats attempted murder any day. Pikelfinger didn't die and it was his goddamn wife who shot him in the first place. This bastard is mine and you know it."

"I'll tell you what, once we get him in custody I'll give you a call."

"Dakota, I want him. You know you got nothing in Flint."

"Look, Cook, Homeland security and the FBI want him. You can be there for the ID but you can't have him. He's mine."

"We can talk about that later. I'm coming to Dallas."

"OK, Kevin, I'm looking forward to seeing you."

"You just love pushing my buttons, don't you?"

"I'm just glad we got him."

The truth was, however, that they did not have him. The CIA was not well liked in South America, so they needed to keep a very low profile. The local authorities would not sanction a pick-up in the airport and insisted that the agents remain outside the terminal. Terry Kingston as Walter Suffolk never left the terminal. He went straight from the commercial section to a private carrier and hopped a local prop plane to Curitiba, leaving the CIA waiting outside in the rain.

"Colonel, I am receiving a very strange data transmission. It seems to be coming from inside Brazil."

"What sort of transmission?"

"I don't know, Sir. It seems to be riding in on the regular satellite transmissions for Channel 12, in Curitiba."

"It does not belong there?"

"No, Sir. It began with the number 153. It was somehow slipped into the regular digital broadcast and appears on the screen, preempting the regular show. At first it was very faint, faded, but it is getting stronger. It only lasts for a couple of seconds but it is getting stronger. I differentiated it from the regular broadcast to locate the source and it seems to be coming from inside Brazil."

"I'll be right there." He hung up the phone and put on his cap. The monitoring station was only a few doors down the hall. "Can you get a closer look?" he asked as he entered the room.

"Here it is again, Sir. Do you see how the static follows it as if there is something else trying to come in but it does not have the power?"

"153. Oje." He whispered, then he barked, "Get out."

"I'm sorry, Sir?"

"I said get out of here. Leave this to me."

The junior officer wasted no time in relinquishing his post to Colonel Zarafina. The colonel had been with the satellite communication division since the beginning and was not known for his patience.

Zarafina worked feverishly on the keyboard, trying to adapt new technology to an old application. He recognized what was going on, but had not seen these signals in years. He had never expected to see them again. He had prayed that he would never see them again. Even with the new technology, he knew he could not blank out the signal, the best he could do was trace it to its source and even that would not be very precise.

During a lull in transmission, Colonel Zarafina switched to different computer and typed a terse e-mail before returning to the receptor.

Monitoring the broadcasts of the television stations had always been considered the best and the worst of positions. Each station had its own room and they were manned by the very finest of failures, slackers and malcontents. Once a man was assigned to this duty, he was assured of going nowhere and advancement in the ranks was out of the question.

Three transmissions in quick succession flashed across the screen: "153 Reporting, 153 Reporting to P…, 153 Reporting to President Stroessner." Then there was no more.

Colonel Zarafina put his head in his hands and waited for General Arridagio. This would not be pretty.

"Hernando. I had thought to see you many days before this and now you call me on my private line."

"I'm sorry, Sir. There was trouble. Call me back on this number and I will explain."

Hernando del Fuego only waited a couple of minutes before the pay phone rang.

"Hernando?"

"Yes, Sir."

"The operation was a success."

"Yes, Sir, but my partner let me down at the border. She had a gun under the spare tire. I did not know about it." Hernando did not mention that Anastasia claimed not to have known about it either.

"I read about that little disaster in the newspaper. They have your photograph."

"I did not have time to destroy their machines. We needed to leave in a hurry."

"Nobody survived?"

"No, Sir, but there is a further situation. I do not know who they are, but we were abducted. First the police took us. No, no, first an American, a big man with red hair, tracked us to a hotel. We escaped him but the police were outside. There is a reward and they did not arrest us but tied us in a garage."

"Go on."

"A man came and took us from there but the other, the American, was hunting us too. I alone escaped. I do not know where my partner was taken but I suspect she is being held at an encampment in the forest. If she is still alive."

"So, you left your partner and now you wish to return home."

284

"She betrayed me."

"I do not want to hear only your side of the story unless there is no other side. Am I making myself clear?"

"Yes, Sir. I will see what I can do."

"No, you will do what you must. I will accept nothing but absolute closure on this. I will see two agents walking into my office or I will see the dead bodies of one or both. I want proof. Then you can come home."

"Yes, Sir. I will make it happen.

"Good. You know if you are captured, we do not know you."

"Yes, Sir, I know."

Hernando hung up the pay phone feeling like he had swallowed acid. He could not be sure now that he would survive a trip home. In any event, without Anastasia Viuda, or proof of her demise, he walked into a sticky wicket across the border.

"Colonel Zarafina, what is it that is so important that I must be disturbed at home?"

"General Arridagio, the last remnant of that super soldier project just popped up."

"Impossible. Those men all died 20 years ago."

"I'm telling you we have something coming in from a number 153"

"How could this happen?"

"I don't know I'm working on that now. You remember the chips were designed to be an intermittent feedback loop that was activated by the fight or flight response in the adrenal cortex. Well, there can be no feedback from a dead man."

"I know this. I was there when the first of the men ran themselves to death because the chip malfunctioned."

"Technically, the chip did not malfunction. The problem started when the increased adrenaline boosted the men's strength and endurance beyond that of a normal man. He would start running and it would feel good and so he would keep running. Some of them ran themselves to death, like a horse. Some of them lifted weights until their bones broke. Some became manic depressive and killed themselves, others could not live in the depressive stage and did more and more dangerous things to evoke the response."

"So this was not a malfunction? Those men died."

"Yes, Sir, they died but not as a result of a malfunction, but as a result of the chip working properly. There was no thought when Professor Scaraboff implanted the chips about dealing with the human psyche. He merely made them into more capable physical specimens. It was their own minds that led them to the excesses that killed them.

"So why is this relevant? Why are we having this discussion?"

"As I said, Number 153 has surfaced and is transmitting. Somehow the transmission is inserting itself into the digital satellite broadcasts of a television station."

"How could this happen? Your mad German scientist died 20 years ago when his laboratory exploded. All his machines were scrapped. I was told all the subjects were destroyed."

"I don't know how it happened. I don't know why it happened. Somehow, one of them escaped our attention. He went underground and has just reappeared, in Brazil and is reporting to President Stroessner."

"What? Stroessner died three or four years ago. He died in Brazil." he ended thoughtfully. "Is there significance there?"

"I cannot say but we definitely need this weed removed from the garden, whoever he is. We cannot have this cancer from the past spoiling our relations with our neighbors. I think, General, that a few men with a tracking device can find and eliminate this thing without creating an international incident. If we try to tell the Brazilian government of the experiment, there is no telling what will happen. Anything from international censure to all out war. This sort of thing must be handled with the utmost care."

"Do we have such a tracking device?"

"We can make one in short order, I think. The problem is that the signal inserts itself into the much stronger television service and so hides itself until it reaches the television set."

"Make it happen. Keep me updated. I will send over a squad. If you need more men we can pull them from my ranks in the Secret Service. No regulars, no civilians. Under no circumstances is this news to be released. If there are questions, 'we are investigating.' Is there anyone else you can think of who might recognize these transmissions? If so, they must be silenced. After all, the whole project was directed toward the creation of assassins."

"The CIA dropped the ball."

"Oh, C'mon Dakota. You're telling me they missed him in Rio?"

"Captain Cook, I have some more evidence, ancillary stuff, that I will send you, but no, I do not have the man himself."

"I can tell when I'm getting swamped. Why are you doing this? Has the Fed got something to do with getting Pikelfinger aced?"

Silence held the line for a second longer than it should have then Brock replied with a hard, gravelly edge in his voice. "Listen, Cook, you're asking questions that are way out of your league. The government has no part in this sort of thing. If we had, it would have been done right and it would have been done by an American. Nobody would ever have found him."

Kevin Cook did not say what he was thinking but remembered another union man who had become the subject of eternal speculation.

"O—K, I get it. Send me copies of what you got. I'll get confirmation that we're looking for the right guy and we'll move from there. Does he know we're after him?"

"We are not, Cook, the CIA and OHS are after him and we will get him. You are invited into this in a support capacity only."

"Ten-four, Special Agent Dakota." Cook hung up without saying goodbye and went to get a cup of coffee from the machine in the hall while muttering about '...shine your shoes, Boss, wash your car...' He could tell he had been cut out of the loop and any further efforts on his part would be ignored.

It was not what Terry had wanted to do, but he knew he only had a couple of minutes before they got the lights back on. There would be no rescue if he ended up in a cell as well. The motorcycle was heading for the gate when he swung his arm out and took the rider off the back of his bike. The bike fell and within seconds Terry had the man's helmet on and was heading for the gate. He was not stopped as he passed through and back into the outside world.

Once he was down the dirt track and onto the road, he opened it all the way and put as much distance between himself and the compound as he could.

Unlike the dumps on the outsides of the major towns and cities, there were no urchins picking through the remains at this site. It was not that there was nothing of value, there were items that could have been put to some use, it was simply that there was nothing close. This dump also held a unique geographical position. It was a flat stone outcropping over a steep crevasse where the garbage piled up for a month at a time until the farmer drove his rusty old tractor the 10 kilometers from his farm and pushed the trash over the edge with his improvised bulldozer blade.

The only man watching this flat expanse of rock that day was the man emptying the industrial trash compactor. He watched carefully as the hydraulic piston pushed out one bundle after another. Then came the moment he had been waiting for. A human body was forced out the back of the compactor. The man walked up to it, grabbed it by both arms and tried to haul it out, but it was too heavy for him and was quickly being buried in trash. Cursing, he shut the hydraulics off and got a milk jug full of water from the cab of the truck. Splashing water on the body animated it, unfastening the snap on his holster reassured the man.

"You are now a free man. I hope you appreciate this for I have ruined my career for you," the man said.

"Don't give me that shit," the form from the garbage responded in English. "You got me out with the promise of a fabulous reward. We're off to see the bloody fuckin' wizard."

"Speak Portuguese. And do not try anything with me, my friend. I only trust you far enough to shoot you if I need to."

"OK. You did your part. I will do mine. Give me the phone." Once on the phone, the man spoke in German. "I need you to be perfectly clear about this and you will need to take notes so it can be relayed to my associate in Portuguese. So get a translator that can speak Portuguese and listen very carefully."

It took a minute for the command to be issued.

"I wish to transfer everything in this account to another account held by me in the name of Andreas Castro. Said monies are not to be accessible by Mr. Castro alone and without my authority. My name is Boris Chercovski. Am I making myself clear?"

"Yes, Herr M… Chercovski. This is perfectly understandable."

"Good. The next part is not to be translated to my associate. In the event that I alone show up, the money will be distributed to me or returned to the original account. If Mr. Castro comes to the bank alone, you are to call this number." A number followed and the banker on the other end of the line assured his client that there would be no trouble.

A few minutes of waiting occurred and then the translator was on the line explaining to Andreas Castro that the account was set up and that the money was his, however, if he were to arrive at the bank without Boris Chercovski, the money would not only not be accessible to him, it would be automatically donated to Doctors Without Borders.

MacMaster took the phone again and thanked the banker on the other end of the line. He thought the Doctors Without Borders thing to be a particularly nice touch and expressed that he wished he had thought of it himself.

"So you see, my friend," he said with only a trace of sarcasm, "if you had any thoughts of leaving me in the forest with a bullet in my brain, you can forget it. That money is yours but only when you show up with me at your side."

"So, now all you need to do is to kill me? Hai, I should never have listened to your snake's tongue."

"But you did, my friend, and I intend to make it worth your while, but first I need to get somewhere that has a shower and a kitchen. I have been starved for weeks and stink like garbage and I want to sleep in a bed."

"There is one other thing. I have your passport. I stole it and mailed it. So you see, you need me as much as I need you. Without me, you will not get out of this country."

"Clever. You are one step ahead of me. Now, about that shower."

The tourist hotels were out of the question. There were hostels and smaller bed-and-breakfast arrangements, but Andreas did not trust them to be impartial. He took Gordon to his sister Rosimar's house. Rosimar was short and wiry with a ready smile and a twinkle in her eye. It occurred to her brother that the twinkle might be for their guest and he warned her in no uncertain terms that it would be a mistake to trust him for a second. He was the key to a new life, but he was dangerous like a jaguar, a killer.

The hot shower ran until there was no more hot water. The red beard that had grown on MacMaster's face stayed there. He ate enough pork chicken, goat and iguana for three men and followed it up with three bottles of Guinness Stout. Rosimar began to complain that she would not be able to keep this one for long. He was too expensive.

"Dom Castro."

"Call me Andreas."

"Andreas, then. Sir, it occurs to me that if they have you on the list for a potential deserter, then it would make sense for them to look at the house of your sister. Our being here throws suspicion her way and puts her in danger as well as yourself. I suggest we move on before someone puts two and two together and comes up with Rosimar. The further north we go, the less likely they are to detect us."

"This is clear. We can take the airplane from Rio de Janeiro."

"No, Dom Castro. I am a fugitive and you are a deserter assisting a fugitive. We would never make it onto the plane. We need to move like ghosts or we will become ghosts. Are there small airports in the north of the country, bush rangers who will fly us across the border?"

"You are being much too cautious. We can go to Rio and fly from there. No one will know who we are. No one is looking for us."

"How can you be sure? I was set to be shot in three days on a murder charge. I think they will take that seriously. In any rate, we cannot stay here in Curitiba, we won't last a week. We can stay in Rio for a while, but we cannot fly out of Rio. They will capture and kill us."

"They will not capture us."

"They will kill us then. We cannot walk into a bank anywhere in Brazil and request a transfer. The days are over when one hand doesn't know what the other hand is doing. With computers and satellite communications, as soon as you give your name to one man, the whole network knows where you are."

"So what is it you suggest?"

"We need to get north, rent a small plane and go over the border to Guyana or Columbia. They will not be looking for us there or care about us one way or the other. That way, we can get on a regular flight out and I can get you to Switzerland and you can get your money. After that, we are quits. I don't care where you go or what you do. We need to get there first."

Rosimar listened to the exchange and decided it was in her interest to tell her stupid brother that he was being duped and used. She got him in the other room and cut into him. "This man will never take you to Switzerland and he will never give you any money. He is leading you around by a ring in your nose and you allow this to happen. He will leave you dead in a field somewhere and thank you for your time. How do you know the money is even where he says it is?"

"The money is there."

"Hai, he is making a fool of you. He could have this money transferred to your account in the Banco National. You could walk in there and take it out and walk away. He is pulling you around."

Andreas Castro thought about it for just a second and realized that his sister was right. He was being made a fool of by this big red-headed foreigner and he needed to stand up and take control of the situation.

"I have been speaking with my sister, Boris, and we both now think you are trying to make me a fool. I want you to get on the telephone and transfer the money you promised me to my account at the Banco National." He pointedly unsnapped the flap of his holster. "All this foolishness of going to Switzerland aids you, but does not help me. I want what has been promised to me and I want it now."

"You are making a huge mistake. The digital trail these transactions leave can be hidden, but to transfer this money into your account will put up a red flag."

"Then put it in my name." Rosimar was angling for what she could get and saw massive opportunity.

"Oh, I can do that but it is up to Andreas to decide what we will do."

"Yes. Nobody is looking for Rosimar. She can get me my money and I can be done with you."

"You still need to get out of the country."

"Not with this kind of money. I can make a fine life for myself without the ghosts of my past."

"OK, but I will not walk into that bank with you. You may have enough disrespect for the system, but I have seen what it can do. I will need a little money though. I cannot disappear without some cash and you both want me to disappear, don't you?"

"Not before our business is concluded." Andreas handed him the cell phone. "Make the call. This time I want the entire procedure done in Portuguese. I do not want you speaking whatever language it was you spoke before."

The call went through to an answering machine that insisted, in French and again in German, that they call back during business hours.

"Colonel Zarafina, what have you accomplished?"

"General, Sir, I have isolated a wavelength that the device is using. I do not know how it is hijacking the bandwidth of the television station. The others never did this. I have no files to work with, so I do not know who this man is or what he might look like, but he must be 40 years old now. I still have no answer as to why this chip is active now."

"Do you have the tracking device?" The General was looking a bit exasperated.

"Yes, yes, yes. We have it but it must be away from the television station that emits the signal, or it masks it. That station is in Curitiba. It will work, even there, if the tracker is within a hundred yards or so of the subject."

"A hundred yards? You could do no better than that?"

"I am working on an improved model but remember, the farther from the television signal, the farther we can read the chip signal."

"Does that station shut down at night?"

"No, it is a 24-hour station."

"Hmm, if it were in this country we could just shut it off for a while. Perhaps we can convince them to shut down for a while."

"But this is not the entire problem, General. We can only get a reading on the chip when it is transmitting and it will only transmit when the adrenaline reaches a certain range. Then it will keep the adrenaline pumping until the danger is past and broadcast in short bursts."

"Will it broadcast anything but hello to a dead man?"

"They were originally designed to broadcast location, I think. It was a long time ago and I had forgotten about the whole program. After all, it died with its creator before Andrés Rodríguez took over from Stroessner."

The mention of General Rodriguez might have been a bad idea. A dark cloud covered General Arridagio's face at his mention. "Find out how to get the coordinates from the broadcast and find this man. I want him eliminated and I want it done now. Five men are in Barracks C3 ready to follow your directions. Get them a tracker and give them your best direction. Explain that they will be able to get a better fix when the television is out but... you know what I am saying, yes?"

"Yes, Sir, General. I will have them outfitted and moving by the end of the day."

"But without a true signal they will be chasing ghosts or sitting on their hands, yes? I am thinking that there should be a way to send a signal back that will activate the chip or help with the location."

"Without notes, I do not know how I will do this, but it is possible, I think. I will work on it while the men are deployed and if anything is discovered, I will make sure both you and they are informed of it immediately."

"Good. The men given this device were driven to excesses that killed them and if we are lucky, so will this one. I still want to know why this one is only active now. There is no telling what was given as a mission to this one. It could turn into another war and nobody wants that. Lopez died over a hundred years ago after almost destroying the country; we cannot allow a dead president to cause another one."

Cell phones are a convenience and Terry often saw them as a necessary evil, but he never liked them much. Text messaging was something he would never engage in for fear it would come back and bite him the way it had so many others already. He had to admit that the truly tech savvy would have applications he never considered, but he never got attached to them.

When Terry turned on his cell phone in Curitiba, there was a message waiting. He accessed the mailbox and a neutral, almost mechanical voice indicated he was to call Germany. There was no city, no number and no name, but there was also no doubt about who and what required contact. The cell phone was clean in that it had been bought for cash, activated under a false name and stocked with minutes from a card. Kingston did not get to speak with Richter that day; he spoke to an aide who told him that there had been an unusual request from a Swiss banker. MacMaster had contacted the bank and the bank had called the number to confirm that it was in operation, and that they were to call that number under a certain set of circumstances. Being a Swiss banker, he was reluctant to explain the circumstances or reveal any more pertinent information but it did seem to confirm that MacMaster had been alive two days ago and at least partially in control of his destiny.

The motorcycle he stole from the army had disappeared into the brush outside town. It would have vanished as quickly if he had left the keys in it on the street but Terry did not want it being found as a possible pointer to his location and identity. Juan would take him wherever he needed to go.

The second call came the following day. Terry was eating breakfast in the dim recesses of a street-side cantina: four eggs with peppers and onions, half a loaf of fresh bread, farofa, tapioca and two beers.

"Stranger?"

"Colonel, how nice to hear your voice." Terry felt gratified in this being one of the only chances he had to practice his German.

"I thought it best to call personally. Our mutual friend has made an arrangement to transfer a large sum of money to Banco National in Curitiba. The banker was kind enough to inform us of this, on his direction, and that transfer will go into effect first thing in the morning, there. The account will be held by Rosimar Castro."

"I see. Is that a man or a woman?"

"I do not know, Stranger."

"Is there a branch in particular this transfer was directed toward?"

"There was no such direction, but to access this sum of money in cash, and I assume that is the plan, it will need to be a wealthy branch."

"Is there a provision for informing you when the account has been accessed?"

"No, we have no such arrangement with the Banco National, unless our mutual friend has made one. Frankly I doubt he has had that opportunity."

"This number will remain active. I assume you are scrambling communications?"

"Of course, Stranger. If there is a further communication, direction or message I will route it to you immediately. Until then, I wish you the best of luck and hope to know something soon."

Communications severed, and an hour-and-a-half before the banks opened, Terry finished his breakfast.

The largest branch of the Banco National in Curitiba was in Central Square. It was an imposing structure with wide, rounded, marble steps and reproductions of Greek statues on each side. There was no auto traffic allowed in Central Square and posts had been erected to keep out the cars. Motorcycles could squeeze through, but were not supposed to. The fountain in the center of the square was old and, though newer than the fountain, the tiles that surfaced the square were both colorful and beautiful. The square was ringed with garment shops and restaurants and the entire north side was taken up by the Royal Grande Hotel.

Terry sat under an umbrella advertising Vermouth and sipped coffee. The young waitress was attentive and obviously attracted to him. The two flirted shamelessly for a while and Terry arranged to take her dancing that night. He knew he could only stay there for a limited amount of time before he raised suspicions. A second light breakfast and coffee with a local newspaper maintained the illusion for a while, but he was not going to wait all day.

The hotel clerk asked to see his identification, but did not demand a credit card as so many hotels did. Terry signed in as the American tourist, Walter Suffolk. Six stories tall, the Royal Grande Hotel had a panoramic view of the steps of Banco National and the entirety of the Central Square. It was perfect for observations, but the sheer number of people investing themselves in the plaza was difficult for one man to monitor.

The rifle scope brought people's faces into focus from across the square, but the closer shops could not be brought into focus. The heat and humidity rose steadily and through the hotel had been air conditioned at one time, it no longer was.

Terry settled in place with his scope balanced on some cushions set on edge on a chair. That vantage kept it focused on the steps of the bank where professionals in business suits and locals in rough clothing streamed in and out.

The bank had been open for about three hours and was about to shut down for lunch when a thin, attractive woman bounced up the steps with an obviously empty canvas bag in one hand. Terry could not help but focus on her form in its tight fitting shorts and exposed midriff. He saw the bag and wondered why else anyone would take such a bag into a bank.

A scan of the perimeter yielded no new information, but it was quite warm now and many of the patrons were escaping the heat in the dark interiors of the restaurants.

The thin woman in the revealing clothing bounced back down the steps of the bank, still holding the empty canvas bag and seeming none the worse for it. At the bottom of the steps, she passed a group of old women wearing widow's weeds. She nodded at them, smiling, and they shook their heads. Terry started following the younger woman with his eyes and noticed that one of the widows was following her. This woman was covered head to toe in draping black, with a veil covering her entire face. The two walked in the same direction without looking at each other until they reached the far end of the square where they rendezvoused, briefly. Then they walked away from each other.

Terry muttered to himself that he would never be able to catch them from this distance even as he tore out the door and down the steps. By the time he reached the corner where the two had obviously spoken, they were nowhere in sight. He spent a few minutes cruising the neighborhood but found neither of them. A small grocery store provided him with a bottle of beer and a fresh pack of cigarettes before returning to his room to continue his observation.

There was only one destination for any one going down that particular dirt road. It did not lead anywhere else. It could have been used as a short cut to the army base if it were a paved road, but the condition of it was such that it would have cost time, not saved it. And there was no place to turn around.

The soldiers at the road block were filled with an intensely foul humor. Very few people traveled this trail and most were carrying supplies. Word traveled fast enough that now no one was following the trail. They were angry and they were bored. The members of this particular base were very fond of the little village they considered theirs and needed some form of action to vent their frustrations. It was acknowledged that whoever had killed their whores and burned their tavern would be hunted like dogs and would die long and horrible deaths.

Hernando del Fuego was travelling this route in search of his erstwhile partner and lover when he approached the road block. He could have turned the Land Rover around if he had a few minutes, but there were few sections of trail on which he could do so. He elected to remain calm and bluff his way through. There had been no official notice of the tragedy at the town that did not exist, so unless one was in touch with the right people, one could not be expected to know.

Bluffing proved to be a bad choice of strategy but the best he could have chosen given the circumstances. If he had decided to turn around and run, he would probably have been shot, but without identification, he stood the chance of being detained. He was, after all, a wanted man. Fortunately for him, there was no laptop computer at the road block that could match his face with the database of criminals maintained by the government. He was not acting suspiciously, other than being where he should not have been. His professed destination was Woodytown but he could provide no answers to the simplest of questions about the layout of the town. He freely admitted he had never been there. As cool as an arctic seal, he smiled and joked and tried to win over the soldiers but was only partially successful.

They determined he was to be taken to the base for questioning.

The soldiers had dropped their guard by the time their final determination had been made. Hernando's joking and friendly demeanor had disarmed them somewhat. When they moved to secure him for transport, he made his move. The nearest man carried an automatic rifle slung around his neck. He dropped like a stone when Hernando kicked him in the side of his right knee and grabbed his rifle. The other three men went down like a synchronized diving team. One after another, their blood painted the trees behind them. The man with the broken knee tried to wrestle his knife from its scabbard but died from a crushed skull before he could manage it.

Hernando knew he had only minutes before the army was on his back so he wasted no more time with the dead. He took the keys from the jeep blocking the trail and threw them into the woods then jumped back into his Land Rover and headed backward toward the road. As soon as he could turn around, he did so and was past the intersection before any soldiers reached it.

Though his mood could not be described as ebullient, his face did hold a grim smile. Even without the details, he could imagine what had happened. He could easily believe that they had tried to subjugate Anastasia and that she had allowed them to underestimate her. The problem he faced was in having no direction for locating her. He needed more information and he needed it before he could make another move.

At the intersection of the road and the trail, he had taken a left. Turning right would have moved him toward the army base. His only course of action for the present was to get to Curitiba, find out what had happened at Woodytown and decide what his next move should be from there.

Cloaked as he was in widows weeds, Andreas could move without attracting attention. He felt invisible and confident. Rosimar had confirmed that the money had been transferred to the account, but it would not be available for a couple of business days. The secret would be to lie low until they could withdraw the cash and then they would move to Rio or Brazilia and set themselves up as someone they were not. As long as they did not become too obvious, he thought they would never get caught.

There was nobody watching the house as far as he could tell. The door had not been forcibly opened. He slipped his key into the lock and went to check on his captive. What he found was that he no longer had a captive. In his confidence, he had tied Gordon MacMaster to a wooden chair. He had tied his wrists and ankles and he had tied him to a chair in such a fashion that he knew the man could not escape. What he had not counted on was that the chair, though solid, was not unbreakable. Somehow the man he knew as Boris Chercovski had shattered the chair, gotten a knife from the kitchen and cut through the ropes that bound him.

It could have been rightly concluded that his captive was waiting somewhere in the two-story house to kill him and retake possession of the money but such was not the case. Gordon MacMaster had rifled the refrigerator for more food and then taken his leave. Andreas did not know if this was for the best or not. He had not intended to allow his captive to live any longer than had been necessary. Penniless in a foreign land, he was afraid the man would be captured and forced to reveal the means and location of his rescuer.

The door opened and in his anxiety, Andreas almost shot his sister as she entered.

"Where is he?" she asked.

"I don't know. He broke the chair and ran away."

"This is a very bad thing. He is a big man and, I think, very dangerous."

"Possibly."

"Very possibly. Shit, Andreas, he could bring the police here and we will be ruined. What good is it to be rich if we are to face a firing squad?"

"Look, he already faces a firing squad. I do not think he will be telling anyone anything unless they capture him. It is true that he is not easy to hide in a crowd. He could not get away with putting on these robes and hiding in them. What did they say at the bank, exactly?"

"They said that the money had been made to an account in my name and that the money was mine, but I needed to wait a couple of days for them to verify that the transfer was legitimate. Once it was verified, I could have the money."

"It doesn't sound right. It sounds like, somehow, that big German bastard set us up. I don't like it."

"Should we go somewhere else for a couple of days?"

"Let me think about it for a minute."

"I think we should keep a watch on the bank so we can tell if the army is there when we go in to get the money."

"Ai, Sister, that is stupid. We could never tell. It is all done over the telephone and the computer systems now."

"But they can't move men, guards into the bank over the telephone. We could get a room and watch the bank or... I've got it, we get the money from a different branch."

"Shut up, sit down and let me think. There is something here I have not considered."

"Don't tell me to shut up. You need me now. That money is in my name."

"That money is mine. If you think you are going to double-cross me, you had better think again. I am the one with the balls to get this money and it is mine. You will have some, but I will be in charge of it. Do not doubt that."

"Yes, brother. You always were smarter."

"I have found her, Señor."

"Juan, you earn your money every day. You are a true friend."

"Señor. I will take you to her house. Now, if you like."

"Do you have a description of her?"

"No, Señor. I have an address. I also have news."

"Yes?"

"The army base has been locked down. They are furious. I do not know what you have done, but the entire area is impassable. They have road blocks. I am told El Jardim de Prazeres was burned to the ground and all the men and women killed. The army is like a nest of hornets poked with a stick."

"What else are they doing?"

"They will do whatever they want, but it is best to stay out of their way. If they find out you did something, they will shoot you and probably shoot me for helping you."

"Meet me at the south end of the Central Plaza, but not until four. Try to get me a description of this Rosimar Castro. I need to know who she is and what she does. She may have powerful friends."

"It will not take long. I will call in an hour."

Terry finished his beer and pulled out another cigarette. He looked at it and returned it to the pack. The bank had been open for half an hour, but he could not get comfortable. He had the feeling he had missed something. He lay on the floor and tried to clear his mind. "Why would MacMaster have burned Woodytown? Why would anyone? Who would have killed everyone in the area? The women might rise up and kill the men for abuse. The one chained to the floor in the cabin had good reason. They all get treated to that from time to time. So they... No, not they, she."

Terry sprang to his feet and grabbed the cigarette he had eschewed minutes earlier. He pulled the photograph out of his bag and squinted at it through the smoke. "It was you, wasn't it? You're the sheila I saw in that cabin. Mrs. Andalucia, Sandiana Torremolinos, Perfecta Navaja. I'll bet those pimps had no idea who they had chained to the floor. Must admit, you didn't look much like yourself. I missed it. So what do we have? Did the Scotsman roll into town and kill everyone and make off with you? No witnesses. Still, not much like him to kill women, unless he had to. Where did you go, then? Are you still alive or did you end up burned? You have a trick of turning it all into a bollix. I wonder if I had pulled you out of there that night, maybe things would... No. Never worry about what you didn't do unless you can go back and do it later."

Terry shook his head and went back to observing the gates to the Bank.

Juan took a little over an hour before calling back. "Señor?"

"Yes, Juan."

"I have it. This one is thin and blonde. She works sewing in the shirt factory by the river. She is not married and has no children."

"She lives alone then?"

"She has a brother in the army. I do not know if she has a lover."

"Good. Keep asking questions. Pick me up at four in the afternoon and we will look into this further."

"What do you want with this one?"

"No questions. You do what I ask and I pay you for it. OK?"

"Yes, Señor."

Terry went back to scanning the square and the customers of the bank but found nothing of interest.

The Banco National closed at 3:30 and Terry put his scope back in his bag, shoved his pistol in his pants pocket and went downstairs to the hotel bar for a beer before leaving. The lobby was empty and the bar was nearly so. Terry put an American $100 bill under his beer and the two photographs of the fugitives next to it. The bartender obviously understood what was being asked but shook his head and did not attempt to take the cash. Terry tipped the man well when he left.

Juan was waiting at the barricade on the south side of the square. He was quick to tell his anonymous passenger that he had gotten a tune up for the cab. It did not bother him that his passenger would not supply him with a name; he had been having more fun in the past week than he could remember, and making more money.

The street Rosimar lived on was wide enough for one vehicle, but there was already one on it. A jeep, painted grey/green held four men in commando attire. It stopped halfway down the block and the soldiers leaped out. One used a post pounder to smash open the front door and three poured in, yelling. A moment's lull presaged a barrage of gunfire.

Terry was three doors away when the cacophony shattered the air. He saw the remaining soldier turn to the doorway and he made a rash decision. He pulled his pistol and shot the soldier between his helmet and his flack jacket. The man went down in a heap.

The gunfire continued unabated from inside the house. Terry bit his lip and relieved the fallen soldier of his automatic weapon. A quick peek inside the house gave him a flash view of three soldiers under the stairs, firing up through the landing while somebody dressed in black fired down at them from above with an identical weapon. There was no time to think, no way to plan. Action was mandated. Now.

Terry crouched just outside the doorway and opened fire with the assault rifle. He fired low, below the bullet-proof vests, catching all three men in the legs. It was too late for the man above, he caught a round under his chin and the top of his head erupted like a volcano. The soldiers were still alive as Terry strode up to them and shot each in the face. The man at the top of the stairs was beyond help or redemption. The bedrooms were empty, downstairs, but the upstairs family room had a stout door, locked. There was no time for finesse and no time to determine who was in the room. Terry blasted the lock out of the door and kicked it open with a roundhouse. The shotgun blast tore through the door as it opened and slammed it shut again. Inside was the unmistakable squeal of a woman.

"Scotsman!" Terry roared. "Is that you?" Knowing it was not.

There was no reply but the sound of the door to the roof slamming.

"Bollix. I knew this was a mistake." Terry leaped over the rail and landed on the bloody corpse of a soldier, slipping to one side momentarily. He heard the tiles sliding from the roof before he saw the figure drop to the street outside. The girl was quick and by the time he got out the door, she was almost to the corner.

Terry dropped the assault weapon and started after his quarry at top speed, only to see Juan step around the corner and punch her in the face, knocking her to the ground. Before she regained her feet, Terry had her. She fought viciously, but was no match for the Australian. He threw her over his shoulder and then tossed her in back of the cab.

"That will cost you extra, Señor." Juan grinned as they tore off down the narrow streets.

Terry had to restrain her as Rosimar struggled. He told her to stop fighting but she continued to bite and scratch. He told her he would not hurt her and that he had just saved her life. Perhaps she did not understand him well enough because she clamped her teeth on the knuckles of his left hand forcing Terry to escalate his reactions. He slapped her hard enough to get her teeth off his left hand, threw her face first on the seat and sat on her back. It did not take long for her to stop squirming.

"Good. Look, you are Rosimar Castro and I have just saved your life."

"You murdered my brother."

"No, I saved your life. I killed four men to get you out of that house. They killed your brother. Soldiers. Why?"

"I don't know."

"You lie."

"I don't know. I have nothing for you. Let me go."

"No. Where is the big red-headed man?"

"I do not know."

"Oh, you know all right. I am going to tell you what I think and you are going to tell me what you know. Is that clear?"

"Let me go."

"There are four ways this will end and only one of them is good for you. I can take you to the army as the sister of a rebel or deserter or whatever it is your brother was and they will kill you. I can take you to that little whore house in the woods and they will chain you to the floor and fuck you to death. You will cause me so much trouble I will kill you myself or you will reveal to me what you know and I will let you live."

"OK. Get off my back."

"Do we have an understanding?"

"I will tell you what I know. Get off me."

"I am done playing. If you do not cooperate, I will kill you with my bare hands."

"Yes, yes, yes. Get off me." Rosimar was much calmer now. "The big man you call Boris has gone. I do not know when he left."

"This is bad. Every word out of your mouth is a lie. Cabbie, take us to the Jardim de Prazeres. I'll sell her for a couple of bucks and watch as the army fucks the truth out of her. How long do you think it will take?"

Juan said nothing but he did turn his way toward the outskirts of town.

"Oje, there is no need for this. I tell the truth already."

"You tell me a little bit and want it to be all. I know a couple of things that you have not mentioned, and the fact that you did not say it means every thing out of your mouth is a lie. So, you tell me everything and I will be kind. Lie to me again and we will go the other way."

"You know, you are a handsome man, I think we could have something together if you just..."

Terry had played the verbal fencing game all he was willing to play. Before the young Miss Castro finished her sentence, he slapped her again. "Look. This man, Boris, is a friend of mine and he is the only reason I am here. I killed those men because I thought he was in the house. All I find is you. You are of no value to me and you want to play games. I do not play games. I kill people. If you do not cooperate, I will kill you. Now, this is your last chance.

Rosimar had emptied her box of tricks and was left with no alternative she could see. "Stop the car. I will tell you what it is you need to know. This Boris left us. Yes, he stayed with us for the night. My brother brought him home."

"Why?"

"I don't know."

"Keep driving. She wants to keep her mouth closed. We'll see how that works when they have kicked all her teeth out and they are fucking her in the face."

"No, no, it is the truth."

"What about the money?"

This was the last straw. The final count she had kept to herself in the hope there would be something left. His words collapsed her into the corner and she started crying.

"Juan, pull the car over. I'm going to kill this bitch right now."

"No, please." The tears ran down her face and sputtered between her full lips. I will tell you. Andreas freed your friend from the army at the risk of his own life and brought him to my house in exchange for money. The money was transferred from Europe and I was to get the money in a couple of days, but Boris is gone."

"Where did he go?"

"I don't know, really, I don't know. We had him tied up, but he escaped."

"And the money?"

"I cannot get the money until Monday."

"What do you think, Juan?"

"She is a tasty little fish. The pimps will give me something for her."

"No," she wailed. "I have told you everything. You said you would let me go."

"You will not survive the three days until Monday if I let you go."

"I'm willing to try."

"I'm sure you are, but I want you alive and I cannot be sure you will be. Bear with us and we will make sure you get what you deserve, and more, that you survive. You have finally given me a reason to keep you that way. If you try to escape, I will kill you myself. If you lie to me again, I will kill you myself. Your money is not important to me; I do not want it. What is important is my friend. If I cannot find him, I will kill you myself. In short, your life depends on my finding my friend. If you anger me in the slightest, your life is forfeit. Do you understand?"

The nature of her dilemma finally sank in completely and she turned her eyes to the floor. "What do I call you, Señor?"

"You call me Boss. I will not abuse you, I will not rape you, but I cannot let you go, yet. Juan, turn this thing around and find me a safe tank to keep this tasty fish in."

"I have just the place."

Juan drove the cab to a house apart from others. Most others shared a wall with their neighbors but this one had a yard with a stone garden and a garage. Inside was a handsome middle-aged woman in an apron, cooking dinner.

"Juan, my love, what have you done, now?"

"Maria, I have need of your help. We can make some real money, but it is imperative that we keep this woman until Monday."

"What woman? Juan, if you have another woman I will kill her before I let her stay here."

"No, Maria, my love, you know you are the only woman for me."

"And your wife?"

"Maria, you know I do not sleep with my wife. She is wife in name only. I will be leaving her soon and we will be together then."

"I have been hearing this for too long. I am beginning to think you play this game with others as well."

"No, Maria, this is not what I do. You are the only one for me. I love you forever. There is no other woman."

"Then who is this woman we must keep until Monday? Is her husband after you? Is he trying to kill you?"

"It is complicated, but I do not even know this woman. She has no husband but she has money and the army will kill her if they find her."

"Then they will kill me as well. What makes you think you can do this to me?"

"He does nothing," Terry said as he entered through the garage door. "I do it."

Maria began speaking so quickly that Terry could not follow what she was saying but it was obvious that she was unhappy.

"Please, Señora, This will make you rich. I am Boss and what I bring you is not a woman but a payday, lottery winnings." Terry's accent and syntax were clumsy but the message was clear.

"So, Señor, you are Boss, eh? Well, you are not my boss and you and your whore are not welcome here. You bring trouble with you and I do not need it." Maria spoke a little slower now, knowing her audience to be a foreigner.

Rosimar began to protest being called a whore, but Terry shook her by the back of her neck and told her that he would bind and gag her if he needed to.

Juan spoke forcefully now. "Maria, this is going to happen. This woman has much money and we will be getting some of it. Boss, here, has much money and he will be paying us for your help. It will only be for three days and when it is over we will be together. She is nothing to me but a means to a payday."

Maria looked over Rosimar's tight little body and blonde hair. Her opinion did not change much but she kept that to herself. "I have a bedroom she can stay in. Will this man be staying with her?"

The hot, humid air between the airport's air conditioning and the interior of the black sedan caused Brock

Dakota to exhale deeply. This was something that would take time to get used to. Rio was about 10 degrees closer to the equator and much hotter.

The two men looked incongruous in the black sedan. They were dressed more like bums than tourists. Brock was dressed in a dark suit and tie, complete with a hat.

"Agent Dakota, Bill Warfield. This is John Fielding." The passenger in the front seat introduced himself and the driver. "We have your man's hotel room under surveillance."

"You found him?"

"We found his hotel room, in Curitiba. That's about 850 K from here. We have not found him. Walter Suffolk rented a hotel room two days ago in the heart of the city. He left yesterday and we have not been able to locate him since. As soon as he returns to the hotel we will have him. Inside his hotel room we found a bag with a rifle scope in it but no rifle. Some clothes that indicate he is six foot or over. The desk clerk verified that he matches the description and we have a man in the lobby and one in the square. We'll get him."

"I'm impressed. This man has been like a ghost for the past year and you get on him in no time."

"We may look like tourists, but we know our jobs. I might suggest you lose the suit and tie. You might as well hang a sign on your neck."

"What kind of sign, 'Spy?'"

"No. It would say 'rob me.' You do look enough like a local though, or you would if you had a bit more of a tan."

"I won't be here long enough to get robbed."

"How do you expect to get him out of the country?"

"I don't."

"Then you had better be ready to get out of the country yourself. I would hate to see you in a Brazilian jail."

"If you really found this man, get me to Curitiba and I'll take care of the rest. By the way, field agents named Warfield and Fielding is like calling a mass murderer Mr. Serial. Choose different names next time."

Chapter Sixteen
As Ye Sow

"Well, this has turned into a hell of a holiday. I've got no bloody ID and the goddamn Brazilian army wants to shoot me." There was a grin on his face as he walked away from the Castro residence but it disappeared quickly. He looked like a bum. His hair was uncut and Andreas' clothes were way too small for him. He had no money, no shoes, no weapons and he knew nobody in town. He had no doubt that to be picked up by the police was to go back to the firing squad, after what was deemed a sufficient amount of torture and degradation by the army. This would involve giving up his accomplice as well, something he was loath to do regardless of the treatment he had received at the Brazilian soldier's hands.

After making sure he was not being followed, MacMaster sought out a commercial area where the streets were lined with cafes and shops. It did not take him long to acquire a cell phone that a woman had laid on the table beside her. He simply lifted it and kept walking. He would not feel comfortable until he had a change of clothes and without identification, he could not access the proper services. He sat outside a café and dialed a number. There was a number of transfers and verification, but he was eventually connected.

"Scotsman! I had given you up for dead."

Gordon spoke in German. "Colonel, I have been put in a bit of a position. I need some help."

"Anything my friend."

"I am in a city called Curitiba. I have no money and no contacts here. My papers were stolen and I need to get undercover quickly."

"Curitiba?"

"Yes."

"You are in luck. I have a man there who will be able to help you if I can contact him. I believe you know him. What is your location?"

"I cannot remain here. I need to keep moving."

"Make your way to the center of the city. I will connect with my contact and we will get to you if I can. Will you be using this phone?"

"For an hour or so. I will be compromised if I keep it."

"If I do not call in one hour, you will need to call me back."

"Yes. I need to move now."

MacMaster rose and walked away as the waiter moved to either take his order or ask him to leave. The center of town was over eight kilometers away. The streets began to burn his feet when he moved out of the shade. He would never make it without shoe leather. Staying to the shadows he cast about for some protection. Clothes lines were strung all over the city like an untidy spider web. There was no way he would find a pair of shoes to fit him but rolling over a low wall gave him access to a pair of pants that fit him better than the ones he had on. He grabbed a tourist shirt from a roadside display while the shopkeeper was inside. He could see why nobody had bought the garment; it was too big for his broad frame. It was not until blocks later he found the sandals outside a back door. To wear these for long would be crippling, they were made from hemp rope and a piece of an old tire, but they would work for a while.

The streets were pretty much deserted at this hour; most honest citizens were taking a siesta through the midday heat. The cell phone rang, but the caller was looking for the owner. Gordon said something rude and hung up. It rang again, but this time the call was appreciated. He spoke a while and then dropped the cell phone down a sewer grate.

The man was not as young as Lula, nor as tall as Anastasia. He had been farming his patch of land since before he was born, his mother pulling weeds with her child in her belly. He would never be a rich man, nor would he make a move to the congestion of the city, but he was an honest man and fearless in his own way.

When the two women had pulled onto his farm looking for gasoline for their motorcycle, he had been only too happy to help them and insisted they stay for a meal. One thing led to another and they stayed longer than they intended. Lula had no problem giving the man a little of her stock in trade as payment for his accommodations, what did surprise her was when Anastasia joined them. The simple farmer lived through a fantasy for a couple of days that would fill his dreams for the rest of his life. Then they moved on.

Curitiba was a logical choice for them. With almost two million people, it provided cover and anonymity. Between the wallets of the dead men and the contents of the cash register, the ladies had enough to live for a couple of weeks, but their ideas of living differed some. Anastasia Viuda was comfortable eating whatever was available for consumption. Survival training had her eating live beetles and roaches though she drew the line at spiders. She had eaten leeches and snakes and could skin an iguana in less than a minute. Lula had no stomach for such a diet. Her idea of roughing it was cooking her own pancakes. She made some allowances for their situation, but she would rather starve than eat the "vermin of the forest floor."

Lula wanted to rent a room in an upscale hotel. Her logic had it that the men in the more expensive hotels will tip better for her services. She tried to convince Anastasia that this would be a good and easy way to make some money, mistaking the Argentine for something she was not. Anastasia was not unable to follow this path, but she was unwilling. It would not take long before some man thought he could own her and that would be another ugly scene.

Lula knew her companion as Sandiana Torremolinos and Sandiana would not talk about her past. In fact, she had been sullen and uncommunicative the entire day before. It looked as though she was coming out of her depression a little on the third day, and Lula tried to console her, but Sandiana had other things on her mind. She took a walk on the morning of the third day, before Lula was out of bed. It took her a while to find a public telephone that worked, but the further she went from the hotel the more comfortable she was using it.

"Agent Viuda, what an unexpected surprise. Is this line secure?"

"Yes. There was trouble at the border or I would have been back weeks ago."

"Yes, we know of the trouble. You will need to coordinate with Agent del Fuego and return to base. What is your location?"

As she spoke, the tingling began in her head. "I am in Curitiba."

"Good. I will direct your partner to join you. Where are you staying?"

The tingling increased, making her scalp itch. "I have a hotel room near the city center. How do I contact Hernando?"

"What is the hotel?"

"Give me Hernando's number, I will contact him. I may need to move on a moment's notice. There has been nothing but trouble. I will coordinate with him."

The voice on the telephone hesitated for a second and the background noise disappeared as if her contact had cupped his hand over the receiver. The tingling in her head became a buzzing that she could feel in her jawbone. Then the man returned with a telephone number. "Hernando will meet with you and the two of you will return home. He has been very concerned about you."

"I'm sure he has."

"Do not call this number again until the two of you meet."

"Affirmative."

Anastasia hung up the pay phone and the vibrations disappeared. She rolled her head and felt the tension in her neck. She wanted to believe everything was going to be as it was, but she knew nothing was the same. She slid some more coins into the slot and dialed the new number.

"Hello?"

As soon as Hernando del Fuego answered the call, the vibrations in Anastasia's head returned with a vengeance. Where it had been a tickle or an itch, it was now more of a miniature jackhammer. She was almost unable to speak.

"Hello?"

"Hello, Hernando."

"Anastasia! How good to hear from you. I hope you are well. We must join up and leave the country. Where can I find you, my love?"

Anastasia bit her lip and tried to concentrate. The feeling in her head was becoming overwhelming. She had not thought it through enough, and knew it. "Meet me in the city center. The Central Plaza."

"I can be there in half an hour."

"No, I cannot make it until Monday morning. This time Monday, in the Central Plaza." She hung up the phone without waiting for a reply, and like the severed connection, the feeling in her head disappeared.

"General."

"Colonel."

"We have another transmission. Actually, two of them, very close together."

"What is the status of the Strike Team?"

"They joined with two agents already in-country and headed toward the area in question. The entire area was locked down by the military, and they were forced to wait. The new transmission is coming from within Curitiba; the target has moved closer to the transmitting tower. The message has changed as well." He finished with a smile. "We are getting coordinates."

"From the broadcast?"

"Yes, Sir. It took a bit of expertise, but we are now getting coordinates. We cannot jam the signal to the television station without killing our own reception, but we are working on that as well. The Strike Team will move back from the previous area and go around to BR476 and into the city this way. The broadcast has ceased for now, but we have a good fix on where it was coming from."

"Carry on, Colonel, and keep me informed at the minute we have something more. I want you on this like a hungry wolf. Am I making myself clear?"

"Perfectly clear, General. As long as we keep getting broadcasts, this man cannot escape us. His grave has already been dug."

Monday morning dawned clear and hot with almost no clouds in the sky. The Central Plaza was abuzz with activity. People sat in the shade and drank coffee, sold food and sundries, made deals, conversed with colleagues and watched.

It was too early for the amorous young people who joined the throng in the evenings to connect with those of their own ages, but the flagstones were covered with humanity.

An umbrella shaded Hernando del Fuego as he sipped his coffee and waited for his erstwhile partner. He had no doubt she would be there. He felt some regret for what he needed to do, but he was given no choice in the matter. If he was to survive, Anastasia Viuda needed to die. He watched the crowd carefully, knowing he was wanted but feeling sufficiently anonymous.

Juan was uncomfortable. He had been listening to Maria's complaints for two days. She had been telling him how wrong he was bringing a woman into her house, and the two foreigners were obviously bandits or drug dealers. She said repeatedly that nothing good was going to come of this and that he was going to end up in prison or dead for consorting with the wrong kinds of men; he was an honest man and he made an honest living driving taxi and that he should forget about these men and their schemes and send them on their way. He had been glad to leave her at the house that morning.

The smaller branch of the bank had refused to allow him to make a withdrawal from Rosimar Castro's account that morning, claiming that the computer system showed no such account, and telling him that he needed to go to the branch where the account had been opened. Rosimar was ready. She had visited the bank Thursday and had no problem other than they needed a couple of days to verify the funds. She was confident the money would be available today. She had agreed to give Juan a large sum of money as long as she could have the rest.

What had surprised Rosimar more than the gentle treatment she was getting at the hands of the foreigner was when Gordon MacMaster strode through the bedroom door. The two men obviously knew each other well; they embraced and all but kissed each other. The blond had told her all he wanted was to find his big red-headed friend, but she was certain that she had just become superfluous. She tried rising and telling them that her part was done and he had promised that she could go, but she was bodily lifted and body slammed on the bed. She would not be leaving before they told her she could. She was not sure that moment would ever come.

Maria had provided them with enough food for 10 men and there was little left when they were done. These big men could eat like there was no tomorrow, yet neither of them carried any fat.

Sunday had come and the man she knew as Boris Chercovski was outfitted with clothes, boots and a cowboy hat. Other clothes were purchased as well.

When they exited the taxi and headed across the plaza to the bank, Juan and Rosimar were both dressed very well. He wore a three-piece suit and she had an expensive dress. She was accented with tasteful, if fake, jewelry. It would not do to have them looking poor if they were withdrawing large sums of money. The two travelled alone; the foreigners stayed with the taxi.

"I don't like this, Terry. Granted the local constabulary is as inefficient as any third world country, but given the amount of blood spilled in the past few days, there is likely to be a flag placed on her account."

"I have a room in that hotel, and nobody knows me here. We can hole up there until we can get you some identification shipped in. Then we can go north and ship out of a smaller port."

"My thoughts exactly. I told Andreas he could not stay here, but he was convinced that money was power and that they would not come after him if he was rich enough."

"Are you sure you don't want to try getting the money back?" Terry asked.

"No. I promised the money to Andreas to get me out of that hole, and I've always been good to my word."

"If you'd just waited a day, I would have gotten you out. I told you I was standing outside the bloody cell when the lights went out."

"And if I had known you were coming... But it's done now. Let them have the money if they can get it, and we will slip out of here in a few days. I should have known better than to take a job while I was on vacation."

The two of them locked the taxi and sauntered around the outside of the square, noting when Juan and Rosimar entered the bank. At that point, they slipped into a store and pretended they were examining the wares near the window as they watched. They were about 50 yards from the corner of the hotel.

Anastasia rolled out of bed on Monday morning with a sense of purpose. Lula grabbed her arm and told her to come back to bed, but there was no time for that. She stepped into the shower and Lula joined her. They spent some time applying make-up afterwards; they both wanted to look their best.

Lula dressed in a very short skirt, high heels and a low cut blouse. Her bright red lipstick and nail polish were arresting. The belly-band holster fit tightly around her midriff and concealed the small pistol. She hoped she would not need to use it, but with her partner's direction, she knew it was ready for action.

Anastasia had gotten quite fond of the tall boots. They had low heels and a wide flare at the top where her knees were covered and looked for all the world like something from a pirate movie. A little glue and a scrap of leather created a good hiding place for a weapon. She also had a pistol in the inside pocket of her calfskin jacket. Her skirt was longer that Lula's and her blouse was tight fitting, accentuating her tight breasts. She did not wear a brassiere so her nipples pushed at the fabric. Her long hair had been dyed back to black and was tied up in a sleek bun.

The two women looked each other over critically and using an American phrase, Anastasia pronounced the two of them "dressed to kill."

A taxi brought them to the plaza and Anastasia's head began to tingle before they reached the end of the street. She had begun to accept the sensation as a reaction to impending danger, and though she had been in dangerous situations before, had no memory of it. Her fear was that it would distract her when the moment of truth arrived. She hoped that the increased adrenaline that accompanied it would see her through the tenser moments. The feeling did not increase as she stepped across the flagstones.

Looking at her partner 15 meters away, Anastasia regretted bringing her, but only for a moment. She had not explained the plans she had for the man they were there to meet, but had made it clear that he was a very dangerous man. There was no hope of counting on Lula in a pinch, but she was definitely worth a distraction. She commanded attention from every man she walked past.

"Well, wrangle and shear me! Isn't that…"
"Quiet. Let her walk past and we'll pick her up from behind. I'll warn you that she's every bit as dangerous as she

looks, but she's wanted as well. She's not going to chance getting picked up.

"You take her right arm, I'll follow. We walk her down the alley next to the hotel. I hadn't planned on this, but we may make out on this after all."

Terry walked out the door and Gordon was right behind him.

"Perfecta Navaja, I thought I would never see you again." Terry said as his left arm grabbed her right arm and he moved so the crowd would not see the knife in his hand. "Come with me or I'll gut you like a pig," he growled.

The danger sense that was becoming such a part of Anastasia clicked into high gear and rattled inside her head like a broken connecting rod. Her breath filled her lungs beyond normal capacity and her mouth hung open, trembling with the rush.

Terry put his arm around his captive's shoulders and guided her into the narrow side street. He had been so focused on Anastasia he had not even noticed Lula a few steps away.

Gordon concentrated on a man who was rising from a table outside the café on the corner. He did not belong there, even though he was dressed as a tourist. The man's attention was on Terry so he did not see Gordon angling toward him.

"Walter Suffolk, freeze. You are coming with me." The man from the café had pulled a pistol from inside his newspaper and adopted a two hand stance. This set off a flurry of simultaneous events so complex that none of the participants knew everything that happened.

Lula had no idea that the man pushing Anastasia into the alley was not the man they were there to see. Further she did not completely understand the plan. She pulled her pistol from under her blouse, pointed it at the man with the gun and yelled "Drop it and get down on the ground," like she was a certified officer.

Across the plaza, Hernando heard the commotion and saw, not Anastasia but the tall red-headed man who had tried to capture them in Porto Alegre. He rose, reached inside his blousy shirt, gripped the pistol secured at his waistband and began walking across the square as nonchalantly as he could. He did not draw the weapon.

Among the five members of the Strike Team there was only one portable detector. The call had come in minutes before and the team was on it instantly. They had been deployed in the center of the city as a means of getting wherever the target was as expeditiously as possible. Their foresight was rewarded with a genuine signal this morning and they had entered the square following it. They all knew that this was not a capture or kill assignment; it was a zero sum game and they were expected to eliminate the man putting out the signal even if it meant none of the team returned to Paraguay.

The man holding the detector got a strong and positive signal dead ahead. He saw a man, about 35 years old, dressed as a tourist and holding a semi-automatic pistol in both hands. The signal was coming from his direction. It had to have been coming from him. There seemed to be no alternative. This was their target. A quick hand signal and the man to his right pulled his own pistol and shot the man through the heart.

At the sound of the gunshot, Terry had turned and seen the beautiful blonde woman with a pistol in her hand. "Lula?" he blurted.

Lula hesitated as the man she was covering dropped to the ground.

Gordon MacMaster launched himself across the alley and slammed her against the wall. His action was the only thing that kept Lula from being shot by the Paraguayans.

The soldiers heading toward the National Bank in search of the deserter and his sister stopped in their tracks at the sound of the report. The Captain ordered one of them to keep going and the remaining three to find out what was going on. The three men charged across the plaza with their automatic weapons locked and loaded.

The one policeman in the square raised his weapon and prepared to fire on the Paraguayan murderer, but he had already been noted. Another member of the Strike Team shot him. That was when the soldiers opened up on them in full automatic. Three members of the Strike Team went down in the torrent of bullets. One of the soldiers dropped from the return fire. At least three pedestrians were struck. Blood spouted and bodies flopped on the cobblestones.

The CIA man guarding the lobby decided he had no business getting involved with the army's problems.

The Captain and his remaining subordinate were at the doors of the bank when the gunfire escalated. They saw the first soldier go down and the other two take cover behind the central fountain. They charged back down the steps toward the battlefield.

Brock Dakota hurtled down the stairs from the fourth floor and was intercepted by the CIA man before he broached the front door.

Anastasia took the split second of surprise to grab Terry's elbow and wrist and try to crank his arm around behind his back, but he was simply too strong to succumb.

Hernando fell to the flagstones and tried to dig a hole in them with his fingers.

Leaving Lula where she was, Gordon grabbed Anastasia's other arm and hauled her down the alley. Lula was not going to be left behind. All four of them ran for their lives. They were a block away before the gunfire ended. Two blocks away, Terry relieved the Argentine of her belly gun.

Rosimar and Juan were being waited on when the gunfire erupted. The cash had already been brought out of the vault and was being counted. The employees and officers hit the floor as soon as they heard the reports, but their customers had been more practical. They had shoveled the money into a pair of canvas shoulder bags, uncounted, and headed for the entrance, ignoring the bank president's protestations. They saw the Captain coming up the steps, and stopped in their tracks; then they saw him turn and head back into the square.

Another of the soldiers died before the last of the Paraguayan Strike Team went down. The captain and the two remaining soldiers secured the area while Hernando del Fuego slipped out. Juan and Rosimar were already long gone.

Chapter Seventeen
The Road to Perdition

Hernando del Fuego was only lucky to have survived the storm in the Plaza. Had his pistol been out of his waistband, somebody would have shot him. Had he moved another 50 feet, he would have been cut down in the crossfire. If he had made it across the plaza Terry, Gordon or Lula would have shot him. He had more reasons to give thanks than he even knew.

The international shit storm that should have arisen from the incident was quelled by the Brazilian government. They did not need the news circulated that paramilitary death squads were roaming the country looking for foreigners. The American government wanted nothing to do with a story about the CIA being involved in armed conflict in South American countries. The Paraguayan government refused to acknowledge that the men had been sent there or even that they existed. They disavowed all knowledge of their actions. By mutual consent the story was diverted and run as a group of Islamic terrorists who had attacked when apprehended.

Implicit in the cover-up was Brock Dakota who wanted nothing to do with the internal or international struggles of these nations. His eye was on the target, but the target was gone and he had never even seen it. Brock's associates in the CIA were forced to furnish the Brazilian Army with a picture of the fugitive, but the army had no knowledge or interest in that one. The army was able to reciprocate with a picture of Gordon MacMaster, though he was still named Boris Chercovski as far as they were concerned. The CIA promised to keep an eye out but had no knowledge of his crimes or whereabouts.

The bodies of the innocent and the guilty were hauled to the morgue and a cadre of sweepers was dispatched to mop up the blood. Within two hours, business in the Central Plaza returned to normal.

"Don't be a fool, Maria. I watched the Boss walk onto the army base like a phantom and come back the next day." Juan's nerves had taken all they could manage already today.

"He's right, Maria." Rosimar acceded. "He walked into my house and shot four or five men like it was ordering fish in the market. Give him what he wants and get him out of here. The less I see of him and Boris, the better I like it. We have the money, give them their cut and let them go."

"I tell you, both of you, you will not make it past today, alive." Maria was furious that Juan would not listen to her. "These men are killers and they will kill us all for the money you think you have. There is no way they will let you keep this fortune. Ai, we are all dead on our feet and only I can see it."

"And because you fear him, we need to shoot him? This man has paid me well. He has done what he says he will do when he says he will do it. I trust him more than I trust..."

"Who? Me?"

"No, my love, no more than I trust Rosimar. Once money is a factor, it changes people."

Maria turned away from her lover and her new friend. She had been playing Juan's game for a long time and she knew it was time for her to accept the reward she deserved. It had been much too long that she had watched her lover go home to his wife while she slept alone. The reward was before her and she wanted her share. Her dead husband had left her the house, but had not left her rich. She had been living on the scraps of society, working for others, sometimes depending on charity. In her mind she deserved her reward more than Rosimar. After all, what had that little tramp done for the money?

For her part, Rosimar could not leave quickly enough. The army was after her and almost had her earlier that day. She had been sure the end was at hand when she saw the Captain at the door of the bank. Her only problem was that she could not go home. The last time she had seen home, the walls were painted with blood and the floor tiled with dead bodies. It was time for her to head to parts unknown and she was anxious to do just that.

"What do you mean 'no more than I trust Rosimar?' I have been straight with you. I gave you your money. This is what we agreed. Now I am going to leave."

"No. You leave when the big men return and have been paid their cut."

"I tell you what, Juan." Rosimar's voice took on a wheedling tone. "I will leave their cut with you and you can pay them."

After a moment's eye contact with his paramour, Juan agreed and Rosimar turned back to place another stack of bills on the table.

The kitchen knife had been sharpened many times in its long life and it had cut much flesh. It was no different to the knife that the flesh was human this time. It did not bother the knife that the flesh was alive rather than already dead and bled. I mattered not to the knife that the flesh was female. The knife was just doing its job.

Mouth open, eyes bulging, Juan stared at his lover as she stabbed Rosimar: once, twice, thrice and again. The younger woman's initial scream died in her throat as her back arched. The blows had hit her low and, while ultimately fatal, they were not immediate. The two women fell to the floor, Rosimar on top, thrashing, but she could not seem to scream.

Blood flew all over the kitchen as she kicked wildly and jerked about trying to reach the blade in her back.

"Help me." Maria growled through gritted teeth but Juan was unable to move. He had been taken as much by surprise as the victim.

A last few powerful heaves and Rosimar's thin, young body went limp. Her wide staring eyes glared at Juan accusingly and he crossed himself and muttered under his breath.

Maria dragged her blood soaked body out from under her victim with the same accusatory stare as Rosimar. They had both expected help and he had assisted neither.

"Well, what did you expect? Do you think I was going to let this little whore walk out of here with all this money that rightfully belongs to us?"

There was no answer in Juan's mind that could encompass all he was thinking. His brain swirled with scenarios, none of which ended with him living well. He saw the Captain, his face triumphant, dropping the sword as the firing squad pulled their triggers. He saw his wife screaming that the money did not belong to him and that he needed to give it to the church. He saw the tall blond Boss shaking his head and saying he was sorry as the huge redheaded Chercovski stepped up with a machete. He saw the most tragic and memorable vision of himself, standing at his own kitchen table, Maria behind him, stabbing him again and again. That was the vision that stuck. That was the scene that turned his mind. That was the one feeling he could not shake.

"Juan, you need to help me dispose of this bitch."

Juan was beside himself. He saw himself standing there, his mouth hanging open, his arms limp and twitching.

"Juan! Help me!"

He saw Maria trying to drag the body toward the counter. He saw himself, frozen, helpless.

"Juan!"

He could not believe it as he saw himself reach out and grab the rolling pin from the wet dough on the counter and swing it into Maria's head. It was a dream, a hallucination. He was cracking from the stress. He realized he was not breathing. When he again took a breath, he was in the kitchen of his lover's house doused with the blood of two women. He was no longer watching himself. He was watching two dead bodies. He saw the rolling pin in his hand and dropped it like it was turned to a snake. It had not been him. It could not have been him. He stood there like a statue of grief, trembling in disbelief, unable to function.

The frozen moment was shattered by the telephone. Juan collapsed on the floor, his back against the counter. It rang five times before he recognized what it was and twice more before he could get it out of his pocket.

"Juan?"

"Uh, Boss. Yes, yes, yes. I, uh, I need a minute."

"We cannot wait. You know the Barking Pelican?"

"Uh, yes, Boss."

"Pick us up there. Now!"

"Yes, Boss, I, uh."

"What is wrong?"

"I will tell you when I get there. I have made a mistake."

Once Juan was again being directed, he moved with a purpose. He stripped off his blood spattered clothing and without washing, put on a clean uniform. He locked the house and drew the curtains before he left, pulled the cab from the garage and locked that after him. He wanted very much to leave, to run away and never return, but that would not be a reasonable course of action. They would hunt him down and kill him. In fact, every moment his mind flashed to the potential futures his life might hold, he saw nothing but being hunted down and killed. He could not believe he was going to pick up two of those who might do exactly what he feared, but he needed help and could not think of anyone else who could do so.

The Barking Pelican was a tavern that fronted a road, but the hillside behind it was built one dwelling on top of another with no passable roads. Steps and alleys separated the buildings that were built of whatever material could be begged, borrowed or bought. The road made an abrupt turn as it reached the inside apex of the arroyo and followed the other wall out without attempting to climb the hill. The Barking Pelican was right at this angle.

Juan had never seen the tactical advantage displayed here. When he drove up, a person standing in front of the tavern could see both sides of the road, coming and going, for a long way. Not that there was anyone in front of the tavern. Juan had little choice but to wait.

Terry Kingston was missing his rifle scope. It would have given him a better view of the incoming traffic. He would have been able to pinpoint anyone waiting in a parked car. He could have been sure there was no one following his ride. As it was, he relied on his eyes and his patience. He let Juan wait 10 minutes before he slid off the roof of the shack where he had hidden. Juan was a seismic wreck by that time.

"What's wrong, amigo?"

"Señor Boss, I have a problem."

"You're shaking like a tree and you stink of blood. What did you do?"

"I killed her."

"Oh. Did you plan on killing Rosimar?"

"No, Señor. I killed Maria."

"Now what did you do that for?"

"I don't know. She stabbed Rosimar and then, I hit her in the head and I killed her. I don't know what I am supposed to do. I have two bodies in my girlfriend's house and I will be taken to the wall and shot if they find out it was me, and the stupid bitch, she went and stabbed the other one, and there is blood all over the floor and the cabinets and the walls and I got it all over me and hit her in the head because I was afraid she was going to stab me too, and if they find out it was me I will be taken to the wall and shot and…"

"Calm down. Did anyone see you do this?"

"No, Señor."

"Drive down there about half a kay. Pull over by that cantina."

Inside the cantina was one large Scot and two beautiful women. The Scot was telling jokes about Irish women and his two associates were laughing. Terry shook his head and wondered how the man did it. They had just walked out of a blood bath and yet here was MacMaster doing a stand-up routine. It was a perfect way to deflect suspicion, but how many people could pull that off and more, how many people could engage an audience who had just gone through the same trauma? The man paid for the drinks and whatever else they had had and the three of them piled into the taxi.

"It looks as though," Terry began, "Juan has made a mess of things."

"Details?" Gordon asked sharply, his comedic demeanor disappearing.

"I'll let him tell you."

Juan was little relaxed and did not want to speak in front of the women. Once he was convinced to speak, he needed to be cut off more than once to determine the extent and implications of his actions. This was the first time he had killed someone and it had to be his girlfriend. The neighbors had all seen him coming and going over the course of their romance, so there was no doubt who would be implicated once the bodies were discovered.

Back in the blood soaked kitchen, the two canvas bags full of money were still sitting on the table. Juan cold not bring himself to touch them. He claimed the money was cursed and that everybody who came near it died. MacMaster smiled grimly and told him that there was a lot of death behind the money and that was where it came from.

"I give you the money freely if you will help me with this problem. I don't know what happened…"

"OK. We get the point. Now is not the time for words, now is the time for action. Get me soap and bleach and a bucket and sponges and rags. When we are done, this will never have happened." At that point Gordon MacMaster shoved his pistol into the back of his waistband. He had been keeping it on his latest acquisition, though she had made no sign of resistance.

Looking as though she were going to voluntarily assist with the cleanup, Anastasia Viuda knelt down with a sponge from the sink in her hand but she stood again, with a small pistol in her hand. She had been carrying it in the top of one oversized boot, waiting for the proper moment. There was no hesitation, no question in her mind about what needed to be done. It was all or nothing. Kill or be killed. The law of the jungle.

Anastasia's finger squeezed the trigger as she rose from the floor. The compact pistol only held six rounds. Her mind ran through the calculations: two in the big man's chest, two in the blond man's chest, one in the cab driver's head, then make sure they were all dead. Unfortunately for her, Anastasia's tall boots had flat soles and the floor was slippery with blood. She slipped just a bit, not more than an inch but enough to throw her shot wide. Her next round would have taken Gordon in the heart if Terry had not swept his leg up and kicked her in the elbow. The second round went through the ceiling.

The two killers were on their captive in an instant, wrenching the weapon from her hand and throwing her into the pooled blood on the floor. Lula and Juan both took one step forward without knowing what it was they were going to do, then they both took two steps back.

"I told you this one was tricky."

Terry did not reply but took a towel from a kitchen cabinet and sliced it up the middle. It served to tie Anastasia's hands behind her back.

"Juan, will any of the neighbors call the police?"

"I don't know, Boss. I think we should go now."

"We cannot leave with this woman dripping blood down the driveway. Where is the bath? She needs a shower." MacMaster took Anastasia into the bathroom and put her in the shower with her clothes on.

Terry got to work with the mop and bucket, slopping up as much of the blood as he could. Lula stripped down to her underclothes, and unselfconsciously kneeled on the floor with a rag and a dishpan. She did not notice Juan standing behind her, biting his knuckles. Terry finally told him to make himself useful and he went to get some suitcases from a room upstairs.

The bodies of Rosimar and Maria were taken to the bathtub, stripped and washed down. The blood soaked clothing was put into a cardboard box.

Soaking wet from the shower, Anastasia was taken to the bedroom for a change of clothes. While Maria's clothing was not the correct size for her, there is always something that can be done. When he untied her hands and she stripped down for him, there was no question that he appreciated her form, but he did not touch her. This surprised Anastasia. She had been hoping he would be overcome with lust as so many other men had been over the years. It had made them easy targets and would have done the same to this one, but he was too professional for that, too disengaged. She vowed that she would find a way to engage him and that it would be his downfall.

Lula was finishing up the kitchen floor when the two came out of the bedroom. Juan was coming out of the bathroom with a leg and stuffing it into a suitcase. Gordon dropped the woman on a chair and stuck his head in the bath.

"Anything I can help you with?"

"Yeah, mate. I'll finish this up but I'll need a new set of clothes. Make sure the hat matches. We'll need a new set of luggage for these little darlings and if you could think of a good destination for them, that would be good. Juan, take him shopping.

Gordon took a stack of bills from one of the two canvas bags sitting on the kitchen table. Juan physically cringed. He had murdered his girlfriend for the money and now he would not touch it. Before he left, Gordon put the bags in the bathroom with Terry. Lula was cleaning the blood off her knees and hands preparatory to garbing herself and Gordon thought it likely that temptation would get the better of her.

The shopping trip went off without a hitch and when the taxi pulled back into the garage it contained two sets of luggage, voluminous bags, and new clothing for the men both formal and informal.

Inside the house, Anastasia was tied to a chair. Apparently she had tried to slip out the door while Terry was finishing his gory chore in the bathroom.

After a shower, Kingston dressed himself in a flowery tourist shirt and shorts. Juan went for the formal attire he had never been able to afford before. He wore the white shirt and tie under a vest and jacket despite the heat. It would not become a long-term trend, but it made him feel better to concentrate on something less dramatic than the situation he had gotten himself into.

Out of hearing of the others, MacMaster lost some of his charm. "Terry, who was the American?"

"I dunno. Smelled like CIA but didn't look the part. Had my name. Maybe from the hotel. This was not a chance meeting, though. He was there looking for me. He was not interested in Perfecta or whatever her name is. He paid no attention to you and if the other man had not shot him, Lula would have."

"Do you think so?"

"I dunno. I don't have a clue who those men were either. They dressed like farmers or fishermen, but they were all armed and went off like a flash. If they had been waiting for me, I would be dead."

"Instead of them."

"Let's face it, mate, the army was on Rosimar. Maybe not Juan. They were distracted by the men who shot the American, or they would have taken them in the plaza."

"There is no connection between Juan and Rosimar." Gordon took over. "So we should be all right here until we leave town. I think we should leave soon. I think we need to take Juan with us. He is rather upset and needs some time to calm down."

Back in the living room, the Scotsman started the conversation. "I wish to take the, uh, evidence to Cascavel. It can be put to some use there."

Juan wanted to know, "How will you get this to Cascavel? It will look stupid to take a cab from Curitiba to Cascavel. It is 500 kilometers away and there are toll booths where the men will see us. I think it is too dangerous a plan. If we steal a car they will know it at the toll booths."

"We will buy one. That is, you will buy one…"

"No, Señor." Juan cut Gordon off and made the sign of the cross. "I will not touch that money. It is cursed. It is only by the will of God that I am alive now, and he knows that if I touch that money again I will die."

"I have no problem touching it." Lula chimed in with her lovely lilting voice and a perfectly charming smile. She had said nothing for a long time, simply absorbing the situation and looking for an opening. She was more comfortable with it than Juan would ever be.

Gordon reverted to English, but with such a heavy Scottish brogue that one could have spoken English and still not understood what he was saying. Terry understood, however, when asked, "Is this man going to compromise our situation?"

Terry shook his head rather than answering.

"If you have the slightest reservations about him, I think perhaps we should decommission him now and save ourselves the trouble later."

Terry pulled back a curtain, just a touch and looked out the window. Gordon changed the subject. "What about the woman?"

"Which one?"

"The brunette is going, for a reward. What about the other?"

"I've met her before. It is almost more of a coincidence than I can justify. In a city this size, I'm going to meet anyone I know is beyond my expectations. Let me give you some history. I saw the look you gave me when I recognized Perfecta. I saw her chained to the floor of a cabin in a little jungle whorehouse they call Woodytown. I was there looking for you. Spent a couple of days with Lula and she helped put me on the right track. She's a whore though, and you know what that means. It might be a good idea to ask them how they survived when everybody else in that little town died."

"There is no reason to ask us. I will tell you," Anastasia interjected. Terry's accent was not so difficult to understand as Gordon's. "It is because we killed them all. Lula and I killed every man and woman in that town, and we will kill you the same way if you do not let us go."

The smile on Gordon's face was not sadistic when he asked if she was going to fuck him like a sheep first. She replied that he had already been fucked like a sheep by a thousand real men.

Terry grabbed Lula by the arm and took her in the bedroom. He asked her pointed questions about the incident at the Jardim de Prazares and got a much more realistic answer. He learned of the death of Roberto Campena de Iguaca, whom he had never met, and the massacre of the inhabitants. Lula made it a point of saying that she had tried relying on men and that they had always fallen short.

While Terry was getting the scoop on Woodytown, Gordon was questioning Anastasia about Hernando del Fuego. He had been with her in the hotel and during the initial accident but had been willing to desert her in the forest. She looked like she was about to open up when suddenly she moaned and closed her eyes. She managed to groan something about danger just before the knock sounded at the door and the police announced themselves.

Gordon grabbed Anastasia by the arm and she did not resist or cry out. He hustled her into the bedroom and told Lula that she was going to be the woman of the house. Juan answered the door in his new three-piece suit and asked the police what they wanted. Lula joined them, charming and sexy. It was a credit to her acting ability that she was smiling and flirting even during such a tense time. Juan was nowhere near as composed, but did not look the part of a ruffian in his three-piece suit.

The officers did not seem to be totally convinced, but they retreated with an admonition to be more careful. They had finally responded to the 'shots fired' call and had been put off with a tale of a couple of backfires.

Gordon slipped upstairs and saw when the car pulled away but pulled around the block to watch the house. They were not subtle about it. They had appeared to have bought the story, but Juan thought they might know Maria, and it was sure they had not seen Lula in the neighborhood before.

He slid back downstairs and watched the look on his captive's face. It had become manic, as if the arrival of the police had recharged a battery within her. She repeatedly tested her bonds, her muscular shoulders flexing in rhythm. He could not help but think she was incredibly sexy the way a caged tiger is sexy.

"I'll go and take care of them if they bother you," she breathed, but he declined with a shake of his head and a smile.

"Look, mate, they didn't buy it. The backfire story didn't fit with the three-piece suit. I'm thinking they're waiting for back up. I say we need to make a move now." Terry was convinced he knew what was best.

"I don't think so, uh, Boss." Gordon could not help smirking at the term. "I think they are waiting for us to panic and make a move. If nothing happens, in a short while they will file their report and move on."

"We'll see. I'm not sure but I don't hear any sirens."

"Relax a little."

"That's easy to say, but we're under surveillance in a dead woman's house with a couple of suitcases full of meat and hostages. I think I have the right to be nervous."

Gordon was right this time and the patrol car moved off after a few minutes. Anastasia relaxed a little. She felt it ironic that the tingling and the heightened awareness had flowed over her when the police came to the door, but that the response all but disappeared after they left. A normal person might have been relieved when the police arrived and more anxious when they departed. She decided it was something about the big redhead's disarming smile and easy, unhurried demeanor that inspired respect. The man had a palpable aura of confidence about him. She looked at him and almost smiled, against her wish. He smiled at her.

"Juan," Terry said, "we need a car, a Volvo. I want to buy it from a private individual, not a dealer. This is important. Car dealers file paperwork. Lula and I will go with you. OK?"

"OK, Boss." Juan was happy to get out of the house. The police were almost more than he could handle tonight. He counted it lucky that he did not know the two who had come to the door. As a cabbie, he knew almost every officer on that side of town.

In an amazing show of disassociation, Lula kept up her perky, flirtatious attitude. Rather than worry about what might happen, she was convinced that the worst was already behind her, and it not only kept a bounce in her step, but heartened those around her. Before she left with Terry, she brought a glass of water for Anastasia and held it to her lips, then she gave her a long and tender kiss on those same wet lips.

The garage door opened and the taxi pulled out with Terry hunkered down in the back seat and Lula riding shotgun. Juan drove carefully and kept his eyes open for the constabulary, but they had indeed retreated.

Anastasia Viuda knew what was coming next. She had seen it so many times it was like a scripted game, a tragedy of human nature that she continually turned to her advantage. The trouble was, this time, it did not.

"Oh, the day has become so hot. Perhaps, if you could loosen my blouse I could get some satisfaction." Bullets would have melted in her mouth, but Gordon MacMaster was unmoved. He loosened a button on her blouse and smiled softly.

"We could have some fun while they are gone. This has gotten me very excited."

Once again, Gordon smiled and it occurred to him that he had been smiling a lot. It seemed very out of place given the circumstances.

"Do you not find me exciting?" she purred.

"Yes, dear. This is where you are going to fuck me like a sheep."

"Oh, yes. I want you to use me. Make me feel much like a woman."

He chuckled. "I think you are very much the woman."

"And you are a real man after all, yes?"

"A real man does not need to tie up his women."

"Then untie me and we will do what comes naturally."

"I think killing me would come more naturally to you than kissing me."

Anastasia began to move as seductively as she could, given her hands were bound behind her. "Why do you deny us this little bit of life?" she asked.

"In the interest of self-preservation. Even the best snake charmer gets bitten from time to time."

"So I am a snake now?"

"No, you are a mark. If it was a simple job, I would have saved myself all this trouble and simply shot you in Porto Alegre." He was not smiling now. "You have become more trouble than you are worth and I may need to shoot you yet."

344

"So, I am nothing more than a mark. You find it easier to kill women than kiss them?"

"What should I call you?" Gordon was slightly uncomfortable with the direction the conversation was taking and did not want her to think he could be manipulated.

"Call me Perfecta." she breathed, sensing his discomfort.

"You can call me Boris."

"But Boris is not your name."

"No more than Perfecta is yours."

She smiled and showed her perfect white teeth. It lit up her face like a beacon.

"We are not much different, you and I," he continued. "We are in the same business, probably for similar reasons."

"And what business is it you think I am in?"

"You, my dear, are a killer. That is how I found you. You know that it is the natural order of things for the strong to kill and eat the weak. Your present mistake is to think I am weak and that you can kill and eat me."

"I would like very much to eat you. I think you would taste good."

"I appreciate your enthusiasm, but I am not on the menu today."

"I need to pee. Do you think I could do that?"

"What you really mean is will I untie you."

"It does make it easier."

"No, I will not untie you, but yes, you can pee." He helped her into the bathroom and pulled her panties down for her.

"A girl needs some privacy."

"No. I will not take advantage of you, but if I give you a minute untied you'll be out of here like the west wind."

"You'll have to wipe me."

He took a wad of toilet paper and gently dabbed her dry.

Again she smiled. She knew she would find a weakness yet. This one was too much of a gentleman to be a true killer and did not make her head vibrate.

Chapter Eighteen
The Devil is in the Details

"Why the fuck didn't he tell us he was going in?"

"He was supposed to watch only. He didn't like wearing the earpiece, so he didn't, but he was only supposed to give us a heads-up. He was specifically instructed not to engage the primary."

"Agent Pierce, you run a sloppy ship down here. You and your men dress like slobs, you don't follow protocol, your communication is slack and you're lax. And now it cost you a man. Don't think this will be overlooked in D.C."

"You look, Agent Dakota, you can't come down here from your ivory tower and tell me what the fuck we're doing wrong. You don't know the first thing about what goes on down here. The corruption, the politics, the system. Yes, I lost a man. I lost my goddamn partner but I will stand by anything and everything he ever did. He saved my ass half a dozen times and not by following your precious protocol, but by using his head. He was 10 times the agent you will ever be and don't you dare forget it. I know he had good reason for drawing down on the subject. In case you missed something, he got caught in a cross-fire. I'll find out what the fuck was going on here and I'll find your man as well, but I want you to stay the fuck out of the way. Lots of people get shot down here without much reason." While he had started speaking vociferously, he ended his speech slowly, carefully enunciating each syllable.

"Are you threatening me, Pierce?"

"I'm trying to teach you something about Brazil, Dakota. It has nothing to do with Washington D.C. It is so different from your velvet lined life that you may get into trouble if you don't pay attention. Now, I'm going down to the morgue to identify my partner's body and I don't want to see you again today. Go get a señorita or get drunk or do whatever it is you do when you're not fucking up my agenda. I'll see you tomorrow."

Dakota literally bit his tongue to keep from launching into a verbal attack on Agent Pierce. He understood the pain of losing someone close and knew that any more conversation with Pierce would alienate his only local connection. What he did do was flip open his laptop and began writing his report. He wanted his to be the first to reach Washington with the details of how he was prevented from leaving the hotel when the shooting started. It was a small point, but he felt it was important. He was not kind to his CIA counterparts in the report, and knew it was a much larger point that the dead agent had not been in contact with his backup.

It was a very short period of time between the encrypted transmission and the reply. The new communication did nothing to sooth his anger. He was told to stand down and return to base. He fired off a quick affirmative and went downstairs to the bar for several doses of liquid pain killer.

After the requisite emotional numbness settled in, Brock made a phone call. "Good afternoon, Chief."

"Good afternoon, Agent Dakota."

"Chief, I have decided I like it down here in Brazil and I would like to take a little vacation here."

"In the future or now?"

"Right now."

"I must say, there is a lot to tempt a man in a place like Brazil. I want you to be absolutely sure you want to vacation there. A man could get in a lot of trouble vacationing in a place like Brazil."

"I understand that, Chief. I have little choice. These Caspers fucked up and would blame it on me if they could."

"Stand down, Agent! There will be no such allegations transmitted into my department by anyone."

"Yes, Sir. I got the same word from them. Stand down."

"Then you have no choice but to go on vacation?"

"I have an itinerary."

"Don't call us if you get sand kicked in your face at the beach. You're on vacation. I don't know you."

"Roger that." Brock hung up the pay phone and wiped the handle almost subconsciously. A tight grin flashed across his face when he thought of the phrase "off the reservation."

It was not difficult to find out the Captain's name and probable location. He was still answering questions at the local police station. He and his surviving men were being held while the ballistic evidence was collated. The local police captain wanted to be sure his officer had not been shot by a member of the army. Dakota knew he would not be allowed immediate access to any of these men. As an agent for Homeland Security he had no jurisdiction in this area of the world. If he had been CIA, he would potentially have been given some restricted access, but currently he could not even claim NSA status.

The day was hot but the better of the local restaurants had air conditioning. Dakota had left a message at the desk for the Captain. He could not be sure it would connect the two of them but it might. He would be able to see the soldiers pulling out; they had brought their truck with them. He waited hours in that restaurant before he finally got a call. Brazilian Portuguese was a little different for him. Dakota spoke a Spanish dialect, like most recently vetted agents.

The call came from the desk. The Captain had agreed to meet him but it would not be until the following day. Brock made an appointment to meet at the Royal Grande Hotel in the plaza, then he caught a cab there. He would be staying in Walter Suffolk's room, breathing in the atmosphere and living as Walter lived. He would figure out why Walter was here, who he was after and how he had intended to do it. Brock Dakota was going to become his target, find him and kill him. He had no intention of bringing the man back alive. He had no jurisdiction, no backup and no business initiating this action. He was a ghost on holiday.

It took the trio longer to find a Volvo for sale than Terry had expected and it was dark when they returned to the deceased Maria's house. Neither Gordon nor Anastasia were sleeping, they were sitting in the living room having a pleasant conversation. It was as though they had been good friends for years.

Juan had relaxed a bit once he was behind the wheel of his cab and Lula was irrepressible. Her bubbly personality was enough to rouse the most dour individual and get them on the dance floor.

It was not clear why Gordon had insisted on the car being a Volvo but he and Terry had not wasted any time going over the details of the plan. MacMaster wanted the car to be a Volvo and Kingston had made sure it was.

The fastest way to Cascavel was to take PR376 to PR277. This would avoid the potential military problems on PR116, but PR277 had multiple toll booths. Juan felt it better to stay on the 376 to Ponta Grossa and then take PR373 South. Terry agreed with him and communicated as much to Gordon. The trip to Ponta Grossa was uneventful with Lula chattering in the front seat, Anastasia rubbing up against the two foreigners in the back seat and Juan doing what he did best, driving.

The motel room was rented for two at the Sword River Motel. The well-dressed man drove a Volvo and paid cash. He had a very pretty blonde woman with him and signed the register as Jose Diaz. She checked out of the room in the morning and they left together.

Anastasia Viuda spent the night with her two escorts in a different motel. They watched her alternately and she slept like a baby. She did not know why they were going in the wrong direction or what Cascavel held for them. She did know that the longer she worked on them, the more likely one of them would make a mistake. She was doing her very best to make them comfortable with her. Without being overt, she tried her best to seduce them as well. It had been one of the lessons she learned early, "Men let their guards down when their pride is up."

Lula was pouting in the morning and Juan was very tight lipped. She complained about having to spend the night with him when there were two others in the group that she wanted to be with. Juan had tried his best to seduce the bubbly blonde, but she was having nothing to do with it. He had eventually tried to pay her for some and that had ignited her fury. Juan did not understand since she came from Woodytown and had been making a living that way for years. What had changed? He did not understand but had given up when she yelled that his last lover was dead. It could not have worked out any better if it had been planned that way.

Breakfast and lunch were eaten in the car, and dinner was room service in the hotel suite. The men were getting more comfortable with Anastasia Viuda as she worked on them, and Lula had made it plain that she would not be sharing a room with Juan. If she could not sleep with Anastasia, she would be sleeping with Terry. Terry felt a little out of sorts being chosen second in line to a woman, but there was no calling a person's preferences.

After dinner, Gordon and Juan left together with a bag of money. Terry remained in the company of two very persuasive women and the thought of having them both was extremely appealing. Lula was disarming and Anastasia had a thrilling, dark sexiness that lured men like spawning salmon. He almost gave in to the temptation, but then it occurred to him that if Lula preferred to be with Anastasia then by the time their little ménage-a-trois was done, there might only be two left alive so he smiled and encouraged them to satisfy each other, which they did not do.

When Gordon returned he had a bit less money but he was driving an almost new Chrysler. He and Lula used the Chrysler in the morning when they went shopping.

"Tell me, Boss," Anastasia drawled sarcastically in English. "Why are we here in Cascavel? What does your friend Boris doing in this town?"

"I think he is repaying a favor. Someone did him a favor once and he is going to do something now to thank him."

"So, it is a good idea to be Boris' friend? I would rather be your friend."

"Perfecta Navaja, your kind of friendship involves the kiss of the blade."

"Ah, it is true to you. I have done many things that some priests would say is beyond confession. I have thought things that are worse. I am thinking some now."

"Stick to Portuguese, I'll try to keep up, but don't think I'm going to fall for your line. I would hate to gag you but I will do what is needed."

Anastasia fell silent. She was not used to men she could not intimidate or seduce. These two were of a different breed from all those she had known, and though she had known men she considered professional killers, when it came to women they were either pliable or hard. They either loved women and suffered for it, or hated women and were already suffering. This pair of killers loved women but would not be played. Her estimation of a true professional was changed as was her strategy for the immediate future. It seemed to her that they were not taking her seriously enough, and that would play well into her hands, but that they also had a cavalier attitude about the fact that they were transporting her to be tortured and killed. It was as though they thought she did not know.

She tested her bonds. The torn towel had been replaced with nylon cord and though there was some give, it was nowhere near enough to free herself. She would be able to get her arms in front of her when the moment arrived but she would not show that card yet.

Thoughts turned to Lula. She was talented with her hands and her tongue, but she was uncommitted. If the adventure they had been through together was not enough to cement her loyalty, then she was too fickle to count on for support. She had verbally thrown her lot in with her, but Anastasia felt that when the chips were down, Lula would prefer to stand with Terry.

The bottom line was that Boss did not have as much respect for her as Boris so he would be the one she went after. If she could just get him to fall asleep in that chair, she would be free in minutes.

It was worth one last try. She slipped off the bed onto the carpet and swayed over toward him. Without saying anything, but holding his eyes with hers, she dropped to her knees in front of him. Her tongue came out and licked her full lips leaving a wet sheen on them. She left no doubt about what she was offering.

Terry smiled and stood up.

Anastasia smiled then opened her mouth further.

Terry reached into his pocket and pulled out another length of rope, pushed Anastasia on her face and tied her ankles. Then he picked her up, returned her to the bed and went back to his chair.

Anastasia finally got the message.

Lula had gone to town with her new friend's bankroll: dresses, skirts, stockings, shoes, hats, jackets, blouses, purses, panties and bras. She was effervescent when she returned to the hotel room and insisted on modeling some of the new clothing for Terry. He had to admit that it fit her well. The clothing was not all hers, however. An assortment of chic outfits for the taller woman was laid out. They represented some of the latest fashion and were not Chinese knock-offs.

Anastasia could not understand why they would dress her in expensive clothing to deliver her to her executioner.

"I'm going to kill that big red-headed motherfucker if it's the last thing I do," Hernando muttered to himself. "And whoever that other pendejo is. I'm going to kill him too." The truth was, Hernando was too drunk to see straight. It had been a long time since he had allowed himself to get so far out of control, and it may have been that he needed to before he could devise a plan of attack. There was no question as to why the hunter had taken his woman, the reward was still being offered. If Hernando thought he could get away with it, he might have turned her in for it himself, but the debacle at the border had eliminated this possibility. He had been anonymous prior to that. So Hernando waited and watched and drank. A sly smile curled his lips when he thought of his enemy doing all the work for him and then setting himself up.

He was about to reach for the bottle again when he saw a vehicle approaching the gate. His eyes were bleary, but he got enough of a focus through the scope of his rifle to see that it was one of Francisco's men driving the children back from school. He cursed and picked up the bottle, realized that if it had been his target that he was too drunk to implement any plan, and put it back down. A noise caught his attention, but it was just the scurrying of rats. The church had been deserted for many years and was falling down in disrepair. Some rats had chewed on the beams but the steeple was constructed of stone. In a different neighborhood, he would have needed to dispossess someone to occupy this vantage point, but it was clear that this neighborhood of Itaborai would not stand for it. While the church was disintegrating, someone still cut the grass and pruned the trees on the property.

Things were going well for Alderman Jose Diaz. He had successfully avoided scandal even though he drank in public and had multiple affairs with less than savory women. He foresaw a day when he would seat himself in the office of the mayor and then, there would be no stopping him. He had stepped on a lot of people on his way up the ladder, but regretted none of it.

The bar was busy that evening. The younger, poorer men vied with their older and better heeled opposition for the favors of the women. Most of the crowd were regulars, and those not seen that often were still known in the neighborhood. It was an old and familiar dance that should have ended in an old and familiar way, but for the injection of whimsy.

Most of the blonde hair in South America is dyed that color. The richer women pay good money to keep up the illusion. The blonde stranger who entered The Watering Hole that evening was no dye job; her eyebrows were blonde and her hair was light all the way to her scalp. This was only the beginning of her appeal. She was dressed in the latest trendy clothing, not gaudy, but stylish and tight fitting. The clothing revealed her tight little body just enough to make it shimmer.

Many were the men who wanted to buy her drinks that evening, she had more alcohol lined up for her than she could possibly consume and was forced to dump much of it as discretely as she could. She was trying not to get drunk, but was failing at it.

The young men trying for her attention had no chance and most of the older men did not even give it try. Jose Diaz would probably have fit into the latter category if she had not come to sit at the bar directly beside him. Had he not been several rounds into his cups, he may have become suspicious. As it was, he bought the illusion that she was interested in him and what he did. He bought the illusion that she wanted to leave the bar with him, and that her designs were to enjoy a hotel room for the night.

The bottle of bourbon that his new love interest retrieved from her car cemented the deal. It was 12 years old and distilled in Kentucky. It was also laced with a sedative. Two shots would not knock a man out, but Jose drank more than that. They never checked into that hotel.

When Alderman Jose Diaz awoke it was to the sound of the motel door being kicked in and the room filling up with the civil guard. When he asked where he was and where the blonde was, the sergeant almost shot him in the face. The box of clothing was what had started the call. It was outside the door of the motel room and contained not only the blood soaked clothing of two women, but a receipt for the Sword River Motel in Ponta Grossa. The suitcases in the room and in the trunk of his car held all the evidence that would ever be needed to convict Alderman Jose Diaz of multiple premeditated murders. His defense was weak as he could not remember what had happened the night before. He insisted that he had never been to Ponta Grossa but the receipt showed a room rented in his name. The clerk of the motel did not remember Jose but he did remember seeing a pretty blonde and knew they had arrived in a Volvo. He got the color wrong, but that did not deter the jury from having the Alderman executed forthwith.

Diaz had some people who owed him some favors but nothing of this magnitude, and no one wanted to admit having been allied with him. Political allies ran for the hills once the scandal was exposed, and those who had opposed him in the past gained favor in the eyes of the voters.

"Lula, that was magnificent. There is a man in Cascavel who owes you a great favor."

"Thank you, Boris, but it was not the favors or the friends I need. I need money."

"Yes, yes. And you will have what was arranged, but not in this town. We need to get you out of here, and you must know that if you are seen by anyone who was in that bar that night, there will be the devil to pay."

"I'll tell you what. You can keep the money and just let Perfecta go. She and I will head out and you will never see us again."

"No." Gordon would not elaborate on his decision.

"Then I will take my money now and leave."

"No."

"What is it you want then, eh?"

"You will stay with us until we get out of Cascavel. I owe you a favor now and that is the only reason I do not kill you and leave you in a ditch somewhere. I like you, but that does not mean I will not cut your throat if you try to do something stupid."

The wide open stare Lula gave Gordon looked very much like a deer in the headlights of a truck. She saw that she had underestimated the man and vowed not to make that mistake again. There was no doubt in her mind that he would follow through with his threat and began to believe that she would never get away with or without the money. She decided she needed a friend and quickly. There was no more being coy.

The bedroom door was not locked so she slipped in quietly and slipped into bed. Terry grunted and pulled his pistol out from under the pillow to place it on the night stand. Then he wrapped his arms around her.

"Why did you do that?" Anastasia asked Gordon.

"Do what?"

"This whole thing in Cascavel. You did not need to come here and it does not even make any sense. We could have dumped those bodies in the river and moved on. We could be in Francisco Modiano's villa right now. He would be pretending to pay you while torturing me and planning to kill you. You know he will never pay you the reward. He is not an honorable man."

Gordon fell silent. It was not the first time he had thought this.

"You will end up with nothing or dead and I will be tortured to death. Does this seem like it is worth your efforts?"

"I don't think I will allow this man to cheat me. As for you, I don't think I will be manipulated. I may need to tape your mouth shut and stick you in the trunk."

"Is that why you bought me these fine clothes? To stick me in the trunk?"

"I have treated you with respect. You killed the wrong man, actually several men, and you will be brought to task for it."

"So, you didn't answer my question." She changed tack. "Why go through this elaborate deception?"

"I owed a man a favor and saw the means to repay him."

"Does he know what you have done?"

"He will."

"So, you went through all this for a favor?"

"Yes."

"I wish we had met under different circumstances. I wish you owed me a favor."

Gordon did not reply. He was thinking about his beautiful captive being tortured to death and did not particularly relish the idea. Then he shook his head to dispel the vision while reminding himself she was a killer. He checked her bonds and, satisfied they would hold her, went into the living room.

"Colonel?"

"Ah, once again, my lost Scottish friend."

"Yes. One might say this job took a bit more of a turn than I would have expected."

"Yes, I got the call from Switzerland. I assumed that you were at least partially in charge of your destiny."

"Things did look chancy for a minute. But the news is better this time."

"Go on."

"I have half of the package, the softer half, in pristine condition and will deliver said package upon receipt of payment in the same Swiss account we just spoke of. You have that number?"

"I do not have the number but I feel certain they will want proof of your claim before initiating the transfer."

"Make the call and I will create proof and mail it. Mail it... Oh. I may have made a mistake. I'm sorry, I was just realizing something."

"Does this affect the timing of the delivery?"

"No. Not at all. I look forward to drinking chilled schnapps."

"And I would relish seeing you again."

"I will call tomorrow."

Captain Bellisario of the Brazilian Army was standing in Walter Suffolk's hotel room in the Royal Grande Hotel looking as professional as he could, given the fact that he had been up the entire night explaining himself repeatedly. He had showered and shaved but he had not slept.

"Agent Dakota, your little operation cost us a great deal and will undoubtedly cost me my next promotion, so tell me, what is it you can do for me that will ameliorate this?" The man's English was better than most American's and his accent was European.

"There is an international terrorist and murderer on the loose. His last known location was Curitiba. We were waiting for him when the shooting started yesterday, and given the fact that a CIA agent was shot while waiting for him, I feel sure that he is responsible."

"I do not know this man and I do not know what your operation was. I am sure it has not escaped your attention that Brazil has no extradition treaty with the United States and that operations here are only to be undertaken by us. Your man was in breach of protocol, international law, civil law and the working arrangement between our countries. He was shot while committing a crime, and if I had known about it, I might have shot him myself."

"Allow me to explain a bit further." Dakota was obviously sliding down the wrong side of this argument. "The man I am seeking is, as I said, a murderer. He is responsible for the brain death of the President of the International United Auto Workers. The UAW has posted a reward for his capture, but the reward is not contingent upon his being alive." The lie was plausible.

"And what is it that you think I am going to do about this? Do you know for sure that he is even here?"

"We are standing in his hotel room. But I have been a poor host. Please, have a seat. Would you like a drink?"

"You have yet to explain who this man is and where he is, since he is obviously not here."

"Ah, yes, that is the problem, isn't it? I do not know where he is. I am looking for your perspective on this. After all, you were in the thick of it while I was not allowed to leave the hotel lobby. I knew he was there, but the senior CIA agent insisted that it was a local matter."

"I am not sure I can help you. I will speak to the men who were closer to the action. Perhaps they have something that will assist us. How much did you say the reward was?"

The reward was substantial in America but a princely sum in Brazil.

"And how would we split this?"

"I am more interested in seeing this man captured or better yet, buried. I would be willing to give you 40 percent."

"You will not be receiving any of this as an official of the Unites States Government, am I mistaken?"

"No, you are not mistaken, but I am not here with an official status. I am on vacation."

"You will take the 40 percent, and I will spread the rest among my assistants. After all, without me you have nothing. Even the CIA is not going to assist you further if you are on vacation." The stress he gave the word indicated he knew exactly what Dakota was up to. "I have expenses that need to be compensated."

"All right. I'll settle for 40 percent, but if we don't find him, we both get nothing."

"I will see what I can do to assist you, in the interest of greater international understanding, and to promote a peaceful resolution to an unfortunate situation."

"This is what we have for a picture. As you can see he is tall and blond. He talks with an English accent. He's also a suspect in a triple homicide in Cleveland, Ohio."

"I thought you said you did not intend to take him to trial?"

"I'm just giving you what I have on him. Believe me, when this guy shows up, the shit starts hitting the fan."

"I understand what you are trying to say, though I do not appreciate your vulgar Americanisms. He is an anarchist."

"He's a stone cold killer and everywhere I followed him, there is a trail of bodies lying in the street. Don't underestimate him."

Captain Bellisario turned on his heel and strode stiffly to the door. He trusted his new American accomplice about as much as he trusted an Amazon Bird Spider, but there were uses for everything if one looked hard enough.

The restaurant owner/cook had not seen the man in the picture. He had seen the man now resting in the morgue, though he had not waited on him. His daughter had waited on him. She was impatient and anxious to get rid of the Captain. She had already given her statement and that should have been enough in her eyes. She had customers and needed to get back to them.

Sitting under one of the umbrellas that sprouted from the café tables, Bellisario grabbed the young woman's arm and told her that she would be sitting in a cell if she did not cooperate with him. Once he explained who he was, and that some of the men who had died the day before were in his command, the waitress was much more willing to assist him.

Yes, the man in the picture was the man that her customer had attempted to apprehend. No, she did not speak English but, yes, the man had said the words "Walter Suffolk."

"I need you to be very sure and very specific about what happened here. You were outside, waiting on whom?"

"It was old man Pablo. He comes around every morning for a cup of coffee. The old bastard likes to come here because I let him pinch my ass from time to time. He is a pretty good tipper and too old to be a threat."

"Has he been here today?"

"In a few minutes. He might not show up after the shooting."

"So what did you see? Take me through everybody's actions including your own. I need to see the scene from your eyes."

"I was talking to Pablo. My back was toward the American."

"How do you know he was American?"

"Americans stick out like the spines of a cactus. He was sitting in that chair. I was over there. That is Pablo's chair, he sits there every day. I hear the legs of the chair scrape and the man yells in English, so I cannot tell you what he said but he was pointing a gun at the other man, the blond one in the picture."

"Was there anyone else near?"

"Now that you say that, yes, there was. The blond man, he was holding on to the arm of a woman. She was tall with long black hair and this tall sexy pair of boots. I did not get a good look at her face. I saw the gun and froze for a second, then I saw the man behind him with the device."

"What device?"

"I told the police... oh, here comes Pablo now. I will get him coffee and be right back." She bounced off faster than Bellisario could stop her but returned soon enough. "The device took all the man's attention, then he tells his friend to shoot the American. His friend pulls out a gun and shoots the American and I run inside. I was hiding under a table after that and the shooting started to get… you know, loud. I was scared and did not look again. I did not see anyone else."

"I will speak with you again later. I need to see Pablo now."

"I will be right here."

"Dom Pablo, how does the day find you?"

"It finds me right where I always am in the morning. I am easy to find."

"I am Captain Bellisario, I was in charge of some of the crew that was killed yesterday. I was hoping you could tell me what you saw."

"I saw the foolishness of the young, thinking they can live forever and killing each other instead."

"Did you see this man?"

"Possibly."

"Yes or no?"

"Captain, I have been on this planet for almost a hundred years. I have seen so many people that I no longer care. My little friend gives me my coffee in the morning and my daughter brings me food for dinner. I no longer need to eat much. My teeth hurt too much most of the time."

"Can we concentrate on yesterday?"

"I don't remember what happened. I do not move very well any more so I sat right here when the men started shooting. I saw the big red-haired man throw the pretty little blonde woman into the wall over there."

"Big red-haired man? Wait," he fished out a picture of Boris Chercovski, "is this the man?"

"Yes. He threw the pretty little girl against the wall over there. I think she had a gun too, but I don't know. I was watching the men who were shooting. I saw them shoot the policeman, and then the soldiers started shooting, and Mrs. Gonzalez got shot and the soldiers shot the men. I was praying. It was my prayers that kept me from getting shot. I pray a lot these days, I will be seeing God soon."

"But this is the man?"

"Yes, this is the man. He was there when the men started shooting. He pushed the nice girl against the wall. He should not have done that. She was pretty. I hope he did not hurt her. God will punish him if he hurt her. God kept me alive. Maybe it was so I could tell you about it. God works in mysterious ways."

"Thank you, Dom Pablo. I may talk to you again if you don't mind."

"I am easy to find. My little friend brings me coffee. I do not eat much any more. My teeth hurt too much and I am getting old."

Captain Bellisario stood to leave as the old man lapsed into a rambling prayer.

The owner of the sundries store was more help. "Yes, I saw this man," he said. "He came in here yesterday, just before the shooting started. He was with a big man with red hair."

Bellisario showed him Gordon's picture.

"Yes, this man. He was not so dirty as in the picture, but it was him. They were looking at the displays by the window when suddenly they saw someone outside and they left in a hurry. They did not buy anything and they did not talk to me and I do not know who they are. I am a simple shopkeeper and one of the bullets broke my window. It was the army who was shooting and they should pay for my window, but I don't know anything about what the men were doing or why they were here or why they left."

"What did the red-haired man look like?"

"Like the picture. He was tall, over two meters and he had hands like hammers. A big, bulging man. I don't know what color his eyes were. He did not look at me. I do not know who he was and I do not know why he was here. Soon after they left the shooting started. I did not see who they were going to talk to. I do not know who they were. I did not go back outside for a long time."

"Good. We have established that you did not know who they were or why they were here. But they were both here, yes?"

"Yes, they were here but they did not buy anything."

It was plain to Bellisario that the shopkeeper was nervous about something. He was probably mixed up in something he should not have been, but it was clearly not germane to the case in hand

The other two soldiers who had survived the firefight in the plaza had pretty much the same story. They had been paying attention to the men with the guns and had not seen the others in the alleyway. They were still in custody at the police station, but they would be released this morning. Bellisario picked them up and witnessed them signing for their possessions, then got them into the truck.

"What is that thing?" he asked one of them.

"What thing, Sir?"

"I saw you sign for it. It is not a cell phone and it is not a power meter. If you are withholding evidence, I will know why, and if you try to cheat me I will have you shot."

"I thought it was a child's toy. I was going to bring it to my son. I forgot I had picked it up."

"Give it to me now."

The chagrinned soldier produced the detector he had picked up at the crime scene and handed it to his captain. In his defense it did look like some sort of child's game. Captain Bellisario had a different idea for it. Somehow this device had told the man that the CIA agent needed to be shot. It seemed far-fetched but the waitress had mentioned it and here it was.

The vibrations in Anastasia's head were all but gone and she was incredibly relieved to be free of them. The additional energy she felt had not compensated for the debilitating feeling. It was like being torn in two directions at once.

Taking stock of her situation, Anastasia decided that yes, she was tied up on a bed in a hotel room, at the mercy of two foreigners who intended to deliver her for a bounty, but the imminent danger that triggered the response did not seem to be there. She would be able to free herself from her bonds because, though they were tied well, she was not without resources. Also, she had faith in her partner's ability to find her.

Danger had always been a part of Anastasia Viuda's life. As far back as she could remember, life had been discipline, self-control and danger. She discovered that she missed the regimented workout and education schedule she had so despised when young. It had been difficult, both physically and mentally. Emotionally, it was a matter of turning off your reactions or hiding them if you could not help having them. Once a subject had been trained to deny fear and grief, turning off the pain responses was next. She began to wonder if the rattling in her head was a response to danger or if it was fear. She had never felt it growing up; it had only manifested itself recently. She began to wonder if she was getting weak.

The tingling began very lightly when her captor reentered the room, and then disappeared. It made no sense to her. This man was the biggest threat to her life she had seen since the massacre in Woodytown, yet he did not trigger the response.

"Boris?" she began softly. "I can see that you are a professional. You handle things like Juan's girlfriend as if they were no more unusual than roasted goat. You have enough money in those bags to live like a king, yet you still continue. Why do you do it? How many times have you done this?"

"Done what?"

"Hunt people down for the price on their heads."

"I have done this a time or two."

"I think we are not that much different, you and I. I think we could join forces and become unstoppable."

"I already have a partner."

"Yes, I see, one who is wanted by the American Secret Services. A man who almost got you shot yesterday. They will be after you now as well. I say you would be better with me as a partner. The blond one, the Boss," she screwed up her mouth, "is a liability and should be sent away."

"And you have the spleen to tell me you are not a snake. Colorful and shiny on the forest floor, like a toy, you are deadly with your mouth."

"I would never try to double-cross you. You are too smart for that. I simply want to be by your side and learn from you."

"Oh, there would be a lesson all right," MacMaster smiled widely. "one I would never get the opportunity to forget, let alone remember."

"I have made the offer. Someday you will regret not accepting it."

Again Gordon MacMaster smiled. He was becoming very fond of his captive, even though he knew her for what she was. He could imagine the two of them walking into a congregation of dignitaries together with a common goal. It was such a pity that he could never trust her.

The local police and the army in Curitiba worked closely, especially in matters that concerned national security.

Captain Bellisario made it his focus to gain all the intelligence he could on the plaza shootings. He and his men had been exonerated by the ballistic evidence, but the bodies of the shooters had yet to be identified. They had no identification on them at all. They had been carrying no wallets and no one had reported anyone fitting their description as missing.

Boris Chercovski's passport had been mailed by Andreas Castro to his sister in Curitiba. The Castro's mail had been diverted to the police after the death of four soldiers at that residence. Bellisario knew then he was looking for the right man. He did not know what the connection was between the two men, but they had been together in the plaza so they must be international terrorists, both of them. Tracking these two down would no doubt restore the captain's status and return him to his place in the promotional hierarchy. All he needed to do now was find them.

And then there was the matter of the reward for the capture of Walter Suffolk. Bellisario did not require Dakota as a go-between for this. He was perfectly capable of contacting the UAW himself and needed no translator. If the truth be told, it might be a good idea to confirm the reward exists beforehand. He remembered clearly that Agent Dakota had said the reward was not contingent upon the man being alive.

"Colonel, the operation was a complete failure. Not only did the undercover Strike Team fail to secure their objective but they ended up being killed by the Brazilian Army. What have you got to say for yourself that will keep me from having you shot as well."

"There have been no official questions yet, General Arridagio. They have not linked the men to Paraguay. As far as the agents know, they have not identified the men at all. I do not think they will. It is unclear what happened, but we have the luck that none of them were left alive to talk."

"Luck! You call that luck? Five men were shot. Our men. They were there to avert an international incident and they caused one instead. This is not luck, this is the worst stupidity and incompetance."

"Yes, Sir. I..." Colonel Zarafina was at a loss for words and grasped for something that would make the situation salvageable.

"Do not sit there like a hooked fish, Colonel. Tell me what the status of the target is."

"Sir, they located the target and shot him, but I think they did not kill him because he is still transmitting."

"This just gets better and better. So how are we coming with the improved detector?"

"That is the good news, Sir. We will soon be able to use the GPS system to zoom in on the target. Once again, this will only be when it is active and the signal is not strong enough to detect all the time, but we will be able to use the transmitter at the television station as a reference. This should be up and running soon. We need a couple more transmissions to lock it in."

"Good. Clean up this mess and you may well survive the ordeal."

Chapter Nineteen
Back to the River

"Juan, you killed your lover and the police can place you in her home. Yes, we framed another man for the killing, but I do not think you can return to Curitiba and resume your life as if nothing happened." Terry was merely being pragmatic.

"Señor Boss, I know all the police in town except for a couple of them. I can report Maria missing. I can tell them she was going to visit someone out of town and she never returned."

"And when they place you in her home on the day she was killed?"

"It will not happen. I just want to go home to my wife and my job. I have had too much of this life. It was fun and exciting but I have had enough. If I return now, nothing ever happened and I will be what I was. I do not want any more of this."

"I don't think you can do that."

"Of course I can. Just drop me off at the house. I will get the cab out of the garage. I cannot leave it there. It links me to Maria. I must take it back to the yard and pay up for the time and distance. If I go missing a couple of days, I can explain it, but if I disappear, I cannot."

"This leaves us with a predicament. Boris, what do you think?"

Gordon MacMaster did not answer the question. He was thinking and Juan would not have liked what he was thinking.

"I need to return the taxi at a minimum. If they find that taxi in her garage, I am going to be arrested for her murder."

Terry spoke softly, "There is no law against prosecuting two men for the same crime?"

"No, Señor. Even if they find me innocent, it will take them years and I have no lawyer. My family will be ruined."

The Scotsman finally spoke. "Juan, you have been a help to us, even if you did kill your girlfriend. I will gladly pay a lawyer for you, and he can pay off whoever needs to be paid off to look the other way. We have given them a guilty man so it will be easy to do. Is there a lawyer you can trust?"

"Ai, this will be with this cursed money?"

"No, Juan, Terr… uh, the boss will take care of it."

"Then I believe we can work something out."

"Remember, if you turn on us, we will come to Curitiba and we will kill your wife, your children, your mother and father and everyone close to you. If they charge you with what you have done and you fold, we are no longer friends. We become the vengeance of the Lord. Are we clear on this?"

"Yes, Señor."

Juan returned to his hotel room to retrieve his clothes. The ladies were in the bedrooms of the suite. Gordon arched his eyebrow at Terry who looked away tight-lipped. They both knew the best way to silence a witness.

There were multiple ways back to Curitiba, the more direct way and the long, meandering way. The men in charge felt safer on the back roads though the trip would take longer. They went north and then south again and met no resistance on the road. Much of the trip was over low mountains and through deep mountain passes where traffic was light. They stayed from behind the diesel trucks growling their way up the hills and made good time. The grazing land and subsistence farms needed little policing and the few officers they saw on the road paid them no mind. Anastasia found it fascinating that she would get a light tingle just before the

372

highway cruiser would be sighted. Thinking back, she realized that she had not seen the officers when they had come to the deceased Maria's door, she had sensed them. This seemed a new development to her, one she felt needed to be developed.

Juan was driving as they entered Curitiba since he had extensive knowledge of the town. Anastasia sat between her two foreign captors in the back seat. She sat bolt upright and watched very carefully what Juan was doing and where he was going. At one point he put his left turn signal on and she said, "There is danger down that way."

Two officers were interrogating a gang of youths on the side of the road half a kilometer down. Lula was the only one who reacted to the incident and she simply asked how Anastasia knew. Anastasia did not answer the question. She could not. This was merely the first time.

Anastasia Viuda began to astound those around her with her ability to predict danger. It was not always the police, either. Gangs of thugs roamed the city selling drugs and women, drinking and stealing. Anastasia could see the danger before they came into view. It became a game for her; it became intriguing for everyone else.

They circled the blocks in Maria's neighborhood to ensure the house was not under surveillance. Anastasia assured them that it was not. She would have been able to feel it.

Juan pulled the taxi out of the garage. He had a pocket full of money and a sincere hope that he never see either of the men he had been involved with again. The excitement was over as far as he was concerned. He had gotten all of that lifestyle he could handle.

Anastasia watched Juan drive off and turned to Gordon. "That is the most dangerous thing you have done all day. You should have shot him in the head before letting him drive off. He does not have what it takes to bluff the police in the long run. As soon as they find him and question him, he will give you up."

"I don't think so," Terry said from the driver's seat. "I don't think he will risk our retribution."

"You have a saying about two birds in the hand... no, two birds in the bush beating..."

"A bird in the hand is worth two in the bush," MacMaster corrected her.

"Exactly. He will turn on you and you will be found and shot."

"Perhaps it would be good for you if it did happen, eh? Oh, but they want you even worse than they want me."

"Why do you think I have not killed you and escaped already?"

"I think you are overestimating yourself."

"I think I am overestimating you."

"We don't shoot our friends."

"We should be friends."

"Perhaps, Perfecta, in another life we would have been, but your mistakes have made that impossible."

In truth, Anastasia Viuda had been trying hard to keep from being noticed. All she needed to do was raise her bound wrists while passing an officer and he would surely have taken some sort of action. She knew it would cost her dearly if she did not have the perfect opportunity, however. Involving the police is never a good thing in Brazil and with every passing hour, she felt her captors relaxing. They did not chance covering her mouth but she knew if she got too loud it would be the trunk for her.

There is 850 kilometers of busy road between Curitiba and Rio with Sao Paolo directly between them. Terry was driving as they left town, wearing a suit and matching hat. There was no need to turn on the heat but he had turned off the air conditioning. Traffic was not bad at this time of night. He was thinking about little other than driving, trying not to think about Juan and the potential liability he represented. He glanced at Lula from time to time. She had fallen silent after chattering all day. They had been on the road for about 14 hours.

Anastasia began to complain about the chafing of her wrists from the rope. Gordon told her to be quiet or she was going in the trunk. The front wheel on the passenger side ran into the dirt twice before Terry announced himself too road-burned to drive any further. He pulled off on the shoulder to switch with Gordon. They both knew it would be a short matter of time before one or both of them was sleeping. It was time to find a motel.

They pulled the car in at the sign of a leaping swordfish and Terry rented two rooms. He had to bribe the old woman in the reception room to get the rooms without presenting identification but cash works wonders in such situations. Terry and Lula took one room, Anastasia and Gordon took the other.

"Boris, I need to shower. I am beginning to stink."

"Yes, I think we both need a shower."

"Join me, we can save water that way." Anastasia's flirting was expected and Gordon didn't even respond any more.

"Get in the shower."

"You won't take the rope off my wrists?"

"No. Just shower."

"But I cannot remove my blouse with my wrists tied."

"All right, come here. I'm tired and sick of this climate. I'll be glad to be done with you."

Anastasia smiled and stepped into the bathroom. The sound of the shower followed for a while, then she stepped out and walked into the bedroom wearing only the water

dripping from her tanned skin. Her smile seemed to light up
the entire room. Gordon felt his manhood start to rise and
reminded himself that he had sworn not to make this mistake.
He found her birthmark very attractive. He told his captive
he needed her to towel off and get dressed but she refused.
She lay on the bed and began to caress herself. Gordon bit
his lip and grabbed the rope from where it lay. He tied her
hands together and, despite her impassioned pleas, tied them
to the bedstead. Then he stepped into the shower. He was a
man of great appetites and Anastasia was wearing down his
resistance. She had already made him hungry.

"I must say," he started smoothly, "that it is a good
thing I will not be with you much longer."

"Oh, why is that?"

"I have a personal code to follow and you are making it
very difficult to focus on my objectives."

"Come out here and focus on this."

"That's precisely what I'm…" The sound of a
smashing table lamp replaced his rumbling voice as he
stepped out of the bathroom. He fell to the floor and,
despite his size and strength, his hands were bound behind
him. It had taken her seconds to immobilize him. Any
thoughts of overpowering her with his feet were dashed as
she pulled his pistol.

"That's very handy work. I wasn't in the shower long."

"You didn't notice the tile with a little piece chipped
off?"

"I saw it but thought nothing of it."

"I broke two fingernails getting that piece out but you
did not notice them when you tied me up. You have been
sloppy and careless."

"You cut the rope with a piece of broken bathroom
tile?"

"We have a saying, 'A man has only enough blood for one head.'" Anastasia was getting dressed as she spoke. She found the car keys in his trouser pocket.

"Very clever girl. What now?"

"You have treated me with some respect. You did not beat me and your reserve is extra ordinary. What has really challenged my decision is when you allowed your driver to leave. I would have killed him. He is of no consequence, yet you paid him well and let him walk with your trust though you did not know him. This tells me things about you. You are not just soft and weak, but you are compassionate as well. A professional would never have allowed that."

"I've never been fond of killing. I do so when needed. Juan had the Boss' protection so it was not my decision to shoot him or not."

"I think he was regretting not shooting the driver too." Anastasia drew the barrel of the gun down her cheek and along her jaw line. "The question remains, what to do with you?"

"Well, you have proved yourself to be superior. A gunshot always attracts attention. Take the car and go, I am no match for you."

A different kind of smile lit Anastasia's features this time. Her inner sunshine was filtered through a mesh of guile. "It takes a lot for a man to admit to that. You are not really Russian are you, Boris?"

"Austrian."

"No. How can we have a relationship if you keep lying to me?"

"Is that what we are going to do, have a relationship?"

"No. I think I should be leaving now and I will be taking your money." She took a pillowcase and tore it into shreds, wadding one piece up and sticking it in Gordon's mouth she tied it in with another. The money was in the small closet by the door and she picked up both bags appreciating the heft.

Moving to the door, she cracked it open and looked out but there was nobody in sight. The insert in her brain was vibrating like thunder. She pushed the button on the pendant causing the doors to the Chrysler to open and the lights to come on. She was outlined in the headlights when she heard Terry's voice telling her she was one step from oblivion. She weighed her options, but each scenario she saw ended up with her getting shot. She had rolled the dice and lost.

"Oy, mate, you let this little thing get the better of you?"

Gordon could say nothing through the gag.

"I don't know what to think of that." Terry was grinning like the Cheshire Cat.

"Boss, I tell you what," Anastasia was speaking English. "We can just take the money. I can give it to you, you can take it. There is enough there so you and Lula can go to a nice village and live like a king."

"I must say, I am getting sick of rescuing you," he said looking at his partner's half naked form and smiling.

Gordon rolled his eyes and Terry loosened the gag.

"Boss, you only have this one chance. If you want, you can have me too, and Lula. You really are the boss and I love you for that." Anastasia was sidling closer as she spoke. Terry had stuck both guns in his waistband, one in front and one in back, while working on Gordon's bonds.

"Sit back down on the bed, woman." Terry said. "I don't want you and I don't want the money. I don't trust you. I turn my back and the next thing you know I'm on my belly with a hole in my head."

Having freed Gordon, both men rose, Gordon working his jaw and Terry continued speaking. "See, darlin', there is nothing in the makeup of mankind that makes me want to trust human nature, but I trust this man. I don't trust easily and I certainly don't trust you. So, save your breath. Turn around and put your hands behind your back."

Anastasia turned around then, as Terry took a step closer she turned half around again and stepped forward. She led with a monkey-paw fist, first knuckles extended, straight toward his throat. He knocked her hand away but jumped when he felt her other hand at his belt line. She was pulling the pistol from his waistband. The safety was on, but the real thing that saved Terry from a bullet in the guts was the big Scotsman grabbing her wrist and forcing it up over her head.

"God bless ya, mate. This one's got more piss 'n vinegar than Manchester United.

It took both of them to gag her and tie her to the bed and neither of them got away without a bruise. She had passed up opportunities to attract attention while in the car because one captor would be as bad as another and most would be worse. She was now only one day from Francisco Modiano's vengeance for the murder of his brother.

"She's good, this one," Gordon observed. "I thought I'd breathed my last."

"You got lucky. I was almost asleep when I heard the lamp smash. She sucked us both in. If I'd been occupied with Lula, she'd have gotten away."

"It's a real shame, such a fireball. I'm tempted to let her go."

"What, after all this?"

"Under different circumstances…" Gordon left the sentence unfinished. He was staring at her bound body. Then he shook his head and smiled. "It's like the lure of the big cats. You can keep one in a cage but you can't get in there with them."

Gordon slept on the floor that night and, in the morning, he went to a local store for a Polaroid instant camera. The photographs of Anastasia Viuda tied to the motel bed would be used to convince Francisco Modiano of the veracity of their claim.

There was still a long drive to Rio and they had to get through the Sao Paolo area as well. It would be past dark when they arrived no matter how fast they drove.

"Colonel, have you been in contact?"

"Scotsman, I have made the call. The buyer is still interested but will not initiate a transfer. He insists on a cash settlement."

"I have plenty of cash."

"I only go between. I am not happy with this either but I only go between. With a transfer, this is simple and automatic but with cash, well, how do I get my commission?"

"I think we can trust each other on this."

"Ah, my friend, do not think it is you I do not trust. I need my commission in case you do not survive this encounter."

"Have you so little faith?"

"Once again, it is not a matter of faith or trust between us. I will need a down payment for the repercussions of a double-cross."

"Very well, 10 percent of half a live delivery."

"That will be sufficient. I will bank this and return it to you if the deal falls apart. Then we have a drink together. If we have a drink together."

"This should not take long. Call the man and tell him I have proof. The contact is Franco Cortico, advisor to Francisco Modiano."

"Good. When can I expect my transfer?"

"I will wire it today from Sao Paolo. Give me an account number."

With the account number in hand, Gordon hung up the pay phone.

"Agent Dakota, we have a break in the case."

"Where can I meet you, Captain?"

"At the police station on Rio do Martin Afonso."

"I know where that is."

"Do not waste time."

"I'll be there as soon as I can." Brock Dakota hung up the phone, fastened his pistol to his ankle, grabbed his hat and headed out. At the police station, Captain Bellisario herded him into a private room with the Chief of Police. The chief was seated behind his desk and Dakota's first thought was "Yon serpent hath a lean and hungry look." The chief did not speak English as well as Bellisario but they were able to communicate well enough.

"Agent Dakota, I hope you understand that except for questioning and testimony, the Government of Brazil had no interest in this man you seek."

"Yes, Captain, we spoke of this before."

"I spoke in the past tense because there are certain developments that may well have changed that."

Brock perked up his ears and raised his eyebrows.

"I will allow Chief Cardosa to elaborate."

"Agent Dakota, this man is wanted for what in your country?"

"Multiple murders."

"So he is, as-you-say, serial killer?"

"No sir, I am convinced he is a paid assassin."

"And you know, that we have no extradition treaty with United States."

"Yes, I am aware of that."

"Then you will not be trying to take the man away?"

"No, sir. I am here in an unofficial capacity. I am merely a concerned citizen doing my duty for the good of mankind."

Chief Cardosa smiled sardonically. "Of course, señor, but as a private citizen you would be able to accept a reward if there was to be offered."

Dakota saw the angle. "No," he replied. "As a federal agent I cannot accept a reward any more than I could accept a bribe. Any monies paid would need to go to someone else. I must point out though that any reward on this man's head is unofficial and I would need to broker the distribution of said monies."

The chief looked at Captain Bellisario for a second and returned his sharp eyes to Dakota. "Unofficial?"

"Yes, sir. You see the UAW charter does not allow for such a thing, but there are interested parties that have put up the money."

"I see. And who are these interested parties?"

"I am not at liberty to divulge their names, but I assure you, their credit is good."

"And I must take your word for this?"

"I'm afraid so."

"Then Captain Bellisario will stick on you like cement. If we are to give you assistance, we will be, uh, compensated."

"I assure you. The money is there but it is not my interest. I wish this man stopped."

"Good. We have found the body of Rosimar Castro. She was found murdered and dismembered in Cascavel. The evidence points to an Alderman in that town but we do not believe he is guilty."

Dakota's silence indicated he had not made the connection.

"The man you are looking for, Walter Suffolk, was seen with another man, Boris Chercovski, in the plaza when all that, uh, unpleasantness occurred."

"I'm sorry, sir, I do not know this Boris Chercovski."

"Allow me. Boris was being held by the army for a murder he committed while in custody. He was to be shot. Somehow he convinced Rosimar's brother Andreas to free him from custody. The passport of Boris Chercovski was mailed to his sister by Andreas Castro. We believe there was a large sum of money involved. Andreas Castro and the five soldiers sent to capture him were murdered. The next week, his sister is making a very large cash withdrawal from the National Bank, in the Central Plaza. Captain Bellisario failed to arrest her and her friend when your man was shot. He was forced to abandon his mission and she escaped."

Dakota took a minute to digest this. Then he asked, "So why do you think Walter Suffolk was involved?"

"He was seen with Boris Chercovski. We believe that Chercovski had Rosimar Castro withdraw this money for him and then killed her, cut up her body and took it to Cascavel along with the body of another woman we have yet to identify."

"So he took it to Cascavel and framed some Alderman he did not know. Why would he do this?"

"I cannot answer all the questions you might have and we have even more, but the fact remains that he killed a woman and someone killed Brazilian soldiers. The details are yet to be proven, but these men must be found and stopped. The pictures are being seen and questions are being asked. I have business to deal with. Captain, take Agent Dakota to a conference room and work with him. I will expect a report soon and I want action."

Dakota and Bellisario sequestered themselves and hashed out what they knew. The more they looked, the more the questions piled up:

Who was the man with Rosimar at the bank?

Who were the men who had shot the CIA man in the plaza and why had they shot him? Officially they had been labeled MST rebels, but the government had no record of the individuals.

Who was the blonde with the gun? Was that Rosimar Castro? If so, then who made the withdrawal at the bank?

Who was Boris Chercovski and what was his connection with Walter Suffolk?

Who was the black-haired woman with the tall boots? Was she the other victim?"

Captain Bellisario had not mentioned the detector to any one. He had gone to the morgue to see if it pointed to the dead agent but it had not. Yet according to the waitress it was the indicator.

The story is older and longer than either of the men acknowledged at first. Then the question came up. "The chief said that the man, Boris, killed another man while in custody, right."

"Yes. He was being held for... ah, I don't know what."

"That might help us unravel this mess. We need to know where and when he was arrested and what the charges were. I'm working with half the information, Captain."

"We will go out to the base and determine the rest of the story. First, I need to take this picture to the plaza and show it to an old man. If he is there."

There is no Brazilian equivalent to the word paydirt, but that is what Hernando del Fuego was thinking. The Chrysler pulling up to the gate was being driven by the very man he wanted to find, but he did not see Anastasia Viuda. His cross hairs were on the back of his head and he was muttering, "Can you feel me, fool? Does the hair on your neck rise? I will be pissing on your corpse, Rojo."

The Chrysler did not go through the gate, only pulled in to deliver an envelope.

"Ah, that is it. You have her and this is your proof. I have you now, you bastard."

He almost lost the American car as he ran down the stone steps of the half demolished church and fired up his stolen motorcycle. He just caught sight of the taillights as it motored back to the south. He found himself wishing he had stolen something faster, though this motorcycle would keep up with most cars without trouble. It was quiet enough for pursuit, however, and that had been a deciding factor in choosing this one.

Following the taillights for 15 minutes was not a difficult job; it was convincing himself that he was far enough back to keep from being identified that was the problem. He passed the vehicle and almost missed it when its driver pulled into the parking lot of a diner. He drove down half a kilometer, pulled over to the side and shut off the engine. His mind went over all the reasons the man would have stopped at this diner.

It was not long before Hernando felt exposed, standing on the street next to his motorcycle. The area was mostly residential and the inhabitants were going to work for the day. Nosy women would be watching him from their kitchens, and he had already been noted by the children on their way to school. He knew he could not go into the diner; his target would recognize him. He was debilitated from lack of sleep and food, so he was running on adrenaline alone and that would not last long.

What Hernando had missed, while concentrating on following the automobile he was chasing, was the automobile that was following him. The guards had not had enough time to mount surveillance on the Chrysler, but they had seen the motorcycle leave in pursuit and had followed that. They had not missed the American car in the parking lot of the diner and had pulled in as well.

The guards were thugs and not chosen for their intelligence. The driver pulled into a spot near their objective and the passenger was on a cell phone. They would clearly make no decision on their own, and it was clear who they were to the man they were following.

Gordon had not left his car; he had simply turned off the engine and ducked down in the front seat. The interior of the diner was not visible from the parking lot, but a glance out the windows would show anyone sitting in a car. The guards shut off their engine and went into the diner to keep an eye on the foreigner, but they could not see where he had gone. He was directly behind them.

"Gentlemen, sit down."

"Uh, what are you talking about?"

"Let us not be foolish, Gentlemen. You followed me from Señor Modiano's house. If you were following me, you must want to talk to me."

Both men sat on one side of a booth. They had obviously not seen this coming and did not know what to say.

Gordon sat down across the table from them and waited a moment for them to speak. As he expected, neither of them said a word. "Coffee," he said to the waitress and indicated the other two with a finger.

"Gentlemen, since you do not seem to have anything to say, I will speak and you will listen. Am I making myself clear?"

The man who had been a passenger nodded his head. The driver was younger and he had a blank look on his face. He was obviously the junior partner of the team.

"I have Perfecta Navaja in my custody. I do not know where the man of the team is. I only know him as a Mr. Andalucia and I have not seen him for a while. He may have been killed in the forest outside Curitiba, I do not know. Do you comprehend what I am saying?"

"You have said, Señor, that you have a perfect knife but do not know where the man who owns it is. Is that what you wanted to say?"

"No. Listen closely. Francisco Modiano wants the woman in the pictures I left at the gate. Her name is Perfecta Navaja. He also wants the man who was with her when she killed his brother, the General. Have I said it correctly now?"

"Yes, I understand now. Dom Modiano will be very glad to hear this."

"Dom Modiano has already heard this. If you were important enough, you would already know this. You are dogs and follow your master's orders."

The younger man half rose in his seat with a grim look on his face.

"Tell your boy to sit down or I will shoot him in the knees and he will never walk again. Make no mistake..." The sound of the hammer being cocked on a double-action revolver left no room for a misunderstanding.

"I intend to drive out of this area and if anyone follows me I will disappear with my prize and those who caused me to do so will suffer the repercussions. This includes the one on the motorcycle. I do not know what Dom Modiano does to those who displease him but I do not think it will be good. Am I clear?"

The elder guard was quick to point out that they had been following the motorcycle when they had seen his car in the parking lot.

The Scotsman knew then that the man was not with these guards and they knew he was not with the foreigner. The guards thought he was lying.

"I expect you to stay here for at least 10 minutes after I leave. If I see you again it will be bad for you. Do you understand?"

They both nodded their understanding. MacMaster called the waitress over and gave her more than enough to cover three meals, told her to give them anything they wanted and walked out the door.

The senior member of the team called back to the house and was connected with Franco Cortico, Francisco Modiano's right hand man. Franco Cortico was not amused, nor was he surprised, to find his men had been picked out. He had been working with the Modiano brothers for a long time and knew intrinsically that the woman who had killed General Modiano was a trained professional. As such, he had never expected to pay a live delivery fee for the assassins. He thought it might be a good idea to recruit any man who could bring him Perfecta Navaja on a silver platter.

When the automobile pulled out from the parking lot and headed back in the direction it had arrived from, Hernando del Fuego was behind it again. He had too much vested interest in this man to lose him now. His stretched mental resources considered that there might have been a switch in drivers at the diner and that he was now following someone else, but he did not let that stop him. He knew he might have walked into a trap in the diner as well. If following the auto did not take him to Anastasia Viuda, then he would convince the driver to do so in whatever manner would be necessary.

The driver took the Chrysler back toward the north, toward the largest of the strip mines that had decapitated the hills in the northern area of Itaborai. Hernando knew before the car pulled into the area that it was a trap. If he pulled down that road he would be riding into a bullet. He had scouted the area and knew there was the exit on the other side, but there was also a clear view of anything driving on that path from the public road half a kilometer away. He cursed the fact that he had left his rifle in the church. Whether he shot the man or not, the scope would give him a positive identification in case they had switched drivers. Or perhaps this is where the exchange had been set up. This would be a good spot for that. The stand of trees on the north side would be a perfect spot for backup to be secreted. He stood with his idling motorcycle underneath him, chewing his lower lip, torn between courses of action. Then he smiled and pulled out his cell phone.

Customer service gave him the number of the local police.

"Hello, I am calling to report a killing. There is a Chrysler in the large mining pit on Christiano Ferreira Braga Road. There is a big man with red hair pulling what looks like a body out of the trunk."

"What is your name?"

"He is over two meters tall with red hair and he is pulling a body out of the trunk. I will meet the police there on a motorcycle." Hernando killed the call and shut off the phone, then he removed the battery. He pulled forward until he had a view of the pit. The Chrysler, sitting about 30 meters from the edge of the trees, brought a grin to his face. He could not see inside the vehicle so he did not know if the driver was in the woods or still inside the car. Either way, he was not going down there yet. He would be a sitting duck on the motorcycle.

The police wasted no time in responding to the call. They had found bodies dumped in pits before and the surrounding neighborhood was very upscale. They were very eager to stop this practice. One cruiser drove in from the north as another pulled up next to Hernando on the south. He pointed to the car and yelled that he would follow them in. The two cars raced up on the Chrysler and three officers jumped out with guns drawn, yelling for the driver to get out of the car and get down on his belly. The forth officer was on the radio confirming that there was a car there and calling in the license plate numbers.

The soldiers who had arrested Gordon MacMaster knew they were in serious trouble. Not only had they deserted their post, more or less, but there was more to it than that. They had thought the affair over when their prisoner was sentenced to death but then the bastard had escaped and now, Captain Bellisario was here with some gringo looking for answers that they did not want to supply. They had practiced their story but once the interrogation started they could not keep their stories straight.

One man said they had arrested their prisoner for rape, the others said kidnapping. They had a statement from a woman called Sandiana Torremolinos that the man, Boris Chercovski had kidnapped her. She had claimed to be the lover of a Colonel Esteban but none of them knew any Colonel Esteban. They had claimed to find the two of them while on patrol and had never been questioned on it, especially after the prisoner had killed Sympatico while trying to escape. His doom had been pronounced and there should have been no more questions.

When the question arose as to where the woman was, they all gave exactly the same answer, word for word. She called a friend from Curitiba and he came and got her.

"This is garbage, Captain. These men are hiding something; they are lying and talking out their asses."

"Yes, you can see this and you do not even speak the same language."

"I speak body language. These men are covering something up. We need to step the pressure up a notch."

"The second man was the weakest. The one who said Boris had raped the woman. I will break him first."

It did not take long once the discrepancies in the stories were brought to light. One after another, the men admitted they were on their way to Woodytown to experience the pleasures of the Jardim de Prazeres: they were within their jurisdiction, but not where they were supposed to be, that they had damaged the vehicle on the way there, and that they had arrested Boris Chercovski there. They were more reticent about the woman who had leveled the charges. Sandiana Torremolinos, it was eventually determined, had been sold to Arturo the whoremaster and the money used to repair the jeep. All five men assumed that the woman had died in the massacre.

The interesting thing to the interrogators was the description of Sandiana Torremolinos. A tall, thin, beautiful woman with big breasts and long black hair. Captain Bellisario asked to use the computer in the office and brought up the picture of Mr. and Mrs. Andalucia. It was confirmed that Mrs. Andalucia was Sandiana Torremolinos, but they could not identify her partner. Shortly after this, the captain insisted they leave. Dakota thought there was more to be gleaned but his Brazilian partner was insistent. They left without consulting with any of the upper echelon about the incident.

"This man was after the reward." Captain Bellisario was pensive as he drove. "There is a large reward on this woman's head, along with her husband or partner or whatever they are.

391

He was there as well, he must have been. He was one of the men who was stealing cars and trucks and crashing buses down the road. Why did the Army not turn Boris over to the police? The lack of decent communication is beyond my understanding. Perhaps they paid off the commander.

"This is not my concern, however. We get better copies of their photographs from the police station. The old dot-matrix printers the army has are almost worthless. Then we confirm this with the witnesses.

"I'll tell you what happened, Agent Dakota. These fools sold this woman, Mrs. Andalucia or Torremolinos, or Navaja, or whatever you want to call her, and her husband found out where she was."

"Where she was? Who the hell is she?"

"Ah, I am sorry. I do not know precisely who she is, but I do know what she is. She is an efficient and cold-blooded killer. Rumor has it that she is responsible for the death of General Modiano. She killed him under the name Perfecta Navaja. That is why his brother, an affluent businessman, has offered an exorbitant price for her head. Dead or alive is the offer. Then she and her husband as a Mr. and Mrs. Andalucia killed six border guards who had detained them for a weapon smuggling charge."

"What? While they were in custody?"

"Yes. I told you they were efficient, did I not?"

"Yes," Brock chuckled.

"I assure you it is no laughing matter."

"I apologize."

"No need, now where was I? Ah, yes. Her husband found out what was done to her and he went to the Woodytown and killed every man and woman there."

"Is he really that good?"

"I think the evidence speaks for itself. The event is not widely publicized; it is actually covered up well, but there were about 20 men and women killed there and then they burned the town."

"They burned an entire town?"

"Well, the Woodytown is not really a town. You will not find it on any map. The Woodytown was a whorehouse in the jungle. This is not to go into any report you file." Captain Bellisario's expression brooked no argument. "It is no secret around here that the Army built the place and supplied it with the necessities. Does this shock you, Agent Dakota?"

"It's nothing we could do in America, but I am a guest in your country. Your customs are not mine to question."

"Good. These two assassins murdered every one in Woodytown and burned the town. The real question is where did they go after this? I suspect that the woman seen with your killer is this same woman."

"That doesn't make much sense."

"Perhaps not, but as they say, birds of a feather nest together."

"Umm. Where did you learn to speak English?"

"In Europe we all speak English."

"So you are not from Brazil?"

"I was born in Brazil. My father was Italian. I spent some of my childhood in London and some in Rome. We need to stay focused on the job at hand."

"So why would this Andalucia be with Walter Suffolk and not her husband?"

"I don't know, perhaps they killed him."

"Maybe. I don't know how good they are."

"Boris Chercovski killed an armed guard in his cell."

"Killing one man and leveling an entire town are two different things."

"I think it would be a good thing not to underestimate these men. First we need to confirm that we are looking at the same things."

The police station on Rio do Martin Afonso in Curitiba provided copies of the photos, but no one in the plaza could confirm seeing either them.

They sat at the café on the corner drinking coffee and plotting. Bellisario was sure of his analysis of the situation. Brock Dakota was less certain. He could not make the connection between Walter Suffolk and Boris Chercovski.

The aged Pablo had not recognized the picture of Rosimar when he had been asked earlier. Between complaining about his teeth and his knees he told them with certainty that this was not the woman that the tall red-haired man had pushed against the wall.

"How many people live in Rio?" Dakota asked.

"About seven million."

"And how is it precisely we will know where to look in a city that size?"

"It is easy. We follow the money. I assure you, your man has left this town. If you wish to stay here I can assign someone else to guide you. You are on vacation, yes?"

"Yes, uh, officially."

"Then there is no reports, no contacts?"

"Right. It has been so long since I took a vacation, I barely know how to act."

"I will tell you how to act. With official protection you are going to Rio to party."

"When do we leave?"

"Waitress! Call us a taxi."

"General Arridagio, we have completed our long-range detector. It is not effective in Curitiba at all, nor will it be in any other city that uses the same wavelength as Channel 12, but it is working perfectly right now."

"How do you know?"

"We have a good signal. We can track this man."

"Once again, Colonel Zarafina, how do you know? Your last detector malfunctioned and almost caused an international incident. Fortunately the men were never traced to our services; fortunately for you that is."

"Yes, General. They blamed it on the Landless Workers Movement, the MST."

"And the MST has denied involvement."

The colonel's enthusiasm was strongly muted but he moved forward anyway. "The signal is constant, not intermittent as it was before and it moves. We have locked the detector to a hand held device so it works like a GPS, sort of. The tech is soldering the last connections now. It shows our target to be in the north of Rio de Janeiro."

"Are you sure of this? I don't care so much about the sacrifice of manpower, I am concerned that our team will be discovered and taken alive. The only thing that prevented disaster last time was that they all died at the scene."

"There will be no such problem this time, General. I need authorization to take a small plane to Rio. There is no telling what our refugee is after there and I think we should find him before he kills someone and implicates us."

"Take a commercial plane. Take three men and yourself, dressed as businessmen."

"Uh, General, you want me to lead the team?"

"Yes, you will be there to prevent what happened last time. If you do not think you can handle the job…?" Arridagio left the sentence unfinished, this was not truly a choice, it was an ultimatum.

"Yes Sir, I will go to Rio as a businessman."

"Of course you will. How many copies of this detection device do you have?"

"We have just the prototype now, but we can make another quickly."

"Give the order, I want one in my hand by the time you touch down in Rio.

"But Sir..."

"Be silent, Captain."

Colonel Zarafina closed his mouth so his teeth audibly clicked. Being called Captain illustrated the fork in the road he was approaching. He would become a good friend of the general, or he would be demoted and sent to some God-forsaken outpost in the jungle to baby-sit the beasts and the bugs.

There had been more than one man in his past who had called Gordon MacMaster crazy and there had been enemies who claimed he was not human, but there was no chance he was going to attempt to run this gauntlet. Blocked fore and aft by policemen with guns trained on him, he had been outsmarted and knew it. Whoever had been following him on the motorcycle had been too cautious to approach him individually.

Placing his hands on the top of the steering wheel and leaving his gun in the newspaper on the console, he controlled his breathing and prepared to be taken into custody.

The police had known the motorcycle was right behind them when they jumped out of their cruiser, but he was the man who had made the call, he was on their side.

The officer facing the Chrysler's front end was the first to die. The half-second of shock was enough time for Hernando del Fuego to shoot both officers facing away from him. The one on the radio in the driver's seat was partially

396

hidden from view and Hernando had to take a couple of steps to the side before he could shoot him through the windshield. In a matter of seconds, all four officers were down. If he had stepped to the driver's side, Hernando would also have expired. Before the third officer had hit the ground, Gordon was rolling out of the car with his pistol in his hand.

Hernando saw the door open and knew enough to keep his feet behind the rear tire of the cruiser. Gordon was squinting through the dust it had kicked up when it had ground to a stop, looking for feet. His adrenaline was so high that time was almost standing still, everything moved in slow motion. He saw the fallen officer on his side of the vehicle reach for the service revolver he had dropped when shot, and reacted. The slug caught the officer between the eyes and blew out the back of his head.

"Hold your fire, Rojo. I do not wish to kill you."

Gordon had heard that voice before.

"Do you hear me, Rojo?"

"I hear you."

"I only want Perfecta."

"You did not seem so, ah, loving, last time I saw you."

"Things changed, Rojo. We can both make this a good thing."

"Then step out, empty hands."

"Ahhh, that is where the problem lies, yes?"

"What, you do not trust me? How could we be partners if you don't trust me?"

Sirens reached their ringing ears from the south. The dead officer had alerted their dispatcher and reinforcements were on their way.

"It is time to go, Rojo. Make a decision."

Gordon half stood and fired through the driver's side window of the cruiser. The glass shattered and the bullet punched through the steel of the pillar behind the passenger's side rear window.

"Oho! Your decision is made! Have some then." He fired twice through the passenger's window to drive Gordon back down and then jumped back on his motorcycle. He did not ride south but ran it directly toward the trees, keeping the cruiser between himself and MacMaster while emptying his clip in the Scot's direction.

Gordon stood and shot once at the fleeing man but missed the first shot and did not get another as the motorcycle entered the trees on what was more than a trail but less than a road. An automobile could not compete with a motorcycle in that terrain.

It was not the backup police cruisers that were next on the scene, but a van, full of reporters and cameramen from the local television station. They drove in on the south road and skidded to a stop almost immediately. The driver was not as gung ho as some of the reporters. They did manage to get footage of the back of the Chrysler, whirling away in a cloud of dust. They never saw the man on the motorcycle. Their story would read that the man or men in the Chrysler had massacred the four officers.

Chapter Twenty
Adjusting for Range

"Dios Mio, I hate these little planes." Captain Bellisario looked green. Some of his four man team did not fare much better.

"They have never bothered me," Brock replied. "My people work high iron, a plane trip is nothing."

"High iron?"

"Structural steel. They build skyscrapers." Nothing more was said about the plane trip. Bellisario's thoughts were his own but he was not being kind in his mind.

They refueled in Sao Paolo and continued to Rio. The sun had gone down when they arrived, and they agreed that they should set up a meeting away from the Modiano compound if that was possible. They would need to wait until the following day to do so.

Dakota was ready to drink and a couple of the team were as well, but Captain Bellisario told them that they would be reprimanded if they did so. The Captain joined Brock for one drink and retreated to his room. Brock stayed in the hotel bar for hours until he was approached by an expensive prostitute. He was drunk enough by then to pay for it and they retired to his room together.

Daybreak came and bright sunshine flooded the city. It came alive like a bee hive, its inhabitants swarming about their business in the coolness of the morning.

Dakota was ready to head out, but Bellisario insisted on breakfast. The troops ate separate from their leaders. Dakota could not help but wonder how any one people could eat so much and remain trim. And they were all trim. The sheer volume of breakfast was staggering.

Over coffee, the American asked his Brazilian counterpart what the plan of action was. They agreed that to go to the gate as a half dozen inquisitors would get them nowhere, but that the only lead they had was the money itself. A denial that the reward existed would leave them in the street. Yet, the only lead they had and the only reason they were in Rio was the woman, and that was no solid thing. A tall beautiful woman with black hair was not a spectacle in Brazil.

"I will be frank with you, Agent Dakota…"

"Please, call me Brock."

"I will be frank with you, Brock. I was hoping you would be of some utility to our cause in this regard. I have not much experience with espionage. I am primarily a soldier, assigned to assist with police work. I have mostly worked with the anti-drug teams in assaulting the jungle hideouts of the coca farmers. In the jungle I am good, but in the city I am not so erudite."

"Don't sell yourself short, Captain. There's more than one way to skin a cat."

"I have no desire to skin cats."

"Right. Uh, let's begin with the basics. One of the ways you get a man to tell you something is to make him think you already know all about it. You still got those pictures, the mug shots from the border?"

"Yes, I have them here."

"I tell you what. I can't do it myself, 'cause I'm not that good, but I'll bet we can find some college student that is."

"Good enough for what?"

"Not for something, but at something. First I need a one-hour processing center.

"Process for what?"

"Stay with me now. Photographs."

"You need to process photographs in one hour."

"Let me guess, you don't do that down here?"

400

"We can probably get this done, yes, but what is it you are looking for, you are being very vague. Do you have a plan or are you feeling the aftereffects of your carousing?"

"No, I have a plan and it involves some legerdemain. When the magician shows you something and then makes it disappear, it is, more often than not gone, because it was not there to begin with."

The man on the motorcycle was clearly in view as he raced across the field on the far side of the trees. Gordon was tearing a cloud of dust with the wheels of his powerful car, knowing it was visible from a distance. He felt certain that his attacker would turn north since the sirens were coming from the south but he was wrong. The motorcycle sped to the south and he was left holding an empty bag.

The dusty road led north for a little while before meeting a paved road. MacMaster had studied the map and saw to his own discomfiture that he was on the furthest north road in the area. A conglomerate farm was all that bounded this area. Traveling further north required a tractor, so he went east. The one saving grace about the area from a fugitive's perspective was the dearth of police personnel. Half the local police force lay dead on the floor of the strip mine; the other half was roaring to the crime scene.

The one thing the Scotsman knew was that he needed to get rid of the car right away. He couldn't drive it around, though he might be able to hide it. Circling around the local police and back into the city was not difficult; the demarcation line was abrupt. One minute he was in the farm belt, he crossed Aveneda Carlos Lacerda and he was in the city. South to BR101 and not wishing to get caught at the Rio Niteroi Bridge, he turned onto BR493 and skirted the bay. It was 20 kilometers further, but took him into Rio proper without hitting any toll booths.

He could have dropped the car off at the edge of the favelas with the keys in it, and it would not have lasted 20 minutes, but that would leave him on foot. He did not have much cash with him, an oversight he was determined to rectify in the future. It had always been a policy that he would carry a wad of cash in his pocket whether he needed it or not. The one time he needed it and did not have it showed him the obvious wisdom of his ways. He pulled up behind an old Chevy Nova idling at a gas station. The driver was in the store buying some cigarettes and an agua de coco. As the man stepped out, Gordon threw him the keys to the Chrysler and stepped into the Chevy. The man was momentarily speechless and that was all Gordon needed to escape.

"Any trouble?" Terry wanted to know when Gordon finally returned to the dumpy furnished second-floor apartment they had rented in Rio.

"Nothing I couldn't handle, but I think there might be a problem."

"Oh?"

"Yes, Mr. Andalucia made things a bit hot for me."

"And he is?"

"He worked with this one." Gordon indicated the bound and gagged Anastasia. "He was the other part of the package."

"Oh, right, Andalucia. So, how did he find you?"

"He was waiting for me. He tried to follow me and some hooligans followed him. Oddly enough he didn't want to kill me, or said he didn't."

"Did you kill him?"

"No, I missed, but he killed four local brassers that he called in to distract me."

"Nice. So what did he want, if not you?"

"Her."

402

"Oh, of course, I can understand that."

"Where's Lula?"

"In the bedroom. She's making noises about getting out of the deal. Taking a package and running."

"I think that won't be long. I wish to conclude this business, first. It's messy and I don't need any loose cannons."

"She's not a bad gal. Not the kind you take home to mother though."

"That's not the question. Can she be left alone?"

"Yeah, as long as she hasn't been paid yet. Alone though, not with the other."

"Umm. Look, Terry, I need to figure out how to finish this without too much exposure. Kidnapping is not my forte."

"And you're hot now."

"I can't be sure but I can't take that chance."

"So you want me to make the exchange?"

"It might be best."

"No worries."

"Good."

"Ai, get those fools out from here! What are you trying to do to me?" The owner of the photography studio was distraught to see the soldiers in the jeep sitting at the curb before his shop.

"You are trying to put me out of business," he said.

Captain Bellisario leaned over the counter and told him with no humor in his voice that if he wanted to put him out of business he would have had the soldiers come in the shop and shoot him. "It is by my good graces that you survive the day. If you have not done the kind of quality job I expect I will shoot you. If it is not done in two hours, I will shoot you and if you tell anyone this job was done, he will shoot you and then I will shoot you. Are we in agreement?"

The man looked at Dakota who wore mirrored sunglasses, observed his hand inside his sport coat and acquiesced without further ado.

Leaving the studio, Brock asked the captain if he didn't think he was a little heavy handed with the man.

"You don't understand the population of Brazil," he replied. "In America, it is all about who gets paid to do what, or what you have on them to make them want to help you. Here, a man must use different motivational tools."

"Motivational tools. I guess I can see that."

"If you do not sufficiently convince a man his life is in danger, then he will look to see what he can do to use the information against you. Perhaps he will sell his information to whoever is willing to pay for it. When the transaction is done for you, it may not be done for him, unless you have convinced him otherwise."

The soldiers had a late breakfast while Perfecta Navaja's face was put on the body of Brock's late night delight.

Hernando del Fuego was terribly disappointed in himself. "If I was only a little more patient, I would have waited until the police had the man in handcuffs. I was so sure of myself that I went in like a bull; full of fury but without direction. I will admit the man was better than I would have expected. He reacted too fast."

Hernando was back in the bell tower of the crumbling church. While it was not across the street from the gate of Francisco Modiano's estate, it still provided a good view due to the fact that the gate formed the fourth leg of the intersection. When he returned to his hallowed hideaway he was happy to see his rifle was unmolested. He had pushed the motorcycle the last half block from the back, to keep quiet, but knew he was no longer safe and hidden. He considered scrapping the job but knew he would be throwing his life and profession out the window. He needed to kill Anastasia Viuda, but his own actions had made that outcome less likely.

Franco Cortico stared at the photograph that had just been delivered. It was his duty as chief advisor to Francisco Modiano to take it to him right away, but it created a paradox. This was the second time, in two days, that a picture of Perfecta Navaja had been delivered to the gate, but they had been delivered by two different people. The two photographs showed the same woman, at least the face was the same, but the bodies were different. They were both tall and slim. They were both bound, one with rope, the other with handcuffs, but they were not the same woman.

"Señor Modiano, we are faced with more questions."

"Franco, have we received a transfer location?"

"No, and I am not sure we can trust any of these people."

"What has occurred?"

"I think someone is trying to play a game on us. First they executed both the butler and the driver, the men who got the best look at the woman that killed your bother." Franco fell silent for a moment as Francisco's pretty little maid poured them both coffee. He began again once they were alone. "This picture was delivered to us this morning."

The manila envelope held nothing but the photograph with a telephone number on the back. Francisco pulled it out and studied it silently while chewing on his lower lip.

"This does not compare perfectly with the photograph that was dropped off yesterday." Franco handed that photograph over. "You see how this woman has thicker ankles, a little more belly and her breasts are smaller. I may be mistaken since one woman has clothes on and the other is naked but I do not know which woman is really Perfecta Navaja."

"So, one of these men is trying to sell us a different woman?"

"I do not understand what is going on. The big rojo shows up yesterday with this one and another man shows up today with this one."

"But this one is a Polaroid, right?"

"Yes, Sir."

"Then this one is the real one. It is difficult to fake an instant picture where any good shop can make this look right. Were we able to follow the man today?"

"He got away before we could get a good fix on him."

"He is the faker. Is he the same man who was hiding in the tower of the church?"

"There is no way to tell. The men never saw his face. He was the only reason they found the man yesterday. From what they said, this rojo is a very dangerous man."

"Any disciplined man would be dangerous to those fools."

"Perhaps, but it seems this man is large and quick, a foreigner of some kind and he takes no chances. If the man in the tower was his backup, then the guards can be glad they did not try to grab him. They would have left widows."

"So, what are we going to do with these men?"

"You still want to get Per…"

"Of course I want this bitch! She shot my brother!"

"Yes, sir, of course. I suggest we make the connection and then eliminate both of them."

"Make it happen, Franco. I am counting on you." Francisco went back to studying the Polaroid. He could understand how such a woman would convince his brother to

406

let his guard down. He did not understand what kind of a woman could do what this one had done. He thought it would be fun to use her for a while before the real torture began.

The morning news showed the site where the four police officers had been shot, complete with the footage of the Chrysler tearing out of the area. The reactions of those involved differed.

The new owner of that vehicle saw the footage and knew why the big man had wanted to trade down. He also knew the driver of the Chrysler had a severely truncated life expectancy, no matter who drove it. It was parked at the side of the street in front of his house and that was enough to implicate him. He grabbed the keys and ran outside, fired the engine, and with no warm-up time drove it four blocks away to a body shop that was rumored to have made other vehicles disappear. He left it blocking the overhead door and walked away as quickly as he could.

As soon as the body shop owner saw the footage and realized what he had, he pulled it in and shut the door. The crew went to work with torches and wrenches. It vanished like sea vapor.

When Franco Cortico saw the footage, he knew it was the same vehicle his men had followed to the diner. He listened very closely to the story again and then called an associate at the newspaper. He wanted to know the entire story before conveying the news to his employer. He expected Francisco Modiano to react with anger, but that was not the case.

Francisco Modiano immediately ordered men sent to the scene of the crime. He was hoping to find something the police had not, the body of Perfecta Navaja.

The captain from Curitiba had no idea what significance the incident represented, and his American partner never even saw it.

Hernando del Fuego was at the end of his rope. The lack of sleep, food and the excess of alcohol had taken their toll. He had slept in the tower, but crept back down the stairs in the morning, and pushed his stolen motorcycle into the street. He fired the engine and ran slowly out of the area to get some breakfast. He should have known that he was being observed but he was too tired and hungry to think straight.

"It doesn't look like they made your face, mate."

"No, not the news men. The cops did."

"News says all four are dead." Terry finished his eggs and started on the fried potatoes.

"I didn't stop to check." Gordon pushed his half full plate aside and poured himself another cup of coffee.

"So, all they have is the footage of the car?"

"No. They have ballistics. I had to shoot one of the brassers in the head."

"You don't think there may be one left?"

"I hope not. This whole bloody thing has gotten so far out of hand, I'm ready to walk away."

"Oy, you already did the work. Take the prize. You're not going soft on me, are you?"

"You're one to talk. You paid off that silly little blonde and let her walk before the job's done. Soft."

"I began to question her loyalties. I think Lula was in love with Perfecta. She was sleeping with me, but you know the way whores get. After a while they don't really like men any more. I didn't trust her."

"Maybe you just weren't man enough for her?"

Terry smiled at his partner and finished his coffee. "I don't think that was the trouble."

"I'm going to check on the prize." Gordon walked into the bedroom where Anastasia Viuda was bound and gagged. He took the gag from her mouth and smoothed back her hair.

"I'm hungry, Boris," she said.

"I'll make you some breakfast."

"Why don't we go out for breakfast?" She was smiling.

Gordon did not reply but in his mind he was admiring her acting skill.

"We could go down to the beach and eat at the Waldorf."

"I don't think I'm ready for a million dollar breakfast this morning," he snorted.

"I let you live when I could have killed you. Can't you return the favor?"

"I'm sorry. I'll get you breakfast."

"You know I didn't kill you because I like you. You go out of your way to help your friends."

"Perfecta," Gordon sat on the bed next to her. "I am a professional. I make mistakes from time to time and I do not always like what I am contracted to do, but I never turn my back on a contract. My reputation as a professional would suffer if I did, and the men I deal with would write me off as a liability if I were to try changing the rules.

"I like you as well. You are one of the most self assured and assertive women I have ever met, and if I had never agreed to this score, we might have become the best of friends. I cannot betray my code however, I must follow through."

"And there is the matter of the money," she said sourly.

"Yes, there is the matter of the money." For the first time, Gordon thought back on his last conversation with Colonel Richter. It had not struck him at the time, but the colonel had said, 'I will bank this and return it to you if the deal does not go down.' He had not questioned it at the time, but his old ally was a very insightful man. Perhaps he smelled real danger in the air.

Breakfast was made and Anastasia was untied so she could eat. Gordon could not deny his fascination with this woman: the way she moved, the way she ate, the way she spoke. He needed to remind himself that one should never step in the cage with a tigress.

Guns are easy to come across in Rio. Colonel Zarafina could have purchased some on the black market if he had not been given a good contact. He and the three with him were armed with Imbel MD2 automatic rifles and extra 20-round clips. They were too long to conceal comfortably, but fired at a rate of 700 rounds a minute. They also packed .45 caliber 1911 style pistols.

The locator was working perfectly although it was still directional. It had no interactive map on it like a GPS locator, but it had a GPS chip in it, so it could be tracked from Paraguay. The signal showed their target to be in a north-eastern section of Rio proper. The four men loaded themselves into their rented car and headed for the target.

When the cell phone rang, there was no doubt who was calling. Only Francisco Modiano had that number. Captain Bellisario answered it.

"Good morning. My name is Franco. You have something that we desire."

"Yes."

"Where can we find it?"

"Where is the money? Once we have the money, you may have what you desire."

"Do you have a place in mind?"

"There is a series of switchbacks on 116 north of Guapimirim. Do you know them?"

"I know the road and I know Guapimirim."

"I will meet you there at 1:00 in the afternoon. Come alone. Bring the money." Bellisario broke the connection but he did not shut off the phone.

"We move, gentlemen. I..." The captain saw a blinking light in his shirt pocket and turned away from the others. The indicator in his pocket was active.

With her breakfast almost finished, Anastasia was holding up her coffee cup to ask for more when she dropped it and buckled forward. Her face was in the remains of her eggs and her hands were holding her head.

Terry and Gordon immediately suspected a trick, but the Scot remembered her description of the sixth sense she had given them while driving through Curitiba. He moved to the window and looked out. A new Toyota was pulling up to the curb and four men in suits stepped out. Three had automatic weapons in their hands and the fourth held a piece of four-inch sewer pipe with a handle welded to it, a door basher.

"Shit!" said Gordon. "A fucking hit squad."

The locating device was directional, but it did not have elevation capability. The door to the upstairs apartment was in the back of the building. The Paraguayans were heading for the front door.

The dirty little alley behind the house was a dead end. The only way to get to the street was down the side of the house.

The choked scream that struggled out of Anastasia's throat sounded as though her lungs were being torn out. It almost covered the sound of the downstairs door being pounded in. Gordon grabbed one arm and Terry grabbed the other expecting to need to carry her through the door and down the alley. She was obviously incapacitated. They were mistaken.

No sooner had the two men grabbed her than Anastasia's head came up off the plate. Her eyes were as round as a full moon. Her lips were drawn back from her perfect teeth in a terrifying death's mask. She twisted left and then right, tearing her arms from her captor's grasp and punching Terry in the side of the head. It knocked him to the floor. Gordon reached for her but he might as well have tried to catch the wind. She moved faster than any man or woman had a right to. With Terry's pistol in her hand, she flew out the back door and down the steps.

Downstairs, the mother was shot in her kitchen before Colonel Zarafina announced that the subject was on the move. He followed it down the side of the building and back to the street.

"Outside, outside," he called and charged for the door, the detector in his left hand and his rifle in his right. Outside he pinpointed the woman running across the street. His mistake was yelling "Stop!"

Anastasia Viuda did not stop; she pulled the most amazing running flip and shot Colonel Zarafina in the middle of his chest while she was upside down and backwards.

The Colonel fell back into his men as they tried to crowd out the door. They tossed him forward again, but that split second was enough for Anastasia to regain her feet, spin around and shoot all three of them between the eyes. Each shot was perfect, dead center of the forehead; a marksman's bulls-eye.

Gordon appeared in the mouth of the alley with his pistol in his hand, but for reasons that could not be fathomed at the time, instead of shooting him as well, this whirlwind of death collapsed in the gutter. He spun to the right, thinking

412

she had been shot and found the pile of bodies blocking the doorway. He tossed his pistol to Terry, without even looking behind him and yelled, "Cover me on the right."

Terry caught the pistol by the grip and spun around the corner looking for an enemy. There was no living target. He turned back to where his partner was scooping his Amazon prisoner from the ground.

The Toyota that the hapless Paraguayans had rented was idling smoothly as Gordon gently placed her in the back seat. Terry ran back upstairs to grab the money and the three of them left the neighborhood in a hurry, but they did not do so anonymously. The spying eyes were multiple.

The conundrum that faced Captain Bellisario was unique to his experience. He had just set up a million dollar payoff, but to make it work he had to leave now. He needed his team in place before the money arrived or there would be no payoff. On the other hand, his sworn duty as an officer was to protect his country and that involved finding the fugitive and taking him down. Somehow the electronic tracker was linked to the fugitive, but he did not know how. Between the two, there was really no contest.

A button on the side of the indicator seemed to lock the location into memory. The Captain handed it to his American counterpart, saying, "Dakota, this thing will lead you to your assassin. You, go with him. You two, come with me. We have work to do, now."

Dakota blurted the beginning of a question to the captain, but the other did not ever turn around. Within seconds he was alone with a driver who only spoke Portuguese. They communicated in hand signals for a few moments before Dakota became frustrated and grabbed the key for the jeep. He vaulted into the driver's seat and cranked the engine. The guard got in beside him hurriedly so as not to be left behind and they scooted off together.

Dakota almost wrecked the jeep several times trying to drive and watch the directional device at the same time. He couldn't make the guard understand what he was doing and felt there was no time. It took him 10 minutes to get to where the device had been locked in for, where they found a crowd of people gathered around the front of a local dwelling.

Dakota stopped in the middle of the road and pulled his pistol from his ankle holster. His guard backed him up with an automatic rifle and the crowd dispersed quickly. The focus of their attention was a pile of bodies in the doorway.

The dispatcher spoke some English so she could direct the officers when she took Dakota's call. Nobody in the neighborhood had telephoned yet. Before the officers arrived, Brock took a quick tour of the downstairs. The woman had been shot multiple times in the kitchen but he doubted the old housewife had been the target. The dead men in the doorway were all dressed in business suits. Some of their arms had been liberated by the local population before Dakota arrived, but there was still one automatic and two pistols. "And another one of these!"

Dakota wiped the blood off the electronic indicator with a kitchen towel and slipped it into his jacket pocket. It was an obviously upgraded model.

Brock did not have any of the mug shots with him but he did have a picture of Terry Kingston. It wasn't bad as surveillance photos go but certainly no portrait. He began to show the photo around to the few people who had not gone back inside at his arrival. Most simply shook their heads but one small boy pointed to the upstairs apartment.

It only took a second for the agent to determine that the access point was the rear of the building; it actually took longer for Dakota and his bodyguard to creep up the steps. The door had been left open and the signs of a hurried departure were plain. Dishes were on the table and in the sink, the coffee maker still had its cheery red bulb glowing, inviting all around to partake of its fragrant bounty. There were men's clothes in one bedroom, and women's clothes in the other. There was also a couple lengths of rope in the woman's bedroom.

Dakota pulled the tracker that Bellisario had given him from his pocket. It was still locked on its previous location, dead center. The button on the side cleared it and it went into search mode but there was no signal. On a whim, he pulled the newer indicator from his pocket and grinned when he saw it was active.

."I've got you now, you bastard. You can run but there isn't a rat hole on Earth that will hide you."

The sound of the approaching sirens perked up both the searchers' ears and they made a quick decision to evacuate rather than face the inevitable questions and possible incarceration. They pulled out of the area just as the local cops pulled in. Dakota wanted very much to tell the locals that the upstairs apartment needed to be dusted for prints but he was not working with the Rio cops; he was working with the police in Curitiba. Once again it seemed that discretion was the better part of valor.

"How the hell did they find us?" Terry wanted to know. "I thought you took precautions."

"I did. There is no way I was followed out of Itaborai. They could not have tagged the car and I swapped it out anyway." Gordon was leaning into the back seat with a napkin, wiping the egg off Anastasia's face. He had been looking for bullet wounds but there had been none. She was barely conscious with her eyes rolled back in her head as if the sudden burst of inhuman speed had wasted all the energy she possessed.

"You know we will need to dump this one within an hour or so. It's a bloody rental, they usually have some sort of GPS in them so they don't lose them."

Gordon chuckled and said, "I don't think they'll be reporting it stolen."

"It still bothers me."

"All right. We'll dump it soon and double back or change direction from there." I don't know how they found us but this is changing the dynamics of the deal. I didn't trust this man before and I certainly don't trust him now. The whole thing stinks." Gordon took another look in the back seat.

"It might be a good idea to tie that wildcat up again."

"Umm, it might be." Gordon agreed but he did not move to tie her up.

"I'll tell you what. I'm going to do what we should have done days ago and get us a van or a panel truck. We've been lucky as hell on the road, but I'm not comfortable now."

"Take a stack of bills and stop somewhere. It may cost a bit to get one without ID, that's all. She looks like she'll be out for a while. Hey, pull in this mall over here. This will only take a second." Gordon hurried into a department store and came out minutes later with a newspaper, a blanket, some rope, an air mattress and two disposable cell phones. Each man activated a cell phone and while they were not secure, they were completely anonymous.

The newspaper pinpointed a fleet of full-sized work vans being sold individually by a local drug store chain. They had no windows and no amenities. The mileage was high and the engine smoked out the tail pipe. A little extra cash satisfied the broker that identification was unnecessary and

Terry drove away in a well-maintained but high mileage vehicle. His first stop was a used furniture store to pick up a mattress, and then he stopped at a sporting goods store and bought a couple of sleeping bags and a couple of blankets.

Gordon was 20 kilometers away, in Nova Iguacu, when Terry called to switch vehicles.

"Where should we meet?"

"Drive north on the 116. Pull off at the Grande Rio Shopping Mall. Meet me in the northern corner of the parking lot."

"Check. I'll be on it in 10 or 15. I need some motor oil. Seals and rings are so loose we'll never need to change the oil, just pour in more."

"Right."

"Is everything all right?"

"I'm not sure, Terry. I pulled so many maneuvers the devil himself couldn't find me. I'll see you at the mall." The concern was evident in MacMaster's voice though the source was unclear.

The mountains around Guapimirim are steep and dangerous. The smaller roads leading through them claim lives every year as unwary motorists plummet into the canyons. The BR116 is the only major road leading north but to negotiate the bluffs, the engineers were forced to include a number of switchbacks. Several of these switchbacks incorporate parking areas for sightseeing and picnicking.

Franco Cortico knew the road between Guapimirim and Teresópolis quite well. He knew the parking areas and the switchbacks. Once, while he was still quite young, he had shot two men at one of the switchbacks, taken their product and sent their truck through a guardrail to the bottom. He knew the drop off was a trap by its very location. He did not know who was setting this trap.

There had been some pretenders approaching since the reward was offered but none of them had a photograph. Now two photos show up in two days. Somebody has at least one of the two wanted killers but Franco was certain it was not the men who wanted to meet him on the mountain.

The choice of a replacement was difficult. He needed someone with enough brains to pull off the illusion but he also needed an expendable hood. Whoever he sent to this exchange would be unlikely to return.

He had a couple of hours to work with and he called in a specialist.

"Good morning, señor. Do you mind if I join you?"

Hernando del Fuego looked up from his breakfast and asked, "Do I know you?"

The smaller of the two men sat across from Hernando while the larger stood. They both wore trench coats and the standing man kept one hand in his pocket. "We are very interested," began the smaller man, "in why you are hiding in the old church and watching the gate to Señor Modiano's house."

"Oh, I am not hiding. I was thrown out of my house as they want to make a road through there and…"

"No. Now you are lying to me. You followed a man in a Chrysler yesterday who had stopped at the gate. There was much commotion. Police officers were killed and we want to know what your interest is and how you are involved."

"Oh. Would you like some breakfast? Please, be seated. I will order coffee. Please, breakfast is on me."

"No. I do not think so. You see, my large friend is not hungry for food and he does not drink coffee. He does, however, have a pistol pointed at your head."

418

"I see." Hernando feigned indifference and went back to eating.

The man standing by the table looked uncomfortable and some of the customers around the area started to get uncomfortable as well. One family left without finishing their meal.

"I don't think you understand. You will be coming with us. This is not a request. If you give us any trouble we will be forced to kill you. I do not wish to kill you, but my friend is quite fond of shooting people."

More people were starting to leave the diner with nervous backward glances.

"More coffee," Hernando called to the waitress, and as she stood between him and the larger man, he threw his hot coffee in the smaller man's face and pulled his pistol from the back of his waistband.

The standing thug shoved the waitress out of the way and fired a round through the fabric of his coat but it missed its target. Hernando had rolled onto the floor, out of the smaller man's sight.

Three rounds punctured the standing man's chest and amid the screaming evacuation of the remaining patrons, he fell. The smaller man jumped on the table in an unexpected move and would have shot Hernando but he had forgotten to rack a shell into the chamber of his semi-automatic pistol. By the time he was ready to fire he was caught by two rounds, one in the crotch and one in the belly. He got off one round after that but it was random. Hernando shot both men through the head for good measure and then turned to offer the waitress his hand. He had intended to assist her in standing, but she was curled up in a screaming ball on the floor and was in no condition to stand.

Before he left, Hernando pulled a large bill from his pocket and laid it on the table. He stole the smaller man's cell phone, expressed his thanks to the helplessly quivering waitress and left the building.

Bellisario hit the callback function on his new cell phone and Franco Cortico answered. The captain told him the location of the exchange was to be the overview within sight of the *Dedo de Deus*, the Finger of God. Franco replied that he knew the spot and would be there, with the money, in 20 minutes.

The rented Toyota was idling with Bellisario standing next to it, gazing at the majesty of the mountains. He saw the Cadillac approach and decided that this must be Franco. Not many men could afford a Cadillac and even fewer would buy one if they could.

The driver of the Cadillac pulled up 30 feet away and stepped out with a briefcase in his hand.

"Franco?"

"Yes."

"You have the money?"

"You have the woman?"

"The money first."

The driver set the briefcase on the ground and opened it. Inside there were neatly stacked piles of large bills.

Bellisario smiled widely and hit the trunk button on his keychain pendant. The trunk opened but instead of a bound and gagged woman, a soldier with a rifle popped up.

"I'm sorry, Señor Franco. I cannot afford to let you live."

"No, I'm not..." was all the imposter got out before Bellisario shot him through the chest.

The soldier in the trunk crawled out and the one on the rocks began to make his way across the road. It was without a doubt the biggest and easiest payday they would ever see.

"Stuff him in the trunk, men. No, not our trunk, the trunk of the Cadillac. That's good. The only problem is," he said as he pulled his pistol back out of its holster, "that when more than one man knows a secret, it is not a secret."

With one man holding the legs and another holding the torso, they had just swung the body into the trunk. They had not even closed the trunk lid when Captain Bellisario shot them both through the chest. The stupid expression on their faces almost brought a smile to his lips as he pushed one face first into the trunk.

As far as Bellisario could tell, there were no witnesses to his perfidy but the BR116 is a busy road. He bemoaned the fact that Cadillacs no longer had the kind of trunks you could stuff an entire family in. He knew the bodies would be found quickly, but it would take the police some time to reach the crime scene. He grabbed the briefcase from the ground, tossed it in the trunk of his rented Toyota and drove off feeling smug and rich.

If the captain had been a criminal he would have known better, but the captain was not. He was reasonably honest man with no more ambition than any other corrupt officer of the Brazilian Armed Services. Bribes, payoffs and kickbacks were business as usual, the expected price of doing business. Extortion, protection and muscle were not always the order of the day, but often encouraged by ranking members who expected a percentage. Drugs were discouraged within the ranks of the services because it led to more problems than the money was worth, but it could be pedaled to the general population without repercussions. Murder was another thing altogether.

Bellisario was quick to realize that he had not thought the whole thing through. He needed to distance himself from the murders. He needed someone to blame for the killings and who better than the arrogant American? So the first order of business is to link up with Dakota.

A career criminal would have known not to use his own telephone to call Brock at this point, but once again, Bellisario did not lean that way. "Agent Dakota?"

"Yes, Captain."

"I have your quarry in sight."

"Excellent. I am sitting in the parking lot of the Grande Rio Shopping Mall. I've been using this electronic tracker. I have your Boris under surveillance right now, he looks like he's waiting for somebody. The tracker led me to him, not Walter. Look, the only reason I haven't called in the Marines is that Walter Suffolk is not here. Do you want me to apprehend him?"

"No, I am following your target. Wait until we get them both together. Be ready for action, I should be there in 15 minutes."

"All right, I'll wait 'till then."

Bellisario drove with all the speed he could afford on the dangerous mountain roads. He knew he could never make it to the mall in 15 minutes, he was still about 60 kilometers away and would be lucky to make that in half an hour. Different plans flew through his head, some quite absurd, where he could push the blame onto someone else. He was actually grinning when he thought that this Walter Suffolk would make the perfect scapegoat. He was associated with known killers and fugitives. The other option was to frame Boris Chercovski for the murders. That would work well enough except that he is obviously in the mall parking lot at the time of the murders and the mall parking lot has cameras. That was when it hit him that the mall parking lot would be such a bad place. He needed to lure one of his potential pigeons out of there if he wanted an alibi. Once they were beyond observation, they would be beyond reproach. You cannot cross-examine a dead man.

"Boris?"
Gordon did not reply.
"Boris!"
"Yes, Perfecta?"
"Boris, we are in danger."
"You need to explain to me how we could be in danger now. Nobody but Walter knows we are here and I trust him implicitly."
"Perhaps your trust is misplaced."
"I don't think so."
"I am telling you that something is wrong. I have a vibration in my head. If it was in my pussy it would be the orgasm of the gods, but it is in my head."
"Yes, you must explain that whole sensing danger business to me some day. I could understand it if you saw an oncoming train and knew it was dangerous, but you knew the men were coming before they got there. That is a real talent and one I'd like to acquire."
"I don't understand the… ah, talent but I have other talents I would like to demonstrate to you as well."
"I'm sure you do, dear, but the thought of going through life as a eunuch comes to mind rather unwillingly."
"You have no idea what I want."
"You, dear, are a woman and it is the jurisdiction of no man to know what you want."
"I will tell you then. I want a cabin in the mountains, in the forests of the mountains where I will be alone with my man. I would have a dog and we would hunt for our food and we could be alone to make love endlessly. And that is for the long term. For the short term, I want to get out of this place. I tell you we are in danger. I can almost smell it."

"Oh, I knew I should have used deodorant."

Anastasia chuckled, amazed that she could find any humor, given the fact that she was tied, wrapped in a blanket and destined to be delivered to her death. Then the feeling became stronger eliciting a whimper. "I am telling you we are in danger and it is getting closer."

Gordon was watching the crowded parking lot and saw the jeep for the third time. He had thought at first that they were security but then he realized that the driver was wearing a suit and the passenger was wearing a uniform. He reached down and turned the key. He had no idea how anyone could follow him in a city of this size but he did not mind testing the theory.

Before exiting the parking lot, he called Terry on his new phone. "Walter, there has been a change of plans. We will meet at the airport. Lot D, in the long-term parking area." He got a confirmation of that. Terry had not even asked why.

The airport was east, that would have been a left on Presidente Dutra Road, BR116. Gordon took a right and exited at the Bela Vista Avenue North. He circled around, got back on the 116 heading east, watching carefully for the jeep. Sure enough, it was following him.

Ordinarily, MacMaster drove carefully, never speeding excessively, never running stop signs, never calling attention to himself. It was a requirement of his chosen profession that he blend in with the population. This did not preclude his being able to drive like a madman. Nobody in a jeep could have tracked that Toyota with that sort of head start unless they were being tracked by satellite. In 10 minutes, he had put three kilometers between Brock Dakota and himself.

"Are we safe now, Perfecta?" he said, only half tongue in cheek.

"Yes… we are safe," she replied. She barely got the sentence out she was breathing so hard.

"Something is wrong?"

"Yes. Something is very wrong. I have a need."

"What is it you need?"

"I need you. It has always been my pleasure to have a man after a job but it was never uncontrollable before. I cannot explain how I feel." She was panting. "I need a man. If you cannot do it, give me to your friend. I need it now."

"I admire your acting ability," he told her. "If I did not know better, I'd fall into that trap face first." Realizing what he had said, he chuckled.

Anastasia did not laugh. She was beginning to moan. "Please, untie me. If I cannot have a man I must use my fingers. Please."

"You should have been in the porno industry. You would have made as much money and wouldn't need to kill anyone."

"Ahhh. You do not understand." Her voice was taking on an edge. "I am going crazy!"

"I think maybe you have some issues that will never be addressed."

"You big faggot, park this car and get back here. I want you now."

"I'm sorry, I told you before, that's against my code."

"Fuck your code, you big bastard. I spared your life twice. If you won't give it to me then find somebody who will. I've never been so horny in my life. It's like I'm possessed by the devil."

"I'll believe that when your head starts doing three-sixties."

"Arrgg," she screamed, arching her back and straining at her bonds and then collapsed, making pitiful, mewling sounds.

Gordon was cautious, especially after having seen what this woman was capable of, but he was becoming concerned now. Until this point she had comported herself capably. Not, perhaps, perfectly ladylike, but completely controlled. Her earlier propositions had clearly been a trap. Now she was acting like a sick animal, writhing in the back seat, her naked feet kicking the door panel. Then she seemed to collapse and lay there unconscious.

The hill rose like a green iceberg in the middle of a sea of houses. It was topped by what appeared to be a Cathedral but there were no other buildings there. The parking lot was to the left, halfway up the hill and quite large. The road went no further. The faithful needed to walk from there. The far end of the parking lot seemed a perfect place to take a rest so Gordon backed the car in, facing the driveway.

Leaving Anastasia in the car for a moment, MacMaster lit a cigar and walked across the parking lot to the entrance. He stood there smoking for a couple of minutes, getting the lay of the land. There was nobody coming up the steep drive and nobody could have seen him from below due to the curve of the drive. It seemed they were alone. Gordon's thoughts were dark. There was only one man who knew they had been in the parking lot of the mall. It made no sense. Terry stood nothing to gain. They had been working together since he was young. Gordon had helped him wipe out the twin crime bosses in Sydney. Neither of them had a reason to suspect the other as far as the Scot knew.

Nobody approached the parking lot from high or low while Gordon stood there so he returned to the car, leaning against the hood and smoking. He looked inside from time to time, but his captive was sleeping. A deep and abiding sadness settled into MacMaster's heart as he thought about needing to kill Terry Kingston. Terry was one of the only men in the world he could call a friend, one of the only men he trusted. As he finished his cigar, two things happened almost simultaneously: Anastasia Viuda screamed in pain and a uniformed soldier stepped out of the surrounding underbrush, his rifle spitting lead.

Gordon had begun to turn when he heard the scream and then finished spinning around and dropping to one knee when the rustle of the underbrush alerted him to the soldier's presence. The bullets raked the air where he had been standing.

Two voices came from the bushes, one Portuguese and one American, both demanding he surrender, but Gordon MacMaster was in no mood to surrender. In a split second, the presence of the enemy had exonerated his long-time friend and ally. He had no time for the rest of the emotions that would flood his psyche. He needed to extricate himself from this position. There was no way he was going back to military prison to be shot.

A somersault brought him to the back of the car and he rose, firing instinctually, taking no time to aim. His first round caught the soldier in the right arm as the man turned toward him. The second round caught the man in the throat. The third and fourth rounds took him in the chest and head, killing him. But there was no other target. He knew there was a second man but he was still hidden in the bushes. He dropped behind the rear axle, lying flat in the gravel, seeking his adversary's feet but they were not there. An uncanny stillness hung for a second in the air as both men strained to hear the other move, to pinpoint their location. Then an unearthly wail came from the interior of the car. Anastasia Viuda was thrashing about inside the car like a snared wolverine.

"Boris Chercovski," rang out with an unmistakably American accent. "We have you surrounded. Give up now or we will be forced to shoot."

Gordon knew he was not surrounded. He would already be dead if he were. He waited, controlling his breathing; in through the nose, out through the mouth. He was sure this man would show himself in a moment, but he did not. Unbidden, Gordon thought, "How can we have a Mexican Standoff in Brazil?" If he could just get into the underbrush he knew he could take this man, but he himself would be exposed. He could see very little from where he was, but he could move like a ghost in trees. He half stood for a second and let three rounds loose into the bushes where his experience best led him to believe his opponent would be and then vaulted through the bushes. He moved quickly and noisily at first, hoping to fool the American into believing he was running away, then he turned and crept around to flank his opponent. He had no idea how the man was armed, but he knew only four rounds remained in his own pistol.

The idea foremost in Gordon's mind as he crept through the woods was that an American, even an experienced hunter, would be clumsy in the woods. Unless this man had Special Forces training, he could take him. Brock Dakota was, however, the exception rather than the rule. While his mother had been a German-American, his father had been full-blooded Shawnee and had taught him how to be like nothing in the woods, to move like the mists of morning.

Brock heard the crashing flight of his quarry initially, but then the forest went silent except for the screaming and thrashing from inside the Toyota. He knew he needed to get far enough away from that distraction to hear. He slipped around in an arc that almost matched his opponent, though neither of them knew it. If neither changed direction, their vectors would intersect perfectly. Then Murphy's Law injected itself.

Dakota's cell phone was set to vibrate but that created enough noise to make him jump. He pulled the phone from his pocket and flipped it into the brush on his left where it continued to vibrate away. A lesser man might have followed the vibration, but Gordon MacMaster was not such a man. He had already pinpointed his opponent and drew down on the tree he was hiding behind. They were only 30 meters apart but they both froze in position, sweating in afternoon heat. Once again they were trying to out wait each other, but the Scottish assassin had the upper hand. He knew where his opponent was.

Hernando was furious. Those ignorant, bumbling thugs had created such a scene that he was sure to be fingered as soon as he popped his head up in Itaborai. Aside from the lack of food and sleep he had been happy hiding in the church. He missed his partner a great deal and for more than the obvious reasons. The two of them could have been watching around the clock, working in shifts. The job was too much for one man. He had expected action sooner. It might even have already happened, how was he to tell?

He rode his stolen motorcycle for half an hour to completely clear the area and then pulled onto a dirt road into the woods. He sat on a gnarled and twisted root sticking from the ground and thought for a second, then he pulled the stolen cell phone from his pocket and scrolled through the names listed. A couple of the names looked promising, primarily Franco. He knew Franco Cortico was Francisco's right hand man so he took the chance and called it. A very irritated Franco answered the phone.

"Yes?"

"Franco Cortico?"

"Who is this?"

"This is the man who was hiding in the bell tower. The man who just shot your two associates in the head. Do I have your attention?"

"Who am I speaking with?"

"My name is of no importance. My interest is in the woman."

"You wish to buy a woman?"

"Do not attempt to play me for a fool again today. If you refuse to have respect then we cannot do business."

"What sort of business is it we would be doing?"

"I am interested in the woman and the man holding her." Hernando took the chance that the exchange had not taken place since the day before.

"And the name of this man is…?"

"That is not important. What I find most important is that you listen to me very carefully. I do not want Perfecta Navaja, your boss can have her. I need proof of her death and I want the fool who brings her to you."

"How do you know anything about this, who are you and what makes you think you can make these absurd demands of me?"

"Franco, Franco, Franco, my demands are simple and easy to accomplish. They cost you nothing. Our goals are identical: the death of the woman and the elimination of the men holding her. I will give you 15 minutes to confer with whomever you need to and I will call back."

Hernando del Fuego hung up the phone and turned it off. He was not sure that what he was doing was going to help his cause, but he was sure that going head to head with the mob was beyond his capabilities. He could hurt them but in the long run it would only sign his own death warrant. His breath caught as he remembered that his death warrant had been signed already.

On the other end of the closed connection, Franco Cortico was wracking his brain to tear loose the identity of a man who had the gall to stalk Francisco Modiano's number one man. He chewed on his thumb knuckle as he watched the screen and thought. "The son-of-a-bitch watches us from the old church. He shot four cops to get at the rojo that probably has Perfecta, yet he didn't kill him. Then he calls me up and says he killed my men?"

The number of the last incoming call confirmed that the cell had belonged to one of his men. The already agitated Franco was beginning to boil. It had taken weeks for anyone to produce even half the team responsible for General Modiano's death but the closer they got to resolution, the worse things got. He jumped as he finally bit his knuckle hard enough to hurt himself. He cursed and lit a cigarette.

When Franco's telephone rang again, it was precisely 15 minutes after the connection had been broken. "Yes?"

"Do we have a deal?"

"Listen, mystery man, we will need to get something out of this deal as well."

"That is only right. I get what I want and you get what you want."

"We need the reward returned to us."

Hernando grinned, thinking he could get his hands on the reward paid for his partner seemed so darkly ironic that it filled him with glee. "Yes, I have no need for the reward. I will kill the mark and return it in exchange for Perfecta's right hand. I don't care if you take it from her before or after death."

"Your man is in the city of Rio. He is pulling into the parking lot of the Grande Rio Mall right now. Do you know where that is?"

"Yes, I can find it."

"Then we have a deal. Return the reward to us and we will provide you with your proof."

The connection was broken.

Franco continued to stare at the screen. The chip in the briefcase would follow it wherever it went, but he expected it to have blinked out already. His man had never called after the one o'clock deadline so he assumed the man was no longer breathing. The light on the console blinked out. After waiting for it to happen, Franco found himself upset that it had not waited a few more minutes. He wished the man on the motorcycle had been there to see it.

It was expected that Brock Dakota would remain in the parking lot or call Captain Bellisario when he left. The man did neither. There was no sign of the jeep, the driver or the American Agent. If he could not manufacture a believable scapegoat, Bellisario would need to leave the country. He was perfectly willing to shoot Bock Dakota, Walter Suffolk, Boris Chercovski or whoever else he needed to, but he needed to have them in his sights to do so.

Sighing, he picked up his cell phone and dialed Brock's number. The call went through but there was no answer and it went to voice mail.

Bellisario could not stand to wait longer, the urge to feel and smell the money was too great. He popped the trunk and walked to the back of the rental car. He reached in and popped the hasps on the briefcase. The top flipped up and he grabbed a stack of bills. He spread the stack and under the top couple of 100 reais notes, the stack consisted of 2 reais notes. The haul, which should have been close to two million reais could not have topped fifty thousand. Cheated, Bellisario's scream of anger was the last noise he made as the plastic explosive in the false bottom of the case ignited. The money he coveted was driven out with such force it scoured the flesh from his bones.

The midday heat was sucking the water from MacMaster's body. The sweat ran down his back in rivers as he waited. It dripped from his brow and stung his eyes. He knew what tree his opponent hid behind but the tension was unbelievable. Minutes ticked by, both men straining for the slightest sound, knowing that their time was critical. Sirens began to wail in the distance. The Scotsman knew he needed to get back to the car and get out of the area before the police arrived. He almost made a move but the American moved first.

Slipping around the tree, pistol in hand, silent on the damp forest floor, Dakota stepped right into the line of fire and MacMaster shot him twice in the chest.

Ordinarily it would have been his policy to confirm death with a head shot but there was no time. He needed to move. He had only seen two men in the jeep and the American in the suit had been one of them. He gambled that those were the only two on his tail and sprinted to the parking lot, eschewing silence for speed. He jumped in the Toyota, fired up the engine and drove at top speed out of the parking lot and down the hill. He did not see the police. They were not following him. It was time to conclude this messy business and get out of Brazil. A check of the back seat found Anastasia Viuda once more unconscious. He pulled out his cell phone.

"Oy, mate, I'm in place but this is no place I want to be. Too many cameras, security, dogs. I need to move."

Terry's voice was almost as much a relief as the air conditioning in the car.

"Terry, get out of there. Get across the bay. There's too much going on I can't explain. Call me back when you're in a good spot and I'll find you. Make it well away from the city."

"I'll dig a rabbit hole and call you back."

The phone went dead. Gordon checked the back seat again but Anastasia was still out cold.

Fifteen minutes later Terry called back and told him to stay on the RJ106 past Niteroi. He was going out past Marica into farm country, about 40 kilometers past Niteroi. An hour after that, Gordon was tossing Anastasia Viuda onto the mattress in the back of the panel van and pushing the Toyota into a stand of trees just off the road. He wiped it down for prints and left the keys in it.

"Do we do it now?" Terry wanted to know.

"No. Tomorrow. I don't know exactly how he did it but there was a jeep following me. Two men. They watched me in the parking lot of the mall. Who knew I was there?"

"I did, mate. Who else knew?"

"I asked myself the same question. They knew who I was. That is they knew I was Boris. Take a right here."

"That takes us to the ocean."

"That's what I want."

Terry pulled over to the side of the road. He reached inside his vest and pulled out his pistol. Gordon was caught by surprise and started reaching for his own gun. Terry popped the clip out onto the floor of the van and then racked out the bullet in the chamber. He flipped it around and handed it to the Scot grip first. "Mate, if you think I had anything to do with you getting fingered at that mall, let's have it right now."

"No, Terry, I'll admit it crossed my mind for a second but I know it wasn't you."

"And I hope you also know it never will be me. I came down here to this God forsaken jungle to save your ass, and now you put me on a spot like I'm some bloody bush pig?"

"I told you, I haven't figured it out yet, but you didn't let me finish. I lost this pair and hid on top of a mountain and then suddenly, there they were. One Brazilian Army and one American. I'm thinking CIA."

"What did they do, what were they after?"

"I don't really know what they were after and it's irrelevant now. They're dead."

"Are you sure you lost the bastards?"

"Yes, at least I was sure at the time."

"Well, crikey, it seems like every time we go to ground somebody is trying to kill us."

As one, both men turned and looked into the bed of the panel van. They were looking at two suitcases full of money and a semi-conscious Anastasia Viuda.

They both moved. Terry was pulling the money out of the suitcases and Gordon was stripping Anastasia. They took the woman's clothing and stuffed it into the suitcases. It was obvious that either the cases or the clothing was bugged. How it had been done and who had done it was unclear, but there could be no other explanation.

A few more kilometers south on RJ118 and they found a dirt road leading to a huge lagoon draining into the ocean through the Rio de Ponta Negra. It was perfect. There was no housing there, just a wide, shallow launch for fishing boats. They pulled into the trees on the north side and placed the suitcases in the trees on the south side. Whoever it was that was tracking them would get what they asked for. They just shouldn't have asked for it.

A couple of hours passed and the sun began to set. Anastasia woke and complained that she was hungry. The men had not thought about it much but once the suggestion was made, they realized that they were hungry as well.

"We passed a supermarket not two kilometers back. If we hurry they'll still be open." Terry said.

"Right. Gag the woman and leave her here with me. Leave the rifle, too. You take the van and go get something to eat."

"Right." Terry started lifting the naked woman out the back doors.

"Hey," she said, sleepily. "I have no clothes on. I know you didn't use me while I was sleeping or I wouldn't still be so horny. Do me a favor and slip me some of what you've got."

"Sorry, darlin' I'd like to accommodate you but it makes things complicated and I don't need anything complicated right now. I do like the birthmark, though, kinda looks like somebody had kissed you on the bottom." He left her lying naked and gagged and completely frustrated.

When Terry returned with the van and some sandwich materials, Anastasia was rolled in the blanket. The mosquitoes that could not fly in full sunlight came out at dusk in swarms. They had covered her naked body. All three of them took refuge in the van with the windows closed.

As soon as Gordon untied her hands from behind her back, Anastasia reached down between her legs. Within seconds she was having a shuddering, gushing orgasm as her perfect body arched backward and she screamed in pleasure. She lay on the mattress for a couple of seconds with her eyes closed and then popped up with a smile. "Ahhh, that's a little better," she said with a twinkle in her eye. "You see, I told you I needed some. Now, how about one of those beers and some food?"

Both men were sitting with their mouths hanging open.

436

Chapter Twenty One
The Payoff

The pain in Dakota's chest was nothing compared to actually being shot but it would have been hard to convince him of that. It felt like he had been punched by a pile driver. He had to roll over before he could even get to his feet. The impact had not just knocked him down, it had knocked him out.

Boris Chercovski was gone, undoubtedly thinking he had killed the agent. Voices from the parking lot commanded his attention and when he turned that way, red and yellow lights flashed in his eyes. He knew there was no excuse for him being there, armed. He would be hauled in and there would be questions he could not answer. He was not officially there. Not moving as silently as he could, he still avoided the attentions of the police as he slipped back down the hill. Despite the bulk and the heat of the Kevlar vest, he swore he would never do field work again without one.

The jeep was still at the bottom of the hill. There was no one around it. Brock was glad that he had the key and that he had been driving. He fired the engine and eased the clutch out in first gear. It was not as quiet as he would have liked but it was gone without attracting too much attention. He knew he couldn't drive the jeep long before some civil servant became curious about what he was doing with it.

The bubbling invective erupted when he realized he had left his phone in the woods. He couldn't be sure the man who had shot him didn't pick it up. He couldn't even call Captain Bellisario. The captain was supposed to be meeting him in the mall parking lot he realized. Maybe he is still there.

As it turned out, the captain was indeed still there. He was not yet loaded into the back of the ambulance because the forensics experts had not finished performing their inspection of his shredded corpse. The sight drew the crowd's eyes like a gory magnet to the north end of the lot and nobody paid any attention when Brock entered the south end.

He pulled in one of the first spots and walked casually into the mall. Once inside he asked a woman in a perfume kiosk what had happened in the parking lot. The woman was more than happy to talk to him about the incident, eyeing him up and down as she did. She did not really know anything substantive; she just wanted the attention. She told him how some soldier had blown himself up, probably smoking while he poured gasoline. Dakota knew that was bullshit. He bought a wide brimmed hat to cover his face from the surveillance cameras and went back out to get a closer look. The area was cordoned off but he could see the remains of the car and the uniformed body. The trunk lid had been blown off by the explosion, and the flesh and hair were torn off Bellisario's head. Dakota had hoped it was one of the other soldiers, not the captain, at least he could communicate with Bellisario. Or he could have.

Shaking his head, Dakota turned around and walked back into the mall. Years back, there had been a row of pay phones on the wall; now there were only two. Dakota felt gratified that his address book had not been stolen and then he realized that he should be more grateful he was still alive. Chercovski had him unconscious in the woods, at his mercy. He wondered if it was an oversight or if the man had thought him dead. He called the police station in Curitiba and asked for Chief Cardosa. Cardosa came on the line after a while and it was necessary for Dakota to work through the language barrier to let him know what kind of trouble there had been.

"Have you captured no one then?" the Chief wanted to know.

"No, no one."

"And yet, Agent Dakota, Captain Bellisario is dead, at least one of his men is dead, and you have been shot?"

"Yes, that is correct."

"Forgive me for a minute, I must take this other call."

Chief Cardosa was off the phone for a matter of a couple of minutes but his demeanor had changed when he returned. He was less upset, less nervous sounding. He asked Brock to go through the scenario again, so that he could get a better handle on it.

As an experienced field agent, Dakota should have known he was being stalled, but he didn't pick up on it quickly enough. Before he was through explaining the entire situation again, four officers of the Rio de Janiero Regional Police surrounded him, hung up the phone and escorted him from the building in handcuffs. By the time the sun went down, he was locked in an interrogation room with representatives of both the army and the local police.

"Señor Dakota, I am Deputy Chief Inspector Llamas. I'm afraid you are in a big trouble."

"I explained to you, gentlemen, that I am working with Captain Bellisario to apprehend a dangerous fugitive, here in Rio de Janiero."

"Yes, señor, we understood that. Perhaps you can explain to us poor policemen why Captain Bellisario is dead?"

"I don't know where he went and I don't know who killed him."

"We have the tapes from the parking lot. We saw you and one soldier in a jeep earlier today. You see, señor, we are following up on your story. We simply need to know for surely that you are telling us everything. So we go through it again, yes?"

"All right. Here we go again." Brock went through it again and again, answering their pointed questions, describing the principal fugitives, naming the other people involved and giving them the same story again and again. He had interrogated enough people in his past to know that there are a couple of things that trip up the guilty: first it was thinking you are smarter than the police, second involves inventing too elaborate a story, third is telling more than one story or changing your original story. While Brock's story was indeed elaborate, none of it contradicted any other part except that he had no idea where the detectors had come from, who had made them or how they worked. He didn't even know what they detected. Fortunately, the newer of the two detectors was still working so he had at least that for corroboration.

The ballistics lab wasted no time processing the shells that had killed the soldiers.

They would have an answer the following day. Until that point, Brock Dakota was to enjoy the hospitality of the state. Brock began to wonder if it would become an indefinite sort of incarceration. He suspected he might become one of those men who disappeared into the system and were never heard from again.

The entire night was spent in the interrogation room. Brock knew he was going nowhere until it could be proved he had not killed anyone. They checked his pistol, to see it had not been recently fired. They examined the bruises on his chest and pulled the two slugs that had caused them from his vest. They took his fingerprints and impressions of the soles of his shoes. And they asked him the same questions a hundred different ways. After all, since he arrived in town the bodies were piling up and the officers needed explanations for their superiors.

Dakota did not know why Chief Cardosa had ordered him incarcerated but it did get him thinking. What, not whom, had blown Captain Bellisario up? He reconstructed the scene from memory and saw the body, which had been physically blown 10 feet from the car. The trunk lid was blown off the car, but the gas tank had not ignited; it wasn't even leaking. The blast had taken the captain's face right off the bone, but his body was barely touched below the shoulders. That told him that the blast was directed up, that it was not in a soft bag, that it was placed in a case that exploded when the lid was raised. Now what sort of case and why? Then he saw the light.

"Inspector, tell me, have you found the two men who were with the captain when last I saw him?"

"You tell me about these two men, yes?"

"Yes. The two soldiers. We flew here with three soldiers. Bellisario took two of them with him when we split up. This is after we had a composite picture made with Mrs. Andalusia's head on this prostitute's body. I was not sure what he was doing but I think I have a clue. Do you have the captain's cell phone?"

"The last call he made was to you, señor."

"That was most likely the call that got me shot. What about before that?"

"He made a call to a local business man."

"I'm going to make a guess. I'm going to say that the call was to whoever offered the reward for Mr. and Mrs. Andalucia."

"What?"

"The team that murdered General Modiano."

Suddenly, Brock Dakota was alone in the interrogation room. The men interrogating him practically ran out of the room. He did not see anyone for over an hour after that. When they returned it seemed they were now at odds over how to proceed. There was a palpable tension in the air that had nothing to do with the early morning hour.

441

"Señor Dakota, we have located your cell phone. It is as you said. The last call was not answered, from Captain Bellisario."

"I have no reason to lie to you gentlemen. The Captain and I were working in concert to eliminate threats to both our national securities. I admit I was more interested in Walter Suffolk and will still consider him my number one target. Boris Chercovski is, however, a wanted man in this country. Uh, wanted for murder, yes?"

"Yes, among other things he is a murderer and an escaped convict. Tell me more about him."

"I don't really know anything about him. I never heard of him before I came to Curitiba. He shot my escort to death and would have killed me if not for the body armor. Ballistics will bear that out. I never got off a shot."

"Yes, that is interesting. Tell me why you never even attempted to shoot this man? You had a loaded pistol brought into this country on the authority of your government yet you never even tried to shoot this killer."

"I never had a shot."

"Of course." The interrogator's sneer was enough to boil blood. "Tell me now, how it was you came to be in the woods with him, yes?"

"You have the detectors. The older one was given to me by Bellisario. I don't know how they work, I don't know what they track. I don't know why the older one only works sometimes and the other one is on all the time. I don't know anything about them except that they led me to the car where Boris Chercovski and this crazy woman were. In the parking lot of the chapel, my escort moved without orders from me and got shot for it."

"Yes, tell me about how you shot him."

"Oh, for Christ's sake. You know I didn't shoot him."

442

"What about the five people in the apartment on Mauricio Avenue? Tell me about them."

"Back to this again. The first direction finder took us there. It was locked in to that location. Bellisario locked it in when he gave it to me. When we got there, the crowd had already gathered around the dead bodies. They scattered when we showed up. I found the other direction finder there, with the dead men. The first one, the one Bellisario gave me had stopped working after leading us there, but the second one led us to the parking lot of the mall, and Boris Chercovski. He got spooked and ditched us but the direction finder led us right to him again, this time on that hill by the chapel. If your rookie hadn't been so gung ho…"

"Be advised that we do not look kindly toward speaking ill of the dead."

"I'm sorry."

"Apology accepted. Now tell us again about where Captain Bellisario went."

On and on it went, backward and forward, the interrogators trying hard to get Dakota to slip or make a conflicting statement or get angry or something but he was too old a hand for that. He stuck to his story. He stuck to his story when the news of Bellisario's men being shot was introduced. He stuck to his story when the added element of the charred bills in the mall parking lot was revealed. He stuck to his story when brow beaten and all but physically assaulted by the interrogation team. He stuck to his story when threatened with a lifetime in a Brazilian prison. He could not be shaken. He stuck to his story.

By the time Hernando del Fuego arrived at the Grande Rio Mall, there was a mess in the parking lot. The police were beginning to tape off the area around the explosion and there was a crowd gathered to witness the gory scene. Rede

Globo had cameramen and reporters on the scene getting footage that may or may not make the evening news. Hernando approached the site with gleeful expectation, only to find that the victim was not the big redhead but a uniformed officer from the army. This was a trap that Franco Cortico had set. If he had been a few minutes earlier and had actually recognized the soldier, Hernando could easily be in the same condition as the dead officer. The level of frustration in the Argentine assassin's head boiled over the top. He was about to take off his helmet when he saw a camera on one of the light poles and decided not to. He pulled back out of the parking lot and zipped down the road just a few minutes before Brock Dakota pulled in.

"Hello?"

"Hello, Franco."

"Hello. Did you get our money back?"

"You know as well as I that the money is spread all over the parking lot of the mall along with some stupid soldier."

"Why, I can't imagine what you are talking about."

"Stop. You planted that bomb and if I had been any closer, it would have killed me, but it didn't. Look, I don't know who that was but he did not have Perfecta Navaja."

"He had a picture of her. She was naked and lying on a bed with her legs open."

There was no way he was going to rise to that bait. Hernando no longer cared what happened to his former partner and lover, he was only interested in saving his own head from the chopping block. "So, you don't have her." It was not a question.

"We will have her soon, señor. I do not think your services will be necessary. Thank you for thinking of us though." Franco hung up the phone.

Without proof of her death, Hernando could not go back home. Until he provided proof he was persona-non-gratis. He needed to find her and kill her but the task seemed more and more difficult by the hour.

The neighborhood was the sort of place that had many more people on the street in the early morning than the early afternoon. Many of the residents were just getting out of bed after a long night. Flashing some cash made for easy access to the suppliers and Hernando purchased some home-cooked methadrine. It was relatively cheap and a few lines would keep a man up for a week. There were some side effects, but the primary effects made all other considerations secondary. It took a few minutes to get his hands to stop shaking after the first healthy snort but once he felt stabilized, he made inquiries about a different kind of contraband. After some additional purchases, he headed back toward Itaborai.

Studying his map of the area, Hernando realized that the neighborhood of Itaborai that housed Francisco Modiano was bordered by the strip mine on the northwest side and a creek to the east. That left only two ways in for a vehicle: First Street and Christiano Ferreira Braga Road. Given the fact that Hernando had shot four police officers in the mine at the far end of Christiano Ferreira Braga, he thought it unlikely his enemy would use that route. The man had been implicated in the killing. That left First Street. There was one farm building and a few trees on First Street but it really provided little cover. It was three blocks long and dead-ended in a field. Anyone driving needed to turn left instead of entering that block.

The only way to pull it off would be with the rifle and scope. He had secured them in the church, but he had been followed from the church so it was no longer safe to ride in there. This was not the sort of neighborhood one could loiter in without good reason. If the police saw him, they would stop him for certain. If Modiano's men saw him they would probably kill him.

Hernando had slept little in the past week and methadrine was the last thing he needed. Mothers grabbed their children and moved to the other side of the street when they saw him pacing up and down on the sidewalk in downtown Itaborai. He looked very much like an unshaven madman as his addled brain worked out a plan of action.

After eating a couple of sandwiches and drinking three beers, Anastasia Viuda, hardly conscious of the fact that she was stark naked, wrapped herself in the blanket and fell asleep. The vibrations in her head were gone, as if she was in no danger whatsoever, belying the fact that she was a captive destined for a horrible death. She did not even wake up when Gordon bound her hands and feet.

Terry and Gordon waited vigilantly for the first couple of hours after the sun went down. If there was a bug in the bags or the woman's clothing, nobody followed it there. Around midnight, Gordon agreed to get some sleep while Terry kept watch. He lay down next to Anastasia and she snuggled up next to him.

Morning came and still there were no arrivals. Terry had not felt comfortable with sleeping next to their victim so he had napped in the passenger seat while Gordon watched.

A thick fog blanketed the area for a very short time, coming off the lagoon. Anastasia expressed that she should be allowed to relieve herself. She had no compunction against being watched while she did so, but did complain that she would like to wipe herself. Gordon walked across the boat launch and got her shirt, soaked it in the lagoon and wiped her clean with that. He also brought her panties to her. There was no easy way a bug could be stowed in a pair of women's panties.

"Thank you, Boris."

"You're welcome, Perfecta."

"You know, I do not understand this situation."

"What's to understand?"

"My head. The noises, well, they are not noises. I get a rattle in my head when danger is near. At first I needed to see it to know that the danger was there, and then the rattle would start. Now, I do not need to see it to know it is there. The rattle starts when danger is near."

"Is that why you screamed, before, when the soldier and the American were there?"

"Oh, Boris, that hurt so bad and then afterward I went crazy."

"I know. You ruined the back seat of that car."

"But now, here, with you, I do not feel the rattle. I do not sense the danger. You are not going to hurt me."

"No, I'm not."

Terry spoke up at this point "Y'know, mate, I never was too fond of a contract on a sheila. I don't take 'em. I know this one is different, but..."

Gordon sighed. "I took the job. I paid the retainer to the colonel. I can't turn my back on it now. Besides it pays like a leprechaun. Let's just get it done today and get the hell out of this bug infested wilderness." Out came the cell phone and in went the number.

"What is it?"

"Dom Modiano?"

"No, this is Franco Cortico. I will be conducting all business on this matter. If you are calling this number, you have something that is of interest to us."

"Correct, and you have something that is of interest to us."

"I would like to speak with the object of our desire, just to confirm its presence."

Gordon took the gag out of Anastasia's mouth and held the phone up to her mouth. He did not expect what she had to say.

"You pitiful little worm," she began, thinking she was speaking to Modiano. "Yes, I killed your brother. I stomped him like the cockroach he was and if I get the chance, I will do the same to you."

After regaining his composure, Gordon asked if he was satisfied.

"Where would you like to make the exchange?" Franco asked.

"Drive south on RJ114 to RJ106 and turn east. The time is 6:30. Call me at 6:50."

Franco started to protest that he would barely be out of Itaborai in 20 minutes but Gordon had hung up his phone and turned it off.

"How's this goin' down? I hold the transfer and you back me up from the point?"

"No, not from the point. There's nowhere to go from there. And this is a natural trap, here. No, we're going back to 106 east and find a nice rest stop. I gave him 20 minutes; if he makes it in 40 he'll be doing well. Here, turn this phone back on at 6:45."

The fog cleared as soon as they got away from the lagoon. Traffic was brisk once they got on the RJ106. A half kilometer past an unexpected bakery on top of a mountain, was a dirt road that seemed perfect.

The telephone rang right on time and Franco Cortico seemed slightly distressed, claiming that he was only halfway to RJ106. He said he was just reaching the top of the mountain range that lay between Itaborai and the ocean. Gordon gave him another 20 minutes, told him to stop at the overlook across the road from the bakery and hung up again.

When the telephone rang again, Gordon asked the caller what he was looking at. Franco hesitated and then said, "The overlook across the road from the bakery."

"Good. Get out and tell me what kind of car is sitting down in the valley."

A man got out of a newer style Cadillac and bent over the rail with his cell phone in his hand, looking for a car. He stopped looking when he heard the hammer being pulled back.

"Give me the cell phone," Gordon said.

The man did not say a word, he simply handed over the instrument. "Dom Cortico? Why are you not here?"

Cortico knew he had been played. "I must say," he began, "that you are much sharper than the last man we dealt with."

"I know nothing of the last man. You are dealing with me now."

"Are you going to shoot my representative?"

"Why? Should I?"

"The last man I dealt with shot my representative."

"I don't see the need for that. I am going to give him back his cell phone and you are going to tell him to cooperate with me, to give me his weapons and to show me the reward."

"He has been instructed to only show the reward when he has seen the woman. This is a great deal of money and we have little proof that she is indeed in your possession and alive."

Another Cadillac pulled into the parking lot and Gordon put the phone back to his ear. "Dom Cortico, you are going to call your other men and tell them to leave the area."

Whether Franco was doing that or not became irrelevant when four men in suits stepped from the Cadillac with MAC10 style weapons in hand. That instant, MacMaster knew there was no money, there was nothing but treachery. There was not a moment to lose. The man in front of him reached into his coat for his pistol and Gordon shot him through the chest. The men behind him lifted their weapons and the lead man pitched forward with a small hole in the middle of his back and a large one blowing out two of his ribs.

Gordon dove over the hood of the first Cadillac scarce inches in front of a spray of lead, then the second of the four fell, his head exploding like a spring flower.

The customers of the bakery were screaming and running and it was a good thing. One of the automatic weapons was turned in their direction and an entire clip of bullets was expended, raking the cars in front and the picture windows. The thug stopped to reload and a rifle slug took him in the throat and smashed out his spine. The last man turned slightly to see who was shooting them from behind and was hit simultaneously by Terry's rifle round in the arm and Gordon's pistol round in the side of his chest.

It took a matter of seconds for MacMaster to shoot each of the five men in the head, jump into the driver's seat of the Cadillac and tear off down the road. The turn off was not half a kilometer down the road, but it was around several turns so it was not visible from the parking lot. He slowed as he made the turn so as to not kick up too much dust, then stopped after the first curve. Out of curiosity he hit the button for the trunk and inside the trunk was a briefcase. He did not open the case. A minute later Terry Kingston came half running, half sliding down the hill with his rifle in his hand. Gordon was in the driver's seat when Terry rolled over the roof, yanked open the door and dove into the back seat.

The van was half a kilometer further and Gordon slid the Cadillac sideways, parked it and tossed the keys into the brush. He popped the trunk and took the briefcase. One kilometer further they turned back onto RJ106 and headed northeast. Terry was driving and Gordon was in the back. Nobody had seen the van, just the Cadillac.

"That, mate, is why I don't like this kind of operation. I don't mind shooting the ignorant bastards, but they were just doing what they were told. The problem is, I don't get paid for that. Anyway, I'm glad you took point on it. I did 'em as quick as I could but I was sure you were gonna eat some lead back there." Terry was smiling.

Gordon was not smiling, he looked grim. He had been shot at, plenty of times, it didn't bother him, but there was usually a reason for it: he was in the wrong uniform, he had just killed someone's best friend, he had even been shot at for screwing someone's daughter. This time it pissed him off though since he was in the right, sort of.

The cell phone in MacMaster's pocket rang and he answered it.

"Well, it seems my men have not followed their instructions," Franco said tensely. "This was supposed to be a simple operation. This was not supposed to happen."

"You have made a mistake this time. Your men may or may not have been following orders, but you have forfeited all trust. I do not think we can do business now."

"No, no, no. You do not understand. The money was there. It was in the trunk of the Cadillac."

"In a briefcase?"

"Yes, yes, in the briefcase. You have the money then?"

"Yes."

"Then you must turn the object over to us. It will solve problems that you will encounter down the road, Señor Chercovski."

"How do you know I am Señor Chercovski?"

"I have my ways, señor. I also know, now, that you have a friend, a blond man named Walter Suffolk. You see, I have contacts in a thousand places. You cannot stop to get a cup of coffee where I do not have friends. So, take the money and deliver the object to us and all will be forgiven. The men you killed were not alone. There were witnesses, more friends of mine. What do you say?"

"I will call you, don't call me." Gordon wrote down the number, shut the phone off and threw it out the window of the moving van.

"Well, shit. This Franco Cortico has our names."

"What names?" Terry wanted to know.

"Boris and Walter."

"Well then, he must have contacts with the bloody CIA."

"I'm not so sure. The American I shot in the woods was working with the Brazilian Army."

"Did you kill him?"

"Huh, I didn't stop to check. I was in kind of a hurry."

"Then he might have contacts with the army. Sure, I can see that. I'm going to pull north over here. We need to get off this road and out of this area. This man might have a lot of friends."

"Oddly enough, that's just what he said."

"So, what do you think is in the briefcase?"

"Do you want to open it?" Now, Gordon was smiling.

"I'll think about it. What, uh, what do you want to do with her?"

"Well, shit. If the son-of-a-bitch paid us, we need to deliver. I'm not sure he did, that's all. I don't know what's in the briefcase and I'm not sure I want to open it."

"Why not have her open it?"

"Now your thinking. She says she's a danger detector, some kind of psychic premonition… thing. Maybe she can tell if there's a bomb in the case."

"The one problem with that is if it goes off. This Modiano gets what he wants and we're left holding the bag… so to speak. Well, find us an empty area."

Gordon gently removed the gag from Anastasia's mouth. She had heard the exchange and had her own ideas on the subject. "Untie me. I cannot do anything with my hands tied behind my back. I need a kit: screwdrivers, tweezers, clippers and a digital voltmeter. Stop at a hardware store. Wait… No. Stop at a hardware store. I want to know for sure that I know what I'm doing.

Terry drove to Macae, a resort town on the ocean, an hour away. Macae seemed perfect for lounging and swimming. The beach was covered with beautiful tanned bodies and the hotels were full of pasty-faced tourists. Terry bought the tools Anastasia had asked for as well as a powerful flashlight, an angled dental mirror, some alligator clips and a roll of 12 gauge wire.

After leaving Macae they drove past a huge Petrobras refinery and Terry made a joke about that being a good place to test explosives. Past the refinery the land rose and they were soon in uninhabited mountain land. An old logging trail provided a good place to stop. The new growth trees grew close together and provided good cover.

It looked a little ridiculous for Anastasia to be wearing panties and Gordon's oversized boots but she could not walk in the woods without shoes. She took the briefcase behind a log and slowly and carefully began examining it.

"There is a small problem here," she said. "I think it is designed to open once and then to explode the second time. There is a piece of tinfoil that will tear the first time. It is grounding the battery the first time but it will tear when opened any further. I think this was the plan. Here take this wire and pull the box open from a distance. Wait, let me get behind the tree. All right, pull it open."

The lack of explosion when the top was pulled back proved her to be correct.

"Well, I must say, I'm impressed." Gordon admitted. "I had thought your sixth sense would have told you of the danger."

"Believe me when I say I was skilled before I started getting jumping beans in my head."

Gordon was forced to laugh. Anastasia smiled at him and there was all but a palpable spark jumping between their eyes.

An inspection of the contents of the case revealed stacks of two reais notes with hundred reais bills on the outside of the stacks. "So," said Gordon, "he has tried to shoot me, blow me up and cheat me all at the same time. There is no honor in that."

"Not only that, there is a GPS signal provider in the case, so he is hunting us as well." Anastasia was about to smash the tracker with a rock but held back at a signal from Gordon.

"Terry, let me use that phone. Anastasia, transfer the money to that suitcase." He stepped away from the others, wincing as he stepped on the forest floor in stocking feet, and spoke in German.

"Good evening."

"Colonel Richter."

"Scotsman! Tell me that this simple little assignment has gotten the better of you."

"No." Then he looked at Anastasia's smooth, almost naked form. "Well, yes, in a way. The man we are dealing with has tried to cheat us and kill us and I have taken some exception to his actions."

454

"Ah, I was afraid there might be some irregularities but I had no proof."

"I picked up some stress from your attitude. I was dealing with Franco Cortico, Modiano's right hand man. Is he anything to you?"

"No, Scotsman, he is nothing to me."

"And Modiano?"

"Ah, Modiano has been the source of some income in the past but if he has become unreliable then by all means do whatever you need to do. After all, you are the kingmaker."

"Please, do not refer to me as that."

Colonel Richter chuckled. "You and a few good men could bring down almost anyone and you know it. With the proper planning and the proper equipment who knows what you could do?"

"I don't think I'm going to be in this business much longer Colonel. I have my eye on something; a piece of land I could retire on."

Again Richter chuckled. "You will retire when the ground pays your pension. You love the thrill too much. It would last six months or a year and then you'll call me up asking for something juicy."

"I don't think so."

"Well, I'll tell you what, I will ask around and see if I can find anyone who wants Modiano dead badly enough to pay your price. All right?"

"Do that for me. I almost gave this job up. I didn't like it. But, I saw it through because…"

"Because you are the consummate professional, I know that. This sort of thing would never happen in Berlin."

"Maybe in Stuttgart, though."

"Uh, maybe," Richter chuckled. "Maybe in Stuttgart and certainly in Paris. I will let you know if anyone has the means to pay for your services. If not, I assume we will be drinking Schnapps together soon?"

"Yes, Colonel, soon." Gordon broke the connection and turned around. He caught Terry's eye and nodded once.

Terry half grinned and half grimaced.

"What is it that you will be doing with me then?" Anastasia wanted to know.

Terry had been standing with the rope in his hand when she asked this. He looked once at it and tossed it to the forest floor.

"Well, I can't leave you out here in the woods naked, could I? That would be terribly uncivilized."

She shocked Gordon by turning around and putting her hands behind her back. "If you wish to bind me I will not protest," she said.

"No. I…"

She turned back around and put one finger against his lips. "This is not your venue. It is clear you have no expertise in the kidnapping trade. You kill people and I think you are good at that. Leave the kidnapping to the experts and stick to what you are good at." She was looking deep into his eyes.

It was Terry's turn to chuckle but he made no comment as he got back into the van and turned the ignition.

Chapter Twenty Two
The New Deal

There had been no sleep that night for Hernando del Fuego. The methadrine was keeping his heart pumping strong but not doing much for his brain. He felt strong and in command. The owners of the house he was in did not feel quite so good about the arrangement. He had slipped in the back window sometime in the early morning and tied up the two parents at gunpoint. Their sole child, a teenage girl, did not survive the night. He had gone into her bedroom and tied her up then decided it would be a good idea to rape her. The problem occurred when he was unable to stiffen his resolve. He blamed her for his performance anxiety and choked her to death on the spot. Then he threw her naked body down the basement stairs.

The home was the closest structure to the Modiano compound. It did not have the elevated view that the church steeple afforded and there were trees between the house and the gangster's front gate but he knew the church's steeple was compromised. He could see the gate from the upstairs bathroom window and had retrieved his rifle from the church so he could get a good look through the scope. The irony of his location touched Hernando's sense of humor. He knew the reward included his head as well as Anastasia's, but considered himself well above worrying about anything so pedestrian.

The boredom of waiting for something he was not sure would arrive threatened to make him pass out. He might have if he were in a comfortable position, but there was no possible way to get comfortable at the bathroom window. The small radio was tuned to the news channel, though most of the reporting was irrelevant.

The army surplus bag sitting on the edge of the tub held everything he was going to need. He only needed to make sure he moved fast enough.

News of the firefight at the mountain top bakery reached Deputy Chief Inspector Llamas quickly and infuriated him. It was not that he cared about the lives of the gangsters, he would have shot them himself given the opportunity, it was the shit that would roll downhill on his head.

The mayor was fit to be tied. He had worked hard to curb the incident rate in Rio. Statistics are only relevant when taken in context but that could never be conveyed with the numbers. The numbers from the past few days showed the town reverting to barbarism. Murders are great for newspaper sales but they are not good for the tourist industry and tourists bring in great volumes of sweet foreign cash. The mayor had already had a conference with the Chief of Police and the Chief had called the inspectors in. The bomb going off in the parking lot of the Grande Rio Mall had made international news and that was completely unacceptable. Tourists do not visit places they see as targets of terrorism.

It had only been an hour since Special Agent Brock Dakota had been hauled to a cell from the interrogation room. He had gotten about 45-minutes of sleep when they came and woke him back up. He was simultaneously surly and groggy.

"Agent Dakota, tell us again about the detector you took from the site of the massacre."

"Again?"

"Yes, Agent Dakota, again. You see, I think if you are capable of helping us, then we will be willing to help you. That is the way it should work, yes?"

"Yes. All right. The first one, the one Bellisario gave to me, only works part of the time. The other one works all the time but it seems to be directional. I don't know how or why it works, but it seems to be tuned to pick up Boris Chercovski. Maybe he has a homing device in his clothing that he does not know about, but it might be a good idea to get on the hunt before he changes his clothes."

"I see. I need to confer with my superiors. Wait here. Sergeant, get this man some coffee and some breakfast. No, no, not that slop, some real breakfast. Send someone to get him some eggs and farofa."

Dakota was just digging into his breakfast when Deputy Chief Inspector Llamas returned looking like he had been browbeaten. His attitude was nowhere near as abusive as it had been the night before. Dakota suspected that Llamas had not slept either.

"So," Dakota said between bites, "are you going to release me?"

"I am going to one better than that. Understand, señor, it was not my decision but I will abide by it."

"What's that?"

"You are to be given a support role in a search team."

"Search and destroy team?"

"That is not what we call them. You are to go with them as an observer and identifier. You will point out this Chercovski and Suffolk and we will take it from there. I hope I am being as clear as I need to be?"

"Perfectly clear, Señor. You get what you want and I get what I want." Dakota hunched over his plate to keep the inspector from seeing the smile on his face.

"As you say, Señor. You will not be issued a firearm. You are to be in a support capacity only."

"When do we start?"

"As soon as you are done with your breakfast."

"I'm done now."

The Town of Carapebus only held about ten thousand permanent residents so the selection of clothing was limited, but Terry managed to get some blouses and a pair of blue jeans that fit Anastasia. There were no shoe stores in town but a pair of tennis shoes from the five and dime sufficed. They picked up some food from the market and some beer and were on their way.

The beaches were rocky in this area and few tourists were interested. It became imperative that they find an area they could blend in with the crowd and Piuma seemed perfect. It had beaches and hotels and night life and tourists. Rather than rent rooms in one of the larger hotels, they rented two rooms in a beachside motel. It was set up in a three sided square with a wrought iron fence around it and a swimming pool in the middle, so the trio sat around the pool with a couple from Holland and another from Sweden. They drank and ate and generally acted as if they were on vacation. Terry turned in first. Finally, after a few more drinks than was necessary, Anastasia took Gordon's hand and led him to the other room.

She was unbuttoning his shirt and kissing his hairy chest when she groaned and all but collapsed on the floor, holding her head. This time there was no question what that meant. Gordon pounded three times on the wall between the two rooms and checked the clip in his pistol. One of the women at poolside screamed. A glance through the curtains revealed no less than eight men in battle gear.

"Queen Ann's tits. They sent the bloody SWAT team."

Five of the eight men were engaged in securing the four tourists that had been sitting about the pool. The other three were approaching Terry's room. Nobody was looking toward Gordon. There was no back way out of the room without smashing the window so there was only seconds to move. As the first man was ready to smash in the door to Terry's room, Gordon cracked open the door and shot the closest man in the foot. Body armor is a wonderful thing but it has limitations, one of which is that it does not cover the feet. The second man in line caught a round in the foot and fell screaming. The lead man turned and did not even get off a round before the door opened and the rifle's barrel slipped between his chest piece and face mask. The round did not seem to do much damage to the man's neck, initially, then the blood began to pump out from both sides in long greasy fountains.

The five men on the other side of the pool turned their weapons toward the assault and opened fire. Gordon grabbed Anastasia and vaulted over the bed with her, hauling the mattress over on top of them with his other hand. He heard the back windows bursting as bullets went straight through the room and out the back wall.

Anastasia was shaking like an earthquake, her lips peeled back from her teeth and her eyes bugging out of her head. Her back arched so only her heels and the top of her head were touching the floor.

The distinctive sound of the high power rifle burst from above, almost hidden by the fire of AK47s. One of the policemen went down with a round through his side. Terry could not get another from there as they rushed the front of the rooms. He stood up and started running along the top of the roof but they opened up on him and he disappeared down the far side of the slope.

The door burst open as one of the men shot out the lock with a shotgun and rushed in. Gordon shot him in the foot from underneath the bed. He dropped his weapon as he fell and Gordon shot him in the throat. A man stuck just his automatic into the room and opened fire but he only had five rounds left in the clip. Gordon's first shot bounced off the armor, the next shot hit the stock of the rifle and there was no third shot.

A scream that would rival the hordes of Ragnarok exploded from Anastasia's mouth, tearing her throat. Gordon thought she had been hit, but it was nothing of the sort. She was back in action. The dead man's shotgun was in her hands and she was heading for the door without the slightest thought for her own skin. The buckshot from the shotgun would not penetrate the Kevlar vests, but it would knock a man down. The one on the left went down first. The two on the right opened fire and as the twin lines of death raced toward her, she fell directly backward with her feet flat on the floor. The firing stopped and she stood back up from there. Not one in a million people can stand from that position, but no sooner had the firing stopped than she was back on her feet, shotgun firing. She knocked the first man down with the blast. She stepped inside the swing of the second man, grabbed both sides of his vest and threw him in the pool. The first man struggling to his feet caught a rifle round in the back of the knee, the second took a pistol round behind the ear. The less gung ho, or perhaps smarter members of the team did not attempt to move as Gordon kicked their weapons into the swimming pool. One of the men who had been shot in the foot insisted on sitting up with his pistol in his hand. Anastasia blew his hand off, still holding the pistol, racked out the empty shell and would have blown his head off if there had been another round. She screamed her frustration and threw the shotgun into the pool while reaching for a dropped rifle. In the throes of her killing frenzy she would have killed all the injured soldiers but for Gordon grabbing her around the waist and hauling her toward the parking lot.

Terry waited until the barrage ended and then jumped from the roof and began to strip the men of clips and grenades.

The tourists were gone from poolside. They had all decided that Europe was as remote a location as they wanted to try in the future. The transport trucks were idling quietly out by the road. Unarmed, Brock Dakota had heard the hostilities commence and stepped out of the back of the truck. He had not been as sure as the assault team had that it would be a simple extraction. He had cautioned them that the men they were after had already killed over a dozen men that he knew of. They had remained confident. By the time the automatic weapons had ceased to fire, Dakota had locked himself back in the truck and told the radio man to call the ambulance.

The assassins were long gone before anyone ventured into the courtyard again. No one saw the gray panel van slipping through the back streets of Piuma and heading north-west out to the BR101. Anastasia sat in the front seat shaking like an epileptic. Gordon had taken the rifle from her and tossed it into the back for fear her shaking would set the weapon off. Terry sat in the back refilling the two automatics they had retrieved instead of sinking. He had a grim smile on his face reflecting the satisfaction of a narrow escape and the acquisition of more firepower.

After about 15 minutes Anastasia sighed, she stopped shaking and rolled her neck. The wild look in her eyes faded and she stretched and yawned as though she had been sleeping. It seemed to take her a second to acclimate herself to her surroundings. She patted herself down to make sure she had not been hit and asked if there was a beer in the back of the van. The matter of fact way she asked it was such a startling change that Terry was speechless. He handed her a warm beer and she drained half of it before belching with great satisfaction.

No one said it but all three of them knew it was impossible for the police to have found them that quickly. Even if there had been an informant turning them in, it would have taken until the next day before the SWAT team showed up. They were only in that motel for a couple of hours.

"I know what it is," Gordon said from the driver's seat. "They have a heat detector and it's homing in on your panties."

"I don't see you complaining." She was growling but she was grinning as well. "Those stupid bastards interrupted me, I should have killed them all just for that."

"Why, Perfecta?"

"What do you mean why? I have needs."

"No, what I mean is what made you… what let you know that I was not going to turn you in… to Modiano."

Anastasia glanced at Terry. ""He probably would have, I got that feeling. I knew you would not."

"That's what I'm asking. How did you know?"

"I don't know. I just know that I have nothing to fear from you. I never had anything to fear from you. Remember, I have a psychic power that detects danger and you do not bump the needle. I had you in my sights twice. I let you live, that's the same as saving your life."

"I tried. I was going to turn you in for the reward, that was the idea. That's what I was going to do. I want to clear the air on that."

"Stupid man. How can you be so smart and so stupid?"

"What do you mean?"

"Somewhere it is written in the stars that we are supposed to be together. Modiano would never have paid you for the job. You learned that. It was never an option for you. The only two courses of action for you are to die or to become my lover."

Now Gordon MacMaster was grinning. "Well, given that choice, I think I took the right path."

"You haven't even taken it yet! But you will, and soon."

An hour up the coast, Vitoria was a city of two million people, capital of the state of Espirito Santo.

Terry got up and staggered into a restaurant to get some coffee and take-out breakfast. He looked out the window and saw that the two people who had been in the front seats of the van were no longer visible. He ordered an extra breakfast and ate it at the counter. By the time he finished eating, both his partners were sleeping soundly, looking incongruous next to the purloined automatic weapons and piles of clips. Terry wished he had taken some of the body armor from the assault team as well.

A city two million strong is enough to hide anyone effectively as long as they have a little money. Vitoria itself is situated on an island and Terry did not drive over the bridge to the island but stayed south of the river in Vila Velha, part of the capital's greater metropolitan area. The larger hotels would insist on a passport but the smaller operations on the fringes had less restrictive practices. Terry could have gotten a room or several rooms but something nagged in the back of his mind. While they had been parked by the side of the lagoon, nobody had disturbed them but as soon as they got a room, the brassers dumped on them. That meant, in his mind, that their pictures must be on the television and the owners of the motels were calling them in, possibly for a reward. His partners were sleeping soundly so he drove to an underground parking garage beneath one of the hotels and parked in a discreet corner where he slept in the passenger seat.

After a couple of hours sleep all three were awakened by the sound of cars starting up and salesmen getting on the road. Breakfast was cold but filling and questions filled the air.

"How did they find us?" Anastasia was the first to ask. "Where did they come from? If they were from Rio de Janiero, they were out of their jurisdiction. Piuma is in Espirito Santo region, not Rio."

"You mean," Terry followed up, "that if the motel owners called the police on us, they would have called local police."

"I mean that if there was an assault team sent after us because the owners called, they would have come from Vitoria, not Rio."

"This tells me," Gordon finished up, "that they are still tracking something we have. Inventory; what could they be following?"

"Money. It has to be the money." Terry was certain. "We changed clothes. I stripped my pistol and cleaned it, no bugs in there. I know they make 'em small now but there's no room to hide one in a pistol. I pulled the cell phone battery. Shit, it was only a disposable anyway. It's got to be the money."

"It's too dark in here. We need to get a room and go through the stacks of bills. We need to find that bug." Gordon resembled a Viking berserker this morning, unshaven and unkempt, radiating power and anger.

"I tell you what gentlemen, if you can get me to an electronics store, we can make a bug detector. They are illegal to buy, but I know how to make one." Anastasia was calm and smiling this morning. She was quite a different woman from the night before.

Terry looked at his huge Scottish associate. He did not trust Anastasia Viuda but he was certain that Gordon did. He could not believe that a little pussy could change the man's attitude so much but it seemed to have done just that.

Set on a course of sorts, they drove around until they found a retail electronics store. Anastasia knew just what she was after and put together the components for a wide bandwidth, amplified sensitivity, radio frequency detector. They also picked up some new disposable cell phones.

Gordon watched her putting the device together and was truly impressed. He was not that in tune with the electronic age. Terry was less impressed but he kept his mouth shut.

"Now then, let's get out of the industrial area. Too many signals come from the electronics. Robots and remote controls cause false signals."

"Are you sure that thing is going to work?"

"Put the battery in your cell phone and make a call. This meter will jump as soon as you push for connection."

"That's all right. I'd rather not." Terry was becoming more suspicious but could not put his finger on why. After all, the woman had killed more men in the last couple of days than either man.

Waving the antenna of the bug detector over the bags of money didn't show a signal, nor did the weapons or any of the clothing. It did move a little from time to time but Anastasia assured them that it was normal background interference and that close proximity to a signal source would show dramatically.

"Well, that was a waste of time. I vote we get rooms, shower and shave and get some food." None of the three doubted what else was on MacMaster's mind.

"I vote no." Terry was calm but firm. "There is something we have not taken into account. This van is clear.

However it is they are tracking us led them to you, not me. We have not found the bug so it is still here, somewhere. Perhaps in the money we got from the briefcase? But we did not have that money when we were attacked the first time. What have we got that has always been there when we were attacked? The money and this woman. She's playing us somehow."

"And how would I be doing that, Walter? I have been bound hand and foot, stripped naked and I cannot even shit without one of you watching. I should have killed you both but I could not bring myself to. I cannot even trust myself, so I understand why you do not trust me. I..." She searched for words to express something she did not understand, her hands moving in little circles.

"There is something pulling me to you." She looked into MacMaster's eyes. "It is like a magnet and it is not some stupid Stockholm Syndrome. It is your... I don't know what."

"Look, I'm for getting out of here. I need to brush my teeth and get a shave and I want a bloody beer. I've heard enough bullshit for one day."

Anastasia looked at Terry with venom in her eye. She knew what she wanted and she always got what she wanted, she simply did not know why she wanted it. If this tall blond man stood between herself and her new love, she would kill him in a heart beat. It was second nature to her.

For Terry's part, he knew something was wrong about this woman. It was not that she was a paid assassin, that didn't bother him, and it was certainly not jealousy. What bothered Terry was the fact that wherever Perfecta Navaja was, death followed her, sniffed her out. From the minute they had laid eyes on her in the plaza, men had begun to die. He had been touching her arm for a matter of seconds when suddenly the CIA had him in their sights and the gunfire erupted. She spoke about being attracted like a magnet, what was really being attracted was trouble and death.

Terry grumbled and drove around Vila Velha while Gordon and Anastasia went through the bundles of cash one by one. They took each one apart, spread them open and scanned them with the radio frequency detector, but they found nothing. They stopped at a drug store for some toothbrushes and deodorant, but otherwise kept moving, each one thinking their own confused thoughts.

Terry turned on his left hand turn signal, intending to drive down the avenue skirting the beach and Anastasia told him not to, that there would be danger down that way. Terry pulled into a parking spot facing the beach and got out of the van. Sure enough the mounted police were patrolling the area between the beach and the hotels. That got him to thinking again.

"Perfecta, how do you do that?"

"I don't know. It just started happening."

"When?"

"When I was chained to the floor in a little rat hole in the jungle."

"So it's nothing you can turn on and off."

"No. It is always there, ever since that day. It hurts most of the time. A rattling in my head that won't stop."

"A rattling?"

"Like a rattlesnake warns its prey, my brain has begun to warn me. When the real danger is there, I feel like I have been plugged into the wall. Like I am being shocked with a cattle prod."

"Do you feel it now?"

"A little bit, but not much."

Terry switched to German. "Brother, run that thing around this woman's head."

Understanding began to dawn in Gordon's mind. He took the radio frequency detector and checked Anastasia's head. Sure enough there was a signal. "That's amazing. You, love, have a transmitter in your head. How long have you known about this?"

"I don't... I..." Anastasia was speechless.

"That's how they found us, mate. They followed her bloody homing beacon. We are going to start calling you LoJack."

"So...?"

"So there is no where in the world you can hide. You're hardwired."

"What does this mean? I can't have a... some thing in my head. No. There is a mistake."

"I doubt it. Watch the needle, mate." Again in German. Terry got back in the van, pulled his pistol and racked a round into the chamber. When he pointed it at Anastasia's head, the needle jumped. When he re-holstered his weapon, the intensity dropped.

"That's it then." Gordon's voice reflected a surge of conflicting emotions. He reached out a hand. Where the signal was the strongest, he felt her scalp through her hair.

"Is there something there?" Terry asked

"It feels like a scar. How big would something like that need to be?"

"I don't know. Pretty big I would think"

"Look, Boris, if there is something in my head I want to get rid of it."

"I don't know what I can do for you. I'm no brain surgeon. I've removed some brains but my tools are a little crude."

"Ah, yes." She smiled despite herself. "But there must be something we can do. How do we block the signal? What do we need? An audio jammer or noise generator?"

"I don't think that's going to work since it's not a listening device. I don't think it's a listening device. It's some kind of frequency transmitter. We need to block the frequency first. I don't know about you but I'm getting sick of being hunted."

"Can we mask it?" Terry wanted to know.

"Sure, I'm going to wear a lead-lined motorcycle helmet for the rest of my life."

"That's not what I meant."

"I tell you what. Get me some scissors and a razor. I will go into the bathroom of the restaurant in this hotel and we will see what we are working with."

"What are you planning?"

"Don't worry, Boris, it will grow back."

The electronics men struggling in the Paraguayan Secret Service had made another breakthrough. The new prototype looked like a large cell phone and was delivered to General Arridagio as soon as it became operational. It was more like a true GPS in that it incorporated satellite tracking as well as signal detection. It had the capability of zooming in and out and represented the best they could envision.

The General took a few minutes to approve the device and then sat back with an unlit cigar in his mouth. He had already lost two such devices, and nine men, including Colonel Zarafina. The men had never been traced back to Paraguay but the possibility still existed. He chewed the end of his cigar, effectively ruining it, without noticing.

The screen showed his target in Vila Velha. The screen jumped a little when he zoomed in to the street level and he had no street names, just the grid of the city but it was a vast improvement over the last tracker. He watched intently as the signal cruised around the streets, stopping from time to time and then moving on.

The telephone rang and his secretary told him that the Diogo Brothers were there to see him.

The men were impeccably dressed, in dark tailored suits and silk ties. They had crisply folded handkerchiefs in their breast pockets and looked for all the world like they had stepped out of a men's magazine. One, the taller one, carried a walking cane which he hung on the coat rack and covered with his hat. Both men had brown hair and handsome but not remarkable faces. The shorter one wore a handlebar mustache. Neither man spoke but merely walked in and took their seats across the desk from General Arridagio.

"Gentlemen, my sources in Brazil tell me you are highly recommended."

Both men merely smiled demurely and nodded their heads.

"What I have is a problem that is in need of your particular talents." He waited for them to speak but neither did.

"I need a man eliminated. He may have gathered others around him for protection, I do not know."

The taller man spoke with a refined accent. "What is the name of this individual?"

"I'm afraid I have no name, but I must warn you that he is quite dangerous."

"I see, you have then, a picture?"

"No. There is no picture."

"I'm sorry, General, how is it we are supposed to locate the target?"

"You will be supplied with a tracking device, ah, two tracking devices. This one indicates the location and this one is directional."

"Forgive me, General, but this is most unusual. How will we know we have eliminated the proper target?"

"When the subject dies, the signal dies. I am no botanist or electrician, but as far as we can tell the signal is powered by the electrical activity of the brain."

The two men looked at each other and then back at the General. "Why are we being brought in on this job?" the shorter man asked.

"Simply for, uh, discretion. I have been told you are quite discreet."

"We have been known for that."

"I am prepared to pay your fees, half up front and half when the job is concluded."

"Surely, a man with your resources has the ability to take care of this without hiring an outside source?"

"Of course. I am contracting this one out, however. I cannot risk an international incident. If members of my staff were to be implicated, the repercussions would be, uh, messy. I cannot afford messy. That is why I have contacted your people and why you are being contracted to do this job. Can I count on your discretion?"

"I think so. Is there anything more we need to know about this man?"

"No."

"Is there anything more that we are allowed to know?" The smaller man asked, stroking his mustache with the back of his index finger.

"The target should be a man in his mid forties. There is nothing further for a description, so do not even ask the questions. You are being paid extremely well for your services and further work will be sent your way if you prove to be effective."

"Very well, make the transfer and we will be in touch."

Each man picked up a locator, assured themselves that they knew how to operate them and slipped them into an outside pocket. They placed their hats back on their heads and stepped out stiffly.

General Arridagio stuck his mangled cigar back in his mouth and ran his fingers through his hair. It rankled him to use outside talent and he did not like assassins in the first place, but he could not afford the potential international backlash. He had confidently sent two teams into Brazil, only to have them tagged and bagged. He would not make the same mistake again.

"I need you to explain to me, Agent Dakota, where you are and how you got my men killed."

"Chief, I assure you that I was not allowed anywhere near the incident. I pointed out where this man was, but I was forced to stay with the van. I did not witness the incident."

"So, what you are saying, then, is that you are not responsible."

"What I am saying, Chief, is that the men went in like cowboys, confident that they knew what they were doing and they got their asses handed to them. I was not allowed to participate, nor have I spoken to any of the men since."

"No. I have, however, gotten the report. And it reads that two men and a woman have chopped up my elite combat team!"

Brock moved the cell phone away from his head as Deputy Chief Inspector Llamas raised his voice.

"Sir…"

"No! I want to know who these people are." His voice was cracking as he screamed into the phone. "Now where are you?"

"I am on my way to kill these men."

"No! I need to know where you are. I need to know how these people can do this and I want to know what you know. If you think you are going to get away with disappearing you are a fool. I will have you thrown into a hole with the scorpions."

"Sir, I can get these men for you. I can take care of it, but I need my weapons. I came down here to take care of this problem and I have been blocked at every turn."

"I am talking to the man who was shot twice in the chest by this Nazi, yes? How am I supposed to have any confidence in you? These creatures, these murderers have been leaving piles of bodies everywhere they go and you want to blame my men? You got my men killed, you arrogant American swine!"

"No, sir, your men got themselves killed. If you allow me to handle this my way I will eliminate this threat." Brock's voice was cold and controlled. He knew he had one chance to get out of this and it was not going to be clean no matter what he did. His only chance consisted of killing Boris Chercovski, Walter Suffolk and Sandiana Torremolinos. His other option, the pit full of scorpions, seemed less appealing.

Llamas was still shouting obscenities into the phone when Brock hung up on him.

"Well, Brock my boy, you've really fucked it up this time," he thought to himself, wishing he had a drink. "It could be worse. If I'd stayed with the truck I'd be back in jail right now."

He took the newer of the directional finders from his pocket and looked up the road toward the capital of Esprito Santo, then got back in his rented Honda and headed north.

Chapter Twenty Three
Dionysus

It caused a little bit of a fuss in the salon when the tall woman with the long black hair asked to be shaved bald. It was not the sort of request they got on a day to day basis. The number one hairdresser tried to change her mind but the woman was adamant. She wanted all the hair cut off and the scalp shaved bald.

The process began with a clamp that gathered the hair together for the clippers to shear. Anastasia suspected that they would be selling the hair to the wig makers but that was the least of her problems. A nice warm shaving cream was smoothed over the stubble and the shaving began. She warned the hairdresser to be careful of this spot and that, where she had picked up some scars over the years.

Outside, in the van, the men watched carefully. They had backed the van into a spot across the street that gave them a good view of the front of the salon. Nothing untoward was occurring as far as they could see.

Terry was pensive and obviously had something to say.

"All right, out with it." Gordon said.

"Look, mate, I'm not one to tell a man where to put his trust but, well... I mean we've been together a long time and we've seen a lot of unpleasant business together. Lord knows, we've pulled each other out of some holes. I value your advice and you've taught me a lot about staying alive."

"You don't trust her, do you?"

"No, mate, I don't trust her. Let's get a look at what we have here. She's got a price on her head. She's wanted for killing. Not that we're not, but that's beside the point. I mean, what do you know about this woman? Where did she come from? Who taught her to move like that? And what's with this science fiction bullshit about something in her bloody head? I think she's crazy and I think she's gonna get us killed."

"I see your point."

"Since when does a little bit of sweet stuff turn you into a quivering koala anyway? That's not the man I know. I'll admit she's not your everyday housewife, but let's face it, you know that yer not some kind of family man. You take off and go on a job and six months later you get back to find some other man in your bed. Then you'd have to kill 'er. How would that make you feel?"

"What on Earth makes you think I'll be marrying this woman? Don't you know me better than that?"

"I see the way you look at her. You got it bad, mate. Then she starts talking about it's inevitable. You'll be my lover or you'll die. I mean what in the name of King Edward is that? She's got an agenda that you don't even know about and it makes me shiver. I need to know what you're planning. I'm not getting my tit in a wringer over this little lost rose."

"I'm afraid both our tits are already in a wringer. You've got the CIA after you and I've got the bloody Brazilian Army after me. I don't know which of us is in a worse pickle."

"Huh."

"What have you got in mind?"

"I just keep thinking that ever since we grabbed this tart the whole thing has gone downhill. I mean, no sooner did I grab her than I got some brasser pointing a gun at me. I say she's bad juju, a fuckin' Typhoid Mary."

"Then we're just looking at this the wrong way. A big fat trout sees a mayfly in the water and he's drawn to it like a magnet. The bass ignores it but the trout is captivated."

"I'm not much of a fisherman."

"Sometimes, that mayfly is not really a mayfly. Sometimes it has a hook in it."

"Oh, you mean like the hook they set for us last time we tried to get a payoff from these bastards? I'm saying she draws trouble like meat draws crocs. I say we put this thing in gear and leave her here. She's not some helpless little thing, she's got a sting like an adder. She'll be all right without us. If she's not a payoff any more, what is she?"

"She's a keeper." Gordon said simply, without meeting Terry's eyes.

"How in hell did she get her hooks so far into you?"

"I can't explain it. She's perfect. She's strong and ruthless and beautiful…"

"So's a damn black widow spider. I'm telling you there's something she's not telling you."

"Shit, brother. She hasn't told me anything yet. She's as much… Uh, check this suit on your ten. He doesn't look like he's up for a haircut." The man went into a haberdashers two doors down.

"Look, Terry, this is a shitty situation. We need to get the hell out of here and I mean to take her with me. If you want to walk then walk, I've got nothing to say. I think we should stick together, but if you need to go, then go."

"Ah fer the lovachrist shut up. I never walked out on you before and I don't mean to now. I just want to cut the deck in our favor and right now it's stacked against us. Am I right?"

"Only because we're not playing it right. We need to stop playing the hunted and start hunting."

"Now yer talkin' mate. That's what I want to hear."

Anastasia's golden tan did not extend to her scalp and she looked a bit ridiculous shaved bald. She stalked across the street more self conscious than usual and slipped into the back of the van.

"I need a hat. I can't walk around like this. I'm attracting attention."

Gordon got in the back with her and Terry got in the driver's seat, put the van in gear and drove off, watching his mirrors closely.

A close inspection of her scalp showed a thin, perfectly square scar with very faint stitching marks around it. It did not look like an accident and it certainly didn't look recent.

They pulled into a strip mall and Anastasia bought a couple of tight fitting pant suits and a variety of hats. She favored the kind with a high dome, thinking there would be a way of putting a masking device inside. They got some food to go and kept moving. At a grocery store they bought some tinfoil but it only seemed to make the signal stronger so they discarded that idea. It occurred to them that a sheet of lead would probably do the trick but they had no idea where to get one. All three were feeling dead tired but Anastasia was passing out so she slept in the back while they drove. They stopped at another hardware store and got supplies for an extended hunting trip in the woods.

The dream came unbidden, but it should not have been unexpected. She was again three years old and tied to a chair while the matron was shaving her head with a straight razor. The care she exhibited with the little girl's scalp belied her rough attitude and words. The woman was saying that it was for her own good and that she should hold still or the razor would cut her. The scene changed to the view from a dirty window. Men were running in formation, climbing ropes, vaulting hurdles, doing push-ups. Other men, in lab coats, were watching them with stop watches and clip boards. Suddenly, the matron was there, behind her, asking why she had stopped studying. The little girl knew that any answer she gave would result in her being slapped so she said nothing and returned to field stripping and oiling an

American M16. She looked up from her task and the scene had changed again. She was in the front row in a classroom full of men. Her hair was beginning to grow back in. She could not tell what the man at the front of the room was trying to say but he frightened her.

The room melted and the men started running around her. There was fire and chaos, guns firing and blood flying. The matron stood beside her like an ethereal vapor, a ghost in a lab coat gripping her arm with a bony hand. She was saying never cry, never cry, never cry like some sort of crow. Then she was gone, replaced by one of the doctors and a kindly young nurse. They had taken the young girl, put her in a car and drove her over a bridge and into a fog.

Twenty years later Anastasia Viuda sat bolt upright on a mattress in the back of a van with tears rolling down her cheeks.

Chemical stimulants can only keep a person awake for a certain amount of time after which sleep becomes mandatory. Some of the world's Special Forces have been trained to go without sleep for extended periods of time, but the brain always suffers. Hernando had slept once in a week. Now he was hyped on the kitchen cooked crank and couldn't sleep. He had eaten two days earlier but had no appetite now.

Two days earlier he had killed the couple's teenage daughter in a fit of rage when his meat would not fill. He felt a little better today, a bit more randy. He took the mother into the kitchen, bent her over the kitchen table, lubed her up with corn oil and raped her from behind, but he could not release. He banged away on her for half an hour, grunting and cursing until his unit lost all feeling and went limp again.

"You fucking whore," he muttered. He let her slip to the floor while he hunted through the kitchen drawers. He

480

found what he wanted, turned, pissed on her prone form and then split her head in half with a cleaver. Once she was done, there was no sense in his mind in keeping the father alive so he went into the bedroom and killed him with the same cleaver. It was a messy process that left him covered in blood so he went upstairs and took a shower. The hot water stimulated his lust again but though he got hard, there was still no feeling in the shaft.

It was while using the victim's shaving kit that Hernando del Fuego thought to turn on his cell phone and see if any messages had been left. He did not really have a plan of action since nobody had shown up to collect the reward on his lovely woman's head.

There were no voice messages on his phone but he did have a text message. Accessing the messaging service brought up *"Love, they have me in cabin. MG214 in the mountains."* He did not recognize the number but there was no doubt in his mind that the message was from Anastasia Viuda. The thought of her strong supple body almost brought the scent of her skin to his nose. He thought it was a terrible pity she should have to die.

Without a map, Hernando could not know where MG214 was and he could never find one cabin compared to every other on a highway. He considered getting some sleep before he moved but there was still no possibility of that. He forced himself to eat some eggs and bacon, then wiped down every surface he could remember touching. It would be dark in a couple of hours and he could leave then. The home owner's car would work just fine for him. "After all, they don't need it any more," he thought with a grin.

"Are we in danger?"

"No, my love, we are not in danger," she said in a tremulous voice. "I had a dream."

The words rang in Gordon MacMaster's head. "No, my love." They had a kind of echo effect giving them a surreal quality. "No, my love."

In the course of a long and exciting life, the Scotsman had bedded lots of women of every color and religion. He leaned back in the passenger's seat and closed his eyes, thinking about all the women who had told him they loved him, all the sweet young things who had tried to make him their exclusive property. The sharper ones had known they stood a better chance of taming the whirlwind and had simply enjoyed his company while he was there. Brazilian women seemed particularly adept at this and he had enjoyed their company a great deal while on vacation.

"But, this one is different," he thought. "Perfecta. No name could be more fitting. Perfecta Navaja. My million-dollar woman. I still don't know who you are. I think I can trust you, but I don't even know you. All I really know is that she's a magnificent woman. A deadly woman."

A vision of her eyes pointing a pistol at him just before she collapsed ran across the inside of his lids like a closed loop reel. She had him. If she had wanted him dead, she could have shot him upstairs. She could have shot him in the motel. She could have shot him downstairs. "Why not? I was taking her to meet her maker and she repeatedly escaped. And yet, there she sits." He glanced back and saw she was still crying.

"Perfecta, what's wrong?"

"I don't know, my love."

There it was again, ringing in his ears like a cathedral bell. "My love, my love, my love"

"I had a dream about having my hair cut off."

"I didn't ask you to do that."

"No, no, when I was young. A child. They cut off my hair."

"Who did?"

"I don't know. I can't remember any names, just isolated scenes. I never dream, or that is I never remember my dreams. I remember this one. Is it any surprise I am crying?"

The dream-memory of the ghostly matron clutching her arm flashed back and her tears dried up. She did not want them to stop, they felt good coursing down her cheeks but they would not start again. The long dead woman with the straight razor had reasserted herself. "You will never cry. You must never cry. You are to be hard like the stones of the mountain," rang in her head. She took a deep breath and wiped her tears away.

Terry was steering the van onto a gravel drive in the mountains well north of Diamantina Centro, a lovely town in the highlands. He had driven most of the day.

The drive led to an attractive cabin, obviously a summer retreat of some sort. It was built better than most of the rough hunting lodges in the area but from the looks of it had not been visited in a while.

"Umm, Mack, it looks like this one has a security system."

"Can you bypass it?"

"It depends. A constant feedback loop is a bit trickier. I think this one is event generated though, y'know, the old style."

"Just cut the phone line then?"

"I'll have a look."

Terry went to see if there was easy access to the phone line while Gordon scouted the immediate area for other cabins or camping areas. He was about halfway around the perimeter when he detected someone coming at him from the front. They were obviously trying to remain undetected, but MacMaster was too good and too patient to be easily thrown off. He simply waited, picking up tiny little sounds: a dead leaf under foot, the swish of a branch on clothing, a shoe scuffing on a rock.

"I would have expected better of you."

Anastasia jumped around and landed in a defensive stance. If MacMaster had been moving toward her she would have caught him but he was not, he was simply leaning against a tree.

"Brought up in this climate, I would have expected you to move more quietly in the woods."

She smiled and stalked toward him, her hips swinging gracefully, her steps sure and solid. "I did not want to sneak up on you. I wanted you to find me."

"Why is that?" he asked as he took her in his arms. The question needed no answer.

By the time they returned to the cabin Terry had gotten the water and electricity turned on and was cooking some steaks. The place was much nicer than they had anticipated, more of a cottage than a cabin, with a separate kitchen, two bedrooms, a tiled bathroom and a fireplace. It was not cool enough to bother starting a fire. After dinner, the Australian retired to one of the bedrooms for a nap.

"Boris," she asked as they sat in the front window watching the empty driveway. "Why did he call you Mack?"

"Who?"

"Walter. Who do you think?"

"Oh, it's a nickname."

"And you got this nickname how? It does not come from Boris Chercovski."

"It's just a nickname."

"I think you are lying to me."

"Why would I do that, Perfecta?"

"Yes, you see, Perfecta is not my real name."

"Andalucia?"

"No…"

"Torremolinos?"

"No. My name is Anastasia."

"Oh, like the Romanoff."

"I do not know Romanoff."

"She was the daughter of Czar Nicholas and the great grand-daughter of Queen Victoria. The last Russian Princess."

"Ah, no, I am not the last Russian Princess."

"Of course not, dear, you'd be over a hundred years old."

Anastasia giggled like a little girl with her hand over her mouth and Gordon felt a flush color his face.

"I am Anastasia Viuda."

"It's a beautiful name even if you are not a princess."

"No, sadly it is not. It means Anastasia the widow."

"Widow? I find it more likely you are a widow maker." Gordon's thoughts jumped to Terry's words as they waited for her outside the salon. "A damn black widow spider."

"Why are you telling me this now?"

"You do not see it?"

"I don't know what I'm looking for."

"Then you will never find it."

Gordon sat reflectively for a second. He knew what she wanted him to see but did not want to acknowledge anything of the sort.

She rubbed her bald scalp which was beginning to itch. "When do we try to get this thing out of my head?

"Oh, I'm afraid there is no cutting that thing out. See, you have the scar there where it was put in, but it is not under the skin. It is under the skull. It was put in there a very long time ago and I have no doubt that if I were to try to remove it, I would kill you."

"Then you could collect the reward for my body."

Gordon looked at her, astonished. While that had been an option for him before, it was not even a remote possibility now. A smile cracked her face, one that included her eyes. He simply shook his head.

"I need to get rid of this thing or we will not be surviving long."

"Don't worry, we'll be fine. I intend to use this thing in your head. You catch more flies with honey than vinegar."

"What on Earth does this have to do with catching flies?"

"Nothing, nothing. Tell me about Mr. Andalucia."

"Hernando. Hernando del Fuego. He was my partner. He was… He was also my lover. If I ever see him again I will kill him where he stands."

"A damn black widow spider," rose to mind again.

"You would kill him?"

"He deserted me. He turned his back on me when I needed him. I was supposed to meet him in the Central Plaza when you so rudely interrupted me. I was instructed to meet him there and return home."

"And where is home?"

"Let us talk about that later."

"He almost killed me as well, you know. I tell you what, Perf… Uh, Anastasia, what do you say we bait a little trap for him? Can you contact him?"

"I can try. I know the number he was using before."

Gordon took out a cell phone and suggested she sent him a text message. As she was dialing in the number, the rains began.

It had been a long, hard drive and Brock Dakota was not ready to tackle such a competent team without rest. He rented a hotel room in Diamantina Centro and had dinner in the hotel dining room. He was beginning to question his own wisdom.

The corruption inherent in the Brazilian system was never so clear. The communications that should have been made, the news reports that should have been broadcast, the support that the Central Intelligence Agency should have received were all predicated on who was going to benefit from them. Everybody wanted to get the bounty and nothing overt was even attempted without the rewards. The corruption was not just involved with law enforcement, either. He had slipped a few dollars extra to the clerk at the hotel and checked in as Mr. Smith.

Sitting in his hotel room he checked his weapon, a Taurus PT 1911 that he had slipped out of the assault van along with two clips and a shoulder holster. Each clip held eight .45 caliber rounds. The weight was more than he was used to, but while it had been used a few times, it was not worn out, just broken in.

The sun was just going down and though he was tired, he did not feel like sleeping. He decided to go out for just one drink.

When the bars finally closed he stumbled back to his room alone with the smell of perfume in his nostrils.

Goaibeiras Airport at Vitoria was busy when the Diogo Brothers transferred onto their local flight to Capelinha. At Capelinha they picked up their luggage and rented a Mercedes. The locators were working perfectly and while one drove the other navigated. They only had about 90 kilometers to drive, but it took them over an hour on the wet mountain road. By the time they reached the driveway, it was well after dark. They parked on the road and walked toward the darkened cottage. Each man carried a 9mm Taurus inside his jacket with 17-round clips locked and loaded.

The night was dark and the rain covered their movements and muted any sounds they may have made as they slipped around to the back side of the cabin. They tried the door and found it unlocked. There was no light in the place but the locators both indicated that this was the place. They slipped inside, congratulating themselves on their ease of entry and confident of a quick and quiet resolution to the job. Then the lights went on.

Both men were caught flat-footed, standing in the kitchen with pistols in hand.

"If you move, you will die," came a voice from the doorway. Both men were trying their best to blink away the sudden assault of light. When they were able to see well enough, what they saw was the business end of an AK47 in the hands of a huge redhead. They had not been able to see the blond standing by the refrigerator holding a .45 caliber pistol on them. Amateurs might have tried to shoot their way out of the predicament, but these men knew there was no hope.

"Drop your weapons and lie on the floor."

The two dapper gentlemen saw no recourse but to do as they were told.

"How many of you are there?"

No answer.

"I will ask you once more and then I will shoot one of you in the head. How many of you are here?"

"Only the two of us. I own this cabin. I saw the van and knew I was being robbed. Please, just let us go and you will never see us again." The taller man was speaking with a decidedly effeminate voice. "We come here to be alone from time to time."

"Humph, queers," said the blond. "I'll find some rope."

The red-haired man kept the AK47 trained on them while the other located some nylon cord in a closet. Both newcomers were tied to steel-tube kitchen chairs.

"What do we have here?" asked the larger man when he discovered a directional device in each man's pocket. He may have been fooled by the GPS style device, but the other one was strictly directional. He chewed his lip for a second and then turned around. The display indicated a single direction. He followed the direction. It pointed directly at Anastasia Viuda where she was just rising from the floor.

"Anastasia," he whispered. "Calm down. I need you calm. I need to know if there is anyone else outside."

"I can't tell. What do you think, I have x-ray vision? I feel the danger is not past but it is not... uh, imminent."

"These men came here to kill us. They came here to kill you. This thing is how they track you. Now, I am going outside to see if they brought help, I want you to watch them. Please don't kill them."

"Turn out the lights. I feel like there is a bulls-eye on my back."

Anastasia watched the two men by the light of an emergency candle while Terry and Gordon took a half hour to search the perimeter. They found no one else, but they did pull the Mercedes into the driveway and parked it next to the van.

"I see you let them live."

"They don't deserve it. I should slit both their throats right now."

"Later. I need some information from them right now. After they convince me they're not lying, maybe I'll let you drink their blood." Gordon said.

"Yuck. I don't want that."

"Of course not. I'm kidding. I do need to get some information from them, though."

"How are we going to stop this? I... I need to go."

"Anastasia, we need to determine what this is all about before you go running all over the place. Once we figure out how to make it stop, then..." He looked at his hands. "Then you can go anywhere you want."

The concentrated look she gave him could easily have been mistaken for hatred it was so intense. "Bah. Men are so stupid."

Interrogation is always a tricky business. Apply too much persuasion and the subject is likely to tell you anything you want to hear because he thinks that is what you want to hear. Apply too little pressure and the information becomes unreliable.

The two dapper assassins were separated to far sides of the cabin for questioning. The real question in their minds was how long they had to live.

Guard duty switched from Gordon to Terry, but Anastasia was too invigorated to sleep. She sat on the sofa looking out the window. Terry sat in one of the kitchen chairs in the middle of the room. They sat in silence for a while before either of them spoke.

"You don't trust me, Walter, do you?" she began, in English.

"How would you take it?"

"What do you mean?"

"Look, first he was hunting you. Now he's boffin' ya. I would have given the man more credit than that. If I remember, you offered me a bit of that as well."

"You would have been sorry if you had accepted the offer."

"I'm already sorry and I didn't accept the offer."

"A woman needs to do what she can to get by in this world." Anastasia said softly. "We are given this lot in life and we need to protect ourselves with what God has given us."

"Well, how about that? God gave you a bloody 'cup runneth over' and you still piss an' moan about your lot in life. You got me bes' mate wrapped around your finger like a schoolboy an' now you think maybe you'll teach me a thing or two about the art of negotiation. It's not going to be that way. No, I don't trust you."

"You are just another stupid man. You cannot see what is right before you. I would not be with you. I have a man and he is more than you." She could not help herself, though she knew there was no benefit to antagonizing Terry.

"And that is the way it will stay. You are not going to drive a wedge between us and you are not going to play me against him. You may have your way with most men but I have your number. Step on my toes and I'll put one between your pretty little eyes."

"No, you see what you want to see. You think you know what is going on and where, but you do not. Yes, I was captured, but I have fallen in love with the man who captured me. He has that something I love in a man."

"Right. Well, he's in the bedroom and I'm sure he will give you some of that something you love from a man."

"Oh, men are so stupid sometimes."

"That's because we only have enough blood for one head."

"Yes, we say that here as well."

"You just watch yourself. You know you're a liability, a magnet for trouble, and we can't keep pulling this off. Every night someone is showing up trying to kill you. Before long, I may need to do the job for them.

"Let us find out why before you pass sentence and execute." There was bitter sarcasm in her voice.

"We'll see. Trot off to bed then and give it your best.

"I'll sit here a while longer. As you say, I am the liability. I bring the trouble. Where do you think they got these things that point only to me?"

"I haven't a clue. Pretty specialized device. Can't get that at Radio Barn."

"Yes. So whoever wants me so bad... badly has a research facility for electronics and the finances to produce this. I do not think Francisco Modiano is responsible for this. He is a thug and very dangerous man, but he is not smart enough to figure this out. The secret is finding out who put this thing in my head and then we will know who is after me this way."

"I was hoping you could tell us where you had this little bit of wizardry installed."

"I cannot remember, only in snatches of dreams and most of them I do not remember. I will try harder."

"That won't be necessary. These three-piece-suits are going to tell us what we want to know. I guarantee it."

Terry stayed awake the rest of the night, watching and waiting. He was watching Anastasia as much as anything else. After a couple of hours she went to sleep sitting on the sofa.

After a cup of coffee in the morning, Gordon went to the shorter of the men and asked him who he was after. The man claimed not to know. He asserted that he and his brother had been given the detection devices and told to eliminate whoever the devices indicated. He would not tell who had given him the devices however.

The taller man was closed mouthed at first. He did not want to give up any information. Anastasia was on hand for the interrogation to ensure a clear translation. Her English was getting much better.

"I assure you, señor, that you will tell us what we wish to know, and it is my fervent desire not to torture you to get it. You appear to be gentlemen, so I am sure you appreciate

the predicament you have contracted yourselves into."
MacMaster was thumbing the edge of a serrated kitchen knife.

"I assure you that we do not know who authorized the contract on you. We were contacted by an intermediary that handled the financial transfer and supplied us with this address."

Gordon did not dignify this with a reply. He stepped forward and systematically cut the suit off the man until he sat before them naked.

"If you had any respect you would not have destroyed my clothing. I paid a tailor a lot of money for that suit."

"How many more are coming?"

"Many more and they will be very upset if you kill us."

"Childish. You two work alone. Now listen to me very carefully, your life depends on it. We have been hounded and pursued across this country and we are getting to the breaking point. Between the three of us, we have killed a dozen men in the past week. This woman killed a dozen more the week before. If you think we have any compunction toward killing you as well, think again. I believe you are a gentleman and I am giving you the opportunity to save yourself. Tell me what I need to know and you will be released. Lie to me again and I will begin to torture you. I think I will begin by making you very ugly. No fancy three-piece suit can make an ugly man attractive. No amount of plastic surgery can fix a face once the lips and nose have been cut off."

"You will kill me when you get the information."

"No, I will not. Once we have the information, we are done with you and you will be free to go. The longer it takes, the less attractive you will be for the rest of your life, however. She says I should start by cutting off the head of your pecker. Can you imagine trying to piss through the scab?"

"What assurance do I have you will release us?"

"None. But if you do not cooperate, you have my word as a gentleman that you will regret it every day of your life until you do expire. You came here to kill us and you deserve the same fate, but we are in the same business and as a nod to the Fraternal Union of Contract Killers, I will leave you alive. Now who sent you here?"

"If we tell you, then he will kill us."

"Oh, you will tell us. There is no doubt about that, the only question is whether or not you leave here with all the pieces you arrived with. I'll give you a couple of minutes to think about it while I heat up a pan to cauterize the wounds. I can't have you bleeding to death."

Gordon left the man alone and went to speak with his brother. "Señor, I do not need to know your name and you do not seem to know ours so it would be best if we left it that way, yes?"

"Yes."

"Now let me explain what I had in mind. I think you two are brothers. I am going to torture your brother. I am not going to torture you until after I am done with him. First I am going to cut off his nose and then his ears. I will cauterize the wounds so he does not bleed to death but he will be ugly after that, yes? Yes. I will then cut off the head of his penis and I will cauterize that. Then I will force feed him some of your delicious Brazilian coffee. How do you think that will feel when he needs to piss? More than that, how do you think you brother is going to feel about the fact that you could have saved him this pain and disfigurement and didn't? Last, I will cut off his lips."

"I have told you what I know."

"No, you have told me what you want me to know. It is time to tell me what I need to know. Who paid you for this job?"

"General Arridagio."

"What branch is he in charge of?"

"Secret Service."

Anastasia stepped in. "You lie. The head of Abin is Paolo Fernando la Costa Lacerda."

"Not the Brazilian Secret Service, the Paraguayan."

Anastasia grabbed her man by the arm and pulled him from the room. They settled in the kitchen and poured themselves more coffee. Terry was in the living room smoking the last cigarette from his last pack.

"It is possible, my love. I did a job in Paraguay a couple of years ago. Perhaps they had... I don't know. It is possible. Arridagio was a major a couple of years ago. I did not know he had been promoted."

"What was the nature of the job? The job in Paraguay?"

"Oh, he was a business man who stole money and was eliminated. It was an easy one."

"And you think this General Arridagio is after you now?"

"It does not make good sense."

"It is progress of some sort, though. Once we get them talking, we can determine if they tell us the truth or not."

"Yes. Ah, Boris?"

"Yes?"

"Does America really have a union for people in our business?"

"No Anastasia, that was a joke."

"You have a very strange sense of humor."

"So they tell me."

Chapter Twenty Four
Modern Love

It was almost checkout time before Brock Dakota managed to slither out of bed. His tongue felt like it had taken a salt bath and his eyes felt as though they had been in a sand storm. He knew the only real cure for a hangover was to drink more, but he realized that there was disaster on that path. He took a shower and brushed his teeth to make himself feel human and then went down to the lobby to check out.

Breakfast was good and filling in a small cantina, and he was able to resist the temptation to have a drink. The coffee was strong and made his stomach feel like he had been drinking battery acid. The pharmacy sold him some antacid tablets to counteract the coffee and he drank a bottle of club soda. Between the antacids and the club soda, he almost threw up a foaming mess, but managed to hold it down.

There was no way of knowing how far the target was since his best locator was directional so he climbed into his rental car and headed north-east on MG367. The map he was using in conjunction with the locator indicated that his quarry was somewhere down the MG214 and that road led directly to the airport in Capelinha. The only other town in that direction was Itamarandiba a small farming town of about 32,000 people. Brock knew if the men he sought were there, it would be no secret. He decided that would be his first destination. Forty minutes later he glanced at his detector and saw he was moving away from his target.

Turning the car around, Brock set both detectors on the passenger's seat. He almost got smashed by a produce truck for paying too much attention to them and not enough to the road. He knew he had the right place when simultaneously the constant detector and the intermittent one both swung to the right. He could see a van and a car in the driveway of a summer cottage, but there was no way he was pulling into that driveway.

"Boris, my love, something is wrong."

Gordon checked both his prisoners to ensure they were carefully bound. Terry checked the driveway. Neither found a problem.

"No, it is fading now. It was not that strong, perhaps a policeman drove down the road, or some soldiers."

"Umm, perhaps. I'm not taking a chance. If you feel it coming on again, let me know right away.

"Yes, my love."

There it was again. The feeling of deja-vu, the feelings of trust and mistrust and desire. He wanted this woman to love him. It was beyond his understanding because he did not want to love this woman. She was too dangerous and in too much danger. After the episodes of the last week, he doubted very much that any of them would get away. He did not want to lose her. That was why he did not want to love her.

Struggling with unfamiliar feelings and the frustration of fear he walked to the storage room at the near side of the cabin and punched the naked man in the mouth. "You will tell me who paid you, now, or I will cut out your brother's right eye."

"Señor, you will not believe me when I say it, but I would appreciate if you did not strike me again."

"Say what you must. My punching you is nothing you can bargain over."

"We were paid by a general in the service of Paraguay. He gave us the devices and told us that you would be here."

"Told you who would be here?"

"I must say, I think it was you he spoke of. A man in

his mid-forties. He did not say you would be a foreigner. I do not think he knew."

Gordon digested this and then spoke to the man with the mustache about it. He got the same story and though stories can be coordinated, the stories were not identical. He asked more, seemingly unrelated questions such as: where they met, what color socks the general had been wearing, how many stars he carried on his shoulders, what he was drinking, what the picture behind him was, whether the flag was on his left or right side and whether he had a beard. The coordination seemed good and both men needed to think about the setting before they could answer the questions.

"I think they're telling the truth, although I don't think I look in my mid-forties," he told Terry.

"Well, it was awfully easy, but then they probably have no real connection to this man. If they were talking about a long-term client or a man they respected, they might not turn it over so quick. On the other hand, Paraguay is a long way off and I can't make the connection... Connection. I'm having a look in their car."

In the trunk of the Mercedes Terry found luggage with airport tags, ticket envelopes but no tickets and two Brazilian passports stamped in and out of Paraguay two days earlier.

"I'd say they had an alibi." Anastasia said.

"Not an alibi, my dear, corroborating evidence."

"Yes, however. We have everything we need from them. Now we shoot them."

"Ah, Anastasia Viuda, I gave my word that I would release them if they told me the truth. As far as I can tell they did so and without too much convincing. I see no reason to kill them."

"But they were coming here to kill you. No, I think they were coming here to kill me too. Why should you let them live?"

498

"You let me live."

"That was different."

"I don't see how."

"You don't see because you are blind and do not look. I throw myself at you like some slut in a bar and you think it is because I am trash, but you do not see. It is just this. You are willing to let these two men go because they did not kill you."

"No, because I promised."

"But, yes, that is it. Your code, your promise, your – how do you say – quality of character. That is why I love you. That is why I did not kill you. That is why, Boris Chercovski, I will stand beside you and fight until the spirits of the dead take my soul."

"Uhhh, okay." Gordon MacMaster was both humbled and elevated by her speech. He was also somewhat speechless. Given the events of the past few days it seemed more likely that the three of them would end up lying dead together than any other scenario. He always knew he would die in battle, but at that point he realized that there was no one else on the planet he would rather die next to. Instead of trying to put his grim thoughts into words, Gordon picked Anastasia up, threw her over one shoulder and headed for a bedroom. In a maelstrom of madness, with the forces of anarchy descending upon them, man and woman will always find a way.

Terry looked out the front window, moved to check on the Diogos, grabbed a parka, his rifle and slipped out the back door. The fancy, impassioned speeches had not convinced him that there was no hidden agenda, but he did trust her instinct for danger. There was no scientific answer and no logical reason that she could sense danger she could not hear or see, but she had done so enough times to qualify as a psychic. She had felt something and then it had gone away, that meant that there was something wrong. Terry was not going to get caught in the cabin during an attack if he could gain a better vantage point.

As good as MacMaster was in the woods, Kingston had grown up hunting rabbits and foxes in New South Wales. He moved through the woods like a phantom, checking the perimeter first and then setting up where he could watch both the driveway and the back of the cottage. With bushes clustered around him like teenagers at a schoolyard fight, he settled in for a long, quiet watch.

Initially he got spooked by the wildlife, until he learned the sounds some of the animals made. He saw foxes and large rodents, glorious sprays of birds and a thousand kinds of insects. He greased his face and neck against the mosquitoes and kept a wary eye on the spiders. He was fascinated by a large, black scorpion driven from under a log by a lizard. He had seen plenty of scorpions in Australia but none came close to this size. It had huge claws so Terry felt confident that it was not very poisonous, but it looked like a nightmare. He knew there would be many more coming out once the sun went down.

After a couple of hours the rains started again, driving the mosquitoes away but limiting his vision and covering the noises of the forest. If anyone had been there they would have thought the man was sleeping, in the forest, in the rain. Terry was listening. He could hear the snuffling grunt of a peccary somewhere behind him and the quick squeal of a rat when something took it to dinner. He could hear through the rain falling on the dead-leaf floor of the semi-deciduous forest. He heard infrequent traffic moving up and down the road but it did not stop. The rain silenced most of the birds.

Terry sat motionless for hours. When he tried to stand his legs would barely function. He shook the tingling, stinging sensations out and slipped back into the cottage.

Dinner was pasta and sauce with some canned sausages on the side. The food was all in cans or jars except the bread. Some cashews sufficed for desert and Terry was ready to go back out.

Anastasia put her hand on Terry's arm and told him that there was no need for him to wait in the rain, that her sixth-sense would detect any danger before it arrived. He told her that it might not be a good thing to get used to it, and he would never rely on it for a final warning. He slipped out into the rain and she stood wondering how she could get this most difficult man to trust her. After all, Boris trusted her. She moved to where he sat in the main room and he told her it was time to call Hernando del Fuego, again. She made the call and as usual it went to voice mail. Making herself sound as scared as she could, she whispered a message into the phone that spoke of being raped like a slave and kept bound in a cottage on MG214. Gordon stomped a boot on the floor and Anastasia hung up the phone and turned it off.

It was two hours shy of sundown when she first felt the tingling. She supposed that it might be Hernando, but she had not told him what cabin, and there was no way to check every cabin down the road. She put her hand to her mouth and told Gordon that it would be necessary only to check the cabins that had cars in front of them. He reassured her that if Hernando had been in the Rio area that he could not have reached the mountain they were on in less than a day. He did not expect to see Hernando del Fuego until the following day at the earliest. She told him that he may have been wrong, that there was something going on, but it seemed like a low level of danger. The tingling was not extreme. It was certainly not the kind of reaction that dropped her to her knees, it was subtle. Like the perpetrator was waiting just inside the range of her senses.

The tingling remained, unchanged until the fall of night when it became stronger, slowly, almost imperceptibly. Gordon turned off the kitchen light and Terry rose from the forest floor. Something was coming and they were going to be ready for it. They waited. An hour went by. Anastasia could not tell if the vibrations in her head had increased or not. Another hour went by. Anastasia was ready to kill something or somebody. Another hour went by and Gordon had to physically keep her from walking out the door and hunting through the woods with a gun.

After the first hour, Terry sat back down. After the second hour he stood back up and started moving. He moved very slowly and carefully, moving a few feet and then waiting and listening. A rainy night in the mountain forests is so black that a blind man could outhunt anyone else. Terry could have crept a hands breadth from his objective and not known he was there. He made a mental note to get some night vision goggles.

After four hours of waiting, Gordon realized that he had a detector of sorts as well. He might not be able to identify his target, but he would be able to determine where the danger lay. First, Anastasia walked from one side of the cabin to the other to determine where the signal was strongest. It seemed strongest to the south. They did not want to outline themselves so they left the lights off, but went to the north side of the house and slipped out a window. Then they slipped up the front of the structure and hid beside the van. Looking into the blackness of the forest gave them the feeling of being lost in space. There was nothing to see. There was no way to navigate without lights.

In the darkness, Gordon slid to the side of the house and at his insistence, Anastasia started both the van and the car and directed the headlights to the south. If the attacker was within a few feet of the tree line he would be revealed. Gordon watched, Terry watched, Anastasia watched.

Brock Dakota watched them attempting to see him. All he could really see was the headlights. He had been sitting on a log, trying to watch the cottage since before sundown. The only movements he made were to keep his circulation flowing. Once darkness fell and the rains started, he knew he was stuck for the night. The darkness made it impossible to move anywhere until the headlights came on.

Knowing that movement would be the first indicator, Dakota froze. As far as he was concerned, there was no possible way they knew he was out there. He had slipped in as quiet as a snake and had done nothing but sit there. After a minute he slid over a few inches to be deeper in the shadows.

The trees reflected the light back at Anastasia as she sat in the car so she could see nothing past the first of them. She moved the car further down the driveway to illuminate a larger section and cross the beams. Gordon was watching for movement but saw none. He saw no reflections from chromed weapons or shiny buttons; he saw nothing but trees. Terry was surprised he had moved as far as he had in the time he had been moving. He had heard the couple slipping out the back window and had waited for someone on that side of the house to move in, but no one had. When the lights came on, they came on toward the other side of the house. They provided enough illumination to detect a python about seven feet away and cause the rat it had been hunting to scurry off into the underbrush, but there was no human other than himself.

Gordon slipped into the forest on the edge of the illumination. The shadows were so sharp and black and the trees so thick that once he was a few feet past the driveway, he couldn't see where to put his feet. He knew there was something in those woods acting on Anastasia's senses but every foot he moved made him it think more likely that this would be his last adventure. His quarry was not running so he was not chasing. Every tree he passed could have a commando behind it for all he knew. The waiting game he had played had been turned over and now something was waiting for him. He turned around and slipped back the way he came. As much as he sympathized with Anastasia's plight and tried to understand what it must be like to live with a constant throbbing in her head, he knew if he went any further, he would not see morning.

When the engines were killed, they stood silent for half an hour, trying to catch a murmur or snap from the forest, but whoever was out there was better than that. They could not catch him in the night.

Morning crept in slowly, illuminating the slate grey sky and the big, fat raindrops that fell with increased fury. The three hunters launched a three pronged attack but found no fish to spear with their trident. They found the spot where someone had sat the night before, watching. They knew he would be back and that he would not be alone, but there was no real indication of who he was. He had been wearing flat-bottomed dress shoes, hardly the optimal style for forest surveillance, yet he had not panicked when the lights went on. He had crept up without Terry noticing his arrival and though he may have arrived while Terry was eating dinner, he still remained halfway through the night without making a sound.

"That's it," Gordon said, looking at the patch of ground where the leaves had been kicked away. "It's got to be the CIA. I'm thinking that it may well be that haggis that tracked me from the mall. I shot him twice in the chest but I never saw any blood. He probably has one of these." He held up one of the devices the Diogo brothers had used.

"We'd better head out then. This is hardly a defensible position. They'd burn us or gas us and we'd be deep in it then." Terry had been in the rain the entire night and needed to dry out and get some sleep.

"Boris, my love, will we then keep running forever? Where do they get these things and why were they ever made and why for the love of Saint Anthony do they point to me?"

Terry was already putting some oil in the van's crankcase and checking the brake fluid. He could see no reason for staying a second longer.

Gordon stuffed everything in bags while Anastasia wiped down the hard surfaces for fingerprints.

"What should we do with Mr. and Mrs. Three-piece-suit?" Terry asked.

"I say they came here with the intention to kill all three of us. They should be made to die." Anastasia was clear.

"She might be right in this case." Terry agreed.

"No, I don't think so. Not in this case. They don't know anything. They couldn't hear us, they couldn't see us much. They don't seem to know who we are. I think we can probably use them. Check their bonds; I want them tied tight. Then let's get out of here before half the damn army comes through the door."

A brief snatch of conversation aimed at convincing one of the Diogo brothers that the team was heading to Brasilia and they were out of there. They flattened two of the tires on the Mercedes before they left.

"Are you aware that there has been a warrant issued for your arrest on the charge of conspiracy to commit murder?"

"No, Deputy Chief Inspector Llamas, I was unaware of that." Dakota's voice hummed with the tension.

"I want you to turn yourself in to the police immediately. We can work this out. I told them it was a mistake, that you had been cooperating with this department and that you were a vital asset in an ongoing investigation, but they would not listen. They claimed that you had fled and so implemented fugitive status for you. As long as you are on the run, they will not listen to reason. I am sure I can convince them otherwise once you turn yourself in."

"I see. Well, I can't make it for at least 18 hours. I'm 800 miles south of you right now."

"Where, Porto Alegre? You can turn yourself in to the police in Porto Alegre and they will transport you here."

"Uh, no, I don't think so. I turn myself in to you or not at all."

"Very well, I look forward to seeing you soon."

"Goodbye, Inspector." Brock hung up the phone and cursed. He was glad he had called the Chief Inspector; it had saved him the embarrassment of being detained again. A sneer curled his lips. "I'm hunting murderous bastards and they put a warrant out for my arrest. Son-of-a-bitch! That means I'm going to need to sneak out of the country when I'm done killing this fucker. And I am going to kill this fucker. In fact, I'm going to enjoy killing this fucker. Then I'm gonna leave this bug infested shit hole forever. I do need some help though."

A call to his CIA contact in Curitiba was no less frustrating. He was told he was off the reservation, that he had no official status, and that he was in deep shit. He was astonished when the agent told him to turn himself in, that he was a wanted man. At that point he hung up without even granting him an answer. He almost called his home office but held back. He could still hear the chief telling him "Don't call us if you get sand kicked in your face at the beach." He would save that for the call of last resort.

The local police did not have a man who spoke English in the office, but Brock was able to give them the address and tell them that someone was breaking in. Apparently it was not a priority for them since it was after noon by the time they showed up at the cottage. They pulled in the driveway and roared up to the cottage. Brock watched from a spot across the road. He did not give the police very good odds; he only expected them to flush the target.

The vantage point across the road was not good for seeing the cottage, but it was a good spot to shoot anyone coming down the driveway and that was what Brock intended to do. Unfortunately, his chickens had already flown the coop. The police were superficially thorough. They checked that the doors and windows on the cottage were closed, wrote down the numbers for the rented Mercedes with the flat tires and left. They did not bother to investigate the inside of the cottage.

Knowing he had been slipped again, Brock took several deep breaths. He had been forced to take anger management classes and learn how to calm himself after beating a suspect in the head with a brick. As far as he was concerned, the suspect deserved it and he would do the same again if confronted with the same situation, but he would not make the mistake of letting the bastard live.

The van was missing from the driveway but the car was still there, that meant one, maybe two, were still in the place. Dakota wished he had some tear gas. That would do the job. He checked his permanent locator. Whoever the device targeted was no longer in the cabin, they had gone south. He couldn't just go running off without clearing the scene. He didn't know what, or who, was left.

Creeping through the woods on the north side of the cottage was easier than it had been the night before. He had almost had a heart attack when they had turned the headlight on him. There was no way they could have known he was there, and yet they did. It scared him rather badly at the time, but they had not so much as seen him before they gave up, so perhaps he was assigning more to the action than it deserved.

The windows all had curtains or cloths of some kind covering them except the kitchen. The kitchen door was in the back of the house. It was locked but certainly took no locksmith to open. Dakota was in the kitchen with his gun drawn within 10 seconds of stepping up to the door. The kitchen sink was dripping. There was a clock in the living room blinking 12:00 over and over again. As quiet as he had tried to be, Brock knew he had not been silent. Anyone in the house knew he had come through that door.

This was certainly not the first time Brock Dakota had gone after a fugitive in a residential structure, but this was by far the worst. The men and woman he was after had already proven themselves to be mad-dog killers who would execute anyone at the drop of a hat. Every door he opened in this cottage was like stepping out on a tightrope.

Imagine his surprise when instead of finding a roomful of stone cold killers, he found one man, stark naked, bound and gagged to a chair. At the other end of the house was another man of similar appearance except for the fact that he was fully clothed in a tailored suit.

Brock took the gags from their mouths but was reticent about releasing them from bondage. He had no idea who they were and why they were there. Both men spoke some English, though not well, and after a while they managed to tell each other that they were engaged in similar endeavors. They were all after blood. The man with the suit on reported hearing his captors say they would be heading to Brasilia.

Brock listened politely as he stood in the living room watching the driveway. He felt like a fish in a bowl. Brasilia was about 750 kilometers to the west, and to head west from where they were, they had to go north or south first. The clothed man assured Dakota that it would be most

508

expeditious to head south first and then head west if Brasilia were indeed the destination. Dakota pulled out his locator and noted the huge smiles both men gained when they saw it. They had obviously seen one before. They asked where he had gotten it and he asked them how common these things were and who made them and how many different people you could track with them.

The Diogo's claimed not to know the answers to most of Brock's questions, but they did manage to convince him that they were of like mind on many things, including the idea that the two men who had tied the Diogos to the chairs should be killed. They differed in the particulars of that death, but they agreed that it was something to be wished by all. Their inventive suggestions convinced Brock that he was speaking with men of little conscience.

Now he was left with a particular situation. Brock Dakota needed to convince these two men that, if they were to work together, then he was going to be in charge, and make it stick. They did not speak the same language and, he feared, they were not used to taking orders. Also, how much could he trust these men? If he turned his back on them, would they kill him for his car and gun?

"Hernando, the number is 42227 on BR214. They left me alone for a minute but I'm handcuffed to a post. I'm going to call the office as well. Ai, the battery is going to die. Please hurry, I don't know how long they are going to keep me alive and they say…" She cut the connection in the middle of the sentence and turned the cell phone off.

"That should send him off in the wrong direction," Gordon muttered.

"Or get him killed," Anastasia replied.

"Could it have been him in the woods last night? I don't think he could have driven that far that fast but he might have flown."

"I don't know. I don't think he has proper identification but he could have gotten it by now. Oh, oh, oh. Stop. That car, that Honda by the side of the road is a rental."

"Can you feel the danger?"

"No, I feel nothing right now."

Gordon grinned, ran across the road and slashed two of the tires on the rental. Then he jumped back in and they resumed their journey south. They were only a couple of kilometers from the cottage.

Anastasia looked into the back where Terry was bundled in a sleeping bag with an extra blanket over him. He did not look good, his face was flushed and he looked like he was trembling in his sleep. "I hope he is not sickened. It is not good to spend so much time in the rain."

"Ah, he's as tough as an old boot. He'll be all right."

When they reached the BR367, they turned left and headed back toward Diamantina Centro. They passed through two small farming communities but did not stop. Small towns made it too easy to be remembered.

As they pulled into Diamantina Centro, Anastasia let out a tortured cry and crumpled onto the floorboard. They had negotiated the cliff with its switchbacks and were in the residential section of town. Gordon took his next right hand turn and then another. He pulled to the side and checked the clip in the AK47 between the engine hump and the seat. There was nobody on the street as far as he could tell. Nobody had followed them from the main road.

With a growl, Anastasia rose from the floor with Gordon's hunting knife in her hand. The look on her face was pure hatred. A line of spittle ran down her chin unnoticed and her wide, unblinking eyes stared back and forth seeking prey.

Gordon tensed himself, thinking she might try to stab him. His immediate thought was she was the closest thing he had ever seen to a werewolf. Then her expression softened, her hand fell and she almost stabbed herself in the leg with the point of the blade. She sighed heavily and leaned back in the seat with her eyes closed. "I cannot live with this. I need to get this thing out of my head."

Exhaling heavily himself, Gordon checked his mirrors and the street ahead but the only person there was an old woman with a cart. The danger seemed to have passed but he was taking no chances. "Walter, spark it up, man. We may have a problem."

"Uh, yeah, Mack, I put oil in the engine."

"No. Get up and get ready."

"Uh, right."

Gordon looked into the back and cursed. Terry's face was beet red but there was no sweat. He obviously had a fever.

"Walter, you do not look so good." Anastasia said, replacing the hat on her bald head.

Terry tried to stand and fell back on the mattress.

"We need to get you to a doctor."

"No, mate, I'll be all right."

"Not from where I'm sitting. You need some penicillin or something."

"Boris, my love, all we need to do is go to a pharmacia. They will sell us penicillin."

"No prescription?"

"No. Perhaps they do that in Austria but here all you need is the need... For the medicine. Anyway, I need a razor. My legs look like the forest and my head is itching."

The pharmacy had very little for sale other than drugs. Even in a relatively small town such as this one, the doors and windows were heavily barred as were the cabinets holding the medicines. The pharmacist was an old man with a limp who smiled widely when Anastasia stalked through the door. She bought penicillin and codeine and walked back out the door, making the old man think of the glory days of his youth.

The grocery store had the shaving cream and disposable razors. She bought some bread, meat, cheese, mustard, guarana soda and two cases of beer. She bought Terry some cigarettes though it did not seem he wanted any right then and she bought Gordon some cigars. While she was there she saw some cans of tire sealant. Thinking of the tires they had flattened in the past few hours, she thought it might be a good idea so she bought five cans of it; one for each tire and one for the spare. They stopped at a gas station afterwards. The attendant filled the tank, put another quart of oil in the crank case and topped off the windshield washer fluid as well as adding the stop leak to the tires. Gordon gave him a good tip and they were back on the road.

An hour after leaving Diamantina Centro they rolled into Curvelo. The rains had stopped along the way. Curvelo did not seem to hold anything for them, so at Anastasia's suggestion, they headed south on the BR135 toward Belo Horizonte. She told Gordon that they have more bars per capita than any other place in Brazil. "They have no seas so they have bars." It took them an hour to reach the outskirts of Belo Horizonte where they got off the main road to take a back road in. It cost them half an hour as the side road was being cleared of cattle herded to the slaughterhouse.

There were indeed all manner of drinking and eating establishments in this huge city, and while it was not like Rio, it had a lively night life. Some of the bars were nothing more than an overhang with wooden crates for tables and chairs and a bubbling pot of beans and pork. Anastasia said she had never been there before but that it had a reputation. Apparently the population had swelled so rapidly that the slaughterhouses that had been well on the outskirts of town were now well within its confines. The iron mines were booming and despite having no port, the city grew exponentially. There was no tourist section, though. It was not really a tourist city since it had no beaches.

Terry had begun coughing, a dry, painful cough, so they stopped and got him some codeine cough syrup. They stopped at a bed and breakfast type arrangement just outside the border of what seemed like a shanty town. It was bordered by a gate that would help keep anyone from stealing the van. When they told the matron that Terry had contracted what looked like pneumonia in the woods, she contacted the local physician. He had no problem making house calls. That was his stock in trade. The price was reasonable and the doctor assured them they were doing the right thing. He gave Terry an injection to boost his immune system and bring his fever down, told him to double his intake of penicillin and drink lots of liquids. He said he would be back the following day to check on his progress.

"I think we should go dancing."

"That might be dangerous."

"Why? First of all, the men who slipped into the back door of the cottage did not know they were looking for a woman. They thought the… things pointed at a man. Second, they will not try to kill me when we are in a room full of people. And, third, we are in a town that is all bars it would look unusual if we did not go out. Don't worry, I will tell you if danger is there, I will protect you as well."

"It did not seem to bother the men in the plaza that there were all manner of innocents about. Though, you're

right, they still don't seem to have figured out that they are
after you. They seem more interested in me." It seemed as
though Gordon were talking to himself more than to her,
until he looked at her. "But, you already look unusual. You're
bald as an egg."

"I don't care," she pouted. "I am going to shave my
legs and my head in the bath and I am going to go dancing.
Are you going with me?"

"Do I need to tie you up again?"

"Maybe later, after we dance, you would like to tie me
up. I don't mind."

"You're not going to dance in that outfit are you?"

"No. You're going to buy me a dress, first. I'm going
to bathe now."

She walked out the door and down the hall to the bath
while Gordon found himself wondering how that had
happened. It had been not long ago when he had made the
decisions.

Hernando pulled past the sign that indicated 42227, put
the car in neutral and killed the engine. It rolled a bit further
and came to a stop. There was nowhere near to hide the
vehicle so he left it at the side of the road and walked through
the forest until he could observe the location. There was a
Mercedes in the driveway with two flat tires and the curtains
were all drawn.

His first reaction had been to toss a Molotov cocktail
through the window and shoot whoever ran out but
Hernando scrapped the idea. He realized that a burned body
was not proof of death. He needed to be able to prove to his
handlers that Anastasia Viuda was dead. He crept around to
the back of the cabin where he could see through the kitchen
windows. There was evidence of activity, some footprints in
the mud. He circled further and came up on the blind side of

514

the kitchen door. Anastasia's last message had said that they had left her alone, but he could not be sure that was true. If she was indeed chained to a post, then any other room in the place might hold a man sleeping.

He felt his eyes starting to glaze over as the methadrine buzz started to leave him. He knew he needed to finish this quickly. He was surprised that the door was unlocked. He crept into the kitchen as quietly as he could but it was not quietly enough. He made almost no noise himself but the increase in the noise of the rain alerted those inside.

Brock Dakota turned from where he was interrogating the still bound Diogo Brothers. He knew there was someone coming in the back door. He stood by the wall waiting for a figure to appear but the latest intruder did not show himself. Like the night before it became a waiting game. Who would be the first to jump?

A creak from the wooden floor of the living room let Hernando know that he had been detected. There was no place in the kitchen that afforded much cover. Hernando stood beside the refrigerator with his pistol trained on the doorway, waiting. He felt his eyes glaze over again and realized he was in no shape to wait much longer.

"Rojo. We can shoot each other here or we can make a deal. You have something I want, but I do not need to take the woman with me." He spoke in English.

Brock had no idea who he was speaking to. The only man who could be called Rojo would have been Boris Chercovski. That told him that the invader did not know who was in the house, did not know that the woman had joined Boris and Walter, and did not know that the Diogo brothers were bound to a pair of chairs. Brock said nothing.

"Come on, Rojo, no hard feelings. Come on out and we can have some coffee. I never wanted to kill you, just keep you from killing me. Our last episode was unfortunate but we can move beyond that."

Everything the man said taught Dakota something more about the man. There was no sense in the American breaking his silence yet.

"Rojo? You know that we are both at the top of the mountain. Just surviving with my lover for as long as you have means you are one of the best. We must have an agreement or one of us is going to die and that is not what I want. I do not even want to kill you; I just need to prove that she has been dispatched."

That was enough for Brock. He was certain, now, that he was facing a very dangerous individual. If he could compare himself with the man who shot him in the woods, then he was not a man to be trusted. "Throw out your weapons and back into the living room."

"Oho, you are not Rojo. You must be the blondie."

"Throw out your weapons and back into the living room."

"I do not think that would be a good idea."

"It is the only option you have. I will kill you if you try to leave and I will kill you if you do not surrender your weapons. If you expect to get out of that kitchen alive, you will do what I say."

"We need to reach an agreement. We must negotiate. I cannot just throw out my pistol because you say I need to. We must negotiate."

Brock suddenly realized that the man on the other side of the wall was Mr. Andalucia from the slaughter at the border. "You are a long way from home, Mr. Andalucia."

"You have me at a disadvantage."

Dakota's mind was working now. "I certainly do. My partner, Boris will be back any minute. Do not think for a minute you can stand against both of us. You are better off surrendering to me now. He will not be so understanding."

"Boris, the name fits him. Perhaps Boris will be even less understanding if I am unarmed."

"I can make him understand that we have similar objectives."

"Perhaps, but he may decide not listen to your reasoning. What assurances do I have that I will survive this if I surrender?"

"The only assurance I can give you is that you will not survive if you do not surrender your weapons immediately."

"I think I should take my chances."

Now it was Brock's turn to be alerted by the creaking of the floor. Hernando moved toward the doorway until he reached the spot he thought parallel to his enemies' and he opened fire through the wall. If Dakota had stood his ground he would have been perforated by .45 caliber hollow points. They lost a lot of energy puncturing both sides of the hardwood paneling, but still carried enough to kill. But they did not strike flesh.

Brock had heard the creak and moved back a few feet. He saw the angle and played it. Nine shots blasted through the boards, then the sound of a clip hitting the floor. Dakota screamed and Hernando came around the corner, leading with his pistol. That was when Brock opened fire.

When Hernando crashed through the kitchen door and headed for the tree line, he was more than a little confused. When he came around that corner, searching for a target, he had expected to see one man, blond, injured and down. What he had seen was two men tied to chairs, one naked, one clothed, and one hard faced man with black hair, pointing a pistol at him. Live rounds followed him into the trees, but the shooter did not.

The action had revived his energy but he knew it would not last. He was crashing fast and when he did, it would be for a long, deep sleep. His muddled mind tried to wrap itself around what was happening. He did not recognize any of the three men he had seen in the cottage and two of them had been tied to chairs. None of them had been either of the men he had seen with Anastasia in Curitiba. Who were they and how had they captured her? Or had they. He tried redialing the number she had called him from, but it went directly to voice mail so he hung up. She had said the battery was dead. The question was did they really have Anastasia chained to a post in the cabin? Had they moved her? Had she ever really been there? Who were the men tied to the chairs? Was Boris the same man he had tried to capture in the strip mine? Who was the man with the gun? He had known that Hernando had gone by the name Andalucia, but he was not Brazilian. His head began to ache. He needed to get somewhere safe so he could sleep. The rain stopped as he sat on a log in the woods trying to make head or tail of what was going on. He had thought he knew who he was facing, at least knew what they looked like, but now he was completely nonplused. He cursed when he realized he had left his spare clip on the kitchen floor.

Colored spots began to float on the edges of his vision and Hernando knew he needed to get out of the area. With the last of his remaining energy, he moved back down to the road, walked back to his car and left. The 8-liter can of gasoline and the glass bottles in the back forced him to admit that his first plan had been better than what he had actually done. He was unsure but began to think that Anastasia Viuda had tricked him and she was not in the cabin at all.

If attracting attention was what they were trying to do, they were going about it the right way. Anastasia was an amazing dancer and coupled with Gordon's strength, they monopolized the stage. There was a space around them, giving them room for the acrobatic display that they performed. The two of them moved like they had been together for years, sliding, flipping, spinning and dipping. They followed no accepted dance format but moved with the music. At one point Gordon wanted to leave and started walking away, but he was dragging the hairless Anastasia on her knees behind him. People actually applauded at that point and Gordon returned to the dance, actually liking the unwanted attention. The lack of pain in her head made Anastasia joyful and wild.

After some drinks and dancing, they stopped in a restaurant for some rice and beans with pork. They were both in wonderful spirits. They made their way back to the bed-and-breakfast and made love tenderly and slowly.

The doctor returned the next day but Terry was no better. He had some kind of jungle fever and would not be in shape to go anywhere for a week or so. More penicillin and vitamins were administered, but he was in bad shape and the doctor thought it best that he stay in bed. Without continued care he would only get worse.

Anastasia felt much better than Terry. For the first time in weeks her head was not rattling. It was like getting rid of a migraine headache, a toothache or back pain. She felt freed from bondage, even though she knew it would probably be temporary,

To say that Gordon MacMaster looked nervous or watchful would be overstating the situation. He looked perfectly at ease, but looks are often merely a façade. He watched everyone and everything around him, more like a predator than prey, though he was not hunting.

Belo Horizonte, or Beaga as it was often called, was planned along the lines of Washington D.C., but had grown to many times that size. Five and a half million people lived in the hilly city surrounded by mountains, ten times the population of the American capital. Without a homing device, the chances of being found in a city of this size were slim. City planning had not prevented the favelas from being constructed, piled on the sides of the mountains like dominos.

Citing the events of the immediate past, MacMaster insisted on accompanying his woman everywhere she went. She got herself clothes, ammunition and food. She bought Gordon cigars and a new pair of boots. She was enjoying the freedom of a couple of free days. Neither of them spoke about the immediate future, the fact that she had a price on her head and that he was a wanted criminal. Most of the problems they had run into with the authorities had been on the edges of the country and they had begun at the south and progressed north.

"You know we're really pretty lucky to be alive."

"I think, my love, that you are lucky and I am good."

Gordon had to laugh and then he looked her in the eyes. He did not want to fall in love with this woman but he could not help himself. She was perfect for him. He shook his head, thinking "Except for the fact that she has men chasing her with electronic homing devices, she is wanted for multiple murders and killing people makes her horny." He laughed again and kissed her.

"Boris?"

"Call me Mack. Boris is wanted."

"Mack. Will they stop hunting us?"

"I don't know. I can't say. When the doctor returns tomorrow, we can ask him about getting that thing out of your head, so shave your scalp tonight. I doubt there is anything he can do but he may recommend a surgeon."

"I cannot pay for that. It is not like I can give them my insurance numbers. I will need to wait until I am back home before I can have that sort of thing done."

"Back home? You are going back home? Where is your home? Wait. You first had a problem crossing the border in Foz do Iguaçu. That's the border with Argentina and Paraguay, right?"

"Yes."

"So which is it, Argentina or Paraguay?"

"Argentina."

"Argentina carries a lot of land. Do you live in Buenos Aires,

"No, I live wherever they send me."

"Where is home then, if you never set down roots?"

"Rosario, I suppose, will do as well as any other. I spent a couple of years there after I got out of the academy."

"They have an academy for killers?"

"No, silly. I am, uh… was Secret Service."

"Well, I'll be! What happened to you?"

"That is a long and complicated story. My parents died when I was young, I think it was a car crash. I was raised by the state to be Secret Service, but not for the protective detail, for the elimination detail."

"Then it is an academy for killers."

"No. They teach us morals and responsibility and strength, personal and emotional strength. They taught me, they gave me a family of sorts. They took care of my needs, my teeth, inoculations, food.

"They were the ones who put that thing in your head then."

"I don't know. I don't remember where it was done, but I am remembering who did it. I remember in my nightmares."

"Are these the same people trying to kill you now?"

521

"I don't know. I don't know if they're trying to kill me or capture me for the reward. They could be trying to kill you for all I know."

"No, my sweet, these locators are tuned to the device in your head. You can feel them coming. Hey! Can you feel these things coming?"

"No. I feel the danger. That is why I know you would never hurt me. You would never have captured me in the plaza if you were really a danger."

"May I point out that it was not I who grabbed you, but my partner."

"Irrelevant. I did not feel you approaching."

"We're back on this again. I wanted to know what happened at the border."

"Ai. I think the owner of the car stashed the gun back there, and we got the gun when we stole the car."

"You were driving a stolen car across the border?"

"It was more of a borrowed car than a stolen one."

"You borrowed it without the owner's knowledge?"

"Yes, my love." Her smile drew him in like a moth to a flame and he needed to kiss her right then and there. They wasted no more words for a while.

The following day the doctor came around and seemed pleased at Terry's progress. He medicated him some more and then had a look at Anastasia's head. He pronounced it a professional job that had been done many years earlier. If there was something remaining in her head he would not think of trying to remove it. The brain would have grown around it and to remove it would cause untold damage. He wouldn't even recommend a surgeon to speak with. Gordon gave him a healthy stack of bills and told him to come back tomorrow.

It was four days later that Terry thought he was well enough to travel. The doctor did not agree with him and since there was no apparent danger in Belo Horizonte, they stayed another day.

It had been almost a week earlier at 42227 on BR214 when Brock Dakota had released the Diogo brothers from their bonds. The man Brock knew as Andalucia had almost shot all three of them and almost been shot himself.

The brothers were not looking so dapper now, since they were forced to wear one suit between the two of them, their weapons had been taken and their tires flattened. It was the loss of image that stung them the most, made them thirst for revenge.

"You know the reward for the man is the same as the reward for the woman?"

"What man?"

"What reward?" The Diogo brothers had already been paid to kill whoever the homing device indicated but there were obviously other monetary circumstances that were not being taken advantage of.

"The reward that was offered for the woman. You really don't know about it then?" Brock did his best with the Portuguese. Sometimes he would throw in an English word they would understand, but communication was spotty and slow.

"We know of no reward."

"Then let me enlighten you. The woman who was here…"

"The bald one?

"Yes, the bald one. She reportedly killed General Modiano. I guess that was a couple, three weeks back. Francisco Modiano has announced a reward for the delivery of the couple. The price doubles if they are alive, but they have proven exceptionally difficult to kill, let alone capture."

"So who are the men protecting her?"

"Walter Suffolk, a contract killer I have been chasing since Cincinnati, Ohio. Do either of you know where Cincinnati is?"

"United States."

"Of course, but Ohio is in the Northeast. Cincinnati is all the way up by the great lakes. On the other side of the country."

"That does not impress us. Which one is he?"

"He is the blond and the bigger man is called Boris Chercovski. He is wanted in connection to a murder on a military base. He had already been sentenced to death when he escaped."

"He escaped death row in a military prison?"

"Yes, the one south of Cascavel."

"That is impressive. What we need to know is how are we going to get out of here? We need new clothes and a car."

"You did not listen. The man who came in the door earlier and almost shot me through the wall has the same objective as we but I think he has a different reason for it. After all, he can't claim the reward that is posted on himself. He claims to want proof that his partner is dead. I do not know what the ramifications of this are for either of them, but I know what they are for us. I want Walter Suffolk. I chased this motherfucker 5000 miles and I want his head."

The Diogo brothers still did not seem impressed. "What is it you are suggesting?"

"This Mr. Andalucia must have a homing device or he could not have found us here, yes?"

"Perhaps."

"Well, that means he will be in our way when we move on the target. He may kill us, spring a trap or just alert the targets. He is a dangerous man and he needs to be eliminated. That brings me back to my first point. He has a reward on his head, payable by Francisco Modiano, dead or alive. Alive pays better."

"And you are saying the woman is also to be rewarded?"

"She had a reward on her head as well. They did the job together." When he mentioned how much the contract on the couple was worth, the Diogo brothers were finally impressed. It was ten times what General Arridagio was paying them for what amounted to the same job. It looked like the best of all possible worlds to the brothers but they needed to get out of there first and they needed some weapons.

They called the rental company and explained the problem to them. It took half the day to get the tires on the Mercedes replaced and then they found that the Honda had been disabled as well. Brock was unwilling to leave his vehicle behind and he had retained the tracking devices so the Diogos were unable to move until he was. The three of them drove to Diamantina Centro and the Diogos got some outfits while Dakota arranged for the tires on the Honda to be replaced. They did not notice they were being followed on the way down.

In the shadows of the cantina, Hernando del Fuego sat, sipping a beer. He had seen the Mercedes driving south and snuck into the cabin but there was nothing to be gained there. When he returned to the road, the Mercedes was being driven away from the Honda with the flat tires.

In Diamantina Centro, the three men got hotel rooms. They would undoubtedly pick up the other car the following day. Hernando knew nothing about the tracking devices but he was convinced that the men knew where his former partner was. He thought that she may have been in the trunk of the Mercedes.

It was not so easy to get weapons in Diamantina Centro as in one of the larger cities. There was no real gang activity here so drugs and unregistered guns were scarce. Dakota was almost broke but the Diogo brothers had access to their bank accounts so money was available. They could have still bought a pistol legally but it would have involved talking with the police and registering the weapon, something the Diogos were not willing to do.

What Brock Dakota had not considered was how badly Deputy Chief Inspector Llamas wanted him and the homing device. Llamas had contacted the rental company and put a trace on the Honda. It had stopped and he had contacted the locals. By the time Brock had returned to the spot, a mile down the road from the cottage, the car had been towed. He called the rental company and determined that the car had been impounded in Diamante Centro. What he had not expected was when he went to retrieve the vehicle he was arrested by the locals and thrown into a holding cell. A warrant for his arrest had been issued from Rio and they had been waiting for him to appear.

Because he was a member of the Homeland Security Team, Brock got what amounted to celebrity treatment in Diamantina Centro. All that really meant was that he got all the phone calls he needed and he did make some calls. The home office told him he was on his own. They had already informed him they wouldn't help if he screwed up. The CIA was no more helpful. They had troubles of their own and would not be assisting with his. The embassy told him they would get him a lawyer when he was settled. Captain Cook could do nothing for him from Cincinnati although he was willing to send him a hundred dollars. The Diogo brothers had no cell phones to contact them on but they wanted the homing devices that were locked up with Brock's personal effects.

A week later Brock was told he would be transported to arraignment in Rio de Janeiro. The transport bus was actually a 15 passenger van. Brock Dakota and one other detainee were being transported to Rio to answer for their deeds. Inside there was a driver and a guard. The road to Rio took them right past Belo Horizonte or it would have if they had made it that far. While traversing the high country on BR259 they were passed by a Mercedes that skidded onto the gravel, half on and half off the road a couple of kilometers further. There was a man in the driver's seat, slumped over the wheel, looking injured.

The driver stopped the van and the guard got out while the driver called in on the radio to report the incident. No sooner had the guard tried to shake the man's shoulder than the accident victim picked up his head and stabbed him through the chest with a skinning knife. The driver fared no better as the other man slipped down the side of the van and smashed his head in with a baseball bat. Seconds later, the only visitors to the spot were both dead and both vehicles were gone.

It was no secret that Brock Dakota was angry but it was equally plain that he could do nothing about it. The tide had turned against him. He was handcuffed and locked in the back of the van so after some initial complaining, he reevaluated his position and shut his mouth. The other prisoner kept his mouth shut. He was being shipped back to Rio to face charges of killing his mother-in-law after being on the run for weeks. He thought if he could get away again he could stay lost.

The taller of the brothers was driving the van, wearing the shirt taken from its driver. He looked as if he belonged and the van attracted little attention as they cruised through Inimutaba and Curvelo. Only one of the homing devices seemed to be functioning, and it was not a GPS style unit but it seemed obvious that their prey was in Belo Horizonte or beyond.

"Ready to roll?"

"I'll be all right, mate. What is it?" Terry was out of bed and getting dressed. He felt weak but he could breathe without coughing.

"Well, we've been here a week and nobody came after us. Why do you suppose that is?"

"Nobody knows we're here?"

Gordon did not look convinced. "Anastasia has not felt any danger except for the proximity of local law enforcement. I've been monitoring the news but I don't see anything relating to us."

"Look, Mack, I say we get the hell out of this country. Take a boat to Grand Cayman and you can stash your cash there. I'm sorry I tied you down but it's time to move."

"No, we need a plan. As long as she has that thing in her head, they can find us."

"Leave her behind. What do you owe her anyway?"

"I can't. I won't."

"You got it real bad now."

"Yeah. I never thought it would happen to me."

"I hope that pussy's worth it. It's gonna get you killed."

"The way I see it, we need to get rid of the reward. Once there is no reward on Anastasia's head, then there will be no danger. Then we can go and not worry about it. I got my eye on a bit of land in the American high desert."

"Oh, right. Gordon MacMaster, sand farmer."

"No, not a farmer, just a retired executive in an area that no one goes to."

"So what are you thinking of, fake a death?"

"No. The trackers prevent that. I'm thinking we need to take care of the primary."

"Like we did in Sydney?"

"Something like that."

"Well, let's get back to business then." Terry picked up the suitcases and headed out the door with Gordon right behind him.

Gordon drove south on BR040 toward Rio. Several kilometers behind him, the Diogo brothers dumped the van with one dead body in it. They had debated killing Brock Dakota as well but had decided against it. They decided to keep him alive for their own purposes. It was not long after that when Hernando del Fuego passed the van. He did not know how the men were tracking the same people he was after but it was obvious to him that they were. He had gotten no further calls from Anastasia so he was using the only source he had. He was not confident they could find his lost love, but he had determined that she was not in the trunk of the Mercedes.

Chapter Twenty Five
Frustration

Just north of the town of Paraopeba on BR040, the Diogo brothers ran into a bit of a snag. The police had set up road blocks in the area looking for fugitives and Brock Dakota had just been added to that list. Along with several other vehicles, they refused to queue up and wait to be inspected. They turned around and headed north again.

The Mercedes served as a warning to Hernando del Fuego a couple of kilometers further back. They did not recognize him in his innocuous Honda, but he noticed them. As soon as they were out of sight, he turned around and followed them. The longer he waited, the more frustrating the situation became. He had reached the point where he was sure he was not progressing in his goals.

"Señor Dakota, we rescued you to regain a tracker. That was when you were of a benefit to us. I fear, now, that you are a liability and that we can no longer be associated with you. We are going to need to leave you behind and take the trackers with us."

"I can see your point but I think you are making a huge mistake. You are going to need me when the rubber hits the road."

"A curious expression. The rubber is hitting the road now." The man in the passenger seat slipped the muzzle of the stolen service revolver next to the head rest to punctuate his statement.

"I'll tell you what, gentlemen, leave me the one that does not work and maybe I can figure out what to do with it. I will be left behind with nothing but we have both rescued the other. After all, if I had not released you from those chairs you would have died in a couple of days from no water. We want the same things, we just want them for different reasons. I may need to hide out for a couple of days or sneak through the fields to avoid the road blocks, but I won't be your problem any more."

"Very well, pull over and we can finish this."

The driver began pulling over to the side of the road. Brock Dakota knew he had seconds to live unless he could pull a miracle out of his hat. Before the vehicle came to a complete stop he had grabbed the bag from the seat next to him and rolled out of the passenger side of the car. The passenger reacted and pulled the trigger, shattering the back window of the car but missing Brock entirely. He was outside the vehicle when the round went off. The forest grew close to the road here and within seconds Brock Dakota had raced into its leafy embrace.

Within seconds, both of the Diogo brothers had jumped out and followed their captive into the woods but they were not woodsmen and their ears rang from the report of the pistol in the confines of the car. Had their target been armed, it would have been their last day breathing but he was not.

Brock's pistol was in the bag but it was unloaded and locked with a trigger lock. The clothes he had been wearing, along with his wallet and ID were in the bag and the tracker that did not seem to function.

Brock slipped silently through the trees and into a wash filled with fallen trees and leaves. He would have been able to follow his trail if it had been laid by someone else, but the Diogos were lost in the woods. Their hunting grounds were paved and illuminated at night. He heard them moving around but they could not find him. He heard them moving back to the road, firing up the engine and driving off. He had never so badly regretted letting anyone live.

"Good day, Scotsman. I have news, though not grand news. Is this line secure?"

"Yes, Sir, a pay phone. Things have become interesting here, Colonel."

"Yes, my sources tell me that twice men have tried to cheat Francisco Modiano and ambushed his couriers."

"Colonel…"

"Do not think for a second that I believe these pieces of trash. My news is that I can get half your usual commission to decommission Modiano. This is the best I could manage and the client is of the same unsavory character as the target."

"That is of no consequence, Colonel. Have the money wired, take your service charge and assure the client the job will be done."

"I can get half the principle wired, he will pay off the balance upon completion of the decommission. Do you have a time line?"

"I'm practically in the neighborhood now. I need some planning and equipment, though. I can't work it through until I get some more effective firepower."

"Do you want me to contact the client in regards to that?"

"No, I don't want to meet him or let him have any knowledge of me."

"I'll leave you to that then and I will contact the client and get the transfer taken care of. Scotsman, you were going to do this anyway, were you not?"

"As I said, things have become both complicated and interesting here. I need an ID package. Make it two German men and one Brazilian woman. Better yet, make the woman Chilean, with stamps showing entrance to Brazil. I will get some photographs done and mail them to Berlin. Once they are done, send them to box 1097 in Petropolis, Brazil."

"I await your photographs. Tell me, old friend, is the woman the original commission?"

"Let's discuss that at another time, over schnapps."

"I thought so. Very well, is there anything else I can do to assist?"

"Airlift in a tank?"

"Ah, those were the days. Call if there is anything I can do."

"I will. I hope to see Berlin soon."

After a few more pleasantries Gordon hung up the phone. "I just got you paid on this one," he said.

"Thanks, Mack. I was ready to do it as a charitable donation if need be." Terry was not smiling but they both felt some satisfaction from it.

"I know. Hey, it's not a really big payday but it'll keep you for a while. I need some passport photos of each of us. The Colonel is going to set us up with ID. I don't know about you, but I'm getting pretty well sick of this miserable climate."

"Yeah, it's a bit moist."

Gordon lit a cigar. Anastasia was looking through a rack of shawls and scarves for some sort of fashion accessory. She had picked up a nice blonde wig.

"Where are we going to get what we need?" Terry asked.

"I have an idea. Let me make another call." Directory assistance gave him the number for Rio Rojo in Porto Alegre and the bartender transferred him to the owner. "Tio Carlos?"

"Who calls?"

"My name is Boris Chercovski. I was brought to the Rio Rojo by your little lost nephew."

"I remember you. You were seeking trouble. Did you find it?"

"Ah yes, I certainly did."

"And I see that you managed to survive it."

"Yes. I am in a market north of Rio and I am about to go looking for more trouble. Tell me, can you help me with something?"

"Possibly. I helped many people when I was younger, but I am getting to be an older man now and fancy myself a bit more of a gentleman. What is it that you need assistance with?"

"A couple of sniper rifles, some explosives. Detonation cord, C4, a trigger."

"I can assist with this. I have some friends. They are trustworthy but not very trusting. I can also find some missiles, if that is something you would be interested in."

"Ah, yes. Very interested. Bring a couple of small pistols and I could also use some manpower if that could be arranged."

"That, Mr. Austria, is the easy part. How many men do you need?"

"Five should be sufficient. Payment will be made in cash. I need men with experience, armed men I can trust to stand fast when the shit begins to roll."

"I have some men in mind. Professionals. They will not be inexpensive but they come highly recommended."

"When and where should we meet to do business?"

"There is a building in the warehouse district. I cannot be there for another two days but I will take a special interest in this. Where can I call you?"

"I will call you back with a new number and we can make arrangements then."

"I await your call."

"Thank you, Tio Carlos. This will be well worth your while."

"Until then."

The three spent that night in Petropolis and got their photographs in the mail. They found it a friendly, if secluded place. It was the first of May and Gordon rented a house there for the two months. If they became separated during the coming action, that was the place to return to. There was a casino in town and all three of them would have liked to hit the tables, but casinos have too many cameras and too many people watching.

The warehouse district off the docks in Rio was huge, confusing and busy. Everything was unloading on the docks from tankers of oil that were pumping into huge storage tanks north of the airport to fishing boats full of shrimp and clams. Diesel trucks hauled freight and freezer trucks hauled food. Bicyclists swerved and dodged through the mess with no apparent instinct for self preservation and huge sweaty longshoremen tossed bundles of this and that into pickup trucks that queued up and down the street.

The address Tio Carlos gave Gordon on the phone was a run down building with a tin roof. It was filled to the eaves with wooden packing crates full of stuff that looked as though it had been there for a long time. Gordon drove the van into the storage area and parked it facing the office. The only man in attendance looked very much like an accountant with thick glasses and a cheap suit. He told Gordon that Carlos was coming but that there had been some delays. He asked if the Scot had brought money with him to affect the purchase whereupon Gordon brought out a metal briefcase stuffed with cash. The accountant separated the agreed-upon amount and Gordon returned the briefcase to the back of the van.

Half an hour had passed with no action before the door opened and four men stepped into the warehouse. They were armed but left their weapons holstered. Carlos was not among them. They moved to the office, two stayed outside and two entered.

"You are Boris?"

"Where is Carlos?"

"He was delayed. Is this the agreed-upon price?"

The accountant answered in the affirmative.

"Where is my merchandise?"

"It is coming. You must be patient." The spokesman for the group reached out and riffled through a couple of stacks of bills, confirming that they were indeed the same denomination.

Gordon took out his cell phone and redialed the only number that had been called on that phone. "Tio Carlos?"

"Boris, my friend, I am sailing into port now. Have my local associates joined you?"

"Yes. I am looking at four armed men but no merchandise. Are these the men we spoke of earlier?"

"No. They are merely backup. You must understand that this business is fraught with dangers that cannot be foreseen. I need to know your intentions are honorable."

Gordon handed the phone to the man he had spoken with and they had a conversation in very fast paced Brazilian Portuguese. When he once again had the telephone, Gordon asked for a time of delivery and Carlos assured him that they would see each other in half an hour.

It was closer to 40 minutes when the overhead door rolled up and an old El Camino was driven in with a packing crate in the back. Carlos got out of the passenger's side and the driver remained behind the wheel.

"Carlos, I am glad to see you."

"Boris. I have been looking forward to seeing you again. I see you have brought the money as agreed. I suppose you would like to see your merchandise now?"

"Is it in the crate?"

Carlos grabbed a crowbar and handed it to his new associate. The top came off the crate but instead of munitions, the crate contained a man with an Uzi.

"Carlos, Carlos, Carlos. What on Earth do you think you are doing?" Gordon was standing in the bed of the El Camino facing the man with the Uzi. The other four men had drawn their weapons and were standing back to back without saying a word, covering the doors and the van. Carlos was fishing a pair of cigars out of his shirt pocket. He handed one to Gordon and bit the end off the other. When he had lit his cigar, he handed Gordon his lighter and walked to the personnel door, swung it open and stood there for a minute, smoking. Then he turned back, closed the door and told his men to stand down.

"One cannot be too careful, as you must know. I was afraid you were working with the locals or perhaps the police. I feared we may have been set up."

"Yes, one cannot be too careful."

"I must say, Boris, that you are very trusting to come here alone. Or do you have men in the van? Oh. I see. You have that canopy added to the top of the van. You have a man inside there."

Panic struck the Brazilians as a pair of hand grenades flipped from inside the canopy and bounced on the floor. They dove behind crates and vehicles. The expected explosion never came, however, since the pins had never been pulled.

"You have a good eye, Carlos. I don't think your men made that call. I was hoping we could do real business together. I'm getting a little tired of killing people for no good reason."

Carlos laughed. He had not scattered when the grenades came out.

"So, where are my rockets?"

"In another warehouse a few blocks away. If you like, we can go there now."

Carlos handed each of the four men a few bills and put the rest into a leather valise. The accountant took the valise and walked out the door. He was heavily guarded as he went to the bank.

Terry did not slide out of the canopy until they had gotten to the other warehouse.

Anastasia appeared from on top of a stack of crates where she had slipped off to while the accountant was verifying the payment. Carlos looked both surprised and appreciative when she walked around the stack, carrying a scoped rifle.

"As you see, Carlos, I am not as trusting as you might like to believe."

"Well, I am satisfied, now. Follow me."

The equipment was close to what had been described: Soviet rockets, Brazilian rifles, pistols, silencers and dynamite, Finnish detonating cord and German blasting caps. As a bonus, Carlos threw in an assault shotgun with a drum clip and a remote control detonator for the blasting caps. There was a hardwired switch in the box, but the remote gave much better range and concealment.

"Are you satisfied with this, Boris?"

"Yes, this will suffice. When can I meet the men you spoke of?"

"They will be here tonight. They will be staying in the Continental Hotel. Five men, professionals. They will want to meet you tomorrow to discuss the details and payment terms. Call room 423."

"I'm not going to look down another barrel, am I?"

"I'm sorry about that, my friend, but we have had no business before and one must be so careful these days."

"I forgive you. I was a bit nervous myself. All right, there is something else I need to take care of." Gordon moved to the back of the van and took out a metal briefcase. It looked identical to the one he had placed in there, half full of cash earlier but he was careful to open it as little as possible before sliding a pair of side cutters in and cutting a wire. "You see, Carlos, if you had double-crossed me, you would have died as well. I am glad we made this bloodless."

Carlos smiled as he tossed the smoldering butt of his cigar on the warehouse floor. The wire had been threaded through a couple of grenade pins so opening the box would have pulled them. It was a crude set up, but effective.

The two men said their good-byes and drove off in different directions, both feeling much tension ebbing away.

Anastasia collapsed on the mattress in the bed of the van. She had said nothing but her hands had been shaking.

Terry was sitting in the passenger's seat. He lit a cigarette as they drove away. "That was as close as I ever came to jumping. How did you know he wasn't going to have you killed?"

"I didn't, but there was nothing I could do about it at that point. I was counting on Anastasia shooting the son-of-a-bitch that popped out of that crate. I'm glad she didn't need to."

"I could have shot him, love," she said wearily. "If I shot him any higher than the bottom it would have gone right through and hit you. If I had shot him in the bottom he would have shot you anyway. The truth is that I didn't have him properly covered from that angle. If the shooting started, you would have died. He would have killed you or I would have killed you but you would have died."

"Well," Gordon said, spitting out the window of the van "that's reassuring."

The Diogo brothers had no problem reaching Rio once they had gotten rid of Brock Dakota. They were not wanted men after all.

After heading north with a shattered rear window, they headed west on BR240 in an effort to circumvent the road blocks and anything associated with them. The only town to deserve the name on BR420 was Pompeu but they had no window for the Mercedes. The brothers had to wait until they reached Papagaios before they could get the repair done. The circumnavigation of the Rio Paraopeba floodplain added about 140 kilometers to the trip and the repair shops were closed when they got there, but they had successfully avoided the police. The shops opened the following day and a rear window was brought in from the local scrap yard and sealed in place.

By the time they reached the Belo Horizonte metropolitan area, their target was long gone. Things had changed considerably since they had been tied to chairs in the cabin, though. They were in possession of a working directional tracker and they were armed. As far as they were concerned, the game was on.

That night was spent in a hotel on the Plaza of Saint Sebastian in Tres Rios. The brothers bought some new clothes and threw away most of the clothing they had with them. They ate well that night and drank deeply. They almost went cruising for young boys but decided that could wait until they had completed their mission. Some of the inherent risks presented by that sort of action might compromise their momentum.

Hernando had been at a loss as to how to proceed. He had turned around to follow the men in Mercedes, knowing they were the only link he had to Anastasia and that big redhead he had sworn to kill. The aftereffects of the amphetamines had worn off and he could think clearly again, but he was unsure as to how he could find his targets.

There had obviously been a problem between the men he was following. The car had been on the side of the road with a smashed rear window when he drove north and there was nobody in it. He considered waiting for the winner or winners of the confrontation but decided against it. He was relatively sure that they did not know he was following them, and a confrontation might have turned against him. He drove a little way up the road and pulled off on a dirt road leading into the woods. The scoped hunting rifle from the trunk gave him a view of the empty Mercedes, but he was far enough back that he was invisible.

It was not long before the two men came out of the woods again. Each of them had a pistol in hand, neither weapon was silenced. Hernando knew he had not heard a shot. That meant either they had not found the other man or they had shot him in the car and dragged him into the woods. It did not make sense to him that they would have shot him inside the car but the rear window was shattered. He concluded that the tables had turned and the man who had shot at him, the man who had tied the other two to the chairs, had been forced to run. This was clearly an opportunity but how should he approach it?

The two men in the car passed his position and continued north. He sat calmly and watched the vehicle disappear and then turned his attention back to the spot where it had been resting. Ten minutes later the hard faced man, dressed as he had been in the cabin, slunk carefully out of the underbrush. A triumphant grin spread across his handsome features as his analysis of the situation proved correct.

After satisfying himself that the men who had hunted him were gone, Brock also started north, on foot. Once he got to a town, he was sure he could get his CIA contacts to help get him out of the country. In a lifetime of lone wolf attitude he had never felt so alone and powerless. It was not beyond possibility that he would spend the rest of his life in a Brazilian prison.

He had not walked far when he heard a familiar voice speak to him from the other side of the road.

"American! I think perhaps it would have been a good idea if you listened to me before, yes?"

Brock turned and looked down the barrel of the rifle Hernando pointed at him. His sense of helplessness and impending doom doubled. He began to wish he had gone to church more often because he was sure he was about to die.

"Come over here, American. I think there is much we have to discuss."

Brock had no choice this time. He knew there was no way he could make it back into the trees before this man shot him in the back. He began to savor every breath he took, knowing it could well be his last.

Much to Brock's surprise, Hernando did not assault him or even tie him up. He had the upper hand, but acted more of a gentleman than would have been expected. He gave Brock a beer.

The rifle went back in the trunk. Hernando made it clear he had no problem shooting Brock but that there were other matters that needed to be attended to as well. After he had finished his beer, Brock got in the passenger side of the Honda and the two of them departed the area.

Hernando del Fuego drove in silence, with his pistol on his lap, until they found a good hiding spot. It was a deserted barn, not far off the road. Pulling the car inside hid the car from view some and Hernando found a tarp that was half disintegrated to conceal it more. The two men sat on stumps and cracked open more beer while the Argentine opened the conversation.

"Why were those two men about to shoot you and who are they? Are you the one who tied them to the chairs?"

"No, Señor Andalucia, I did not tie them to the chairs, I found them that way. They claim they were contracted to eliminate whoever the trackers led to."

"What trackers?"

"The electronic trackers. The devices, like the one you took from me."

"This thing? How does it work? Who is it tracking? Why were they contracted? Who contracted them and who are they? Wait, first, who are you?"

"I am an agent of the American Homeland Security Agency. I came to Brazil looking for Russell O'mara. He is going by the name of Walter Suffolk, here."

"Now I believe you are lying to me. Homeland Security does not involve itself with foreign countries. If you had said CIA I might have believed you but you are working toward your own end."

"I came down here to work with the CIA, but they cut me loose after the slaughter in the Central Plaza in Curitiba."

"What do you know about that?" Hernando said sharply.

"Not much really."

"You know something and if you don't tell me something I want to know I am going to leave you here in this deserted barn with a bullet in your head. The animals will have eaten your flesh and scattered your bones before anyone even knows you were here."

"I get the picture. What do you want to know that you think I know?"

"The men, Rojo and Blondie, who are they?"

"The big man calls himself Boris. Boris Chercovski."

"Um, Boris. I thought this Boris was your partner? That is what you said in the cottage."

"I lied."

"Yes, American Secret Agent, I think maybe everything you say is a lie."

"No, no, no. I promise you, I will tell you everything you want to know. Everything I know. I came down here to get a man, a killer I tracked across two continents and then once I get here, the fucking CIA cut me loose. Stupid bastards. Everywhere this man goes, dead bodies start piling up. I started working with the police in Curitiba, but they seem more interested in the reward offered for your wife."

"Ah, yes. And how is Mrs. Andalucia?"

"As far as I can tell, she is thick as thieves with the two men. When I first saw her, she seemed to be the prisoner of Boris Chercovski, but the Diogo brothers tell me that is no longer the case. I cannot verify this; I can only report it."

"Are you trying to tell me that these men would give up that kind of a payoff for something that's going to get worn out after a couple more years?"

"I can't confirm it, only report it."

"So the men tied to the chairs…?"

"The Diogo brothers, Juan and Jose. Juan is the taller one, Jose is shorter and wears a handlebar mustache. They were paid kill someone else; they did not know about the reward on your head, although they do now. They were paid to kill whoever he tracker leads them to. They would not tell me who had hired them and I didn't press it that far. I tried to work with them."

"Umm. Tell me about Blondie."

"As I said, that one passed himself for Russell O'mara in the States. He seems to be Australian and he's going by the name Walter Suffolk down here."

"And what was your plan?"

"That's where the problems began. It's like it's impossible to sneak up on these people. Every time I get near them, they are on the alert. Every team that gets near them ends up dead. That's where I got the other tracker from originally. I picked it up off a dead body at the bottom of a pile of dead bodies. This one came from another dead body, in the square in Curitiba."

"Ah, full circle. We are back to Curitiba. I did not see you in the square that day so how did you get the tracker?"

"You where there?"

"Yes, I was there, trying very hard not to get shot. I was there to meet Mrs. Andalucia. This is where I see these two men as they intercept her. Then the bullets began to fly. From what I saw, however, these men were not the ones killing."

"No, it would seem not. That was where the trouble started. We were waiting for Walter Suffolk…"

"Blondie?"

"Yes. We were waiting for Blondie…"

"Who is we?"

"The CIA was with me. We lost a CIA agent in that scuffle and I still don't know why. That was the beginning of the problems and when I got cut off from all official recognition and assistance."

"So, you tell me now that you are working on your own to find and eliminate this Blondie?"

"I told you, I was working with the police but they turned on me as well, after getting a whole strike team gunned down. I spent a week in jail and the only reason I'm out now is the Diogo brothers sprung me from the bus."

"Unless I have made a mistake, it was they who were about to shoot you like a dog in the street, yes?"

"Yes. Once they had the tracker, I became a liability because I am a wanted man. There was a road block they avoided, but I am still wanted for whatever stupid charges they decide to level against me."

"Mr. American Secret Agent, you have already admitted to me that you are here to kill a man. What more serious charges do they need than that?"

"But I have killed no one. I am trying to stop the killing which just keeps on."

"So, the Diogo brothers were tied to chairs in the cottage. Did you do that?"

"No, Señor Andalucia. I rescued those ungrateful bastards from that situation and they turned on me like rats. I would have been better off just shooting them in the head."

"And that is something you would be comfortable doing?"

"No. I have never been the kind of cold-blooded killer needed for that. I will shoot Walter Suffolk without a second thought because he is a cold-blooded killer who escaped justice, but I'm not a mad dog."

"So you wouldn't shoot them given the opportunity?"

"You make your point well. If it were them or me, yes, I would kill them, but it is not my job to hunt them here."

"I put it to you that it is not your job to hunt Blondie here either and yet, here you are. Perhaps you would like to explain that to me?"

"He is a foreign national who has endangered the national security of the United States and I will hunt him down wherever he goes."

"You are a strange man, but a loyal one. The CIA has made a mistake. They would be better off cultivating your friendship than disavowing your actions. The question I have is what do I do with you now that I no longer need you?"

Brock did not know how to answer that. He felt his rectum tighten and his spine stiffen. He knew the odds were good that his odyssey would end right there in that deserted barn at the hands of an unknown killer. Chances were good that they would never identify the body and the animals would scatter his bones as his captor had said.

Then, Hernando del Fuego smiled at him, disconcertingly. "I think you and I have the same goals, generally. You want Blondie and I want, uh... Mrs. Andalucia, and I want Boris Chercovski. We have different reasons but I think we could work together since we are not at odds with each other, yes?"

"Yes. I have no interest in her or the reward. I want what you want."

"You are going to drive. Be aware, if you fail to follow my directions, I will shoot you. If you lie to me, I will shoot you. I am a wanted man as well, but I will not allow you to be captured; I will kill you first. Have you heard what I am saying?"

"Yes. I will, however, be of much more value armed. We are working from a disabled base if I am unarmed. While I do have ID, I am a wanted man."

"So you are saying you would shoot the police?"

"You are asking a question I cannot answer until the moment presents itself. I would prefer not to."

"Then you do not need to be armed. If I cannot count on you to work with me then I may as well leave you here."

"Señor Andalucia, you cannot go against these men alone. They will not hesitate to shoot you."

"But you might hesitate."

"No. I will shoot these men in a New York minute. I will shoot the Diogo brothers as well. Your question was if I would shoot a police officer. I merely said I did not want to, I did not say I would not."

"Very well. Now, tell me, how does this tracker operate?"

"I'm not sure. I don't know who it tracks. I think it is Boris Chercovski. This one has led me to him before, but it has a limited range. The other one, the one the Diogo brothers have is a better model. It has a better range. I was lucky to get this one."

"You were lucky to escape with your life."

"That was not luck, that was skill. Juan and Jose Diogo could not match me in the woods. I am an expert tracker and as such, a valuable asset. You will learn to appreciate what I can do for you before this is all over."

Thus it was that an uneasy alliance was formed between the out-of-favor Homeland Security Operative and the out-of-favor Argentine Secret Service Operative. Neither really trusted the other but they both felt overmatched and desperate. They spent the rest of the day getting to know each other better and sharing everything they knew about the men they were after. Brock ran out his experience in the woods, where they could not have known he was there, but had. He told of Captain Bellisario's untimely demise in the mall parking lot and of subsequently being shot in the bullet-proof vest by Boris Chercovski. He began to tell Hernando of the events that had brought him to Brazil, but was cut off.

Hernando told his new associate of trying to cross the border into Argentina and being arrested because of the gun in the trunk. He skipped having met Boris Chercovski in the hotel hallway, but went into some detail about being taken to the police officer's garage in Porto Alegre. He was careful to explain that this was why he needed to know if Brock could shoot an officer. He went over it more than once, explaining that the level of corruption in South America was endemic and inherent.

The conversation moved to being chased by both Boris Chercovski and Roberto Campena de Iguaca. He put a spin on the story that alleviated him of culpability in the ultimate outcome of the confrontation. He told Brock of being driven off by the army and of them taking his partner and Boris Chercovski prisoner. The two of them spoke at length of the telephone calls Hernando had gotten from Anastasia and the possibility of her allegations being real. Brock told of the Diogos' assertion that she was not their prisoner, but their accomplice.

Their next order of business was to formulate a plan to terminate their respective targets.

The lobby of the Continental Hotel was bright and airy. It had a high, glass ceiling and a huge crystal chandelier, evoking memories of the earlier part of the previous century. The rooms were no longer the classy suites they had been when it was newer, however. The walls had been patched and the sinks had been washed until the glaze was worn through. The restaurant still served good food and the bar was well cleaned.

The beer was good and cold and Terry was enjoying his second in a booth when Gordon sauntered up to the bar and ordered Kentucky bourbon. Anastasia followed him a minute later and sat at the other end of the bar. She did not even have the opportunity to pay for her own drink as a fat, sweaty businessman had taken the opportunity before she was even seated. He came and sat next to her as she was being served. She softly asked him if he would sit on the other side. She did not tell him that he would be blocking her shot.

After his first drink, Gordon asked for the room phone and told the man who answered that he was in the bar. A few minutes later an eclectic crew entered and took a table. He joined them and told the waiter that the drinks were on him. They sat for a moment as he surveyed the men Tio Carlos has brought in for him. Two of them were obviously local and dressed in rough, farmers clothing. Two looked like mercenaries, a short blond with blue eyes and a massive black man with a scar that covered one eye. The fifth member of the team was a woman dressed in jeans and a tee shirt with no bra. She had tattoos of naked women covering both arms and the shoulders of a professional wrestler.

"Uncle Carlos tells us you have a job that needs to be done?" The short man in camouflage seemed to be the spokesman. He spoke with a Texas accent.

"Yes, a little something. Why don't you tell me a little about yourselves?"

"Why don't you tell me who the fuck you are and what you want done?"

"I, my friend, am the man who pays for this sort of work and since I am the one who pays, I would like to know I am getting what I pay for."

"Fair enough. SAS then?"

Gordon smiled and said nothing as the waiter brought drinks. He signaled for another bourbon and lit a cigar while he waited for it. It would not take long to determine if there was a member of the crew who was too nervous or inexperienced for this sort of work. "I am not affiliated with any of the government agencies at present, I am working freelance" he said after a while.

"At present?" one of the men dressed as a farmer asked. "That means that you are at some point working with a government." His English was heavily accented.

"I have, upon occasion, leased my services to some of the more clandestine agencies but I am not currently so affiliated."

"Well, aren't you a Fancy Dan?" growled the woman. "I think he's a faggot." Her accent was pure New York City.

"I assure you my sexual preferences are none of your business as are yours. We are not here for an orgy, although it has been described as wet work."

The black man guffawed and banged on the table once. "I'm up for some," he said with a deep Caribbean accent.

"We all are, Milton. That's why we're here. Maybe we should go upstairs to discuss this?" The blond seemed afraid they would draw attention to themselves. He was obviously used to keeping them in line.

"I like it right here," Gordon said. "It makes me feel safe."

"You got some issues with that?" the woman asked.

"No. What do I call you?"

"Call me Sadie Hawkins. I chase what I want and I usually get it." The woman's leer was both suggestive and sadistic.

"Call me Boris Chercovski."

"My name is Chico," said the farmer who had spoken earlier.

"They call me Boom-Boom," said the other Hispanic.

"Why Boom-Boom?" Gordon asked.

"Because I make things go boom-boom-boom."

"Now we're getting somewhere. I'm pleased to meet you Boom-Boom."

"I'm Hans and this is Milton."

"Pleased to meet you, Hans, Milton, Chico and Sadie. What have you done to recommend you, Sadie?" Gordon was staring right in her eyes.

"I've done it all, baby. I reached into my mother's cunt and pulled out my baby brother."

"Once again, Sadie, I don't want to know anything about your sexual proclivities, I want to know what you can do for me."

"I can rock you like you never been rocked before."

551

Hans spoke up before things got out of hand. "Boris. I call you Boris? Yeah. Sadie here can take most men hand-to-hand. She's big but she's fast. I never saw a man that could take her with a knife. She's like a fuckin' ninja with a sword. Plus it throws most men off to fight a woman. She plays around inside their heads first. We'all been together for a while now. We work well together."

The waiter showed up to replenish the drinks. Gordon told him to keep them coming.

"Boom-Boom makes things go boom. Milton is for physical persuasion. I tend to stay back and shoot things from afar while Chico tends to slide in and shoot things up close. We are all capable in all arenas of endeavor but there are things we prefer to do." Hans had not touched his second drink.

"Yeah." Sadie whispered. "I like to look a man in the eye when I cut out his gizzards." The smile on her face seemed to say she was reminiscing at that point.

When the waiter showed up again, Gordon was surprised to realize that he was the only one who had finished his drink. He decided that it would be his last.

Chapter Twenty Six
The Exchange

They did not leave the barn until after dark. They had found much to talk about and had both been surprised to find that each liked the other. It is difficult to like someone you do not trust but they agreed on many points

They turned off onto the BR135 toward Curvelo. Between Curvelo and Paraopeba was 85 kilometers of mostly ranch land. The police did not bother patrolling the ranch land since the cows didn't break many laws.

Curvelo was a mid-sized town where a man could stay for a while without evoking any interest. They wiped clean and dumped the stolen Honda. Hernando had been driving it too long. They found a hotel for the night. Brock had not slept so well in weeks.

There were no automobiles ripe for the picking in Curvelo. It was not that populous a town. A large grocery store parking lot is usually a good place to troll for one if such is your need. The problem is the owner coming out with a bag of groceries and finding their car gone will usually call the police right away creating a bad scene. It is easy to get a car; getting away with it is the trick.

Kidnapping is not uncommon in Brazil, much less common than in Mexico, but still not uncommon. The penalties are as severe as might be imagined and prison anywhere south of the Rio Grande is Hell on Earth but that does not stop the crime.

Some of the newer gas stations have security cameras but not the older ones. It is not uncommon in Brazil to have an attendant at an older gas station, but many of the stations are moving to the more modern way of doing things, cutting out the service. This opens the way for the scurrilous and thieving.

The older gentleman was obviously proud of his Chevrolet Suburban. He kept it clean and waxed, the fluids were full and the tires were properly inflated. There was no telling how long he had saved just to get the down payment on this vehicle or what privations his family had endured to keep the thirsty engine in gasoline, but these were not issues Hernando del Fuego was prepared to address. He walked up to the pump where the man was filling the tank and shoved his gun in the man's face. The view from the cashier's window was obscured by the bulk of the truck. Brock took the man's wallet and paid for the gasoline.

Brock was driving and Hernando kept his eye on the owner in the back seat. The owner kept his mouth shut knowing that his number might already have been rolled. Hernando thought he was in charge of the situation. What he did not know was that Brock Dakota had found the owner's loaded revolver in the map pocket of the door and slipped it into his jacket pocket.

Without knowing if the road block was still in place north of Paraopeba, neither man could risk driving in that direction so they took a circuitous route. It added a few kilometers but ended in a suburb of Belo Horizonte. Along the way, they stopped at a church that had no outbuildings or living quarters nearby. They took the owner of the truck inside the church and tied him to a pew. He may have been able to free himself or, at worst, he would be freed on Sunday when the first of the faithful arrived for the service. This was a compromise arrived at through some negotiation between Brock and Hernando. Brock had been willing to leave the man at the side of the road and Hernando had been willing to leave his body by the side of the road. The church was a reasonable middle ground they could both agree on.

The tracker had not been activated in two days so they agreed that their targets had probably headed further south.

554

By the end of the day, Saturday, they were back in Rio but had no further direction.

"Dom Modiano, there has been another set of photographs delivered. I cannot tell who these are from, they came in the post, but I assume they come from the one who killed all those men at the bakery"

"So, he still thinks he can get a payoff, eh?"

"I must assume so. They are Polaroids, very difficult to fake."

"Leave them, Franco. I will take a look after breakfast. I assume there was no return address. Was there a telephone number?"

"Yes, a number. Different from the last one. How do you want to handle this?"

"Give me a minute. We lost too many men over this stupid bitch. She needs to die horribly. I have lost the respect of some of my associates over the affair."

"Perhaps it would be best to simply pay the reward. Things have gotten bad, as you said. The family that was killed practically across the street, the Captain we blew up, the men we lost. It is getting very messy and needs to come to a close."

"Have we that much cash on hand, Franco?"

"Yes, Señor. I have kept some aside in case you felt this was necessary."

"Well then, put it together and let us put this thing behind us. It has gone on way too long and hurts us every day it continues."

"Yes, Dom Modiano. I will take care of it immediately."

Breakfast was finished and Francisco Modiano slipped the Polaroids out of the envelope. They were similar to the one that was delivered before, Perfecta Navaja tied, naked, to a hotel bed. He gave them a cursory examination as he finished his coffee but the third picture caused him to drop his cup right in his lap.

"Aye, Maria!" he exclaimed and crossed himself. "This cannot be!"

The Chief of Police for Itaborai Township, Ignacio Dumond, was fit to be tied. He had been in office for a couple of years and had enjoyed a lucrative assignment. He had been taking care of the town with a mix of heavy-handed justice and judicious blind sight. Itaborai was an upscale neighborhood separated from the bay by the lower class, mountainous neighborhoods of Niteroi. The wealthier citizens paid well for the police to work in their best interests. Having a family butchered practically across the street from Francisco Modiano's villa was terribly bad form and the repercussions could be explicitly painful.

The news that the family's car had been located in Curvelo did nothing to alleviate the stress since there were no fingerprints on the car. Ignacio Dumond knew that there needed to be a scapegoat for the crime. He had been waiting for someone to spot the car and they would prosecute and execute whoever was driving it but it was found wiped clean, 500 kilometers away. That complicated things. He had no arrangement with the police department in Curvelo other than inter-jurisdictional cooperation. He did not know the Chief of Police there.

Juan and Jose Diogo reached Rio on Saturday and had seen the signal moving in different directions. They agreed that to try to follow a signal that kept changing directions was futile. It would be best to wait until night time when the people they were hunting settled down. The signal headed out of town before the night was old and they were too tired and wary to chase it into the countryside. They rented rooms and stayed in Rio that night.

Sunday morning looked more promising. The signal moved to the Continental hotel and stabilized. They had no way of telling what room their prey was in so they waited outside, expecting to see one or all of them exit. The tracker pointed solidly at the building.

A telephone call informed General Arridagio that the job would be completed sometime that day.

"Well then, Mack, what do you think?" Terry asked nonchalantly, his mouth half full of steak.

"They are relatively cautious. An unusual group; they would stand out in any crowd. At least the woman would."

"That black fellah would to. He's big as a house."

"They didn't want to discuss the job in public. They went back to the room expecting me to follow."

"You goin' up?"

"We could use the help. They seem professional enough though a bit eccentric."

"But can we trust 'em?" Terry drained another beer to follow his steak.

"They don't act like a regular group of mercenaries, I'll grant you that. They speak English, I imagine that's why they were steered toward us. Lord knows there are enough men in this country that will kill for cash."

At the bar, Anastasia was telling her suitor that he had bought her enough drinks and that she was through drinking. As she expected the businessman was not willing to let her get away so easily. He kept talking and when she stood, he grabbed her arm. Her first reaction would have hospitalized him, her second choice would have seen him buried, but she restrained herself. Discretion, she reminded herself, is the better part of valor.

"Señor," she began. "I simply wish to introduce you to one of my friends. Over here." She tugged his hand gently and he followed her across the barroom floor.

"Sandiana?" Gordon said as she approached, knowing that was the name she gave her new friend.

"My love." She leaned over the table to plant a kiss on his lips. "This man seems to think that he has bought me a couple of drinks and now has some claim to me."

"Is that right?" Gordon met the man's eyes but only for a second, as the man turned and waddled his way back across the floor. He knew when to leave well enough alone.

"Boris, there is some danger. The feeling in my head is there."

"I was afraid of that." Terry asserted.

"It is not from the crew you were talking to," she continued.

"With." Gordon corrected her.

"What?"

"It was not from the crew I was speaking with. If I was giving a speech, I would be talking to them but it was a conversation."

"Now is not the time, lover. The conversation you were speaking with was almost over before I felt this thing in my head. I do not think this crew is the danger. I think there is someone else. It is unchanging so someone is waiting somewhere."

"You two stay right here. I'm getting a look at the street. Order me another beer." Terry walked to the front of the bar and into the men's room. After returning some of the beer he had consumed, he stepped into the lobby and asked the concierge if there were any messages for Santino Stromboli. As he turned to look, Terry took in the view through the windows.

The concierge could find no messages for Santino Stromboli and Terry thanked him for his time and walked back into the bar.

"Get this, mate. There is a Mercedes Benz parked over and down the street and I think there are two men in it. They might have seen me but I doubt it. They probably already checked out the basement so they know the van is down there. I swear it's the same bloody car we left up in the woods with the same bloody Fleet Street Bankers we left tied to the chairs."

"I said, my love, that we should have shot them both."

Gordon took a deep breath through his nose and exhaled the same way. He looked at both his companions and asked. "How did they follow us without one of these devices? Well, shit, I don't think that is the important thing right now. I let them live once and they came back like a herpes sore. I'm gonna cauterize them this time." Gordon moved to the bar and asked again for the room phone.

Ten minutes later, Chico and Sadie were back in the bar. Gordon was sitting where he had been, but it did not escape notice that the woman with the wig, from the bar, was now drinking with the blond in the booth.

"You claimed that you are both sneaky and quiet, right?"

"What's the deal, Red? You just met us, you haven't outlined a job yet and now you got something on the burner?" Sadie did not look happy.

"You said you were professionals. I'm giving you the chance to prove it."

"Why do we need to?"

"Because you're getting paid to prove it. If you don't want the job, that's fine. This country is full of men who will take the job for less and probably do a better job."

"Well, hold on now," Chico said. "Let us not get ahead of ourselves. What is the job in question before we go jumping the gun?"

"There is a Mercedes parked across the street and down a way. In it are two men. One will have a handlebar mustache and they will both be dressed well. A warning, they will probably both have hats in their laps and pistols under the hats. This has not been confirmed. I am not going to tell you how this job will be done, but I want them both decommissioned."

"That's gonna cost you…" Sadie began.

"No, it is not. This is part of the job and will be eaten as part of the cost of doing business. This is not an additional job; it is part of the job."

"But, Boris. You do not mind if I call you Boris, do you?" Chico was speaking quietly and slowly. "We have not accepted the job. You have not laid it out for us. We do not know what we are expected to do and we have not agreed on compensation. I think you are trying to get us to do a free job and then you will disappear out the back door with all the cash and none of the blood on your hands. I must agree with Sadie that without some compensation, we are taking a chance for nothing but your word."

"If you're as good as you say, there is no taking a chance. You just take care of business. Consider it a gesture of good faith."

"I think we need to consult with Hans. He is the negotiator." Chico seemed to think that reasonable.

"I'm going upstairs to tell him about it. This whole deal stinks like ass." Sadie stood. "You sit right there, Boris Blowjob. I'll be right back."

"She certainly is colorful." Gordon commented.

"It is part of her charm." Chico replied. "She does a little song and dance and then cuts a man down like bamboo."

It took five minutes for Hans to return to the bar. He did not bring Sadie Hawkins with him; he brought Milton, the muscular black man.

"Sadie tells me you are looking for a freebie. That you have something going that we knew nothing about."

"In my defense, I knew nothing about it before. It seems we have been followed by a pair of men that I spared previously and never expected to see again."

"And who are these men?"

"Assassins. Killers that have been contracted to decommission a friend of mine."

"So they are not after you?"

"Oh, I think they would be happy to end my story as well."

"And you expect us to do this thing for you, why?"

"As a gesture of good faith. As proof of your efficiency and dedication. As proof of your abilities and value to my cause."

"And yet, you have yet to tell us what the job involves. We have, as yet, no agreement, no details and have seen no money."

"That is correct." Gordon stubbed the nub of his cigar out in the ashtray. "I need to know who I am working with."

"You're not dealing with chumps. No deal."

"Good. I would have been disappointed if you were green enough to fall for it. I will meet you in your room in 10 minutes to go over the details."

"So, this was a test? Who do you think you're dealing with, pal?"

"I needed to be sure. I don't work with cowboys."

"You're making the crew very nervous. I'm ready to call this one off and forget I ever met you. Either we are going to do business or we vamoose."

"We do business. I'll see you in 10 minutes."

The three men left the bar, but only two of them took the elevator to the fourth floor. Hans left the building instead, turning right out of the lobby he walked down the street surreptitiously observing everything on the street. He saw the Mercedes with the two men in the front seat, calculated the angles from the hotel, the corner, and several different attack points. He took careful note of the vendors and shops along the block with concealment and efficiency of operation in mind. At the end of the block he turned right again and made his way around the block, coming up on the back door of the hotel. It was the kind of door that only opened from the inside, but he pulled it open nonetheless thanks to the little wooden wedge that had been jammed in the locking mechanism earlier.

Inside the hotel, Hans looked into the bar to see if his new associate had left yet. Gordon was no longer there although the pair at the booth remained and the fat businessman who had been working on the woman with the wig was still drinking at the bar.

Gordon was sitting in room 423 when Hans returned. He had a case with him that he had not been carrying in the hotel bar.

"If we had a room in the front of the hotel," Hans said, "I could have seen the Mercedes from the window."

"You have seen it then?"

"There are two men sitting in a Mercedes, just as you said. I did not get close enough to see if they had hats on their laps, but they are dressed in business suits. They look more like detectives than hit men."

"No, they are assassins. I never expected to see them again and now that I do, I never want to see them again."

"You have made some very powerful enemies, Boris Chercovski. People get killed in this town all the time, but not by professionals. These guys are no stupid gang bangers. We'll take 'em out for full price but no less and no package deal."

"Wait till after dark." Gordon tossed a bundle of cash from the case across the room. "Full price, two men. I don't care who does it and I don't really care how it gets done, but I think having cops swarming all over the neighborhood would not be in our best interest."

"Now we're negotiating," Hans said, "but it's going to be full price one man. You are going to take the other. As a show of good faith. To show who you are. To demonstrate your efficiency?" He tossed the bundle of cash back.

Gordon sat for a moment weighing the situation. He was convinced this unusual team was not affiliated with the government in any way, but if he had wanted to kill the Diogos himself, he would have already. He needed to get them out of the way, however, every time a team of killers was eliminated, another team showed up. It would have been better to misdirect them if he could, but there was no way to get the device out of Anastasia's head. Killing them was the only option left.

"All right, Hans. If I'm in on it then we do it my way."

"Tell me your way and then we play." Hans was grinning.

"The tracker is active. The target is south-east of us."

"Why is it active now?" Hernando wanted to know.

"I think it has a limited range. Pull over. I need to know if they are moving or stationary. I can lock it in but I don't know if that's a good idea."

"It will take us to where they are or where they were. You can unlock it, no?"

"Yes. It looks like they are not moving. I'm locking it in now."

"How do you feel about this, Agent Dakota? Are you ready to spill some blood?"

"More than ready, and if you don't mind, I'm more than ready to get out of this country too. The heat and humidity make me feel like a sponge."

"I take no offense. I am used to a slightly drier climate myself."

Brock digested that and drew his own conclusions silently.

"Is there any way of telling how close we are?"

"No, I don't think so. Not without driving all over hell and triangulating the angles from center and all that shit is useless. If we are going to take care of this situation, then we need to move."

"Wait, let us think about this for just a moment. The tracker begins working but the target it is tracking is not moving? That means it is something other than distance that makes it work. Like it was tracking a cell phone or a bug. Leave it locked in. The signal may die again for some reason we don't know."

"The other one, the one the Diogos took, was active all the time. It did not fade this way. There is a constant signal that that one follows."

"If I had known that, I might have been less likely to let them go."

"But then you wouldn't have picked up a partner."

"Is that what we are, Agent Dakota, partners?"

"Yes, I think so. You didn't shoot me and I didn't shoot you as you slept while I drove."

"You think you could have taken the gun from me?"

"No. I didn't need to. I have one right here." Brock pulled out the pistol he had secured from the map pocket of the truck.

"I see. A very fancy gun, a stainless steel Smith and Wesson revolver."

"Loaded with .357 hollow points, it would have made a mess, but you would have been out of my life forever."

"True. I suppose then I must consider you an ally."

"It's my pleasure, Señor Andalucia, I need all the friends I can get."

"Call me Hernando."

"Hernando then. You can call me Brock."

"I shall be honored."

"I must say, Hernando, despite my earlier assessment, I am very glad to know you."

"And I am glad to be making your acquaintance as well, Brock."

The telephone call came at noon. Franco Cortico took the call but Francisco Modiano wanted to speak with the hunters personally this time.

"This is Francisco Modiano. Who am I speaking with?" he said in English.

"That is not of your concern. Be advised that I am in possession of the female half of the team you seek and I am willing to turn her over for half the promised reward."

"It seems that the game is different now. I will no longer accept either of the refugees in damaged condition. They are to be whole and in good health."

"I was told you had no problem accepting a certified corpse."

"That is no longer the case. I want the woman delivered immediately. The man is of less interest to me. Where does the transfer take place?"

"Central Avenue runs between the lagoons and the beaches. Do you know it?"

"Are we speaking of the town of Marica?"

"Yes, the shore south of Marica."

"You have the woman with you?"

"She will be in the trunk."

"Ai, she will die in the trunk of a car in this heat."

"Then I suggest you do not come late. At three this afternoon I will call back. I will expect you to be on Central Avenue with the money. If you are not, you will find this bitch in the trunk at the bottom of a lagoon."

"Wait…" Francisco said but the caller had hung up. "Franco. Get me a map, get the money and get me some men."

The Diogos had only been waiting an hour when the signal began to move. The smoky old fleet van pulled out of the parking ramp under the hotel. Jose stroked his handlebar mustache and smiled while Juan started the engine and pulled away from the curb. It was a long and arduous task for them to follow the van without getting too close and yet not losing sight of it. They drove east to a major expressway and then north toward the airport. They took the President Costa E. Silva Bridge across the bay to Niteroi and then drove up the mountain on the RJ106.

Jose was of the opinion that they should cut the van off on the mountain road and shoot everyone in it, but Juan was more cautious at this point. He reminded his brother that they were dealing with professionals. He further reminded him of what had happened the last time they had underestimated their opponents. Juan would never forget the humiliation of having his suit cut from him and being forced to sit naked in that chair. He assured Jose that he wanted the targets dead, but that the time had to be right or humiliation would be the least of their worries. Juan had stopped trying to keep the van in sight and had backed off, relying on the tracker to tell them if their targets had left the main road.

The van did not stop on the mountain but continued back down the far side. It turned off the RJ106 once they reached sea level and headed through the residential section toward the beach on Central Avenue. The Marica Lagoon was on their left and the beach on their right. It had taken them two hours to get to this point.

Jose was starting to get nervous. It felt like a trap to him. "If they know we are back here, they could stop at any point and what are we going to do? Drive slowly through here, let them have the lead. I do not know where they are going but I do not like this."

"I do not think they know we are back here," opined Juan. "We have not seen them so they could not have seen us. I think they are going swimming or fishing. I think we have the arrogant bastards now."

The locked in tracker signal led Brock and Hernando unerringly to the Continental Hotel but when they had arrived, the signal had moved on. The signal was still there but it was on the move now. They had not seen the van leave the parking area, nor had they seen the Mercedes following it. Their directions were, therefore, less precise and they were much further behind the van than the Diogo brothers were. They passed their exits and needed to turn around repeatedly. The clogged surface roads bogged them down and left them behind, but the signal did not die. It got weaker and weaker as their objective moved further away, but it stopped fading so much once they were on the bridge across the bay.

They did manage to save some time taking the Velha de Marica expressway to the RJ106 but they still trailed the other vehicles by half an hour.

Franco Cortico had been waiting for an hour already and still had 45 minutes remaining before the meeting was scheduled. He was not a happy man. The last two attempts to recover this woman had ended in death. They had lost eight men to this fiasco already and were no closer to their objective than they had been.

Lighting another cigarette from the burning filter of the last one, Franco spat out the window of the Cadillac. He could not understand his boss' insistence on having the woman brought to him in good condition. He had been planning on torturing her to death. That is until he saw the new photographs. What had changed? It was the same woman.

People were leaving the beach to escape the blazing afternoon sun. The taverns were doing a lively lunch time business, but the frying pan hot sidewalks were emptying. The Cadillac had an evaporating pool of water under the engine from the air conditioning.

Whoever had the woman now must be different from the one who had her last, the one who killed five men at the mountain bakery. There is no way a professional such as that one would set himself up in a pipe this way. Something had happened and Perfecta Navaja had changed hands.

The digital clock slowly changed its glowing red number until it read 2:45 and then the call came in.

An older, gravel road paralleled Central avenue for a about a kilometer on its north side. Various entrances and exits had been worn into the scrub grass along the way, giving drivers plenty of access to the old road and people used it for parking so they could have picnics on the lagoon. Across the road was a heavily forested area between the road and the beach. There was another unimproved road that ran down the beach. Many had been the young couple that took advantage of the beachside forest for their private trysts. There was no cover on the north side, so nothing hid the van parked on the gravel.

"There it is," said Jose. "Look, the engine is running. I see smoke from the tailpipe. They are still in there. What do you think they are doing in there?"

"I don't know if both men are in that van or not. They are probably fucking that whore."

"That would be perfect for us."

"No. I don't trust those bastards. They could be waiting for us to show. They could open that back door and take us out with a couple of shotguns. We will wait."

They did not wait long. It took about two minutes before a Cadillac pulled up on the other side of the street from them. A well-dressed man got out with a cigarette in his mouth and a briefcase in his hand.

The brothers looked at each other and then back at the man who had opened the briefcase to show them it was full of bank notes. The man took a paper bag out of his jacket pocket, opened it, and began transferring stacks of bills into it from the briefcase.

"We're being set up. Get the hell out of here," Jose yelled. Juan put the car in gear and the tires spit gravel as they spun back onto the road.

Franco froze. He was standing there with a paper bag half full of money and a briefcase with stacks of bills in it. He had feared for his life at the hands of these men, but he had not expected them to race off without the cash. It took him seconds to realize there was more going on than he knew about and by that time it was too late. A minivan pulled up to the spot where the Mercedes had been. It had side doors on both sides and the driver's side sliding door was already open. A short blond man with a bandanna over his face and an AK47 in his hands was standing in the opening. Franco remained frozen, there was nothing he could do. If he tried to escape, he would die.

"Finish putting the money in the bag," the man said. "If you try anything stupid you will die! If I see a weapon you will die! Move, move, move!"

Franco finished transferring the money to the bag and then said, "Where is the woman? I need the woman."

"Shut up. You will get the woman. Bring the bag over here or you will die!"

"If I give you this money and do not have the woman I will die anyway, in a much more horrible way than getting shot. Produce the woman or I will leave."

As they spoke, the van on the old gravel road was backing up toward them. The back door opened and out stepped Anastasia Viuda. She had her hands behind her back and nothing but a peach-fuzz of black hair on her head. She was dressed in a dark jump suit, belted at the waist.

It only took Franco a second to determine that it was indeed the woman he was looking for, though she looked considerably worse for wear. He walked the bag of cash across the street and handed it to the masked man with the rifle. That man pulled out a wad of bills and verified that they were all a similar denomination then told his driver who was also blond and masked, to drive off.

It looked to Franco as if he was finally going to see an end to this charade. The woman he knew as Perfecta Navaja walked with her head held high, straight toward him. The other van had not left yet.

"Please get in the car," Cortico said, opening the back door for her.

Anastasia took Franco completely by surprise when instead of getting in the car, she brought a fighting knife out from behind her back, grabbed his hair with her other hand

and placed the tip on his throat. "Take out your gun and drop it on the ground."

Franco had not had to fight hand-to-hand for a long time, but in his day he had been very effective. He knew he could not be beaten by a woman, regardless of who they were or what advantage they had. He moved swiftly, knocking the blade to the side with his right hand and grabbing Anastasia's throat with his left, but he did not properly secure the weapon, instead he punched her in the eye. As he brought his fist back for another strike, he felt the blade bite through his jacket, his vest, his shirt and his skin. Five inches of double-edged blade slid under his ribs and into his liver. With a strangled cry he doubled forward, reached under his jacket and pulled out his gun but he never got a shot off. Anastasia was under his arm in a flash and this time the knife point went between the ribs into his heart. A look of incredulity spread across his features, he tried to breathe but could not. He fell to his knees and his lungs emptied in their death rattle.

"Stupid man. All I wanted was your gun and your cell phone. Was that worth dying for? I have them anyway." Anastasia was in the front seat of the Cadillac in a flash and heading west. Gordon turned the van around on the tarmac to follow her, but their run was temporary. Less than two kilometers down the road, where it turned north at the west side of the lagoon, two cars had nosed together blocking traffic.

The traffic toward the beach was backing up, but they had released the traffic heading north, away from the ocean. The Cadillac was recognized immediately, as soon as it came around the corner and screamed to a halt. The trap they had set for the Diogo brothers had been turned back on them and they were now in a cage.

The west end of the somewhat square lagoon is much steeper than the other sides. The west side faces the mountains and there is no beach there, just a rocky drop off. It was the perfect place for an ambush.

Gordon MacMaster drove his smoky, worn out van around the corner with all the power it still had in it. He knew as soon as he saw the roadblock that he had miscalculated and the other end of the pipe would be blocked as well. It might have served them better to leave the vehicles and walk into town, but it was too late for that now. He drove that van with everything it had into the tail of the right hand car, hoping to spin it around and allow Anastasia to get the Cadillac through. The plan was a failure all the way around. The van caromed off the back of the car it struck and headed nose first into the deepest part of the lagoon. Anastasia did make it through the road block, but the Cadillac took a bullet in the passenger's side rear tire and threw sparks and shredded rubber two kilometers down the road.

The men at the roadblock had no trouble pacing her disabled vehicle and eventually just pinned both sides of the car. She unleashed a volley of lead out both sides, not knowing or caring why they did not shoot back. She shot the driver of the car on the driver's side and he swerved into the front of her car, forcing her toward the other car. That car slammed on the brakes and she drove directly into the corner of a brick building. If she had a few seconds more she could have recovered and gone on the offensive again but she did not. She was overwhelmed while still groggy from the impact. Anastasia Viuda was once again a prisoner.

Five kilometers down the road the Mercedes that had left the area so precipitously was at a dead stop. A bus had been pulled across the road and there was no way around it. There was also no escaping the shotguns that opened up on them from the interior of the same bus. Slugs slammed into their bodies, bathing the interior with blood. Men ran from either side of the road, Juan and Jose each took a pistol round to the head ensuring their demise. The trunk was popped and the interior searched but the men found neither the woman nor the money. The bus was pulled off and left by the side of the road. The killers left in a hurry.

No attention was paid to the minivan that crawled around the perforated Mercedes a moment later.

Chapter Twenty Seven
Payday

"Explain to me again how the money escaped." The drug kingpin was obviously upset by the turn of events and the elation he felt at having captured Anastasia did not seem to soothe his anger. Franco Cortico had been his right hand man for many years and had handled much of the high level negotiations. Losing him was a blow that would take some time to recover from and the knowledge that Francisco Modiano himself was responsible for putting the man in harm's way was infuriating him.

The man before him explained how they had gotten the call. Franco had told both teams that the men responsible were in a Mercedes and that they were to be eliminated and the money recovered.

"I was with the team on the west end of the road and we never saw the Mercedes. We saw Franco's Cadillac come racing down the road and thought everything was working properly until we realized that the woman was driving and Franco was nowhere in sight. I think the money must have been in the van that tried to run the road block and ended up in the lagoon. We knew the priority was the woman so we followed the Cadillac and stopped it. We got the woman but the money was not in the car."

"So, nobody went back to check out the van?" Modiano said, tight lipped.

"No, Señor. The lagoon is deep at that end and we had no diving equipment with us."

"Have the divers been dispatched yet?"

"Yes. They left a half hour ago. They should be getting there soon. I do not know if the police are on the scene or if the man driving the van drowned. We got a couple of shots off at it, but I don't know if we hit the driver.

He was a big man with red hair and he was in the van when it went into the water. We were occupied with chasing the Cadillac so no one saw if he came out or not."

"It was all a set up from the beginning. Who were the men in the Mercedes?"

"I don't know, Dom Modiano."

"Find out!" he yelled. "The police don't care if the drug addicts in the favelas slaughter each other, but this was in a tourist area. You know how they feel about that."

"Yes, Señor, right away." The man turned hand headed for the door, glad to be leaving the room with his head on his shoulders. He had acted the way he had seen best and had brought the prisoner in, but it seemed it had not been enough.

The next man brought into the room was the captain of the east side team. He explained how he had commandeered a bus and blocked the road and taken out the two men in the Mercedes, just as he had been ordered to, but that there had been no money in the car and no woman. The two teams had been kept separate since the incident as a precaution. That kind of money made people do really stupid things.

Modiano decided his new second in command was to be Giorgio Pereira, a long time associate. The man was dependable and loyal, but not as well-respected as Franco Cortico had been. Also, he didn't have the same head for numbers. Giorgio had not been with either team that day.

The day wore on and Francisco satisfied himself that the men who had been on the scene were telling the truth. Each told the same story although in a slightly different way, each depending on their memories and view point.

Now was the time he turned his attention to his newest interest, Anastasia Viuda.

"I need to admit that I called Boris wrong. I thought he was a bit daffy, but it looks like he got us a bloody payday and a half." Hans was looking into the shopping bag full of bundles of cash and all but drooling.

"You just leave that bag on the front seat, mate. Boris is the one to decide who gets what on this." Terry was driving the minivan through Marica.

"This is quite a haul. We could split this up and be set for a while."

"What, just you and me?"

"Just you and me."

Terry was fully aware of the fact that the man behind him was armed. A glance in the rear view mirror confirmed that the weapon was pointed at the back of the driver's seat. There was no way he could survive pulling his pistol and shooting the American. "What sort of split did you have in mind?"

"Fifty-fifty works all right. I got my eye on a ranch back home and this would make a fine down payment."

"Are you in the habit of double-crossing your partners?"

"Naw. Never did before."

"Then why are you trying to now?"

"I'm just fishin'. Wanna know what your feelings are about it."

"You saw what was left of the two men in the Mercedes, right?"

Hans gave a short laugh.

"If you want to spend the rest of your life wondering if today is the day you end up like that, then you can double-cross Boris Chercovski. He's not a very forgiving man."

"Shit brother, I just want to know I can trust you."

"Well I don't trust you much, but you know as well as I that if we're going in on a job, I need to be sure you have my back."

Hans grunted, put his AK47 on the floor between the front seats and sat in the passenger's seat with the bag of money on his lap. "Pull over up here somewhere and call him. I'm in for the long haul."

"Good." Terry pulled into the parking lot of a grocery store and made the call. The system told him it was unable to complete the call. He tried three times with the same result.

"Well then, what do you reckon we do? I'm for going back to the hotel and getting me a beer."

"Take one of those notes and head into in the shop here. Pick us up some tucker and beer."

"If you think I'm going in there and leaving you out here with all this loot your crazy as a sun-baked lizard."

"Your right. We need to get out of this area, sharp."

"Back to the hotel?"

"No, I don't think so. I've got a bad feeling about this."

"Well, I'm not sure I want to stay here."

"No, but the hotel's too far off. Let's find something a bit closer."

"Back by the bay?"

"No, this side of the mountains."

"Well, I'm sorry to tell you this, Colonel Kangaroo, but it's all mountains over here. Once you get away from these tidal pools it's all uphill."

"I'll tell you what, Captain Cactus," Terry replied with a smile, "we're both going into that sports place over there and getting us some fishing rods."

There was no need for ID when purchasing a fishing license. The rods, reels, line and bait were not cheap but the cover was easily worth it. Back in the van, Hans expressed that they couldn't fish without beer. Terry agreed but told his new fishing buddy he knew a place. Within 20 minutes they were parked on the east side of Lagoa de Ponta Negra, drinking beer.

Terry kept trying Gordon's number but repeatedly got the same message.

"Hey, Colonel Kangaroo…"

"Call me Terry."

"Not Walter?"

"No. If we are going to work together, you need to trust me. Call me Terry."

"All right, Terry, I gotta tell you, this job started, as far as I'm concerned. Not just for me but for my crew. Even if it goes no further than this, I expect everybody to get paid the agreed price."

"I wouldn't have it any other way. The job is going on regardless. You will be paid but the job is going to happen."

"So when are we going to find out what the job is?"

"We're going to take down a major drug dealer in Itaborai."

"Itaborai? That means you're going after Modiano."

"Right."

"He's a major player. I need to check with the team to see if the money is right for a job like this."

"Not on the air. Cell phones are too easy to hack."

"Don't worry. I never say shit on the air." Hans called his hotel room. "Heads up," he said. "The wedding cake is real. The wedding is on. Everybody get your tux's ready." Then he hung up.

"Ready for action?"

"All set, lock and load. Now can we go?"

"Hell no. I'm here to catch dinner."

With the almost certain assurance that he was going to be filled with lead, Gordon MacMaster stayed in the sinking van until the pocket of air trapped inside disappeared. The seals on the doors were badly worn so it did not take long. He took a deep breath and swam under water as far from the van as he could before surfacing. When he popped up it was only to get more air and he went down again. When he surfaced the second time it was against the stone wall of the lagoon. The water had slightly undercut the rock face so he had a little protection from above. As quietly as possible he moved away from the site of the crash until he could climb up on the shore. He saw a couple of people standing on the edge, looking toward the spot where the van had plunged, but they were not gangsters; they were obviously a family. Trees grew near the edge and the Scot slipped into their concealing embrace thankfully.

Water ran out of his cell phone and Gordon had neither the tools nor the patience to take it apart and dry it out. He wiped it down and left it under a log. He kept his pistol, though he was certain that the bullets had gotten as wet as he had and would not fire. He pulled his boots off and drained them, wringing his socks out as well. One of his cigars was still dry and with a little attention, his butane lighter would work, but he did not light it up.

Peering back out of the woods verified that the family had returned to their car and were driving off. The police would not be on the scene for quite some time since they had much more important duties to attend to. Traffic was moving again, but Gordon knew nobody was going to pick him up soaking wet except perhaps those he did not wish to see.

A kilometer down the shore line and across the shallow entrance of a canal was a residential neighborhood. While he did look out of place, the men he was sure were still hunting him would not be likely to find him there. His clothing was tightening up as it dried and he took his first opportunity to buy something else. As it turned out this was a rough woven poncho since there were no actual clothing stores in that area. He bought a hat against the heat but could not find a pair of jeans of any description. His boots were beginning to feel slimy on the inside as well.

The neighborhood was named Imbassai. It was really more of an offshoot of Marica. There was one main road running through, but there was no way Gordon was going to venture out there. He took the back streets and began a long walk toward the commercial section of town. At one point a gang of kids surrounded him and began begging. He made a deal with them to get him to a store where he could get some boots and pants. They were happy to accommodate him. He gave them some cash for their troubles and they called him Clint and left him there wondering what they were talking about.

Close to the shoe store was an electronics store. Try as he might, the manager of the store would not allow him to purchase a cell phone without a contract. They did not have a disposable model he could purchase minutes for and toss when he was done. He stood in the store trying out one of the models after determining he could not get one without entanglements and called Terry's number. Twenty minutes later the minivan was there to pick him up.

"So, I tried to catch you some fish for dinner, but all we pulled out were some evil-looking catfish and I wasn't sure about them."

"Where's Anastasia?"

"Damned if I know. She was with you last I saw."

"She took off in the man's Cadillac but we hit a snag."

"Nowhere near the snag those blokes in the Mercedes hit." Terry drew his finger across his throat."

"That's what I'm afraid of. Anastasia's in his hands now and I'm terrified what he might do to her."

Hans jumped into the conversation. "It's about four hours before sundown. I already called the team and told them to get ready but I didn't tell them it would be tonight. Jumping in on a moment's notice might not be such a fine idea. Especially if they know we're coming. A rescue operation changes the dynamic of the whole job."

"He's right you know." Terry followed his line of reasoning. "Just taking him down could have been done with explosives and fire but with your lady somewhere in the house, it makes it, uh… dicey. And you're saying it's only possible? She might have gotten away?"

"I don't think so." MacMaster looked grim. "If she was free she would have called me."

"Look, mate, you just called me, so they may have been complications."

"I ended up in the water and the cell phone shorted out. Shit! I should never have let her talk me into that. We need another vehicle. The van is at the bottom of the lagoon. The first car you see for sale pull over. We haven't got time to waste."

Terry took a sideways glance at his mentor, friend and business associate. The Scot was usually the calmest person in a frantic situation. When everybody is running and screaming, Gordon MacMaster would calmly analyze the situation and take the appropriate action. Terry had never seen his friend get hooked by a woman, though they had wined and dined many. He found it ironic that the one woman who really got to him was one he didn't trust enough to tell his real name.

The first auto for sale that Terry spotted was not functional, but the next one ran well enough. They purchased the brown Ford Taurus Sedan and drove it off without plates. Hans took the minivan and headed back to Rio to pick up his team. They were to meet at the abandoned strip mine in Itaborai that night.

It was almost 80 kilometers to the house in Petropolis where they had stashed the explosives, guns and cash, but that was as the crow flies. Between the beach and that mountain valley was another mountain range. The map showed the most direct route, but that road was a disaster. What should have taken an hour or two took almost four hours. It was nine o'clock when they reached Petropolis.

The first thing Gordon did upon entering the house he had rented was find the GPS tracker he had taken from the Diogo brothers. There was no doubt now, the signal was coming directly from the north end of Itaborai.

The trip back to Itaborai was faster. The mountain roads still snaked and twisted but they were in better shape. Traffic had died some as the truckers pulled off for the night. They remained in contact with the team who reported they could be ready as early as 7:30. Gordon advised them to get some dinner first; that it was going to be a while before they would arrive with a layout of the grounds.

Brock was watching the tracker and Hernando was driving when the tracker suddenly did an about face. They were on their way out of the mountains when the signal suddenly changed direction. It took a few kilometers before they reached a break in the center guard rail where they could turn around and then they got stuck behind the inevitable line of trucks crawling their way up the mountain. The left lane moved only marginally faster.

Despite some traffic delays, Brock and Hernando were more confident by the minute. The signal was strong and steady and pointed to the road above them. They finally got around the trucks close to the top of the hill and left the line behind them, only to find another group crawling down the other side. They took the chance of taking the Velha de Marica expressway back down since it was clear of trucks, but their target had obviously not done the same. When they reached the bottom of the valley, the tracker showed their target to be on the right. They drove down the RJ104 to the RJ106 interchange but the target had turned in the other direction. They drove down out of the mountain valley, through the northern suburbs of Niteroi and into Itaborai.

"He has them," Hernando said as they approached the north end of town.

"Who?" Brock wanted to know.

"Francisco Modiano, the man who put a price on my head. He has wanted her since the job we did in Rio. It looks like he has taken all of them now."

"That is not the way I read it. He has the one the tracker leads to. I thought it was Boris but I may have been wrong."

"Let me tell you what I saw in the Central Plaza. Blondie was holding Anastasia…"

"Wait. Walter Suffolk was holding who?"

Hernando realized he had slipped but it hardly seemed to matter now. "Mrs. Andalucia. The CIA man, the first man to be shot was standing right behind both of them. Boris was off to the left side. Some blonde woman pulled out a gun and started yelling at the CIA man to drop his weapon. That was when the other men, the men with the tracker, shot the CIA man. That tells me that either Blondie or Anastasia is the target of the tracker."

"I see. It must be the woman then, not the men. I don't really understand this whole thing. The Diogos said they had been hired by the Paraguayan military to kill whoever the tracker pointed to. I suppose it makes more sense that it would point to her. The reward was offered for her and the tracker is pointing to the man who offered the reward…"

"The reward was offered for me as well. I need to either rescue her from this man's house or return with proof that she is dead."

"Damn. How the hell do you expect to do that? We might have been able to pull it off before, but this place is a fucking fortress. I have no intention of trying to get in there."

"We need to get out of here. If they find me here my life is over." Hernando drove to the nearest hotel and got a couple of rooms. Room service provided dinner and they sat together in one room thrashing out the details of what they knew over a bottle of Russian vodka.

Chapter Twenty Eight
Assault

The entire north-west section of Itaborai was pock marked with strip mines. Some of them had pools filled with fresh water that made for good swimming holes; others had shelves of shale that made good seating for parties. The police would patrol them looking for bonfires and roust the young revelers from time to time. The mines were all accessible from the road so they also made good spots to dump dead bodies. The largest of the strip mines was separated from the Modiano compound by a kilometer thick line of trees. It was also the spot where Hernando had shot four officers. Since that day, chains had been erected at both entrances to keep cars out. The unintended consequence of that was denying the police access to the area as well.

The Modiano compound was two kilometers away from the south entrance to the barricaded strip mine, but it was only one kilometer from the north entrance and that entrance looped through the trees before reaching the mine. That made it a good spot to stage an attack but a natural trap as well. Gordon had not been to this spot since the encounter so he had no idea that the entrances had been blocked.

With a diagram of the compound and an overhead view from the internet, six men and a woman laid out the plan. Gordon had agreed to pay a premium for the rescue operation since that had not been part of the original agreement. The plan had not taken into account the chains at the entrances, however and when they arrived, in three separate vehicles, it stalled the operation momentarily until Boom-Boom brought out the solution. A couple of twists of phosphorus cutting cord and the chain on the south side fell to the ground. Once they were inside, they took a twist of light wire and wired the chain back up. It would pass muster at a casual glance. They had left the north entrance chain in place when they had seen it and changed their plan slightly.

Chico stayed with the vehicles while the rest of the team slipped through the woods using shrouded flashlights. The night was much too dark to make their way through the initial section without some form of illumination. As they got closer to the drug dealer's compound, the lights from the perimeter shed enough light to move by.

Recent events had caused Modiano to have more guards put on. Franco Cortico took pride in coordinating the guard assignments himself, but no one had done it today. It was not that Giorgio Pereira was lazy or incompetent, it was merely a matter of available time. There were guards on the perimeter and around the house, but they were usually on 2-hour shifts and these men had been there since 6 pm. They were tired and inattentive by 11 when Gordon MacMaster slipped up to the edge of the woods.

The front of the property was faced with a 9-foot stone wall and a massive wrought iron gate. The sides and back were ringed with an 8-foot chain link fence. The guards made regular rounds inside the fence but with nowhere near military precision. They were gangsters, not soldiers and resented that particular assignment, especially today. The captain of the guard had promised to bring up the matter of the short shifts tomorrow, but did not wish to disturb the men of power tonight. Many of the men who would ordinarily be available had been pulled off to search the hotels and bars for the big red-headed foreigner.

Divers had gone down and examined the van while it was still in the lagoon. Even Modiano's influence with the police was not enough to get this facet of the investigation speeded up given the other events so close to the beach. Disruption of the tourist industry could not be tolerated and the police had their suspicions about who was responsible for the killings. It was no secret that Franco Cortico was Francisco Modiano's right hand man. Ideas were thrown around in the precinct that he had some sort of falling out with his boss and it led to his demise. Finding the man's car wrecked further down the road led to the conclusion that he was possibly car-jacked, but there were no witnesses willing to come forth. The police would get around to questioning Modiano on the subject later.

While the guards were off in different towns searching for Gordon MacMaster, he was crouching in the woods, watching the remaining men make their rounds. The south-west corner of the compound was where the trees grew closest to the fence, it was also the corner furthest from the main house. Between the house and the south-west corner was a one-story building that contained rows of cots, a kitchen and a game room. On ordinary days, the guards not patrolling would be in there playing pool or cards or napping. Tonight it was empty.

Boom-Boom had wanted to use the phosphorous cord on the fence but the others had outvoted him on that. It attracted too much attention. Three pairs of fencing pliers had been brought for that job and while not as fast, they were much less flamboyant.

The four perimeter guards' regular rounds did not bring them together at the corner, but had them pass each other in the middle of the sides and back. On any other night they would have been more regular, but they were definitely off schedule tonight. The two men passed each other close to the corner, grumbled at each other for a second and moved away. Behind them, a door was being cut in the fence.

Five men headed for the back of the guards' quarters and quickly around the one end that was deep in shadows.

Sadie stayed in the shadows of the trees with a silenced rifle. She had complained about being left behind but had acquiesced before long. Her argument would have been sound except they did not expect to see much hand-to-hand fighting.

From the shadows of the guards' quarters, they waited until the two guards on the outside of the house were in close proximity to each other. There was too much light and too much lawn to sneak up on them so they were shot from a distance. Gordon shot one and Hans shot the other. No sooner had they hit the ground than Milton and Terry ran across the intervening lawn with knives to finish the job.

A yell from behind them indicated one of the perimeter guards had seen the muzzle flash. Gordon turned, sighted him in and shot him as well. From outside the fence, Sadie shot the one on the other side. The guns were silenced but the guard's yell had alerted the others. Two more men were patrolling the outside of the house and two more were on the perimeter and they came running. Additional lights came on outside the house and, where the invaders had been in shadows before, they were outlined by halogen bulbs now. The time for subtlety was over.

Sadie moved to the hole in the fence and yelled. As the men ran toward her, she shot one in the head and another in the chest, then she turned and ran back into the woods. One of the guards ran around the corner and impaled himself on Milton's knife. He took a breath to scream, but the big man delivered a backhanded chop to the throat that silenced him forever. The last of the eight guards made the mistake of following Sadie into the woods. The police found him in the morning with his throat cut.

Having no way of knowing how many guards were in the house, Gordon threw a grenade through the kitchen window and ducked as it made a mess of the stainless steel counters. Boom-Boom slapped a piece of plastic explosive on the kitchen door and blew the lock off it. Within seconds they had eliminated the guard patrols and gained entrance to the house.

Things got a little trickier from there. If it had been a simple decommission they could have charged through the house with bullets and bombs until they had taken out the target. With the added element of the rescue operation they had to be a little more careful who they shot. Not much more careful however.

Two guards downstairs stood in the short hallway at the kitchen entrance and opened up with automatics but there was no one in their line of fire. Boom-Boom tossed a flash-bang at them which blinded them momentarily. They kept firing until their clips went empty then Milton stepped up and decisively eliminated the danger.

The mansion was built like a hotel. It was three stories tall with the bedrooms on the third floor. The ground floor was cooking and cleaning facilities, the second, entertaining and game rooms. The outer structure was made of field stone while the inside was done in exotic hardwoods. There was no reception area with wide arcing stairways. There was an elevator the serving staff used and the stairways were small and narrow. There was also an elevator from the third floor to the underground garage. That one had no access from the second floor and was hidden on the ground floor.

The two guards at the gate had hesitated just long enough to seal their fates. When they came charging through the immense oak door they were already covered. Hans shot them both.

Milton had pulled on a ski mask and was busy rounding up the cooking and cleaning staff and locking them in the laundry. Gordon was investigating the second floor; he found a billiards room, a library filled with antique leather bound editions, a cards room and several well cared for reading rooms. The long hallways made it easy enough to clear from one side to the other. Terry watched his back and kept the hallway clear. There were no guards on the second floor. The narrow stairwells would have been a perfect ambush spot if there had been a guard on the top floor but there was not. Francisco Modiano liked to have guards on the premises but not in his personal space. The guards stayed on the ground floor, a tactical error that might have been corrected if he had known the assault was imminent.

Most of the bedrooms on the third floor had not been slept in for some time. The beds were made but the blankets would be changed before anyone used them. Gordon found room after empty room with not a stitch out of place. It was as though he was in a house of ghosts. He finally found evidence of habitation when he got to the other end of the house. The beds were disheveled and the pillows had been slept on. There was, however, no Francisco and no Anastasia. When he found the elevator in the largest of the bedrooms, the power had been turned off to it. He heard the chains that opened the front gates just as he realized his quarry had given him the slip. Racing to the front of the house he saw an armored limousine exiting through the opening in the stone wall.

This close, the GPS locator had ceased to be of utility. The directional tracker was still functional though. Pulling it from his pocket, Gordon saw the signal leaving with the limo. He gave the signal and the team left the premises almost as fast as they had entered.

The police had been alerted, though it was hard to say who had done so. They were coming in the front gate while the team was exiting the hole in the fence. One pair of patrolmen knew the best way to assault the compound would have been from the north entrance to the strip mine but the chain was still in place and there were no cars on the road. They turned around and went to the front gate. The team drove out the south entrance to the strip mine and turned away from the scene. In 10 minutes they were heading out of town, in 20 they were in Magé, a small town to the northwest of Itaborai. They stopped by the side of the road just outside of town.

"Hans," Gordon began, "weren't you supposed to be covering the garage?"

"Yeah, and if I could have found it I would have."

"It's right here on the plans."

"Right. But when I got to where I thought it should be, I was in a store room full of cans and crates. If there was a door there, I couldn't find it and I'll tell you, the damn thing had a sewer grate for a door on the outside. If we had time, Boom-Boom could have blown it off its hinges but by the time we got out there, it was opening up and that limo was heading out. No telling where it is now."

"Not true. I know exactly where it is." Gordon pulled the directional tracker from his pocket and Terry produced the GPS locator.

"Brock, my friend, wake up. We have a signal again and it is on the move."

"Shit. What time is it?"

"Almost midnight."

"Oh. My head hurts."

"Too much of that vodka will do that. See, the signal is moving. It looks like it is moving past us."

Brock looked at the tracker, ran his hand through his hair and made a decision. "We need to follow it. Don't lock it in."

"I agree. Let us get moving."

Brock grabbed what was left of the vodka and took a swig to clear his mouth and his mind and grabbed his pistol and the car keys. They both knew their best chance for closure on this was to acquire the targets while they were outside the compound.

It was plain that Hernando should drive since Dakota did not seem to be in any condition to do so. The signal led them east and they took the chance of getting on the BR101 toward Tangua and Rio Bonito. The signal was weak but improved once they were cruising on the expressway. The direction remained a more or less constant east-north-east.

They passed through Tangua and 30 kilometers outside of Itaborai, the signal swung north. They had passed the turn off and needed to proceed to the next exit and turn around. Northeast of Rio Bonito was a warehouse district. The Honda looked incongruous among all the diesel tractor-trailers. After locating the particular warehouse, they locked the location into the tracker. That warehouse had several cars parked near the office. They reconnoitered the area and drove out to where the road turned from blacktop to dirt. They drove into a grove of trees and shut the engine off.

"I saw five cars in addition to that limo," Brock began. "That tells me we have at least six unfriendlies in there."

"Unfriendlies, is that a word?"

"Enemies, guards, hoodlums, gangsters. It doesn't matter what you call them if there are six of them it makes it difficult."

"What I would like to know is why are they here? Why did they move from the safety of Modiano's house to this place?"

"I don't know and I don't care. What we need to focus on is, what are we going to do and how are we going to do it?"

"These places lock up very securely to keep out the thieves. Many of them have security on guard all the time. This one might be difficult to get inside."

"Then what we need to do is get them outside."

"And how do you suggest we do that?" Hernando cocked an eye at his American partner. "We could set the place on fire."

"No, I don't think so, too crude. Look, they have a gate to the area but it was open. That means they get deliveries at night. Maybe we can use that."

"We would need to know the schedule and we would need a truck. I don't see this as working all that well. Also, once you get through the door to the office, there is probably an inside door that is locked and they might be able to lock the outside door remotely. That would trap us at the driver's window in the shipping and receiving office. Sitting geese."

"Sitting ducks."

"Geese, ducks, pigeons, who cares. We would be trapped."

"I get the point. Can you drive one?"

"A truck? Certainly. It can't be much worse that a military transport truck."

"That's how we're getting in there. We just need to deliver something special."

"We've gone in the wrong direction." Terry asserted. "We should be heading east. It looks as though they have her going down this road here. Where's the map? Ah, here. It looks like they went down to the BR101 and headed east from there."

The crew gathered around the map on the hood of the car and peered at it under the beam of the flashlight.

"We're about 20 miles behind them." Hans concluded.

"When did you get the chance to tag him car?" Milton asked.

"It's not the car it tracks, it's the woman." Gordon replied.

"Ya man. Das the way to be keeping an eye on dem women." Milton was grinning, showing his big white teeth.

Sadie opened her mouth to say something but Gordon cut her off. "Terry, you take the lead car with the GPS. Chico, you're driving with me and Sadie. Boom-Boom, follow us and try to keep up."

Boom-Boom grinned. "It may be a van but I got that baby souped. I can take either of those cars and leave 'em behind. Don't you worry about me."

When the team pulled on the BR101, the GPS tracker indicated their objective was moving through Tangua. By the time they had reached Tangua, the signal had stabilized northeast of Rio Bonito. All three vehicles rolled around the block where the warehouse was located and pulled into a dark parking lot a block away. A quick conference among the team settled on a course of action. Munitions were distributed, head sets were mounted and they moved to get in place for the action.

Of the eleven people in the warehouse that night, one was the shipping and receiving clerk, one was a woman and one was the boss. The other eight were armed with AK47s as well as their personal firearms. These men had not been at the house when the team made their way inside; they'd been shaking down the local bars and hotels looking for the leader of the team while he was assaulting their boss's house. They showed up in four different cars at different times and had seen nothing suspicious when they arrived. They sat on chairs around lunchroom tables on the warehouse floor, smoking, playing cards and joking. None of them believed their enemies knew where they were.

The clerk was watching the parking lot, but he could only see one side of it through the shipping and receiving window. That window did not face the outside, but into a little antechamber with a glass door and a big window. The shipping docks were empty so he had a good view of the entrance. The window that had a view of the other half was blocked by a trailer. The trailer had been received and was empty. The clerk planned on having the next drop-off swap that one out and take it with him, but that was not scheduled until seven in the morning. One of the problems with hiding in a working warehouse is that the trucks still need to load and unload.

The warehouse was owned by Francisco Modiano as were several others. The difference with this one was that it never served as a storage or transport hub for drugs. Francisco was a great believer in plausible deniability. He had not been anywhere near the source of his wealth for years. This warehouse was filled with construction materials such as bags of concrete, sheets of plywood, crates of tiles and buckets of grout. These materials do not have a fast turn-over rate like fresh fruit or fish and can remain in storage for a long time. With an adequate parking lot, trucks can drop their trailers, hook an empty and roll off without ever needing to open the dock door.

Chico's quiet voice came over the headset. "Boris, I can't pick this lock. It is electronic. If I short circuit the electrics it will lock automatically." Chico was on the back side of the building at the fire door. He had expected to be able to pick the lock and shoot whoever was guarding the exit. There was similar door on the north end of the building but Milton said it was electronic as well.

"This changes things." Gordon broadcast. "We're still going in but if we can't do it quietly, we'll need to be very loud. Boom-Boom, can you take out the doors?"

"Sure thing, Boss, but it would be easier to go in through the walls than the doors. The doors are reinforced and set on the load bearing members. The walls are sheet metal. Give me a few minutes and I'll rig us up some doors. How many you want?"

"Three, but make sure you can go through them after you blow them. There might be stock behind them."

"I'll do what I can but there are no windows. I could make some windows first but someone might notice."

The crew stayed to the shadows. Milton and Hans were on the north side, Chico and Sadie were on the back side and Terry and Gordon were on the end of the adjacent warehouse. Boom-Boom had to sneak back to his van to get more phosphorous cord and primacord. The primacord would set the intensely hot phosphorous cords off almost simultaneously.

Gordon and Terry slunk over to the location Boom-Boom had chosen for one of his impromptu doors and waited while he set up for three of them. He deliberately made each of the planned openings twice as wide as most pallet loads to ensure there would be some free space behind it when it blew. The set up was almost ready when they first heard the truck fire up. It was to the north of them and would have no business coming down either side of the warehouse.

The gears ground horribly when the clutch was engaged but the truck didn't stall. The team hugged the shadows as it pulled out. It was a Peterbilt with a long-nosed cab. They could not see it pulling in the dock side of the warehouse but they could hear it as it came around the corner, up-shifted and charged down the lot. The crash that ensued told of mangled metal and breaking glass.

"Boom-Boom, blow it now!" Gordon hollered.

"I'm almost done." He replied.

"Now!"

The primacord flashed and the phosphorous burned its way through the sheet metal wall in two places. The setup on the north end was not complete but the time was obviously right. An oval of metal fell out in front of Sadie and Chico and they slipped inside. The entrance formed in front of Gordon and Terry held for a second but Gordon stomped it in. It fell with a clatter.

When the truck smashed into the cars on the dock side of the building, everybody inside jumped like they had been electrocuted; everybody but Anastasia, who collapsed and fell off her chair. The guards grabbed their guns and six headed for the door, two ran to an overhead dock door where one pushed the buttons to open it.

Brock Dakota had been standing on the running board of the Peterbilt and had jumped off just before it impacted the parked cars. Hernando was driving but the impact was negligible inside the cab. When the men began running out the door, the pair was ready for them, pistols in hand.

Brock shot the lead man when there were three men through the door and two down the galvanized steps. Hernando shot the second and third men while standing on the driver's side running board. The fourth man saw his compatriots downed and shot back straight through the side window. The AK47 sprayed the truck, forcing Hernando to jump back inside and slide out the passenger's side. The driver's side window exploded behind him as the men at the dock door fired long bursts at him from there.

The two men at the dock door had the misfortune of being outlined perfectly from behind and as Chico and Sadie came to the end of the aisle they had entered in, they shot them both in the back.

The three remaining guards were in the antechamber where drivers were usually served by the clerk. The door had

locked behind them and there was no window in it. They
could not see their comrades fall and the noise of their
automatic weapons deafened them. They were blasting holes
in the truck in hopes of punching through and hitting the two
men hiding behind it. The window was gone and the glass
door was spider-webbed from the return fire.

When the shooting began, Francisco Modiano had
grabbed his pistol and backed against the wall. He saw
Anastasia collapse on the floor but did not move to assist her.
Francisco saw Chico and Sadie come around the corner of
the aisle and shoot the two men at the dock door and,
knowing his number was being called, slipped into the
women's bathroom which was attached to the office with a
door at each end.

On the north end of the building, Boom-Boom blew
the final hole in the wall but there was nothing behind it but
pallets of concrete. The stock was pushed all the way up to
the wall and offered no way in.

Gordon went in first with Terry right behind him.
They moved more toward the center of the building and
crept down the aisle to the back wall of the office. On the
right, Gordon saw Sadie shoot once and then she moved out
of his sight. He could hear the deafening roar of the gunfire
from the other side of the office that almost drowned out the
scream from around the corner.

Chico and Sadie both saw the woman rise from behind
the table, screaming wildly. They did not know if she was
screaming because she had been tortured or if she was really
just a lunatic. They kept their weapons pointed at the front
of the building, ready to meet any challenge that appeared,
except for the one that did. Anastasia Viuda leaped on the
table and cleared half the distance between them in one
bound. She hit the ground running and hit Chico first. She
had no weapons in her hands but truly needed none,

especially because the invaders had not expected her to attack. Anastasia's first strike was a kick in the stomach, doubling Chico over, her next blow was actually a sweep that took Sadie's legs out from under her. A back-handed punch broke Sadie's nose. Chico was trying to rise when a forward kick caught him on the tip of his chin and rang his bell. He collapsed unconscious. Sadie was on her knees, shaking her head and wiping her eyes, trying to get around the effects of having her nose broken. A round house kick to the side of the head broke her neck and ended her life.

Gordon came around the corner just in time to see Anastasia end Sadie Hawkins' life. Anastasia was moving faster than seemed humanly possible. She scooped up the fallen Chico's pistol and turned just as Terry came around the corner. The only thing that saved Terry's life was his proximity to Gordon. If the Aussie had not been behind the Scot, she would have shot him. Casting about for another target and seeing none, she leaped for the dock door, rolled once and jumped out.

The guards behind the shattered glass saw her leap out the dock door and run up the sloping ramp. One of them made the mistake of pointing his weapon at her. She spun and emptied her newly acquired pistol into the area, killing one man and injuring another in the left shoulder. Before they could readjust to the new threat, Anastasia was off and running with preternatural speed.

The two behind the truck could not hear the silenced pistol Anastasia had used so they had no idea she was there or that the men in the driver's service area had been shot. Brock Dakota used the next-to-last round in his pistol and shot the last uninjured man in the face as that man was shooting at the retreating Anastasia Viuda. The man who had been shot in the shoulder got a round off at the same time and Brock Dakota felt the burning impact of a 7.62mm round tearing through the flesh of his thigh. He went down and rolled under the cab of the truck.

Hernando knew he was in deep trouble now. He had no way of knowing the men on the dock had been shot. He could not know that two of the three men in the driver's service area were dead and the remaining one was shot. He was certain he had bitten off more than he could chew and was about to die, but he had gotten out of tough spots before and was willing to keep going. He had about seven rounds left in his last clip. He looked down and saw the slide on Brock's pistol open, so he knew that weapon was empty. A grim downward smile fixed on his face as he stepped onto the running board and pointed through the shattered side windows of the truck. He saw five or six men on the floor of the warehouse. Looking through the windshield, he saw one blood spattered guard swinging his weapon around. He dropped back to the ground as the guard expended the rest of his clip into the cab of the truck, and Hernando stepped around the front of the vehicle in time to shoot the man in the chest as he was trying to change clips one handed.

Gordon and Terry got the news that Milton and Hans were coming around to the side since they could not enter the end of the building. Chico and Sadie were pulled off the floor and into an aisle. Chico was coming around but Sadie never would.

None of the team knew who had crashed the truck or why there was a firefight going on at the shipping dock. Milton came through the warehouse with the drum fed repeating shotgun in his hand. Gordon pointed at the door where the automatic weapons had just been firing and Milton put half a dozen slugs through the door. The automatic weapons ceased firing. Milton did not know it was Hernando who had finished the last of them.

"Move out, teams of two. Milton and Hans, north end. Chico and Boom-Boom South end. We're gonna find out who drove that truck. If you find Modiano, shoot him." Gordon was moving to the dock door, cautiously. Two dead guards lay in the drain area of the slope. He could not see Bock underneath the truck but Brock could see him. Through the searing pain of his leg wound, the Homeland security agent saw Gordon and then Terry move in. All he could think of was after all the tracking, the death and pain these men had inflicted, here they were and he was almost unarmed.

Hernando del Fuego had heard the shotgun going off in the building and had peered around the front bumper of the truck. He saw no one in the antechamber and took the opportunity to run as fast as he could. He used the wrecked cars for cover and ran to the protection provided by the tandem wheels of the empty trailer in the receiving dock.

Brock made his decision. He was here to kill the blond, the Australian. His chances of getting out of the situation alive were negligible. The last act of his life would be one of honor; his last public service. He took aim and with his last round he shot Terry Kingston in the chest.

Gordon MacMaster saw the muzzle flash from under the wrecked cab of the truck and saw Terry go down. He emptied a full clip into the shadows and there was no more gunfire from there. He pulled Terry back behind the wall and tore off his vest. The wound was long and diagonal. The bullet had glanced off the handle of one of the twin pistols holstered under the vest and torn a furrow upward across his chest. He was bleeding badly but was not critically injured.

Lying on the ground under the cab, Brock did everything in his power to remain silent. Two rounds from the dock had caught him in the chest and once again his body armor had saved his life but he was in no condition to continue the fight. He could barely breathe and was unsure of whether he could walk or not. Worst of all, in his mind, he was now unarmed.

Hernando crawled into the shadows under the trailer expecting to see the guards behind the glass but could see only one man, through the newly shattered glass of the door, and he was obviously dead. Something was wrong. He knew he and Brock had not killed all these men. Then he saw the shotgun holes in the door and knew someone else was here. Someone else had attacked this warehouse and they were still inside. It could only be Boris and Walter. Then he saw the single flash from under the wrecked truck and the muffled reports of the pistol returning fire from the open dock door. He was certain now that he was alone. His American partner had just breathed his last.

Then the lights went out both inside and outside the warehouse. Anastasia Viuda had run to the south end of the building and around the end. In her enhanced state, there was no real planning in her mind, it was all reaction. Somehow people had entered the warehouse from the back side so she was going to find out where they had come in and come up behind them. She found the first hole Boom-Boom had blown in the wall and slipped inside. She picked up a four-foot length of half-inch rebar as she moved down the inside wall. A faint sound led her toward the other side of the building where she saw two armed men, obviously searching the building. She waited, trembling, at one end of an aisle, behind a rack of dry wall. When the small man dressed in farmer's garb came to the end of that aisle, she swung the rebar fiercely. The small man went down gasping; she had hit him square in the chest, but when she moved to stab him through the throat with the rebar, the other man opened up with his pistol, forcing her to run. When she reached the east side of the building she practically ran into the main power panel for the lights. A quick pull of the lever drowned both the building and the truck lot in darkness.

"Boris, this is Chico. That crazy bitch we're supposed to be rescuing is in the building and trying to kill us."

"Don't shoot her."

"I did. I mean, I tried. She was going to kill Boom-Boom. I think she turned out the lights."

"Stand down, stand down. Get the hell out of here. Hans, Milton, evacuate."

Chico shoved his gun in his belt and helped Boom-Boom to his feet. It took a few seconds for the emergency lights to come on, the batteries were weak, and they didn't provide much illumination but it was enough to keep them from running into the racks.

Once they had holstered their weapons, Chico and Boom-Boom did not register as a threat so Anastasia did not go after them, but the sense of threat was real and immediate so she did not miss a beat. Her enhanced senses almost provided direction in the darkness and once the emergency lights came on she was back at full speed. She raced through the warehouse to the shipping dock where Gordon was just rising from an injured Terry Kingston's prone body. He saw her come out on the floor with the rebar in her hands and the crazed look in her eye. It took him a second to determine that she was not going to attack him. She stood there casting her head back and forth like a hunting lioness, looking for the source of the impending danger.

Hearing something toward the back of the building, she started moving that way but stopped when Gordon spoke her name.

"Anastasia, they are not the enemy. They are not the enemy. Where is Modiano?"

Anastasia froze and turned toward Gordon. She was shaking like a leaf. "No, you cannot," shuddered out of her. "You cannot. He is my brother."

Chapter Twenty Nine
Epiphany

The gunfire had ceased outside the office and the muffled shot from Chico's gun could not be heard inside the block and tile of the bathroom. Francisco Modiano had been squatting on one of the seats, waiting for whoever won the encounter to enter the room but no one had. With pistol in hand he carefully put his feet back on the floor and opened the door to the stall. He knew there was no protection in the office area if the lead started flying. The cubicle walls limited vision only.

When the lights went out, Hernando del Fuego saw opportunity. The lot was black but the emergency lights were starting to flicker on inside. Slipping out from under the trailer he crept past the smashed hulk of a car. There was no way he was going through the driver's entrance. Every man who had entered that spot was currently dead. There was no one in sight on the loading dock; he had a good view of it. There was a couple of rows of stock waiting to be loaded and it was possible someone was hiding behind them but they were not in line with the open door. He hustled down the length of the trailer he had driven in and around the back side of it. He caught sight of one man lying on the floor by the wall and the big redhead just moving out of sight and into the middle of the floor.

"If nothing else, I get to kill that son-of-a-bitch," he thought to himself.

The pool of light that spilled out of the open dock door would have outlined him against the white of the trailer. He could not risk that. Instead he crept halfway down the slope of the dock and over toward the open door.

Knowing he could not hide forever and that if his guards had been killed, he was next, Francisco Modiano moved to the door of the bathroom. Crossing himself and kissing his gun hand, he pushed the painted metal door open and began firing. The first shot flashed between Anastasia and Gordon. The second shot went wide as the door bounced back at him. The third shot went through the open dock door and into the already perforated trailer.

Hernando could practically feel the bullet fly by him as he crept up to the border between light and shadow. He saw the man firing from the women's bathroom and naturally assumed he was the target. His first shot ricocheted off the metal of the bathroom door but the second and third shots caught Francisco Modiano in the chest and head.

The scream Anastasia voiced must have rivaled all the harpies in Hell. Suddenly she was not standing and shuddering but running. She ran for the dock and Hernando del Fuego.

"Ana!" he yelled. "It's me."

Anastasia did not slow an iota.

Hernando opened fire on her but she would not have been stopped by anything less than a fatal shot. One round creased her arm, one flew through the stubble on her head and the third went between her legs as she vaulted from the edge of the dock with the length of rebar gripped in both hands. She came down directly on top of him, driving the knotty piece of steel between his collar bone and his neck, straight through the intervening muscle and sinew and into his heart.

Brock Dakota played dead when the headlights from the cars raced into the lot. He had pushed his luck as far as he possibly could and the fact that he was still alive actually surprised him. He had been given a perfect view of Anastasia flying through the air and impaling his partner. It convinced him that he was hallucinating from lack of blood and that the end was near so he simply lay there like a dead man.

Gordon MacMaster was lying on the floor looking for a target but found none. Francisco Modiano was hanging half in and half out of the ladies' room. Anastasia was standing over the body of her former partner shaking like an epileptic. Terry was rising from the floor slowly and painfully.

Gordon had time to check Modiano's body for a pulse but found none. Terry moved to the driver's door and opened it in time to see the shipping and receiving clerk jump off the shelf in the office and dash through the shattered door. He pulled a pistol from under his vest and stepped forward but the floor was covered with blood and bodies. He slipped and then fell backward.

The clerk was not a gangster; he was just affiliated with gangsters. If he had stayed under his desk, in the office, he would have been unmolested but he could not have known that. He jumped over the bodies on the stairs and ran directly toward the road. The only thing he saw between himself and safety was a tall woman and he knew he could take care of her. On the other side of the wrecked truck, two cars were pulling up. He ran directly at her, thinking he would be able to dash directly past but he was mistaken. She moved faster than any man or woman had a right to. She reached out and wrapped her long left arm around his neck. She stepped behind him and locked that arm in with her right arm. Squeezing both sides of his neck that way would have knocked him out in a matter of seconds, but he had an ace up his sleeve. He reached back over his shoulder and pressed the electrodes of a 90,000-volt stun gun against her skull. Unfortunately for him, since they were in contact with each other, the voltage ran through him as well. His muscles cramped and he was unable to release the trigger so they stood there, racked and quaking with the shock, until they both collapsed.

"Terry, we're done here. Get your ass into the car and let's go. Anastasia, where are you?" There was no reply to Gordon's question.

Terry rolled to the edge of the dock and slid to his feet on the ground. "She's here. I'll get her, you get that other nasty bitch and let's go."

Gordon walked to the body of the woman he had known as Sadie Hawkins and threw her body over his shoulder. He walked to the edge and sat her down, almost tenderly.

Hans came around the end of the truck and helped Terry move the unconscious Anastasia to one car. Milton came around the other end and stopped Gordon from picking Sadie back up. He cradled her in his arms and moved her to the other car. The team left the warehouse district with their wounded and their dead five minutes before the police arrived.

"Agent Dakota, we told you that there would be no assistance, that you have been disavowed. It was your choice to go on vacation, to leave the ranch and now you need to deal with the repercussions of that decision." Agent Pierce showed no remorse or compassion for his fellow American.

"All I'm asking for is bail money so I can get a lawyer. If I stick with the lawyer they give me I'll spend the rest of my life in prison." Brock was speaking from a hospital bed where he had been lying for a week.

"Repercussions, Dakota. This is what I was talking about. You once told me I run a sloppy ship down here. Well, it looks like your boat just capsized. I tried to tell you, explain to you how it works down here, but you wanted to go all cowboy on us."

"Can you at least get me a lawyer?"

"Yeah. I guess we can do that for you. You can't have one of ours though, for obvious reasons. I'll get in touch with someone discreet and send him over. I can't bail you out though. Besides, you haven't been arraigned yet. I don't even know what you're charged with."

"I've got two officers outside my door, I'll be charged with something."

The next day, instead of a lawyer, the chief of police for Rio Bonito stopped by in the morning. He spoke excellent English, though with a Caribbean accent and they spoke behind a closed door.

"Agent Brock Dakota?"

"Yes, sir."

"My name is Chief D'artuille."

"I'm pleased to meet you."

"No, you should not be. First, I hope you understand you are in a lot of trouble."

"Yes, sir, I was afraid of that."

"You and this clerk, this Manuel, were the only men alive when the police reached that warehouse and he was unconscious."

"If I might explain…"

Chief D'artuille held his hand in the air to forestall any further conversation from the American. "Agent Dakota, there are things that you have not yet learned about this little problem."

Dakota kept his mouth closed, sensing that some truly bad news was about to be divulged. He could imagine what he and his department would do in a similar situation.

"It seems you have some very powerful and influential friends. Your solicitor visited me this morning and made a powerful case for your release. I am taking it under advisement for now and will be speaking with the prosecutor about it."

Now Dakota did not know what to say. He could not imagine what Agent Pierce might have done or said to get this sort of reaction from the Chief.

"You have not yet been arraigned and depending on verification of your solicitor's statements, it is possible that you will not be." Chief D'artuille pursed his lips thoughtfully. "This is speculation, of course. It would also be contingent upon your leaving this country and never returning to Brazil. If you were to again find yourself in this country, I could not be held responsible for the outcome."

"Given an exit, Chief, I would never again set foot south of the Rio Grande."

"I assume you speak of the border of Mexico and Texas?"

"Absolutely. I would never again step foot south of Texas."

"Once again, this is speculation and I have no way of confirming the veracity of your solicitor's assertions. If this were to happen, you will never speak of it again, and if pressed, will deny ever being in Brazil. Am I making myself clear?"

"Perfectly clear. Like glass."

"Good. I will leave you now, to recover. It never does a man good to get shot. Where was it you said you got shot?"

"In the leg."

"Not what I asked."

"Oh. In Kansas City, Missouri."

"That is what I thought you said." The man turned with military precision and walked to the door. "If you are lucky, we will never speak again. If we meet again, I will regret what I will be forced to do."

Later that day, a thin man in a cheap suit visited Brock. His English was as poor as Brock's Portuguese. He said that Brock was in a lot of trouble and thought he might be able to work some sort of deal with the prosecutor and get Brock a maximum of 20 years in prison. He assumed that the confused look on the American's face was due to the language barrier. He promised to bring an interpreter the following day and apologized, saying that Agent Pierce had not mentioned that Brock could not speak Portuguese.

After he left, Dakota was more confused than before.

Late that night, another lawyer visited him. This man was much better dressed and spoke much better English, with a Boston Accent.

"Agent Dakota?"

"Yes sir."

"I am here to allow you to understand precisely where you find yourself and the ramifications thereof. I will speak and you will listen then I will ask you some questions. Your answers to these questions will determine your future for the rest of your life. Am I making myself understood?"

"Yes, sir, I think so."

"Good. You have never been to Brazil. You have never met anyone from Brazil. You were on vacation in Hawaii. You had a wonderful time in Hawaii. Now, where have you been?"

"I, uh, I was on vacation in Hawaii. I rented a room at the Marriott."

"No. You were in Hawaii, that is all. Do not complicate things with lies that can be checked with a simple phone call. As a lawman, you know that lies lead to more lies and then you need to remember all the lies you told and they begin to contradict themselves. You were in Hawaii and that is all anyone needs to know. Where were you?"

"I was in Hawaii."

"Good. You never heard of Walter Suffolk. You have never met a Walter Suffolk. You do not know anybody with that name. Have you ever heard of Walter Suffolk?"

"No, sir. I don't know anybody with that name.

"You have never heard of Boris Chercovski."

"I have never heard of Boris Chercovski."

"You have never heard the names Perfect Navaja, Andalucia, Torremolinos or Viuda."

"I'm sorry, I didn't catch those names. I don't think I ever heard of those, uh, men. Do they live in America?"

"I think you understand me. Now let me explain that there has been a sizeable donation made in your name to a policemen's benevolent fund. I have the exact details of this donation, who made it and who benefited from the benevolence. I have connections at Harvard, The Boston Herald, the New York Times and the FBI among others. If it is discovered you were ever looking for any of these people that you have already admitted not knowing, the details of this donation would be made known to them. I will never be implicated in any of this because I have never been here. You have never met me. The records of this case are sealed and only your actions can unseal them. Have I made myself clearly understood?"

"Am I to believe…?"

"Sir, was there a section in my instructions that included you asking me questions?"

"No, sir."

"I believe, then, that our business is concluded. I never expect to see you again. If I do, it will set in motion a series of events that will not be to your liking. The alternative, 20 years in a Brazilian prison, might be preferable. Now, can you walk?"

"Not well, but I think I can make it a ways."

"Good. The only thing you will remember is that you have friends who wish to remain anonymous and you will stop at nothing to keep them that way." The lawyer picked up his briefcase and walked out the door without looking back.

Two hours later, two men wearing off-the-rack suits came into his room and disconnected the intravenous tube from his arm, handed him a suit of clothes and told him to get dressed which he did without further question.

The suit fit him very well and felt very good after the backless hospital gown. It did not include a holster or pistol although his identification and badge were in the pocket of the jacket.

Brock Dakota would never forget a minute of his little trip to Brazil, but no matter how drunk he got or how close were the friends he was holding company with, did he ever tell another living soul that he had ever been to Brazil. The only men who knew, outside of Brazil, were his Deputy Chief and Captain Cook. He swore to never work with Captain Cook again and did not get the chance since he was transferred to the Canadian Border Patrol in Northern Idaho before the end of spring.

Gordon MacMaster paid his team in cash and bid them adieu. Before they left, Hans told him that if they had the opportunity to work together again, they might consider it but that they would never work with his woman. Feelings ran deep over the death of Sadie Hawkins and it would be better if they never had to be in contact with Anastasia. He agreed and they parted as amicably as could be expected under the circumstances.

The wound across Terry's chest needed some stitches and Gordon provided them after anesthetizing him with codeine and alcohol. It would leave a noticeable scar after it healed but there was little to be done about that.

It took three days before Anastasia could get out of bed in Petropolis. She had no appetite for that time and her speech was stumbling and slurred. After three days she began to come around again and a week later she was almost her old self. There was one major difference however. She could no longer detect danger. She could not warn her comrades about the police or the army. After a little thought, Gordon checked the tracker and was satisfied that it no longer pointed to her. He had spent a week looking through the curtains with a gun in his hand in case another team of mercenaries, soldiers or assassins came looking for her. The only explanation he could use to explain the sudden loss of signal was that the clerk's stun gun short-circuited her implant. He took an entire day and night and slept like a baby.

The payoff for Francisco Modiano was transferred to Gordon's account and the passports arrived in the post office box. They were exactly as ordered, two German men and one Chilean woman with stamps indicating their arrival in Brazil. Along with them was a marriage certificate from a chapel in Sao Paulo.

"Damn," Gordon said. "I didn't carry you over the threshold. Oh, actually, I guess I did."

"Always the romantic," Anastasia replied.

Terry arrived at that point. He had been gone all day. "I got it done."

"They agreed to it?" Gordon asked.

"I don't know yet. The lawyer will be giving me a call later to verify the entire process."

"What did you do?" Anastasia asked.

"I paid that stupid Homeland Security Agent's way out of the country."

"Who?"

"He was the man under the truck; the one who shot me. It turns out he had a vest on and while he did catch a couple in it, he didn't die. He caught one in the leg too."

"What did, uh, does he look like?" she asked.

"Hell, I don't know. He was in the shadows, I never saw the bastard."

"Why, then, have you helped him?"

"I helped him to help us. You see, if we kill a CIA man we end up with a whole pile of shit flowing down hill. I know he's not CIA but he's still American Secret Service of some kind. I would rather pay a few thousand dollars than have those bloodthirsty bastards on my ass."

"What about the one Boris shot?"

"Shit, mate, you haven't told her yet?"

"What have you not told me, love?"

"My real name is Gordon. Gordon MacMaster."

"And when was it that you were going to tell me this, Gordon?" The venom that dripped off her lips shocked him.

"I, uh, well I was waiting for the right time." He looked away.

"And when was that going to be? What are you afraid of? Was I going to hunt you down and kill you?"

"Hell, darling, you might just do that still." He was grinning now.

"Oh, you are the stupidest man I have ever met. How could God conspire to make me fall in love with such a stupid man?" She began ranting in Spanish and Portuguese and some other languages that the men did not recognize as she stormed off into the bedroom.

General Arridagio had been a happy man for a week. The news that the Diogo brothers had been killed had put him into a fury for a while. After all, he had paid those incompetent bastards and they had not fulfilled the contract.

Three teams had died chasing this phantom super-soldier and he was still alive! Then, inexplicably, the signal had died quicker than it had appeared. He had been assured that the only thing that would cause the signal to die was the death of the target. Someone had done the job for him. He may never know who or why but he appreciated the service. The mad science experiments of the previous administration were no longer threatening to disturb Paraguay's international relations with its neighbors.

The Secret Service in Argentina got the news about Hernando del Fuego's untimely demise. Notice of Anastasia's involvement did not accompany the information. The sole living witness to the affair had the misfortune of being murdered in prison before he could testify and the files were sealed permanently. They waited a while for Anastasia to return but eventually concluded that Francisco Modiano had disposed of her body before his own violent end. The men in power hoped she would never surface, for while she was a competent agent, her face had become too well known once the reward was offered.

"So what was that 'He's my brother' bollix she gave you? I waited to ask, thinking you might tell me."

"Ah, I didn't know you heard that." Gordon spoke in a subdued voice. "Apparently the Modiano brothers' mother gave birth to their sister, or more properly, half-sister, when they were about 20 or 25 years old. This sister disappeared when she was very young, still in diapers. It seems this half-sister had a birth mark on her bottom that looked like a pair of lips had kissed her there and that was what made Francisco think she was his sister. He saw the birth mark in one of the naked pictures we sent him."

"So, is she really related to them?"

"I don't know. She seems to think it's a possibility but it depresses the hell out of her to think that she was the cause of the death of her only living relatives she knows about. The worst is the thought that she killed her own brother."

"There's ways to verify that, now."

"Sorry, I didn't think to get a sample as I was checking his neck for a pulse."

"Umn. Well then, what is it now?"

"Being frank with you, I'm getting a wee sick of this life. I may take one or two little jobs, simple stuff, but I think I'll be ready to retire soon. I'd like very much to take this one," he pointed to the bedroom where Anastasia was pouting, "I'd like to take her to the States and settle down."

"Why America?"

"Taxes are low, the gun laws are pretty good and I don't think I have any one there that wants to kill me."

Terry laughed.